Anansi Boys

Also by Neil Gaiman and available from Review

MirrorMask: The Illustrated Film Script (*with Dave McKean*)
American Gods
Stardust
Neverwhere
Smoke and Mirrors

Anansi Boys

Neil Gaiman

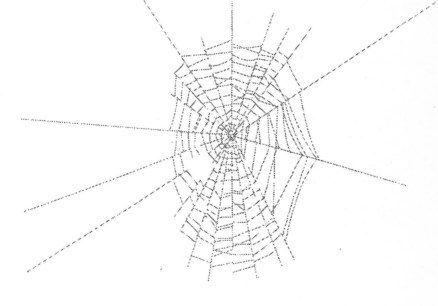

review

First published in Great Britain in 2005
by REVIEW

An imprint of Headline Book Publishing

1

Cataloguing in Publication Data is available from the British Library

ISBN 07553 0507 8 (hardback)
ISBn 07553 0508 6 (trade paperback)

Typeset in ZapfElliptical by Avon DataSet Ltd,
Bidford on Avon, Warwickshire

Printed and Bound in Great Britain by
Mackays of Chatham plc, Chatham, Kent

Headline's policy is to use papers that are natural, renewable and recyclable
products and made from wood grown in sustainable forests. The logging and
manufacturing processes are expected to conform to the environmental
regulations of the country of origin.

HEADLINE BOOK PUBLISHING
A division of Hodder Headline
338 Euston Road
London NW1 3BH

www.reviewbooks.co.uk
www.hodderheadline.com

Dedication

You know how it is. You pick up a book, flip to the dedication, and find that, once again, the author has dedicated a book to someone else and not to you.

Not this time.

Because we haven't yet met/have only a glancing acquaintance/ are just crazy about each other/haven't seen each other in much too long/are in some way related/will never meet, but will, I trust, despite that, always think fondly of each other . . .

This one's for you.

With you know what, and you probably know why.

Note: the author would like to take this opportunity to tip his hat respectfully to the ghosts of Zora Neale Hurston, Thorne Smith, P. G. Wodehouse, and Frederick 'Tex' Avery.

Chapter One

Which Is Mostly about Names and Family Relationships

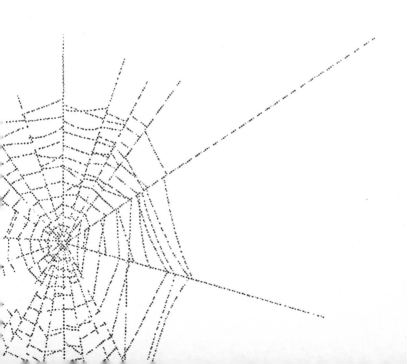

It begins, as most things begin, with a song.

In the beginning, after all, were the words, and they came with a tune. That was how the world was made, how the void was divided, how the lands and the stars and the dreams and the little gods and the animals, how all of them came into the world.

They were sung.

The great beasts were sung into existence, after the Singer had done with the planets and the hills and the trees and the oceans and the lesser beasts. The cliffs that bound existence were sung, and the hunting grounds, and the dark.

Songs remain. They last. The right song can turn an emperor into a laughing stock, can bring down dynasties. A song can last long after the events and the people in it are dust and dreams and gone. That's the power of songs.

There are other things you can do with songs. They do not only make worlds or recreate existence. Fat Charlie Nancy's father, for example, was simply using them to have what he hoped and expected would be a marvellous night out.

Before Fat Charlie's father had come into the bar, the barman had been of the opinion that the whole karaoke evening was going to be an utter bust; but then the little old man had sashayed into the room, walked past the table of several blonde women with the fresh sunburns and smiles of tourists who were sitting by the little makeshift stage in the corner. He had tipped his hat to them, for he wore a hat, a spotless green fedora, and lemon-yellow gloves, and then he walked over to their table. They giggled.

'Are you enjoyin' yourselves, ladies?' he asked.

They continued to giggle and told him they were having a good time, thank you, and that they were here on vacation. He said to them, it gets better, just you wait.

He was older than they were, much, much older, but he was charm itself, like something from a bygone age when fine manners and courtly gestures were worth something. The barman relaxed. With someone like this in the bar, it was going to be a good evening.

There was karaoke. There was dancing. The old man got up to sing, on the makeshift stage, not once, that evening, but twice. He had a fine voice, and an excellent smile, and feet that twinkled when he danced. The first time he got up to sing, he sang 'What's New Pussycat?' The second time he got up to sing, he ruined Fat Charlie's life.

***

Fat Charlie was only ever fat for a handful of years, from shortly before the age of ten, which was when his mother announced to the world that if there was one thing she was over and done with (and if the gentleman in question had any argument with it he could just stick it you know where) it was her marriage to the elderly goat that she had made the unfortunate mistake of marrying and she would be leaving in the morning for somewhere a long way away and he had better not try to follow, to the age of fourteen, when Fat Charlie grew a bit and exercised a little more. He was not fat. Truth to tell, he was not really even chubby, simply slightly soft-looking around the edges. But the name Fat Charlie clung to him, like chewing gum to the sole of a tennis shoe. He would introduce himself as Charles, or, in his early twenties, Chaz, or, in writing, as C. Nancy, but it was no use: the name would creep in, infiltrating the new part of his life just as cockroaches invade the cracks and the world behind the fridge in a new kitchen, and like it or not – and he didn't – he would be Fat Charlie again.

It was, he knew, irrationally, because his father had given him the nickname, and when his father gave things names, they stuck.

There was a dog who had lived in the house across the way, in the Florida street on which Fat Charlie had grown up. It was a chestnut-coloured boxer, long-legged and pointy-eared, with a face that looked like the beast had, as a puppy, run face-first into a wall. Its head was raised, its tail-nub erect. It was, unmistakably, an aristocrat amongst canines. It had entered dog shows. It had rosettes for Best of Breed, and for Best in Class, and even one rosette marked Best in Show. This dog rejoiced in the name of Campbell's Macinrory Arbuthnot the Seventh, and its owners, when they were feeling familiar, called it Kai. This lasted until the day that Fat Charlie's father, sitting out on their dilapidated porch-swing, sipping his beer, noticed the dog as it ambled back and forth across the neighbour's yard, on a leash that ran from a palm tree to a fence-post.

'Hell of a goofy dog,' said Fat Charlie's father. 'Like that friend of Donald Duck's. Hey, Goofy.'

And what once had been Best in Show suddenly slipped and shifted. For Fat Charlie, it was as if he saw the dog through his father's eyes, and darned if he *wasn't* a pretty goofy dog, all things considered. Almost rubbery.

It didn't take long for the name to spread up and down the street. Campbell's Macinrory Arbuthnot the Seventh's owners struggled with it, but they might as well have stood their ground and argued with a hurricane. Total strangers would pat the once-proud boxer's head, and say, 'Hello, Goofy. How's a boy?' The dog's owners stopped entering him in dog shows soon after that. They didn't have the heart. 'Goofy-looking dog,' said the judges.

Fat Charlie's father's names for things stuck. That was just how it was.

That was far from the worst thing about Fat Charlie's father.

There had been, during the years that Fat Charlie was growing up, a number of candidates for the worst thing about his father: his roving eye and equally as adventurous fingers, at least according to the young ladies of the area, who would complain to Fat Charlie's mother, and then there would be trouble; the little black cigarillos, which he called cheroots, which he smoked, the smell of which clung to everything he touched; his fondness for a peculiar shuffling form of tap-dancing only ever fashionable, Fat Charlie suspected, for half an hour in Harlem in the 1920s; his total and invincible ignorance about current world affairs, combined with his apparent conviction that sitcoms were half-hour-long insights into the lives and struggles of real people. None of these, individually, as far as Fat Charlie was concerned, was the worst thing about Fat Charlie's father, although each of them had contributed to the worst thing.

The worst thing about Fat Charlie's father was simply this: he was embarrassing.

Of course, everyone's parents are embarrassing. It goes with the territory. The nature of parents is to embarrass merely by existing, just as it is the nature of children of a certain age to cringe with embarrassment, shame and mortification should their parents so much as speak to them on the street.

Fat Charlie's father, of course, had elevated this to an art form, and he rejoiced in it, just as he rejoiced in practical jokes, from the simple – Fat Charlie would never forget the first time he had climbed into an apple-pie bed – to the unimaginably complex.

'Like what?' asked Rosie, Fat Charlie's fiancée, one evening, when Fat Charlie, who normally did not talk about his father, had attempted, stumblingly, to explain why he believed that simply inviting his father to their upcoming wedding would be a horrendously bad idea. They were in a small wine bar in South London at the time. Fat Charlie had long been of the opinion that four thousand miles and the Atlantic Ocean were both good things to keep between himself and his father.

'Well . . .' said Fat Charlie, and he remembered a parade of indignities, each one of which made his toes curl involuntarily. He settled upon one of them. 'Well, when I changed schools, when I was a kid, my dad made a point of telling me how much he had always looked forward to Presidents' Day, when he was a boy, because it's the law that on Presidents' Day, the kids who go to school dressed as their favourite presidents get a big bag of candy.'

'Oh. That's a nice law,' said Rosie. 'I wish we had something like that in England.' Rosie had never been out of the UK, if you didn't count a Club 18-30 holiday to an island in, she was fairly certain, the Mediterranean. She had warm brown eyes and a good heart, even if geography was not her strongest suit.

'It's *not* a nice law,' said Fat Charlie. 'It's not a law at all. He made it up. Most states don't even have school on Presidents' Day, and even for the ones that do, there is no tradition of going to school on Presidents' Day dressed as your favourite president. Kids dressed as presidents do not get big bags of candy by an Act of Congress, nor is your popularity in the years ahead, all through middle school and high school, decided entirely by which president you decided to dress as – the average kids dress as the obvious presidents, the Lincolns and Washingtons and Jeffersons, but the ones who would become popular, they dressed as John Quincy Adams or Warren Gamaliel Harding, or someone like that. And it's bad luck to talk about it before the day. Or rather it isn't, but he said it was.'

'Boys *and* girls dress up as presidents?'

'Oh yes. Boys and girls. So I spent the week before Presidents' Day reading everything there was to read about presidents in the *World Book Encyclopedia*, trying to choose the right one.'

'Didn't you ever suspect that he was pulling your leg?'

Fat Charlie shook his head. 'It's not something you think about, when my dad starts to work you over. He's the finest liar you'll ever meet. He's convincing.'

Rosie took a sip of her Chardonnay. 'So which president did you go to school as?'

'Taft. He was the twenty-seventh president. I wore a brown suit my father had found somewhere, with the legs all rolled up and a pillow stuffed down the front. I had a painted-on moustache. My dad took me to school himself that day. I walked in so proudly. The other kids just screamed and pointed, and somewhere in there I locked myself in a cubicle in the boys' room and cried. They wouldn't let me go home to change. I went through the day like that. It was Hell.'

'You should have made something up,' said Rosie. 'You were going to a costume party afterwards or something. Or just told them the truth.'

'Yeah,' said Fat Charlie meaningfully and gloomily, remembering.

'What did your dad say, when you got home?'

'Oh, he hooted with laughter. Chuckled and chortled and, and chittered and all that. Then he told me that maybe they didn't do that Presidents' Day stuff any more. Now, why didn't we go down to the beach together and look for mermaids?'

'Look for . . . mermaids?'

'We'd go down to the beach, and walk along it, and he'd be as embarrassing as any human being on the face of this planet has ever been – he'd start singing, and he'd start doing a shuffling sort of sand-dance on the sand, and he'd just talk to people as he went – people he didn't even know, people he'd never met, and I hated it, except he told me there were mermaids out there in the Atlantic, and if I looked fast enough and sharp enough, I'd see one.

' "There!" he'd say. "Did you see her? She was a big ol' redhead, with a green tail." And I looked, and I looked, but I never did.'

He shook his head. Then he took a handful of mixed nuts from the bowl on the table and began to toss them into his mouth, chomping down on them as if each nut was a twenty-year-old indignity that could never be erased.

'Well,' said Rosie, brightly, 'I think he sounds lovely, a real character! We have to get him to come over for the wedding. He'd be the life and soul of the party.'

Which, Fat Charlie explained, after briefly choking on a Brazil nut, was really the last thing you wanted at your wedding, after all, wasn't it, your father turning up and being the life and soul of the party? He said that his father was, he had no doubt, still the most embarrassing person on God's Green Earth. He added that he was perfectly happy not to have seen the old goat for several years, and that the best thing his mother ever did was to leave his father and come to England to stay with her Aunt Alanna. He buttressed this by stating categorically that he was damned, double damned, and quite possibly even thrice damned if he was going to invite his father. In fact, said Fat Charlie in closing, the best thing about getting married was not having to invite his dad to their wedding.

And then Fat Charlie saw the expression on Rosie's face and the icy glint in her normally friendly eyes, and he corrected himself hurriedly, explaining that he meant the second-best, but it was already much too late.

'You'll just have to get used to the idea,' said Rosie. 'After all, a wedding is a marvellous opportunity for mending fences and building bridges. It's your opportunity to show him that there are no hard feelings.'

'But there *are* hard feelings,' said Fat Charlie. 'Lots.'

'Do you have an address for him?' asked Rosie. 'Or a phone number? You probably ought to phone him. A letter's a bit impersonal when your only son is getting married . . . you are his only son, aren't you? Does he have e-mail?'

'Yes. I'm his only son. I have no idea if he has e-mail or not. Probably not,' said Fat Charlie. Letters were good things, he thought. They could get lost in the post for a start.

'Well, you must have an address or a phone number.'

'I don't,' said Fat Charlie, honestly. Maybe his father had moved away. He could have left Florida and gone somewhere they didn't have telephones. Or addresses.

'Well,' said Rosie, sharply, 'who does?'

'Mrs Higgler,' said Fat Charlie, and all the fight went out of him.

Rosie smiled sweetly. 'And who is Mrs Higgler?' she asked.

'Friend of the family,' said Fat Charlie. 'When I was growing up, she used to live next door.'

He had spoken to Mrs Higgler several years earlier, when his mother was dying. He had, at his mother's request, telephoned Mrs Higgler to pass on the message to Fat Charlie's father, and to tell him to get in touch. And several days later there had been a message on Fat Charlie's answering machine, left while he was at work, in a voice that was unmistakably his father's, even if it did sound rather older, and a little drunk.

His father said that it was not a good time, and that business affairs would be keeping him in America. And then he added that, for everything, Fat Charlie's mother was a damn fine woman. Several days later a vase of assorted flowers had been delivered to the hospital ward. Fat Charlie's mother had snorted when she read the card.

'Thinks he can get around me that easily?' she said. 'He's got another think coming, I can tell you that.' But she had had the nurse put the flowers in a place of honour by her bed, and, several times since, had asked Fat Charlie if he had heard anything about his father coming and visiting her before it was all over.

Fat Charlie said he hadn't. He grew to hate the question, and his answer, and the expression on her face when he told her that, no, his father wasn't coming.

The worst day, in Fat Charlie's opinion, was the day that the doctor, a gruff little man, had taken Fat Charlie aside and told him that it would not be long now, that his mother was fading fast, and it had become a matter of keeping her comfortable until the end.

Fat Charlie had nodded, and gone in to his mother. She had held his hand, and was asking him whether or not he had remembered to pay her gas bill, when the noise began in the corridor – a clashing, parping, stomping, rattling, brass and bass and drum sort of noise, of the kind that tends not to be heard in hospitals, where signs in the stairwells request quiet and the icy glares of the nursing staff enforce it.

The noise was getting louder.

For one moment Fat Charlie thought it might be terrorists. His mother, though, smiled weakly at the cacophony. 'Yellow bird,' she whispered.

'What?' said Fat Charlie, scared that she had stopped making sense.

' "Yellow Bird",' she said, louder and more firmly. 'It's what they're playing.'

Fat Charlie went to the door, and looked out.

Coming down the hospital corridor, ignoring the protests of nurses, the stares of patients in pyjamas and of their families, was what appeared to be a very small New Orleans jazz band. There was a saxophone, and a sousaphone and a trumpet. There was an enormous man with what looked like a double bass strung around his neck. There was a man with a bass drum, which he banged. And at the head of the pack, in a smart checked suit, wearing a fedora hat and lemon-yellow gloves, came Fat Charlie's father. He played no instrument, but was doing a soft-shoe shuffle along the polished linoleum of the hospital floor, lifting his hat to each of the medical staff in turn, shaking hands with anyone who got close enough to talk or to attempt to complain.

Fat Charlie bit his lip, and prayed to anyone who might be listening that the Earth would open and swallow him up, or failing that, that he might suffer a brief, merciful and entirely fatal heart attack. No such luck. He remained among the living, the brass band kept coming, his father kept dancing, and shaking hands, and smiling.

If there is any justice in the world, thought Fat Charlie, *my father will keep going down the corridor and he'll go straight past us and into the genito-urinary department*; however, there was no justice, and his father reached the door of the oncology ward and stopped.

'Fat Charlie,' he said, loudly enough that everyone in the ward – on that floor – in the hospital – was able to comprehend that this was someone who knew Fat Charlie. 'Fat Charlie, get out of the way. Your father is here.'

Fat Charlie got out of the way.

The band, led by Fat Charlie's father, snaked their way through the ward to Fat Charlie's mother's bed. She looked up at them as they approached, and she smiled.

' "Yellow Bird",' she said, weakly. 'It's my favourite song.'

'And what kind of man would I be if I forgot that?' asked Fat Charlie's father.

She shook her head slowly, and she reached out her hand and squeezed his hand in its lemon-yellow glove.

'Excuse me,' said a small white woman with a clipboard, 'are these people with you?'

'No,' said Fat Charlie, his cheeks heating up. 'They're not. Not really.'

'But that *is* your mother, isn't it?' said the woman, with a basilisk glance. 'I must ask you to make these people vacate the ward momentarily, and without incurring any further disturbance.'

Fat Charlie muttered.

'What was that?'

'I said, I'm pretty sure I can't make them do anything,' said Fat Charlie. He was consoling himself that things could not possibly get any worse, when his father took a plastic carrier bag from the drummer, and began producing cans of brown ale and handing them out, to his band, to the nursing staff, to the patients. Then he lit a cheroot.

'Excuse me,' said the woman with the clipboard, when she saw the smoke, and she launched herself across the room at Fat Charlie's father like a Scud missile with its watch on upside down.

Fat Charlie took that moment to slip away. It seemed the wisest course of action.

He sat at home that night, waiting for the phone to ring or for a knock on the door in much the same spirit that a man kneeling at the guillotine might wait for the blade to kiss his neck; still, the doorbell did not ring.

He barely slept, and slunk in to the hospital the following afternoon, prepared for the worst.

His mother, in her bed, looked happier and more comfortable than she had looked in months. 'He's gone back,' she told Fat Charlie, when he came in. 'He couldn't stay. I have to say, Charlie, I do wish you hadn't just gone like that. We wound up having a party here. We had a fine old time.'

Fat Charlie could think of nothing worse than having to attend a party in a cancer ward, thrown by his father with a jazz band. He didn't say anything.

'He's not a bad man,' said Fat Charlie's mother, with a twinkle in her eye. Then she frowned. 'Well, that's not exactly true. He's certainly not a good man. But he did me a power of good last night,' and she smiled a real smile and, for just a moment, looked young again.

The woman with the clipboard was standing in the doorway, and she crooked her finger at him. Fat Charlie beetled down the ward towards her, apologising before she was even properly within earshot. Her look, he realised, as he got closer to her, was no longer that of a basilisk with stomach cramps. Now she looked positively kittenish. 'Your father,' she said.

'I'm sorry,' said Fat Charlie. It was what he had always said, growing up, when his father was mentioned.

'No, no, no,' said the former basilisk. 'Nothing to apologise for. I was just wondering. Your father. In case we need to get in touch with him – we don't have a telephone number or an address on file. I should have asked him last night, but it completely got away from me.'

'I don't think he has a phone number,' said Fat Charlie. 'And the best way to find him is to go to Florida, and to drive up Highway A1A – that's the coast road that runs up most of the east of the state. In the afternoon you may find him fishing off a bridge. In the evening he'll be in a bar.'

'Such a charming man,' she said, wistfully. 'What does he do?'

'I told you. He says it's the miracle of the loafs and the fishes.'

She stared at him blankly, and he felt stupid. When his father said it, people would laugh. 'Um. Like in the Bible. The miracle of the loaves and the fishes. Dad used to say that he loafs and fishes, and it's a miracle that he still makes money. It was a sort of joke.'

A misty look. 'Yes. He told the funniest jokes.' She clucked her tongue, and once more was all business. 'Now, I need you back here at five-thirty.'

'Why?'

'To pick up your mother. And her belongings. Didn't Dr Johnson tell you we were discharging her?'

'You're sending her home?'

'Yes, Mr Nancy.'

'What about the, about the cancer?'

'It seems to have been a false alarm.'

Fat Charlie couldn't understand how it could have been a false alarm. Last week they'd been talking about sending his mother to a hospice. The doctor had been using phrases like 'weeks not months' and 'making her as comfortable as possible while we wait for the inevitable'.

Still, Fat Charlie came back at 5.30 and picked up his mother, who seemed quite unsurprised to learn that she was no longer dying. On the way home she told Fat Charlie that she would be using her life's savings to travel around the world.

'The doctors were saying I had three months,' she said. 'And I remember I thought, if I get out of this hospital bed then I'm going to see Paris and Rome and places like that. I'm going back to Barbados, and to Saint Andrews. I may go to Africa. And China. I like Chinese food.'

Fat Charlie wasn't sure what was going on, but whatever it was, he blamed his father. He accompanied his mother and a serious suitcase to Heathrow airport, and waved her goodbye at the International Departures gate. She was smiling hugely as she went through, clutching her passport and tickets, and she looked younger than he remembered her looking in many years.

She sent him postcards from Paris, and from Rome and from Athens, and from Lagos and Cape Town. Her postcard from Nanking told him that she certainly didn't like what passed for Chinese food in China, and that she couldn't wait to come back to London and eat *proper* Chinese food.

She died in her sleep, in a hotel in Williamstown, on the Caribbean island of Saint Andrews.

At the funeral, at a South London crematorium, Fat Charlie kept expecting to see his father: perhaps the old man would make an entrance at the head of a jazz band, or be followed down the aisle by a clown troupe or a half-dozen tricycle-riding cigar-puffing chimpanzees; even during the service Fat Charlie kept glancing back over his shoulder, towards the chapel door. But Fat Charlie's father was not there, only his mother's friends and distant relations, mostly big women in black hats, blowing their noses and dabbing at their eyes and shaking their heads.

It was during the final hymn, after the button had been pressed and Fat Charlie's mother had trundled off down the conveyor belt to her final reward, that Fat Charlie noticed a man of about his own age standing at the back of the chapel. It was not his father, obviously. It was someone he did not know, someone he might not even have noticed, at the back, in the shadows, had he not been looking for his father . . . and then there was the stranger, in an elegant black suit, his eyes lowered, his hands folded.

Fat Charlie let his glance linger a moment too long, and the stranger looked at Fat Charlie and flashed him a joyless smile of the kind that suggested that they were both in this together. It was not the kind of expression you see on the faces of strangers, but still, Fat Charlie could not place the man. He turned his face back to the front of the chapel. They sang 'Swing Low, Sweet Chariot', a song Fat Charlie was pretty sure his mother had always disliked, and the Reverend Wright invited them back to Fat Charlie's Great-Aunt Alanna's for something to eat.

There was nobody at his Great-Aunt Alanna's whom he did not already know. In the years since his mother had died, he had sometimes wondered about that stranger: who he was, why he was there. Sometimes Fat Charlie thought that he had simply imagined him . . .

'So,' said Rosie, draining her Chardonnay, 'you'll call your Mrs Higgler, and give her my mobile number. Tell her about the wedding and the date . . . that's a thought: do you think we should invite her?'

'We can if we like,' said Fat Charlie. 'I don't think she'll come. She's an old family friend. She knew my dad back in the Dark Ages.'

'Well, sound her out. See if we should send her an invitation.'

Rosie was a good person. There was in Rosie a little of the essence of Francis of Assisi, of Robin Hood, of Buddha and of Glinda the Good: the knowledge that she was about to bring together her true love and his estranged father gave her forthcoming wedding an extra dimension, she decided. It was no longer simply a wedding: it was now practically a humanitarian mission, and Fat Charlie had known Rosie long enough to know never to stand between his fiancée and her need to Do Good.

'I'll call Mrs Higgler tomorrow,' he said.

'Tell you what,' said Rosie, with an endearing wrinkle of her nose, 'call her tonight. It's not late in America, after all.'

Fat Charlie nodded. They walked out of the wine bar together, Rosie with a spring in her step, Fat Charlie like a man going to the gallows. He told himself not to be silly. After all, perhaps Mrs

Higgler had moved, or had her phone disconnected. It was possible. Anything was possible.

They went up to Fat Charlie's place, the upstairs half of a smallish house in Maxwell Gardens, just off the Brixton Road.

'What time is it in Florida?' Rosie asked.

'Late afternoon,' said Fat Charlie.

'Well. Go on then.'

'Maybe we should wait a bit. In case she's out.'

'And maybe we should call now, before she has her dinner.'

Fat Charlie found his old paper address book, and under H was a scrap of an envelope, in his mother's handwriting, with a telephone number on it and, beneath that, 'Callyanne Higgler'.

The phone rang and rang.

'She's not there,' he said to Rosie, but at that moment the phone at the other end was answered, and a female voice said 'Yes? Who is this?'

'Um. Is that Mrs Higgler?'

'Who is this?' said Mrs Higgler. 'If you're one of they damn telemarketers, you take me off your list right now or I sue. I know my rights.'

'No. It's me. Charles Nancy. I used to live next door to you.'

'Fat Charlie? If that don't beat all. I been looking for your number all this morning. I turn this place upside down, looking for it, and you think I could find it? What I think happen was I had it written in my old accounts book. Upside down I turn the place. And I say to myself, Callyanne, this is a good time to just pray and hope the Lord hear you and see you right, and I went down on my knees, well, my knees are not so good any more, so I just put my hands together, but anyway, I still don't find your number, but look at how you just phone me up, and that's even better from some points of view, particularly because I ain't made of money and I can't afford to go phoning no foreign countries even for something like this, although I was going to phone you, don't you worry, given the circumstances—'

And she stopped, suddenly, either to take a breath, or to take a sip from the huge mug of too-hot coffee she always carried in her left hand, and during the brief quiet Fat Charlie said, 'I want to ask my dad to come to my wedding. Getting married.' There was silence at the end of the line. 'It's not till the end of the year, though,' he said. Still silence. 'Her name's Rosie,' he added, helpfully. He was starting to wonder if they had been cut off; conversations with Mrs Higgler were normally somewhat one-sided affairs, often with her doing your lines for you, and here she was, letting him say three whole things uninterrupted. He decided to go for a fourth. 'You can come too if you want,' he said.

'Lord, Lord, Lord,' said Mrs Higgler. 'Nobody tell you?'

'Told me what?'

So she told him, at length and in detail, while he stood there and said nothing at all, and when she was done he said, 'Thank you, Mrs Higgler.' He wrote something down on a scrap of paper, then he said, 'Thanks. No, really, thanks,' again, and he put down the phone.

'Well?' asked Rosie. 'Have you got his number?'

Fat Charlie said, 'Dad won't be coming to the wedding.' Then he said, 'I have to go to Florida.' His voice was flat, and without emotion. He might have been saying, 'I have to order a new cheque book.'

'When?'

'Tomorrow.'

'Why?'

'Funeral. My dad's. He's dead.'

'Oh. I'm sorry. I'm so sorry.' She put her arms around him, and held him. He stood in her arms like a shop-window dummy. 'How did it, did he . . . was he ill?'

Fat Charlie shook his head. 'I don't want to talk about it,' he said.

And Rosie squeezed him tightly, and then she nodded, sympathetically, and let him go. She thought he was too over-come with grief to talk about it.

He wasn't. That wasn't it at all. He was too embarrassed.

***

There must be a hundred thousand respectable ways to die. Leaping off a bridge into a river to save a small child from drowning, for example, or being mown down in a hail of bullets while single-handedly storming a nest of criminals. Perfectly respectable ways to die.

Truth to tell, there were even some less-than-respectable ways to die that wouldn't have been so bad. Spontaneous human combustion, for example: it's medically dodgy and scientifically unlikely, but even so, people persist in going up in smoke, leaving nothing behind but a charred hand still clutching an unfinished cigarette. Fat Charlie had read about it in a magazine: he wouldn't have minded if his father had gone like that. Or even if he'd had a heart attack running down the street after the men who had stolen his beer money.

This is how Fat Charlie's father died.

He had arrived in the bar early, and had launched the karaoke evening by singing 'What's New Pussycat?', which song he had belted out, according to Mrs Higgler, who had not been there, in a manner that would have caused Tom Jones to be festooned in flung feminine undergarments, and which brought Fat Charlie's father a complimentary beer, courtesy of the several blonde tourists from Michigan who thought he was just about the cutest thing they'd ever seen.

'It was their fault,' said Mrs Higgler, bitterly, over the phone. 'They was encouragin' him!' They were women who had squeezed into tube tops, and they had reddish too-much-sun-too-early tans, and they were all young enough to be his daughters.

So pretty soon he's down at their table, smoking his cheroots and hinting strongly that he was in army intelligence during the war, although he was careful not to say which war, and that he could kill a man in a dozen different ways with his bare hands without breaking a sweat.

Now he takes the bustiest and blondest of the tourists on a quick spin around the dance floor, such as it was, while one of her friends warbled 'Strangers in the Night' from the stage. He appeared to be having a fine time, although the tourist was somewhat taller than he was, and his grin was on a level with her bosom.

And then, the dance done, he announced it was his turn again, and, because if there was one thing you could say about Fat Charlie's father, it was that he was secure in his heterosexuality, he sang 'I Am What I Am' to the room, but particularly to the blondest tourist on the table just below him. He gave it everything he had. He had just got as far as explaining to anyone listening that as far as he was concerned his life would not actually be worth a damn unless he was able to tell everybody that he was what he was, when he made an odd face, pressed one hand to his chest, stretched the other hand out, and toppled, as slowly and as gracefully as a man could topple, off the makeshift stage and on to the blondest holidaymaker, and from her on to the floor.

'It was how he always would have wanted to go,' sighed Mrs Higgler.

And then she told Fat Charlie how his father had, with his final gesture, as he fell, reached out and grasped at something, which turned out to be the blonde tourist's tube top, so that at first some people thought he had made a lust-driven leap from the stage with the sole purpose of exposing the bosom in question, because there she was, screaming, with her breasts staring at the room, while the music for 'I Am What I Am' kept playing, only now without anyone singing.

When the onlookers realised what had actually happened they had two minutes' silence, and Fat Charlie's father was carried out and put into an ambulance while the blonde tourist had hysterics in the ladies' room.

It was the breasts that Fat Charlie couldn't get out of his head. In his mind's eye they followed him accusatively around the room, like the eyes in a painting. He kept wanting to apologise to a roomful of people he had never met. And the knowledge that his father would have found it hugely amusing simply added to Fat Charlie's mortification. It's worse when you're embarrassed about something you were not even there to see: your mind keeps embroidering the events, and going back to it and turning it over and over, and examining it from every side. Well, yours might not, but Fat Charlie's certainly did.

As a rule, Fat Charlie felt embarrassment in his teeth, and in the upper pit of his stomach. If something that even looked like it might be embarrassing was about to happen on his television screen Fat Charlie would leap up and turn it off. If that was not possible, say if other people were present, he would leave

the room on some pretext and wait until the moment of
embarrassment was sure to be over.

Fat Charlie lived in South London. He had arrived, at the age of
ten, with an American accent, which he had been relentlessly
teased about, and had worked very hard to lose, slowly
extirpating the last of the soft consonants and rich Rs, while
learning the correct use and placement of the word 'innit'. He had
finally succeeded in losing his American accent for good as he
had turned sixteen, just as his schoolfriends discovered that they
needed very badly to sound like they came from the 'hood. Soon
all of them except Fat Charlie sounded like people who wanted to
sound like Fat Charlie had talked when he'd come to England in
the first place, except that he could never have used language like
that in public without his mum giving him a swift clout round the
ear.

It was all in the voice.

Once the embarrassment over his father's method of passing
began to fade, Fat Charlie just felt empty.

'I don't have any family,' he said to Rosie, almost petulantly.

'You've got me,' she said. That made Fat Charlie smile. 'And
you've got my mum,' she added, which stopped the smile in its
tracks. She kissed him on the cheek.

'You could stay over for the night,' he suggested. 'Comfort me,
all that.'

'I could,' she agreed, 'but I'm not going to.'

Rosie was not going to sleep with Fat Charlie until they were
married. She said it was her decision, and she had made it when
she was fifteen; not that she had known Fat Charlie then, but she
had decided. So she gave him another hug, a long one. And she
said, 'You need to make your peace with your dad, you know.'
And then she went home.

He spent a restless night, sleeping sometimes, then waking, and
wondering, and falling back asleep again.

He was up at sunrise. When people got in to work he would
ring his travel agent and ask about bereavement fares to Florida,
and he would phone the Grahame Coats Agency and tell them
that, due to a death in the family, he would have to take a few
days off and yes, he knew it came out of his sick leave or his

holiday time. But for now he was glad that the world was quiet.

He went along the corridor to the tiny spare room at the back of the house, and looked down into the gardens below. The dawn chorus had begun, and he could see blackbirds, and small hedge-hopping sparrows, a single spotted-breasted thrush in the boughs of a nearby tree. Fat Charlie thought that a world in which birds sang in the morning was a normal world, a sensible world, a world he didn't mind being a part of.

Later, when birds were something to be afraid of, Fat Charlie would still remember that morning as something good and something fine, but also as the place where it all started. Before the madness; before the fear.

Chapter Two

Which Goes into Some of the Things that Happen after Funerals

at Charlie puffed his way through the Memorial Garden of
Rest, squinting at the Florida sunshine. Sweat stains were
spreading across his suit, beginning with the armpits and
the chest. Sweat began to pour down his face as he ran.

The Memorial Garden of Rest did, in fact, look very much like
a garden, but a very odd garden, in which all the flowers were
artificial and they grew from metal vases protruding from metal
plaques set in the ground. Fat Charlie ran past a sign. 'FREE Burial
Space for all Honorably Discharged Veterans!' it said. He ran
through Babyland, where multicoloured windmills and sodden
blue and pink teddy bears joined the artificial flowers on the
Florida turf. A mouldering Winnie-the-Pooh stared up wanly at
the blue sky.

Fat Charlie could see the funeral party now, and he changed
direction, finding a path that allowed him to run towards it.
There were thirty people, perhaps more, standing around the
grave. The women wore dark dresses, and big black hats trimmed
with black lace, like fabulous flowers. The men wore suits
without sweat stains. The children looked solemn. Fat Charlie

slowed his pace to a respectful walk, still trying to hurry without moving fast enough for anyone to notice that he was in fact hurrying, and, having reached the group of mourners, he attempted to edge his way to the front ranks without attracting too much attention. Seeing that by now he was panting like a walrus who had just had to tackle a flight of stairs, was dripping with sweat, and trod on several feet as he went by, this attempt proved a failure.

There were glares, which Fat Charlie tried to pretend he did not notice. Everyone was singing a song that Fat Charlie did not know. He moved his head in time with the song and tried to make it look as if he was sort of singing, moving his lips in a way that might have meant that he was actively singing along, *sotto voce*, and he might have been muttering a prayer under his breath, and it might just have been random lip motion. He took the opportunity to look down at the casket. He was pleased to see that it was closed.

The casket was a glorious thing, made of what looked like heavy-duty, reinforced steel, gun-metal grey. In the event of the glorious resurrection, thought Fat Charlie, when Gabriel blows his mighty horn and the dead escape their coffins, his father was going to be stuck in his grave, banging away futilely at the lid, wishing that he had been buried with a crowbar and possibly an oxyacetylene torch.

A final, deeply melodic hallelujah faded away. In the silence that followed, Fat Charlie could hear someone shouting at the other end of the memorial gardens, back near where he had come in.

The preacher said, 'Now, does anyone have anything they want to say in memory of the dear departed?'

By the expressions on the faces of those nearest to the grave, it was obvious that several of them were planning to say things. But Fat Charlie knew it was a now or never moment. *You need to make your peace with your dad, you know*. Right.

He took a deep breath and a step forward, so he was right at the edge of the grave, and he said, 'Um. Excuse me. Right. I think I have something to say.'

The distant shouting was getting louder. Several of the

mourners were casting glances back over their shoulders to see where it was coming from. The rest of them were staring at Fat Charlie.

'I was never what you would call close to my father,' said Fat Charlie. 'I suppose we didn't really know how. I've not been part of his life for twenty years, and he hasn't been part of mine. There's a lot of things it's hard to forgive, but then one day you turn around and you've got no family left.' He wiped a hand across his forehead. 'I don't think I've ever said "I love you, Dad" in my whole life. All of you, you all probably knew him better than I did. Some of you may have loved him. You were part of his life and I wasn't. So I'm not ashamed that any of you should hear me say it. Say it for the first time in at least twenty years.' He looked down at the impregnable metal casket lid. 'I love you,' he said. 'And I'll never forget you.'

The shouting got even louder, and now it was loud enough, and clear enough, in the silence that followed Fat Charlie's statement, for everyone to be able to make out the words being bellowed across the memorial gardens.

'Fat Charlie! You stop botherin' those people and get your ass over here *this* minute!'

Fat Charlie stared at the sea of unfamiliar faces, their expressions a seething stew of shock, puzzlement, anger and horror; ears burning, he realised the truth.

'Er. Sorry. Wrong funeral,' he said.

A small boy with big ears and an enormous smile said, proudly, 'That was my gramma.'

Fat Charlie backed through the small crowd mumbling barely coherent apologies. He wanted the world to end now. He knew it was not his father's fault, but also knew that his father would have found it hilarious.

Standing on the path, her hands on her hips, was a large woman with grey hair and thunder in her face. Fat Charlie walked towards her as he would have walked across a minefield, nine years old again, and in trouble.

'You don't hear me yellin?' she asked. 'You went right on past me. Makin' a embarrassment of yourself!' The way she said 'embarrassment', it began with the letter H. 'Back this way,' she said. 'You miss the service and everythin'. But there's a shovelful of dirt waiting for you.'

Mrs Higgler had barely changed in the last two decades: she was a little fatter, a little greyer. Her lips were pressed tightly together, and she led the way down one of the memorial garden's many paths. Fat Charlie suspected that he had not made the best possible first impression. She led the way and, in disgrace, Fat Charlie followed.

A lizard zapped up one of the struts of the metal fence at the edge of the memorial garden, then poised itself at the top of a spike, tasting the thick Florida air. The sun had gone behind a cloud, but, if anything, the afternoon was getting hotter. The lizard puffed its neck out into a bright orange balloon.

Two long-legged cranes he had taken initially for lawn ornaments looked up at him as he passed. One of them darted its head down, rose up again with a large frog dangling from its beak. It began, in a series of gulping movements, to try to swallow the frog, which kicked and flailed in the air.

'Come on,' said Mrs Higgler. 'Don't dawdle. Bad enough you missing your own father's funeral.'

Fat Charlie suppressed the urge to say something about having come four thousand miles already that day, and having rented a car and driven down from Orlando, and how he had got off at the wrong exit and whose idea was it anyway to tuck a garden of rest behind a Wal-Mart on the very edge of town? They kept walking, past a large concrete building that smelled of formaldehyde, until they reached an open grave at the very furthest reaches of the property. There was nothing beyond this but a high fence, and, beyond that, a wilderness of trees and palms and greenery. In the grave was a modest wooden coffin. It had several mounds of dirt on it already. Beside the grave was a pile of mud, and a shovel.

Mrs Higgler picked up the shovel and handed it to Fat Charlie.

'It was a pretty service,' she said. 'Some of your daddy's old drinkin' buddies were there, and all the ladies from our street. Even after he moved down the road we still kept in touch. He would have liked it. Of course, he would have liked it more if you'd been there.' She shook her head. 'Now, shovel,' she said.

'And if you got any goodbyes, you can say them while you're shovellin' down the dirt.'

'I thought I was just meant to do one or two spadefuls of dirt,' he said. 'To show willing.'

'I give the man thirty bucks to go away,' said Mrs Higgler. 'I tell him that the departed's son is flying in all the way from Hingland, and that he would want to do right by his father. Do the right thing. Not just "show willing".'

'Right,' said Fat Charlie. 'Absolutely. Got it.' He took off his suit jacket and hung it on the fence. He loosened his tie, pulled it over his head, and put it into the jacket pocket. He shovelled the black dirt into the open grave, in Florida air as thick as soup.

After a while it sort of began to rain, which is to say that it was the kind of rain that never comes to a decision about whether it's actually raining or not. Driving in it, you would never have been certain whether or not to turn on your wipers. Standing in it, shovelling in it, you simply got sweatier, damper, more uncomfortable. Fat Charlie continued to shovel, and Mrs Higgler stood there with her arms folded across her gargantuan bosom, with the almost-rain misting her black dress and her straw hat with one black silk rose on it, watching him, as he filled in the hole.

The earth became mud, and became, if anything, heavier.

After what seemed like a lifetime, and a very uncomfortable one at that, Fat Charlie patted down the final shovelful of dirt.

Mrs Higgler walked over to him. She took his jacket off the fence, and handed it to him.

'You're soaked to the skin, and covered in dirt and sweat, but you grew up. Welcome home, Fat Charlie,' she said, and she smiled and she held him to her vast breast.

'I'm not crying,' said Fat Charlie.

'Hush now,' said Mrs Higgler.

'It's the rain on my face,' said Fat Charlie.

Mrs Higgler didn't say anything. She just held him, and swayed backward and forward, and after a while Fat Charlie said 'It's OK. I'm better now.'

'There's food back at my house,' said Mrs Higgler. 'Let's get you fed.'

He wiped the mud from his shoes in the parking lot, then he got into his grey rental car, and he followed Mrs Higgler in her maroon station wagon down streets that had not existed twenty years earlier. Mrs Higgler drove like a woman who had just discovered an enormous and much-needed mug of coffee and whose primary mission was to drink as much coffee as she was able to while driving as fast as possible, and Fat Charlie drove along behind her, keeping up as best he could, racing from traffic light to traffic light while trying to figure out more or less where they were.

And then they turned down a street, and, with mounting apprehension, he realised he recognised it. This was the street he had lived on as a boy. Even the houses looked more or less the same, although most of them had now grown impressive wire-mesh fences around their front yards.

There were several cars already parked in front of Mrs Higgler's house. He pulled up behind an elderly grey Ford. Mrs Higgler walked up to the front door, opened it with her key.

Fat Charlie looked down at himself, muddy and sweat-soaked. 'I can't go in looking like this,' he said.

'I seen worse,' said Mrs Higgler. Then she sniffed. 'I tell you what, you go in there, go straight into the bathroom, you can wash off your hands and face, clean yourself up, and when you're ready we'll all be in the kitchen.'

He went into the bathroom. Everything smelled like jasmine. He took off his muddy shirt, and washed his face and hands with jasmine-scented soap, in a tiny washbasin. He took a wash-cloth, and wiped down his chest, and scrubbed at the muddiest lumps on his suit trousers. He looked at the shirt, which had been white when he put it on this morning and was now a particularly grubby brown, and decided not to put it back on. He had more shirts in his bag, in the back seat of the rental car. He would slip back out of the house, put on a clean shirt, then face the people in the house.

He unlocked the bathroom door, and opened it.

Four elderly ladies were standing in the corridor, staring at him. He knew them. He knew all of them.

'What you doing now?' asked Mrs Higgler.

'Changing shirt,' said Fat Charlie. 'Shirt in car. Yes. Back soon.'

He raised his chin high, and strode down the corridor and out of the front door.

'What kind of language was that he was talkin?' asked little Mrs Dunwiddy, behind his back, loudly.

'That's not something you see every day,' said Mrs Bustamonte, although, this being Florida's Treasure Coast, if there was something you did see every day, it was topless men, although not usually with muddy suit trousers on.

Fat Charlie changed his shirt by the car, and went back into the house. The four ladies were in the kitchen, industriously packing away into Tupperware containers what looked like it had until recently been a large spread of food.

Mrs Higgler was older than Mrs Bustamonte, and both of them were older than Miss Noles and none of them was older than Mrs Dunwiddy. Mrs Dunwiddy was old, and she looked it. There were geological ages that were probably younger than Mrs Dunwiddy.

As a boy, Fat Charlie had imagined Mrs Dunwiddy in Equatorial Africa, peering disapprovingly though her thick spectacles at the newly erect hominids. 'Keep out of my front yard,' she would tell a recently evolved and rather nervous specimen of *Homo habilis*, 'or I going to belt you around your earhole, I can tell you.' Mrs Dunwiddy smelled of violet-water and beneath the violets she smelled of very old woman indeed. She was a tiny old lady who could outglare a thunderstorm, and Fat Charlie, who had, over two decades ago, followed a lost tennis ball into her yard, and then broken one of her lawn ornaments, was still quite terrified of her.

Right now, Mrs Dunwiddy was eating lumps of curry goat with her fingers from a small Tupperware bowl. 'Pity to waste it,' she said, and dropped the bits of goat-bone into a china saucer.

'Time for you to eat, Fat Charlie?' asked Miss Noles.

'I'm fine,' said Fat Charlie. 'Honest.'

Four pairs of eyes stared at him reproachfully through four pairs of spectacles. 'No good starvin' yourself in your grief,' said Mrs Dunwiddy, licking her fingertips, and picking out another brown fatty lump of goat.

'I'm not. I'm just not hungry. That's all.'

'Misery going to shrivel you away to pure skin and bones,' said Miss Noles, with gloomy relish.

'I don't think it will.'

'I putting a plate together for you at the table over there,' said Mrs Higgler. 'You go and sit down now. I don't want to hear another word out of you. There's more of everything, so don't you worry about that.'

Fat Charlie sat down where she pointed, and within seconds there was placed in front of him a plate piled high with stew peas and rice, and sweet potato pudding, jerk pork, curry goat, curry chicken, fried plantains, and a pickled cow foot. Fat Charlie could feel the heartburn beginning, and he had not even put anything in his mouth yet.

'Where's everyone else?' he said.

'Your daddy's drinking buddies, they gone off drinking. They going to have a memorial fishing trip off a bridge, in his memory.' Mrs Higgler poured the remaining coffee out of her bucket-sized travelling mug into the sink, and replaced it with the steaming contents of a freshly brewed jug of coffee.

Mrs Dunwiddy licked her fingers clean with a small purple tongue, and she shuffled over to where Fat Charlie was sitting, his food as yet untouched. When he was a little boy he had truly believed that Mrs Dunwiddy was a witch. Not a nice witch, more the kind kids had to push into ovens to escape from. This was the first time he'd seen her in more than twenty years, and he was still having to quell an inner urge to yelp and hide under the table.

'I seen plenty people die,' said Mrs Dunwiddy. 'In my time. Get old enough, you will see it your own self too. Everybody going to be dead one day, just give them time.' She paused. 'Still. I never thought it would happen to your daddy.' And she shook her head.

'What was he like?' asked Fat Charlie. 'When he was young?'

Mrs Dunwiddy looked at him through her thick, thick spectacles, and her lips pursed, and she shook her head. 'Before my time,' was all she said. 'Eat your cow foot.'

Fat Charlie sighed, and he began to eat.

***

It was late afternoon, and they were alone in the house.

'Where you going to sleep tonight?' asked Mrs Higgler.

'I thought I'd get a motel room,' said Fat Charlie.

'When you got a perfectly good bedroom here? And a perfectly good house down the road? You haven't even looked at it yet. You ask me, your father would have wanted you to stay there.'

'I'd rather be on my own. And I don't think I feel right about sleeping at my dad's place.'

'Well, it's not my money I'm throwin' away,' said Mrs Higgler. 'You're goin' to have to decide what you're goin' to do with your father's house anyway. And all his things.'

'I don't care,' said Fat Charlie. 'We could have a garage sale. Put them on eBay. Haul them to the dump.'

'Now, what kind of an attitude is that?' She rummaged in a kitchen drawer, and pulled out a front door key with a large paper label attached to it. 'He give me a spare key when he move,' she said. 'In case he lose his, or lock it inside, or something. He used to say, he could forget his head if it wasn't attached to his neck. When he sell the house next door, he tell me, don't you worry, Callyanne, I won't go far, he'd live in that house as long as I remember, but now he decide it's too big and he need to move house . . .' and still talking she walked him down to the kerb, and drove them down several streets in her maroon station wagon, until they reached a one-storey wooden house.

She unlocked the front door and they went inside.

The smell was familiar: faintly sweet, as if chocolate-chip cookies had been baked there the last time the kitchen was used, but that had been a long time ago. It was too hot in there. Mrs Higgler led them into the little sitting room, and she turned on a window-fitted air-conditioning unit. It rattled and shook, and smelled like a wet sheepdog, and moved the warm air around.

There were stacks of books piled around a decrepit sofa Fat Charlie remembered from his childhood, and there were photographs in frames: one, in black and white, of Fat Charlie's mother when she was young, with her hair up on top of her head all black and shiny, wearing a sparkly dress; beside it, a photo of Fat Charlie himself, aged perhaps five or six years old, standing beside a mirrored door, so it looked at first glance as if two little

Fat Charlies, side by side, were staring seriously out of the photograph at you.

Fat Charlie picked up the top book in the pile. It was a book on Italian architecture.

'Was he interested in architecture?'

'Passionate about it. Yes.'

'I didn't know that.'

Mrs Higgler shrugged and sipped her coffee.

Fat Charlie opened the book, and saw his father's name neatly written on the first page. He closed the book.

'I never knew him,' said Fat Charlie. 'Not really.'

'He was never an easy man to know,' said Mrs Higgler. 'I knew him for what, nearly sixty years? And I didn't know him.'

'You must have known him when he was a boy.'

Mrs Higgler hesitated. She seemed to be remembering. Then she said, very quietly, 'I knew him when I was a girl.'

Fat Charlie felt that he should be changing the subject, so he pointed to the photo of his mother. 'He's got Mum's picture there,' he said.

Mrs Higgler took a slurp of her coffee. 'Them take it on a boat,' she said. 'Back before you was born. One of those boats that you had dinner on, and they would sail out three miles, out of territorial waters, and then there was gamblin'. Then they come back. I don't know if they still run those boats. Your mother say it was the first time she ever eat steak.'

Fat Charlie tried to imagine what his parents had been like before he was born.

'He always was a good-looking man,' mused Mrs Higgler, as if she were reading his mind. 'All the way to the end. He had a smile that could make a girl squeeze her toes. And he was always such a very fine dresser. All the ladies loved him.'

Fat Charlie knew the answer before he asked the question. 'Did you . . . ?'

'What kind of a question is that to be asking a respectable widow-woman?' She sipped her coffee. Fat Charlie waited for the answer. She said, 'I kissed him. Long, long time ago, before he ever met your mother. He was a fine, fine kisser. I hoped that he'd call, take me dancing again, instead he vanish. He was gone for what, a year? Two years? And by the time he come back, I was married to Mr Higgler, and he's bringing back your mother. Is out on the islands he meet her.'

'Were you upset?'

'I was a married woman.' Another sip of coffee. 'And you couldn't hate him. Couldn't even be properly angry with him. And the way he look at her – damn, if he did ever look at me like that I could have died happy. You know, at their wedding, is me was your mother's matron of honour?'

'I didn't know.'

The air-conditioning unit was starting to bellow out cold air. It still smelled like a wet sheepdog.

He asked, 'Do you think they were happy?'

'In the beginning.' She hefted her huge thermal mug, seemed about to take a sip of coffee and then changed her mind. 'In the beginning. But not even she could keep his attention for very long. He had so much to do. He was very busy, your father.'

Fat Charlie tried to work out if Mrs Higgler was joking or not. He couldn't tell. She didn't smile, though.

'So much to do? Like what? Fish off bridges? Play dominoes on the porch? Await the inevitable invention of karaoke? He wasn't busy. I don't think he ever did a day's work in all the time I knew him.'

'You shouldn't say that about your father!'

'Well, it's true. He was crap. A rotten husband and a rotten father.'

'Of course he was!' said Mrs Higgler, fiercely, 'But you can't judge him like you would judge a man. You got to remember, Fat Charlie, that your father was a god.'

'A god among men?'

'No. Just a god.' She said it without any kind of emphasis, as flatly and as normally as she might have said 'he was diabetic' or simply 'he was black'.

Fat Charlie wanted to make a joke of it, but there was that look in Mrs Higgler's eyes, and suddenly he couldn't think of anything funny to say. So he said, softly, 'He wasn't a god. Gods are special. Mythical. They do miracles and things.'

'That's right,' said Mrs Higgler. 'We wouldn't have told you while he was alive, but now he is gone, there can't be any harm in it.'

'He was not a god. He was my dad.'

'You can be both,' she said. 'It happens.'

It was like arguing with a crazy person, thought Fat Charlie. He realised that he should just shut up, but his mouth kept going. Right now his mouth was saying, 'Look. If my dad was a god, he would have had godlike powers.'

'He did. Never did a lot with them, mind you. But he was old. Anyway, how do you think he got away with not working? Whenever he needed money, he'd play the lottery, or go down to Hallendale and bet on the dogs or the horses. Never win enough to attract attention. Just enough to get by.'

Fat Charlie had never won anything in his whole life. Nothing whatsoever. In the various office sweepstakes he had taken part in, he was only able to rely on his horse never making it out of the starting gate, or his team being relegated to some hitherto unheard-of division somewhere in the elephants' graveyard of organised sport. It rankled.

'If my dad was a god – something which I do not for one moment concede in any way, I should add – then why aren't *I* a god too? I mean, you're saying I'm the son of a god, aren't you?'

'Obviously.'

'Well then, why can't I bet on winning horses or do magic or miracles or things?'

She sniffed. 'Your brother got all that god stuff.'

Fat Charlie found that he was smiling. He breathed out. It was a joke after all, then.

'Ah. You know, Mrs Higgler, I don't actually have a brother.'

'Of course you do. That's you and him, in the photograph.'

Although he knew what was in it, Fat Charlie glanced over at the photograph. She was mad all right. Absolutely barking. 'Mrs Higgler,' he said, as gently as possible, 'that's *me*. Just me when I was a kid. It's a mirrored door. I'm standing next to it. It's me, and my reflection.'

'It is you, and it is also your brother.'

'I never had a brother.'

'Sure you did. I don't miss him. You were always the good one,

you know. He was a handful when he was here.' And before Fat
Charlie could say anything else she added. 'He went away, when
you are just a little boy.'

Fat Charlie leaned over. He put his big hand on Mrs Higgler's
bony hand, the one that wasn't holding the coffee mug. 'It's not
true,' he said.

'Louella Dunwiddy made him go,' she said. 'He was scared of
her. But he still came back, from time to time. He could be
charming when he wanted to be.' She finished her coffee.

'I always wanted a brother,' said Fat Charlie. 'Somebody to play
with.'

Mrs Higgler got up. 'This place isn't going to clean itself up,' she
said. 'I've got garbage bags in the car. I figure we'll need a lot of
garbage bags.'

'Yes,' said Fat Charlie.

He stayed in a motel that night. In the morning, he and Mrs
Higgler met, back at his father's house, and they put garbage into
big black garbage bags. They assembled bags of objects to be
donated to Goodwill. They also filled a box with things Fat
Charlie wanted to hold on to for sentimental reasons, mostly
photographs from his childhood and before he was born.

There was an old trunk, like a small pirate's treasure chest,
filled with documents and old papers. Fat Charlie sat on the floor
going through them. Mrs Higgler came in from the bedroom, with
another black garbage bag filled with moth-eaten clothes.

'It's your brother give him that trunk,' said Mrs Higgler, out of
the blue. It was the first time she had mentioned any of her
fantasies of the previous night.

'I wish I did have a brother,' said Fat Charlie, and he did not
realise he had said it aloud until Mrs Higgler said, 'I already told
you. You *do* have a brother.'

'So,' he said. 'Where would I find this mythical brother of
mine?' Later, he would wonder why he had asked her this. Was he
humouring her? Teasing her? Was it just that he had to say
something to fill the void? Whatever the reason, he said it. And
she was chewing her lower lip, and nodding.

'You got to know. It's your heritage. It's your bloodline.' She
walked over to him and crooked her finger. Fat Charlie bent down.

The old woman's lips brushed his ear as she whispered, '. . . need him . . . tell a . . .'

'What?'

'I say,' she said, in her normal voice, 'if you need him, just tell a spider. He'll come running.'

'Tell a spider?'

'That's what I said. You think I just talkin' for my health? Exercisin' my lungs? You never hear of talkin' to the bees? When I was a girl in Saint Andrews, before my folks came here, you would go tell the bees all your good news. Well, this is just like that. Talk to spider. It was how I used to send messages to your father, when he would vanish off.'

' . . . Right.'

'Don't you say "right" like that.'

'Like what?'

'Like I'm a crazy old lady who don't know the price of fish. You think I don't know which way is up?'

'Um. I'm quite sure you do. Honestly.'

Mrs Higgler was not mollified. She was far from gruntled. She picked up her coffee mug from the table, and cradled it, disapprovingly. Fat Charlie had done it now, and Mrs Higgler was determined to make sure that he knew it.

'I don't got to do this, you know,' she said. 'I don't got to help you. I'm only doing it because your father, he was special, and because your mother, she was a fine woman. I'm telling you big things. I'm telling you important things. You should listen to me. You should believe me.'

'I do believe you,' said Fat Charlie, as convincingly as he could.

'Now you're just humouring an old woman.'

'No,' he lied. 'I'm not. Honestly I'm not.' His words rang with honesty, sincerity and truth. He was thousands of miles from home, in his late father's house, with a crazy old woman on the verge of an apoplectic seizure. He would have told her that the moon was just some kind of unusual tropical fruit if it would have calmed her down, and meant it, as best he could.

She sniffed.

'That's the trouble with you young people,' she said. 'You think because you ain't been here long, you know everything. In my life

I already forget more than you ever know. You don't know nothin' about your father, you don't know nothin' about your family. I tell you your father is a god, you don't even ask me what god I talking about.'

Fat Charlie tried to remember the names of some gods. 'Zeus?' he suggested.

Mrs Higgler made a noise like a kettle suppressing the urge to boil. Fat Charlie was fairly sure that Zeus had been the wrong answer. 'Cupid?'

She made another noise, which began as a sputter and ended in a giggle. 'I can just picture your dad wearing nothin' but one of them fluffy diapers, with a big bow and arrow.' She giggled some more. Then she swallowed some coffee.

'Back when he was a god,' she told him. 'Back then, they called him Anansi.'

* * *

Now, probably you know some Anansi stories. Probably there's no one in the whole wide world doesn't know some Anansi stories.

Anansi was a spider, when the world was young, and all the stories were being told for the first time. He used to get himself into trouble, and he used to get himself out of trouble. The story of the tar-baby, the one they tell about Brer Rabbit? That was Anansi's story first. Some people think he was a rabbit. But that's their mistake. He wasn't a rabbit. He was a spider.

Anansi stories go back as long as people been telling each other stories. Back in Africa, where everything began, even before people were painting cave-lions and bears on rock walls, even then they were telling stories, about monkeys and lions and buffalo: big dream stories. People always had those proclivities. That was how they made sense of their worlds. Everything that ran or crawled or swung or snaked got to walk through those stories, and different tribes of people would venerate different creatures.

Lion was the king of beasts, even then, and Gazelle was the fleetest of foot, and Monkey was the most foolish, and Tiger was the most terrible, but it wasn't stories about them people wanted to hear.

Anansi gave his name to stories. Every story is Anansi's. Once, before the stories were Anansi's, they all belonged to Tiger (which is the name the people of the islands call all the big cats), and back then the tales were dark and evil, and filled with pain, and none of them ended happily. But that was a long time ago. These days, the stories are Anansi's.

Seeing we were just at a funeral, let me tell you a story about Anansi, the time his grandmother died. (It's OK: she was a very old woman, and she went in her sleep. It happens.) She died a long way from home, so Anansi, he goes across the island with his handcart, and he gets his grandmother's body, and puts it on the handcart, and he wheels it home. He's going to bury her by the banyan tree out the back of his hut, you see.

Now, he's passing through the town, after pushing his grandmother's corpse in the cart all morning, and he thinks, *I need some whisky.* So he goes into the shop, for there is a shop in that village, a store that sells everything, where the shopkeeper is a very hasty-tempered man. Anansi, he goes in and he drinks some whisky. He drinks a little more whisky, and he thinks, I shall play a trick on this fellow, so he says to the shopkeeper, go take some whisky to my grandmother, sleeping in the cart outside. You may have to wake her, for she's a sound sleeper.

So the shopkeeper, he goes out to the cart with a bottle, and he says to the old lady in the cart, hey, here's your whisky, but the old lady she not say anything. And the shopkeeper, he's just getting angrier and angrier, for he was such a hasty-tempered man, saying get up old woman, get up and drink your whisky, but the old woman she says nothing. Then she does something that the dead sometimes do in the heat of the day: she flatulates loudly. Well, the shopkeeper, he's so angry with this old woman for flatulating at him that he hits her, and then he hits her again, and now he hits her one more time and she tumbles down from the handcart on to the ground.

Anansi, he runs out and he starts a-crying and a-wailing and a-carrying on, and saying my grandmother, she's a dead woman, look what you did! Murderer! Evil-doer! Now the shopkeeper, he says to Anansi, don't you tell anyone I done this, and he gives Anansi five whole bottles of whisky, and a bag of gold, and a sack of plantains and pineapples and mangos, to make him hush his carrying-on, and to go away.

(He thinks he killed Anansi's grandmother, you see.)

So Anansi, he wheels his handcart home, and he buries his grandmother underneath the banyan tree.

Now the next day, Tiger, he's passing by Anansi's house, and he smells cooking smells. So he invites himself over, and there's Anansi having a feast, and Anansi, having no other option, asks Tiger to sit and eat with them.

Tiger says, Brother Anansi, where did you get all that fine food from, and don't you lie to me? And where did you get these bottles of whisky from, and that big bag filled with gold pieces? If you lie to me, I'll tear out your throat.

So Anansi, he says, I cannot lie to you, Brother Tiger. I got them all for I take my dead grandmother to the village on a handcart. And the storekeeper gave me all these good things for bringing him my dead grandmother.

Now, Tiger, he didn't have a living grandmother, but his wife had a mother, so he goes home and he calls his wife's mother out to see him, saying, Grandmother, you come out now, for you and I must have a talk. And she comes out and peers around, and says what is it? Well, Tiger, he kills her, even though his wife loves her, and he places her body on a handcart.

Then he wheels his handcart to the village, with his dead mother-in-law on it. Who want a dead body? he calls. Who want a dead grandmother? But all the people they just jeered at him, and they laughed at him, and they mocked him and when they saw that he was serious and he wasn't going anywhere, they pelted him with rotten fruit until he ran away.

It wasn't the first time Tiger was made a fool of by Anansi, and it wouldn't be the last time. Tiger's wife never let him forget how he killed her mother. Some days it's better for Tiger if he's never been born.

That's an Anansi story.

'Course, all stories are Anansi stories. Even this one.

Olden days, all the animals wanted to have stories named after them, back in the days when the songs that sung the world were still being sung, back when they were still singing the sky and the rainbow and the ocean. It was in those days when animals were people as well as animals that Anansi the spider tricked all of them, especially Tiger, because he wanted all the stories named after him.

Stories are like spiders, with all they long legs, and stories are like spider-webs, which man gets himself all tangled up in but which look so pretty when you see them under a leaf in the morning dew and in the elegant way that they connect to one another, each to each.

What's that? You want to know if Anansi looked like a spider? Sure he did, except when he looked like a man.

No, he never changed his shape. It's just a matter of how you tell the story. That's all.

Chapter Three

In Which There
Is a Family Reunion

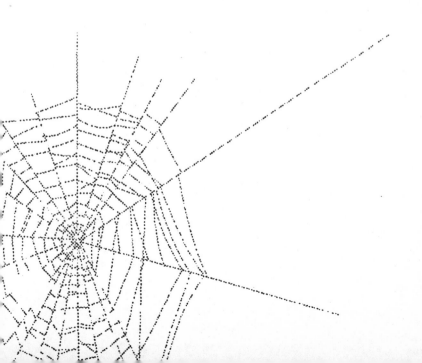

Fat Charlie flew home to England; as home as he was going to get, anyway.

Rosie was waiting for him as he came out of the Customs Hall carrying a small suitcase and a large taped-up cardboard box. She gave him a huge hug. 'How was it?' she asked.

He shrugged. 'Could've been worse.'

'Well,' she said, 'at least you don't have to worry about him coming to the wedding and embarrassing you any more.'

'There is that.'

'My mum says that we ought to put off the wedding for a few months as a mark of respect.'

'Your mum just wants us to put off the wedding, full stop.'

'Nonsense. She thinks you're quite a catch.'

'Your mother wouldn't describe a combination of Brad Pitt, Bill Gates and Prince William as "quite a catch". There is nobody walking the earth good enough to be her son-in-law.'

'She likes you,' said Rosie, dutifully, and without conviction.

Rosie's mother did not like Fat Charlie, and everybody knew it. Rosie's mother was a highly strung bundle of barely

thought-through prejudices, worries, and feuds. She lived in a
magnificent flat in Wimpole Street with nothing in the enormous
fridge but bottles of vitaminised water and rye crackers. Wax fruit
sat in the bowls on the antique sideboards, and was dusted twice
a week.

Fat Charlie had, on his first visit to Rosie's mother's place, taken
a bite from one of the wax apples. He had been extremely
nervous, nervous enough that he had picked up an apple – in his
defence, an extremely realistic apple – and had bitten into it.
Rosie had signed frantically. Fat Charlie spat out the lump of wax
into his hand and thought about pretending that he liked wax
fruit, or that he'd known all along and had just done it to be
funny; however, Rosie's mother had raised an eyebrow, walked
over, taken the remains of the apple from him, explained shortly
just how much real wax fruit cost these days, if you could find it,
and then dropped the apple into the bin. He sat on the sofa for the
rest of the afternoon, with his mouth tasting like the inside of a
candle, while Rosie's mother stared at him to ensure that he did
not try to take another bite out of her precious wax fruit, or
attempt to gnaw on the leg of a Chippendale chair.

There were large colour photographs in silver frames on the
sideboard of Rosie's mother's flat: photographs of Rosie as a girl,
and of Rosie's mother and father, and Fat Charlie had studied
them intently, looking for clues to the mystery that was Rosie. Her
father, who had died when Rosie was fifteen, had been an
enormous man. He had been first a cook, then a chef, then a
restaurateur. He was perfectly turned-out in every photograph, as
if dressed by a wardrobe department before each shot, rotund and
smiling, his arm always crooked for Rosie's mother to hold.

'He was an amazing cook,' Rosie said. In the photographs,
Rosie's mother had been curvaceous, and smiling. Now, twelve
years on, she resembled a skeletal Eartha Kitt, and Fat Charlie had
never seen her smile.

'Does your mum ever cook?' Fat Charlie had asked, after that
first time.

'I don't know. I've never seen her cook anything.'

'What does she eat? I mean, she can't live on crackers and
water.'

Rosie said, 'I think she sends out for things.'

Fat Charlie thought it highly likely that Rosie's mum went out at night in bat form to suck the blood from sleeping innocents. He had mentioned this theory to Rosie once, but she had failed to see the humour in it.

Rosie's mother had told Rosie that she was certain that Fat Charlie was marrying her for her money.

'What money?' asked Rosie.

Rosie's mother gestured to the apartment, a gesture that took in the wax fruit, the antique furniture, the paintings on the walls, and pursed her lips.

'But this is all yours,' said Rosie, who lived on her wages working for a London charity, and her wages were not large, so to supplement them Rosie had dipped into the money her father had left her in his will. It had paid for a small flat, which Rosie shared with a succession of Australians and New Zealanders, and for a second-hand VW Golf.

'I won't live for ever,' sniffed her mother, in a way that implied that she had every intention of living for ever, getting harder and thinner and more stonelike as she went, and eating less and less, until she would be able to live on nothing more than air and wax fruit and spite.

Rosie, driving Fat Charlie home from Heathrow, decided that the subject should be changed. She said, 'The water's gone off in my flat. It's out in the whole building.'

'Why's that then?'

'Mrs Klinger downstairs. She said something sprung a leak.'

'Probably Mrs Klinger.'

'*Char*lie. So, I was wondering – could I take a bath at your place tonight?'

'Do you need me to sponge you down?'

'*Char*lie.'

'Sure. Not a problem.'

Rosie stared at the back of the car in front of her, then she took her hand off the gear stick, and reached out, and squeezed Fat Charlie's huge hand. 'We'll be married soon enough,' she said.

'I know,' said Fat Charlie.

'Well, I mean,' she said, 'there'll be plenty of time for all that, won't there?'

'Plenty,' said Fat Charlie.

'You know what my mum once said?' said Rosie.

'Er. Was it something about bringing back hanging?'

'It was *not*. She said that if a just-married couple put a coin in a jar every time they make love in their first year, and take a coin out for every time that they make love in the years that follow, the jar will never be emptied.'

'And this means . . . ?'

'Well,' she said. 'It's interesting, isn't it? I'll be over at eight tonight with my rubber duck. How are you for towels?'

'Um . . .'

'I'll bring my own towel.'

Fat Charlie did not believe it would be the end of the world if an occasional coin went into the jar before they tied the knot and sliced the wedding cake, but Rosie had her own opinions on the matter, and there the matter ended. The jar remained perfectly empty.

* * *

The problem, Fat Charlie realised, once he got home, with arriving back in London after a brief trip away, is that if you arrive in the early morning, there is nothing much to do for the rest of the day.

Fat Charlie was a man who preferred to be working. He regarded lying on a sofa watching *Countdown* as a reminder of his interludes as a member of the unemployed. He decided that the sensible thing to do would be to go back to work a day early. In the Aldwych offices of the Grahame Coats Agency, up on the fifth and topmost floor, he would feel part of the swim of things. There would be interesting conversation with his fellow workers in the tea-room. The whole panoply of life would unfold before him, majestic in its tapestry, implacable and relentless in its industry. People would be pleased to see him.

'You're not back until tomorrow,' said Annie the receptionist, when Fat Charlie walked in. 'I told people you wouldn't be back until tomorrow. When they phoned.' She was not amused.

'Couldn't keep away,' said Fat Charlie.

'Obviously not,' she said, with a sniff. 'You should phone Maeve Livingstone back. She's been calling every day.'

'I thought she was one of Grahame Coats's people.'

'Well, he wants you to talk to her. Hang on.' She picked up the phone.

Grahame Coats came with both names. Not Mr Coats. Never just Grahame. It was his agency, and it represented people, and took a percentage of what they earned for the right to have represented them.

Fat Charlie went back to his office, which was a tiny room he shared with a number of filing cabinets. There was a yellow Post-it note stuck to his computer screen with 'See me. GC' on it, so he went down the hall to Grahame Coats's enormous office. The door was closed. He knocked, and then, unsure if he had heard anyone say anything or not, opened the door and put his head inside.

The room was empty. There was nobody there. 'Um, hello?' said Fat Charlie, not very loudly. There was no reply. There was a certain amount of disarrangement in the room, however: the bookcase was sticking out of the wall at a peculiar angle, and from the space behind it he could hear a thumping sound that might have been hammering.

He closed the door as quietly as he could, and went back to his desk.

His telephone rang. He picked it up.

'Grahame Coats here. Come and see me.'

This time Grahame Coats was sitting behind his desk, and the bookcase was flat against the wall. He did not invite Fat Charlie to sit down. He was a middle-aged white man with receding very fair hair. If you happened to see Grahame Coats and immediately found yourself thinking of an albino ferret in an expensive suit, you would not be the first.

'You're back with us, I see,' said Grahame Coats. 'As it were.'

'Yes,' said Fat Charlie. Then, because Grahame Coats did not seem particularly pleased with Fat Charlie's early return, he added, 'Sorry.'

Grahame Coats pinched his lips together, looked down at a

paper on his desk, looked up again. 'I was given to understand that you were not, in fact, returning until tomorrow. Bit early, aren't we?'

'We – I mean, I – got in this morning. From Florida. I thought I'd come in. Lots to do. Show willing. If that's all right.'

'Absatively,' said Grahame Coats. The word – a car crash between *absolutely* and *positively* – always set Fat Charlie's teeth on edge. 'It's your funeral.'

'My father's, actually.'

A ferret-like neck twist. 'You're still using one of your sick days.'

'Right.'

'Maeve Livingstone. Worried widow of Morris. Needs reassurance. Fair words and fine promises. Rome was not built in a day. The actual business of sorting out Morris Livingstone's estate and getting money to her continues unabated. Phones me practically daily for hand-holding. Meanwhilst, I turn the task over to you.'

'Right,' said Fat Charlie. 'So, um. No rest for the wicked.'

'Another day, another dollar,' said Grahame Coats, with a wag of his finger.

'Nose to the grindstone?' suggested Fat Charlie.

'Shoulder to the wheel,' said Grahame Coats. 'Well, delightful chatting with you. But we both have much work to do.'

There was something about being in the vicinity of Grahame Coats that always made Fat Charlie a) speak in clichés and b) begin to daydream about huge black helicopters first opening fire upon, then dropping buckets of flaming napalm on to the offices of the Grahame Coats Agency. Fat Charlie would not be in the office in those daydreams. He would be sitting in a chair outside a little café on the other side of the Aldwych, sipping a frothy coffee and occasionally cheering at an exceptionally well-flung bucket of napalm.

From this you would presume that there is little you need to know about Fat Charlie's employment, save that he was unhappy in it, and, in the main, you would be right. Fat Charlie had a facility for figures which kept him in work, and an awkwardness and a diffidence which kept him from pointing out to people what it was that he actually did, and how much he actually did. All about him, Fat Charlie would see people ascending implacably to their levels of incompetence, while he remained in entry-level positions, performing essential functions until the day he rejoined the ranks of the unemployed and started watching daytime television again. He was never out of a job for long, but it had happened far too often in the last decade for Fat Charlie to feel particularly comfortable in any position. He did not, however, take it personally.

He telephoned Maeve Livingstone, widow of Morris Livingstone, once the most famous short Yorkshire comedian in Britain and a long-time client of the Grahame Coats Agency. 'Hello,' he said. 'This is Charles Nancy, from the accounts department of the Grahame Coats Agency.'

'Oh,' said a woman's voice at the other end of the line. 'I thought Grahame would be phoning me himself.'

'He's a bit tied up. So he's um, delegated it,' said Fat Charlie. 'To me. So. Can I help?'

'I'm not sure. I was rather wondering – well, the bank manager was wondering – when the rest of the money from Morris's estate would be coming through – Grahame Coats explained to me, the last time – well, I think it was the last time – when we spoke – that it was invested – I mean, I understand that these things take time – he said otherwise I could lose a lot of money—'

'Well,' said Fat Charlie, 'I know he's on it. But these things do take time.'

'Yes,' she said. 'I suppose they must do. I called the BBC and they said they'd made several payments since Morris's death. You know, they've released the whole of *Morris Livingstone, I Presume* on DVD now? And they're bringing out both series of *Short Back and Sides* for Christmas.'

'I didn't know,' admitted Fat Charlie. 'But I'm sure Grahame Coats does. He's always on top of that kind of thing.'

'I had to buy my own DVD,' she said, wistfully. 'Still, it brought it all back. The roar of the greasepaint, the smell of the BBC club. Made me miss the spotlight, I can tell you that for nothing. That was how I met Morris, you know. I was a dancer. I had my own career.'

Fat Charlie told her that he'd let Grahame Coats know that her bank manager was a bit concerned, and he put down the phone.

He wondered how anyone could ever miss the spotlight.

In Fat Charlie's worst nightmares, a spotlight shone down upon him from a dark sky, on to a wide stage, and unseen figures would try to force Fat Charlie to stand in the spotlight and sing. And no matter how far or how fast he ran, or how well he hid, they would find him, and drag him back on to the stage, in front of dozens of expectant faces. He would always awake before he actually had to sing, sweating and trembling, his heart beating a cannonade in his chest.

A day's work passed. Fat Charlie had worked there almost two years. He had been there longer than anyone except Grahame Coats himself, for the staff turnover at the Grahame Coats Agency tended to be high. And still, nobody had been pleased to see him.

Fat Charlie would sometimes sit at his desk and stare out of the window, as the loveless grey rain rattled against the glass, and he would imagine himself on a tropical beach somewhere, with the breakers crashing from an impossibly blue sea on to the impossibly yellow sands. Often Fat Charlie would wonder if the people on the beach in his imagination, watching the white fingers of the waves as they wriggled towards the shore, listening to the tropical birds whistling in the palm trees, whether they ever dreamed of being in England, in the rain, in a cupboard-sized room in a fifth-floor office, a safe distance from the dullness of the pure golden sand and the hellish boredom of a day so perfect that not even a creamy drink containing slightly too much rum and a red paper umbrella can do anything to alleviate it. It comforted him.

He stopped at the off-licence on the way home, and bought a bottle of German white wine, and a patchouli-scented candle from the tiny supermarket next door, and picked up a pizza from the Pizza Place nearby.

Rosie phoned from her yoga class at 7.30 p.m. to let him know that she was going to be a little late, then from her car at 8.00 p.m. to let him know she was stuck in traffic, at 9.15 to let him know that she was now just around the corner, by which time Fat Charlie had drunk most of the bottle of white wine on his own, and consumed all but one lonely triangle of pizza.

Later, he wondered if it was the wine that made him say it.

Rosie arrived at 9:20, with towels, and a Tesco bag filled with shampoos, soaps and a large pot of hair mayonnaise. She said no, briskly but cheerfully, to a glass of the white wine and the slice of pizza – she had, she explained, eaten in the traffic jam. She had ordered in. So Fat Charlie sat in the kitchen, and poured himself the final glass of white wine, and picked the cheese and the pepperoni from the top of the cold pizza while Rosie went off to run the bath and then started, suddenly and quite loudly, to scream.

Fat Charlie made it to the bathroom before the first scream had finished dying away, and while Rosie was filling her lungs for the second. He was convinced that he would find her dripping with blood. To his surprise and relief, she was not bleeding. She was wearing a blue bra and panties, and was pointing to the bath, in the centre of which sat a large brown garden spider.

'I'm sorry,' she wailed. 'It took me by surprise.'

'They can do that,' said Fat Charlie. 'I'll just wash it away.'

'Don't you dare,' said Rosie, fiercely. 'It's a living thing. Take it outside.'

'Right,' said Fat Charlie.

'I'll wait in the kitchen,' she said. 'Tell me when it's all over.'

When you have drunk an entire bottle of white wine, coaxing a rather skittish garden spider into a clear plastic tumbler using only an old birthday card becomes more of a challenge to hand-eye coordination than it is at other times; a challenge that is not helped by a partially unclothed fiancée on the edge of hysterics, who, despite her announcement that she would wait in the kitchen, is instead leaning over your shoulder and offering advice.

But soon enough, despite the help, he had the spider inside the tumbler, the mouth of which was firmly covered by a card from an old schoolfriend which told him, 'YOU ARE ONLY AS OLD AS YOU FEEL' (and, on the inside humorously topped this with 'SO STOP FEELING YOURSELF YOU SEX MANIAC – HAPPY BIRTHDAY').

He took the spider downstairs and out of the front door, into the tiny front garden, which consisted of a hedge, for people to throw up in, and several large flagstones with grass growing up between them. He held the tumbler up. In the yellow sodium light, the spider was black. He imagined it was staring at him.

'Sorry about that,' he said to the spider, and, white wine slooshing comfortably around inside him, he said it aloud.

He put the card and the tumbler down on a cracked flagstone, and he lifted the tumbler, and waited for the spider to scuttle away. Instead, it simply sat, unmoving, on the face of the cheerful cartoon teddy bear on the birthday card. The man and the spider regarded each other.

Something that Mrs Higgler said came to him then, and the words were out of his mouth before he could stop them. Perhaps it was the devil in him. Probably it was the alcohol.

'If you see my brother,' said Fat Charlie to the spider, 'tell him he ought to come by and say hello.'

The spider remained where it was, and raised one leg, almost as if it was thinking it over, then it scuttled across the flagstone towards the hedge, and was gone.

* * *

Rosie had her bath, and she gave Fat Charlie a lingering peck on the cheek, and she went home.

Fat Charlie turned on the TV, but he found himself nodding, so he turned it off, and went to bed, where he dreamed a dream of such vividness and peculiarity that it would remain with him for the rest of his life.

One way that you know something is a dream is that you are somewhere you have never been in real life. Fat Charlie had never been to California. He had never been to Beverly Hills. He had seen it enough, though, in movies and on television to feel a comfortable thrill of recognition. A party was going on.

The lights of Los Angeles glimmered and twinkled beneath them.

The people at the party seemed to divide neatly into the ones with the silver plates, covered with perfect canapés, and the ones who picked things off the silver plates, or who declined to. The ones who were being fed moved around the huge house gossiping, smiling, talking, each as certain of his or her relative importance in the world of Hollywood as were the courtiers in the court of ancient Japan – and, just as in the ancient Japanese court, each of them was certain that, just one rung up the ladder, they would be safe. There were actors who wished to be stars, stars who wanted to be independent producers, independent producers who craved the safety of a studio job, directors who wanted to be stars, studio bosses who wanted to be the bosses of other, less precarious studios, studio lawyers who wanted to be liked for themselves, or, failing that, just wanted to be liked.

In Fat Charlie's dream, he could see himself from inside and outside at the same time, and he was not himself. In Fat Charlie's usual dreams he was probably just sitting down for an exam on double-entry book-keeping that he had forgotten to study for in circumstances which made it a certainty that when he finally stood up he would discover that he had somehow neglected to put anything on below the waist when he got dressed that morning. In his dreams, Fat Charlie was himself, only clumsier.

Not in this dream.

In this dream, Fat Charlie was cool, and beyond cool. He was slick, he was fly, he was smart, he was the only person at the party without a silver tray who had not received an invitation. And (this was something that was a source of astonishment to the sleeping Fat Charlie, who could think of nothing more embarrassing than being anywhere without an invitation) he was having a marvellous time.

He told each person who asked him a different story about who he was and why he was there. After half an hour, most of the people at the party were convinced that he was the representative of a foreign investment house, seeking to buy outright one of the studios, and after another half an hour it was common knowledge at the party that he would be putting in a bid for Paramount.

His laugh was raucous and infectious, and he seemed to be having a better time than any of the other people at the party, that was for certain. He instructed the barman in the preparation of a cocktail he called a 'Double Entendre' which, while it seemed to begin with a base of champagne, he explained was actually scientifically non-alcoholic. It contained a splash of this and a splash of that until it went a vivid purple colour, and he handed them out to the partygoers, pressing them upon them with joy and enthusiasm until even the people who had been sipping fizzy water warily, as if it might go off, were knocking back the purple drinks with pleasure.

And then, with the logic of dreams, he was leading them all down to the pool, and was proposing to teach them the trick of Walking on the Water. It was all a matter of confidence, he told them, of attitude, of attack, of knowing how to do it. And it seemed to the people at the party that Walking on the Water would be a very fine trick to master, something they had always known how to do, deep down in their souls, but they had forgotten, and that this man would remind them of the technique of it.

Take off your shoes, he said to them, so they took off their shoes, Sergio Rossis and Christian Louboutins and René Caovillas lined up side by side with Nikes and Doc Martens and anonymous black leather agent-shoes, and he led them, in a sort of a conga line, around the side of the swimming pool and then out on to its surface. The water was cool to the touch, and it quivered, like thick jelly, under their feet; some women, and several men, tittered at this, and a couple of the younger agents began jumping up and down on the surface of the pool, like children at a bouncy castle. Far below them the lights of Los Angeles shone through the smog, like distant galaxies.

Soon every inch of the pool was taken up with partygoers – standing, dancing, shaking or bouncing up and down on the water. The press of the crowd was so strong that the fly guy, the Charlie-in-his-dream, stepped back on to the concrete poolside to take a falafel-sashimi ball from a silver plate.

A spider dropped from a jasmine plant on to the fly guy's shoulder. It scuttled down his arm and on to the palm of his hand, where he greeted it with a delighted *Heyyy*.

There was a silence, as if he was listening to something the spider was saying, something only he could hear, then he said, *Ask, and you shall receive. Ain't that the truth?*

He placed the spider down, carefully, on a jasmine leaf.

And at that selfsame moment, each of the people standing barefoot on the surface of the swimming pool remembered that water was a liquid and not a solid, and that there was a reason why people did not commonly walk, let alone dance or even bounce on water, viz., its impossibility.

They were the movers and the shakers of the dream machine, those people, and suddenly they were flailing, fully dressed, in from four to twelve feet of water, wet and scrabbling and terrified.

Casually, the fly guy walked across the pool, treading on the heads of people, and on the hands of other people, and never once losing his balance. Then, when he reached the far end of the pool, where everything dropped into a steep hill, he took one huge jump and dived into the lights of Los Angeles at night, which shimmered and swallowed him like an ocean.

The people in the pool scrambled out, angry, upset, confused, wet, and in some cases, half drowned . . .

It was early in the morning in South London. The light was blue-grey.

Fat Charlie got out of bed, troubled by his dream, and walked to the window. The curtains were open. He could see the sunrise beginning, a huge blood orange of a morning sun surrounded by grey clouds tinged with scarlet. It was the kind of sky that makes even the most prosaic person discover a deeply buried urge to start painting in oils.

Fat Charlie looked at the sunrise. *Red sky in the morning*, he thought, *sailor's warning*.

His dream had been so strange. *A party in Hollywood. The secret of Walking on the Water. And that man, who was him and was not him . . .*

Fat Charlie realised that he knew the man in his dream, knew him from somewhere, and he also realised that this would irritate him for the rest of the day if he let it, like a snag of dental floss caught between two teeth, or the precise difference between the words 'lubricious' and 'lascivious', it would sit there, and it would irritate him.

He stared out of the window.

It was barely 6.00 in the morning, and the world was quiet. An early dog-walker, at the end of the road, was encouraging a

Pomeranian to defecate. A postman ambled from house to house
and back to his red van. And then something moved, on the
pavement beneath his house, and Fat Charlie looked down.

A man was standing by the hedge. When he saw that Fat
Charlie, in pyjamas, was looking down at him, he grinned,
and waved. A moment of recognition that shocked Fat Charlie to
the core: he was familiar with both the grin and the wave,
although he could not immediately see how. Something of the
dream still hung about Fat Charlie's head, making him
uncomfortable, making the world seem unreal. He rubbed his
eyes, and now the person by the hedge was gone. Fat Charlie
hoped that the man had moved on, wandered down the road into
the remnants of the hanging morning mist, taking whatever
awkwardnesses and irritants and madnesses he had brought
away with him.

And then the doorbell rang.

Fat Charlie pulled on his dressing gown, and he went
downstairs.

He had never fastened the safety chain before opening a door,
never in his life, but before he turned the handle he clicked the
head of the chain into place, and he pulled the front door open
six inches.

'Morning?' he said, warily.

The smile that came through the crack in the door could have
illuminated a small village.

'You called me and I came,' said the stranger. 'Now. You going
to open this door for me, Fat Charlie?'

'Who are you?' As he said it, he knew where he had seen the
man before: at his mother's funeral service, in the little chapel at
the crematorium. That was the last time he had seen that smile.
And he knew the answer, knew it even before the man could say
the words.

'I'm your brother,' said the man.

Fat Charlie closed the door. He slipped off the safety chain and
opened the door all the way. The man was still there.

Fat Charlie was not entirely sure how to greet a potentially
imaginary brother he had not previously believed in. So they
stood there, one on one side of the door, one on the other, until

his brother said, 'You can call me Spider. You going to invite me in?'

'Yes. I am. Of course I am. Please. Come in.'

Fat Charlie led the man upstairs.

Impossible things happen. When they do happen, most people just deal with it. Today, like every day, roughly five thousand people on the face of the planet will experience one-chance-in-a-million things, and not one of them will refuse to believe the evidence of their senses. Most of them will say the equivalent, in their own language, of 'funny old world, isn't it?' and just keep going. So while part of Fat Charlie was trying to come up with logical, sensible, sane explanations for what was going on, most of him was simply getting used to the idea that a brother he hadn't known he had was walking up the staircase behind him.

They got to the kitchen and stood there.

'Would you like a cup of tea?'

'Got any coffee?'

'Only instant, I'm afraid.'

'That's fine.'

Fat Charlie turned on the kettle. 'You come far, then?' he asked.

'Los Angeles.'

'How was the flight?'

The man sat down at the kitchen table. Now he shrugged. It was the kind of shrug that could have meant anything.

'Um. You planning on staying long?'

'I haven't really given it much thought.' The man – Spider – looked around Fat Charlie's kitchen, as if he had never been in a kitchen before.

'How do you take your coffee?'

'Dark as night, sweet as sin.'

Fat Charlie put the mug down in front of him, and passed him a sugarbowl. 'Help yourself.'

While Spider spooned teaspoon after teaspoon of sugar into his coffee, Fat Charlie sat opposite him, and stared.

There was a family resemblance between the two men. That was unarguable, although that alone did not explain the intense feeling of familiarity that Fat Charlie felt on seeing Spider. His brother looked like Fat Charlie wished he looked in his mind, unconstrained by the faintly disappointing fellow that he saw, with monotonous regularity, in the bathroom mirror. Spider was taller, and leaner, and cooler. He was wearing a black and scarlet leather jacket, and black leather leggings, and he looked at home in them. Fat Charlie tried to remember if this was what the fly guy had been wearing in his dream. There was something larger than life about him: simply being on the other side of the table to this man made Fat Charlie feel awkward and badly constructed, and slightly foolish. It wasn't the clothes Spider wore, but the knowledge that if Fat Charlie put them on he would look as if he were wearing some kind of unconvincing drag. It wasn't the way Spider smiled – casually, delightedly – but Fat Charlie's cold, incontrovertible certainty that he himself could practise smiling in front of a mirror from now until the end of time and never manage a single smile one-half so charming, so cocky, or so twinklingly debonair.

'You were at Mum's cremation,' said Fat Charlie.

'I thought about coming over to talk to you after the service,' said Spider. 'I just wasn't certain that it would be a good idea.'

'I wish you had.' Fat Charlie thought of something. He said, 'I would have thought you would have been at Dad's funeral.'

Spider said 'What?'

'His funeral. It was in Florida. Couple of days ago.'

Spider shook his head. 'He's not dead,' he said. 'I'm pretty sure I'd know if he were dead.'

'He's dead. I buried him. Well, I filled the grave. Ask Mrs Higgler.'

Spider said, 'How'd he die?'

'Heart failure.'

'That doesn't mean anything. That just means he died.'

'Well, yes. He did.'

Spider had stopped smiling. Now he was staring down into his coffee as if he suspected he was going to be able to find an answer in there. 'I ought to check this out,' said Spider. 'It's not that I don't believe you. But when it's your old man. Even when your old man is my old man.' And he made a face. Fat Charlie knew what that face meant. He had made it himself, from the inside, enough times, when the subject of his father came up. 'Is she still living in the same place? Next door to where we grew up?'

'Mrs Higgler? Yes. Still there.'

'You don't have anything from there, do you? A picture? Maybe a photograph?'

'I brought home a box of them.' Fat Charlie had not opened the large cardboard box yet. It was still sitting in the hall. He carried the box into the kitchen and put it down on the table. He took a kitchen knife and cut the packing tape that surrounded it, Spider reached into the box with his thin fingers, riffling through the photographs like playing cards, until he pulled out one of their mother and Mrs Higgler, sitting on Mrs Higgler's porch, twenty-five years earlier.

'Is that porch still there?'

Fat Charlie tried to remember. 'I think so,' he said.

Later, he was unable to remember whether the picture grew very big, or Spider grew very small. He could have sworn that neither of those things had actually happened; nevertheless, it was unarguable that Spider had walked into the photograph, and it had shimmered and rippled and swallowed him up.

Fat Charlie rubbed his eyes. He was alone in the kitchen at six in the morning. There was a box filled with photographs and papers on the kitchen table, along with an empty mug, which he placed in the sink. He walked along the hall to his bedroom, lay down on his bed and slept until the alarm went off at 7.15.

Chapter Four

Which Concludes
With an Evening of
Wine, Women and Song

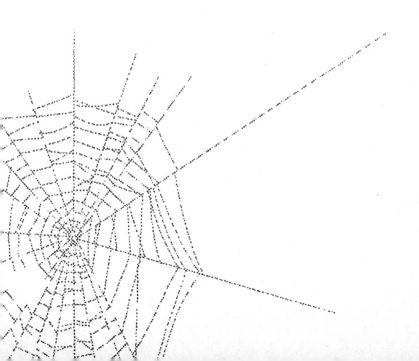

F at Charlie woke up.

Memories of dreams of a meeting with some film-star brother mingled with a dream in which President Taft had come to stay, bringing with him the entire cast of the cartoon *Tom and Jerry*. He showered, and he took the tube to work.

All through the work day something was nagging at the back of his head, and he didn't know what it was. He misplaced things. He forgot things. At one point, he started singing, at his desk, not because he was happy, but because he forgot not to. He only realised he was doing it when Grahame Coats himself put his head around the door of Fat Charlie's closet to chide him. 'No radios, Walkmans, MP3 players or similar instruments of music at the office,' said Grahame Coats, with a ferrety glare. 'It bespeaks a lackadaisical attitude, of the kind one abhors in the workaday world.'

'It wasn't the radio,' admitted Fat Charlie, his ears burning.

'No? Then what, pray tell, was it?'

'It was me,' said Fat Charlie.

'You?'

'Yes. I was singing. I'm sorry—'

'I could have sworn it was the radio. And yet I was wrong. Good Lord. Well, with such a wealth of talents at your disposal, with such remarkable skills, perhaps you should leave us to tread the boards, entertain the multitudes, possibly do an end-of-the-pier show, rather than cluttering up a desk in an office where other people are trying to work. Eh? A place where people's careers are being managed.'

'No,' said Fat Charlie. 'I don't want to leave. I just wasn't thinking.'

'Then,' said Grahame Coats, 'you must learn to refrain from singing – save in the bath, the shower, or perchance the stands as you support your favourite football team. I myself am a Crystal Palace supporter. Or you will find yourself seeking gainful employment elsewhere.'

Fat Charlie smiled, then realised that smiling wasn't what he wanted to do at all, and looked serious, but by that point Grahame Coats had left the room, so Fat Charlie swore under his breath, folded his arms on the desk and put his head on them.

'Was that you singing?' It was one of the new girls in the Artist Liaison Department. Fat Charlie never managed to learn their names. They were always gone before then.

'I'm afraid so.'

'What were you singing? It was pretty.'

Fat Charlie realised he didn't know. He said, 'I'm not sure. I wasn't listening.'

She laughed at that, although quietly. 'He's right. You should be making records, not wasting your time here.'

Fat Charlie didn't know what to say. Cheeks burning, he started crossing out numbers and making notes and gathering up Post-it notes with messages on them and putting those messages up on the screen, until he was sure that she had gone.

Maeve Livingstone phoned: could Fat Charlie *please* ensure that Grahame Coats phoned her bank manager. He said he'd do his best. She told him pointedly to see that he did.

Rosie called him on his mobile at four in the afternoon, to let him know that the water was now back on again in her flat, and to tell him that, good news, her mother had decided to take an interest in the upcoming wedding, and had asked her to come round that evening and discuss it.

'Well,' said Fat Charlie, 'if she's organising the dinner, we'll save a fortune on food.'

'That's not nice. I'll call you tonight and let you know how it went.'

Fat Charlie told her that he loved her, and he clicked the phone off. Someone was looking at him. He turned round.

Grahame Coats said, 'He who maketh personal phone calls on company time, lo he shall reap the whirlwind. Do you know who said that?'

'You did?'

'Indeed I did,' said Grahame Coats. 'Indeed I did. And never a truer word was spoken. Consider this a formal warning.' And he smiled then, the kind of self-satisfied smile that forced Fat Charlie to ponder the various probable outcomes of sinking his fist into Grahame Coats's comfortably padded mid-section. He decided that it would be a toss-up between being fired and an action for assault. Either way, he thought, it would be a fine thing . . .

Fat Charlie was not by nature a violent man; still, he could dream. His daydreams tended to be small and comfortable things. He would like to have enough money to eat in good restaurants whenever he wished. He wanted a job in which nobody could tell him what to do. He wanted to be able to sing without embarrassment, somewhere there were never any people around to hear him.

This afternoon, however, his daydreams assumed a different shape: he could fly, for a start, and bullets bounced off his mighty chest as he zoomed down from the sky and rescued Rosie from a band of kidnapping scoundrels and dastards. She would hold him tightly as they flew off into the sunset, off to his Fortress of Cool, where she would be so overwhelmed with feelings of gratitude that she would enthusiastically decide not to bother with the whole waiting until they were married bit, and would start to see how high and how fast they could fill their jar . . .

The daydream eased the stress of life in the Grahame Coats Agency, of telling people that their cheques were in the post, of calling in money the agency was owed.

At 6.00 p.m. Fat Charlie turned off his computer, and walked down the five flights of stairs to the street. It had not rained. Overhead, the starlings were wheeling and cheeping: the dusk chorus of a city. Everyone on the pavement was hurrying somewhere. Most of them, like Fat Charlie, were walking up Kingsway to Holborn tube. They had their heads down, and the look about them of people who wanted to get home for the night.

There was one person on the pavement who wasn't going anywhere, though. He stood there, facing Fat Charlie and the remaining commuters, and his leather jacket flapped in the wind. He was not smiling.

Fat Charlie saw him from the end of the street. As he walked towards him everything became unreal. The day melted, and he realised what he had spent the day trying to remember.

'Hello, Spider,' he said, when he got close.

Spider looked like a storm was raging inside him. He might have been about to cry. Fat Charlie didn't know. There was too much emotion on his face, in the way he stood, so the people on the street looked away, ashamed.

'I went out there,' he said. His voice was jagged. 'I saw Mrs Higgler. She took me to the grave. My father died, and I didn't know.'

Fat Charlie said, 'He was my father too, Spider.' He wondered how he could have forgotten Spider, how he could have dismissed him so easily as a dream.

'True.'

The dusk sky was cross-hatched with starlings; they wheeled and crossed from rooftop to rooftop.

Spider jerked, and stood straight. He seemed to have come to a decision. 'You are so right,' he said. 'We got to do this together.'

'Exactly,' said Fat Charlie. Then he said, 'Do what?' but Spider had already hailed a cab.

'We are men with troubles,' said Spider to the world. 'Our father is no more. Our hearts are heavy in our chests. Sorrow settles upon us like pollen in hay fever season. Darkness is our lot, and misfortune our only companion.'

'Right, gentlemen,' said the cabbie, brightly. 'Where am I taking you?'

'To where the three remedies for darkness of the soul may be found,' said Spider.

'Maybe we could get a curry,' suggested Fat Charlie.

'There are three things, and three things only, that can lift the pain of mortality and ease the ravages of life,' said Spider. 'These things are wine, women and song.'

'Curry's nice too,' pointed out Fat Charlie, but nobody was listening to him.

'In any particular order?' asked the cabbie.

'Wine first,' Spider announced. 'Rivers and lakes and vast oceans of wine.'

'Right you are,' said the cabbie, and he pulled out into the traffic.

'I have a particularly bad feeling about all this,' said Fat Charlie, helpfully.

Spider nodded. 'A bad feeling,' he said. 'Yes. We both have a bad feeling. Tonight we shall take our bad feelings and share them, and face them. We shall mourn. We shall drain the bitter dregs of mortality. Pain shared, my brother, is pain not doubled, but halved. No man is an island.'

'Seek not to ask for whom the bell tolls,' intoned the cabbie. 'It tolls for thee.'

'Whoa,' said Spider. 'Now that's a pretty heavy koan you got there.'

'Thank you,' said the cabbie.

'That's how it ends, all right. You are some kind of philosopher. I'm Spider. This is my brother, Fat Charlie.'

'Charles,' said Fat Charlie.

'Steve,' said the cabbie. 'Steve Burridge.'

'Mr Burridge,' said Spider. 'How would you like to be our personal driver, this evening?'

Steve Burridge explained that he was coming up to the end of his shift, and would now be driving his cab home for the night, that dinner with Mrs Burridge and all the little Burridges awaited him.

'You hear that?' said Spider. 'A family man. Now, my brother and I are all the family that we have left. And this is the first time we've met.'

'Sounds like quite a story,' said the cabbie. 'Was there a feud?'

'Not at all. He simply did not know that he had a brother,' said Spider.

'Did *you*?' asked Fat Charlie. 'Know about me?'

'I may have done,' said Spider. 'But things like that can slip a guy's mind so easily.'

The cab pulled over to the kerb. 'Where are we?' asked Fat Charlie. They hadn't gone very far. He thought they were somewhere just off Fleet Street.

'What he asked for,' said the cabbie. 'Wine.'

Spider got out of the cab and stared at the grubby oak and grimy glass exterior of the ancient wine bar. 'Perfect,' he said. 'Pay the man, brother.'

Fat Charlie paid the cabbie. They went inside: down wooden steps to a cellar where rubicund barristers drank side by side with pallid money market fund managers. There was sawdust on the floor, and a wine list chalked illegibly on a blackboard behind the bar.

'What are you drinking?' asked Spider.

'Just a glass of house red, please,' said Fat Charlie.

Spider looked at him gravely. 'We are the final scions of Anansi's line. We do not mourn our father's passing with house red.'

'Er. Right. Well, I'll have what you're having then.'

Spider went up to the bar, easing his way through the crush of people as if it was not there. In several minutes he returned, carrying two wine glasses, a corkscrew and an extremely dusty wine bottle. He opened the bottle with an ease that left Fat Charlie, who always wound up picking fragments of cork from his wine, deeply impressed. Spider poured from the bottle a wine so tawny it was almost black. He filled each glass, then put one in front of Fat Charlie.

'A toast,' he said. 'To our father's memory.'

'To Dad,' said Fat Charlie, and he clinked his glass against Spider's – managing, miraculously, not to spill any as he did so – and he tasted his wine. It was peculiarly bitter, and herby, and salty. 'What is this?'

'Funeral wine, the kind you drink for gods. They haven't made it for a long time. It's seasoned with bitter aloes and rosemary, and with the tears of broken-hearted virgins.'

'And they sell it in a Fleet Street wine bar?' Fat Charlie picked up the bottle, but the label was too faded and dusty to read. 'Never heard of it.'

'These old places have the good stuff, if you ask for it,' said Spider. 'Or maybe I just think they do.'

Fat Charlie took another sip of his wine. It was powerful and pungent.

'It's not a sipping wine,' said Spider. 'It's a mourning wine. You drain it. Like this.' He took a huge swig. Then he made a face. 'It tastes better that way, too.'

Fat Charlie hesitated, then took a large mouthful of the strange wine. He could imagine that he was able to taste the aloes and the rosemary. He wondered if the salt was really tears.

'They put in the rosemary for remembrance,' said Spider, and he began to top up their glasses. Fat Charlie started to try to explain that he wasn't really up for too much wine tonight, and that he had to work tomorrow, but Spider cut him off. 'It's your turn to make a toast,' he said.

'Er. Right,' said Fat Charlie. 'To Mum.'

They drank to their mother. Fat Charlie found that the taste of the bitter wine was beginning to grow on him; he found his eyes prickling, and a sense of loss, profound and painful, ran through him. He missed his mother. He missed his childhood. He even missed his father. Across the table, Spider was shaking his head; a tear ran down Spider's face, and plopped into the wineglass; he reached for the bottle and poured more wine for them both.

Fat Charlie drank.

Grief ran through him as he drank, filling his head and his body with loss and with the pain of absence, swelling through him like waves on the ocean.

His own tears were running down his face, splashing into his drink. He fumbled in his pockets for a tissue. Spider poured out the last of the black wine, for both of them.

'Did they really sell this wine here?'

'They had a bottle they didn't know they had. They just needed to be reminded.'

Fat Charlie blew his nose. 'I never knew I had a brother,' he said.

'I did,' admitted Spider. 'I always meant to look you up, but I got distracted. You know how it is.'

'Not really.'

'Things came up.'

'What kind of things?'

'Things. They came up. That's what things do. They come up. I can't be expected to keep track of them all.'

'Well, give me a f'rinstance.'

Spider drank more wine. 'OK. The last time I decided that you and I should meet, I, well, I spent days planning it. Wanted it to go perfectly. I had to choose my wardrobe. Then I had to decide what I'd say to you when we met. I knew that the meeting of two brothers, well, it's the subject of epics, isn't it? I decided that the only way to treat it with the appropriate gravity would be to do it in verse. But what kind of verse? Am I going to rap it? Declaim it? I mean, I'm not going to greet you with a limerick. So. It had to be something dark, something powerful, rhythmic, epic. And then, I had it. The perfect first line. *Blood calls to blood like sirens in the night*. It says so much. I knew I'd be able to get everything in there – people dying in alleys, sweat and nightmares, the power of free spirits uncrushable. Everything was going to be there. And then I had to come up with a second line, and the whole thing completely fell apart. The best I could come up with was *Tum-tumpty-tumpty-tumpty got a fright*.'

Fat Charlie blinked. 'Who exactly is Tum-tumpty-tumpty-tumpty?'

'It's not anybody. It's just there to show you where the words ought to be. But I never really got any further on it than that, and I couldn't turn up with just a first line, some tumpties and three words of an epic poem, could I? That would have been disrespecting you.'

'Well . . .'

'Exactly. So I went to Hawaii for the week instead. Like I said, something came up.'

Fat Charlie drank more of his wine. He was beginning to like it. Sometimes strong tastes fit strong emotions, and this was one of those times. 'It couldn't *always* have been the second line of a poem, though,' he said.

Spider put his thin hand on top of Fat Charlie's larger hand. 'Enough about me,' he said. 'I want to hear about you.'

'Not much to tell,' said Fat Charlie. He told his brother about his life. About Rosie and Rosie's mother, about Grahame Coats and the Grahame Coats Agency, and his brother nodded his head. It didn't sound like much of a life, now that Fat Charlie was putting it into words.

'Still,' Fat Charlie said, philosophically, 'I figure that there are those people you read about in the gossip pages of newspapers. And they are always saying how dull and empty and pointless their lives are.' He held the wine bottle above his glass, hoping there was just enough of the wine left for another mouthful, but there was barely a drip. The bottle was empty. It had lasted longer than it had any right to have lasted, but now there was nothing left at all.

Spider stood up. 'I've met those people,' he said. 'The ones from the glossy magazines. I've walked among them. I have seen, first-hand, their callow empty lives. I have watched them from the shadows when they thought themselves alone. And I can tell you this: I'm afraid there is not one of them who would swap lives with you at gunpoint, my brother. Come on.'

'Whuh? Where are you going?'

'We are going. We have accomplished the first part of tonight's triune mission. Wine has been drunk. Two parts left to go.'

'Er . . .'

Fat Charlie followed Spider outside, hoping the cool night air would clear his head. It didn't. Fat Charlie's head was feeling like it might float away if it wasn't firmly tied down.

'Women next,' said Spider. 'Then song.'

* * *

It is possibly worth mentioning that in Fat Charlie's world, women did not simply turn up. You needed to be introduced to them; you needed to pluck up the courage to talk to them; you needed to find a subject to talk about when you did, and then, once you had achieved those heights, there were further peaks to scale. You needed to dare to ask them if they were doing anything on Saturday night, and then when you did, mostly they had hair that needed washing that night, or diaries to update, or cockatiels to groom, or they simply needed to wait by the phone for some other man not to call.

But Spider lived in a different world.

They wandered towards the West End, stopping when they reached a crowded pub. The patrons spilled out on to the pavement, and Spider stopped and said hello to what turned out to be a birthday celebration for a young lady named Sybilla, who was only too flattered when Spider insisted on buying a birthday round of drinks for her and for her friends. Then he told jokes ('. . . and the duck says, *Put it on my bill? WhaddayathinkIam? Some kinda perrvert?*') and he laughed at his own jokes, a booming, joyful laugh. He could remember the names of all the people around him. He talked to people, and listened to what they said. When Spider announced it was time to find another pub, the entire birthday group decided, as one woman, that they were coming with him . . .

By the time they reached their third pub, Spider resembled someone from a rock video. He was draped with girls. They snuggled in. Several of them had kissed him, half-joking, half-seriously. Fat Charlie watched in envious horror.

'You his bodyguard?' asked one of the girls.

'What?'

'His bodyguard. *Are* you?'

'No,' said Fat Charlie. 'I'm his brother.'

'Wow,' she said. 'I didn't know he had a brother. I think he's amazing.'

'Me too,' said another, who had spent some time cuddling Spider, until forced away by the press of other bodies with similar ideas. She noticed Fat Charlie for the first time. 'Are you his manager?'

'No. He's the brother,' said the first girl. 'He was just telling me,' she added, pointedly.

The second ignored her. 'Are you from the States as well?' she asked. 'You've sort of got a bit of an accent.'

'When I was younger,' said Fat Charlie, 'we lived in Florida. My dad was American, my mum was from, well, she was originally from Saint Andrews, but she grew up in . . .'

Nobody was listening.

When they moved on from there, the remnants of the birthday celebration accompanied them. The women surrounded Spider, enquiring where they were going next. Restaurants were suggested, as were nightclubs. Spider simply grinned and kept walking.

Fat Charlie trailed along behind them, feeling more left out than ever.

They stumbled through the neon and striplight world. Spider had his arms around several of the women. He would kiss them, as he walked, indiscriminately, like a man taking a bite from first one summer fruit, then another. None of them seemed to mind.

It's not normal, thought Fat Charlie. *That's what it's not.* He was not even trying to keep up, merely attempting not to be left behind.

He could still taste the bitter wine on his tongue.

He became aware that a girl was walking along beside him. She was small, and pretty in a pixyish sort of way. She tugged at his sleeve. 'What are we doing?' she asked. 'Where are we going?'

'We're mourning my father,' he said, 'I think.'

'Is it a reality TV show?'

'I hope not.'

Spider stopped and turned. The gleam in his eyes was disturbing. 'We are here,' he announced. 'We have arrived. It is what he would have wanted.' There was a handwritten message on a sheet of bright orange paper on the door outside the pub. It said on it: 'Tonight. Upstair's. KAROAKE.'

'Song,' said Spider. Then he said, 'It's showtime!'

'No,' said Fat Charlie. He stopped where he was.

'It's what he loved,' said Spider.

'I don't sing. Not in public. And I'm drunk. And, I really don't think this is a really good idea.'

'It's a *great* idea.' Spider had a perfectly convincing smile. Properly deployed, a smile like that could launch a holy war. Fat Charlie, however, was not convinced.

'Look,' he said, trying to keep the panic from his voice. 'There are things that people don't do. Right? Some people don't fly. Some people don't have sex in public. Some people don't turn into smoke and blow away. I don't do any of those things, and I don't sing either.'

'Not even for Dad?'

'Especially not for Dad. He's not going to embarrass me from beyond the grave. Well, not any more than he has already.'

''Scuse me,' said one of the young women. ''Scuse me but are we going in? 'Cause I'm getting cold out here, and Sybilla needs to wee.'

'We're going in,' said Spider, and he smiled at her.

Fat Charlie wanted to protest, to stand his ground, but he found himself swept inside, hating himself.

He caught up with Spider on the stairs. 'I'll go in,' he said. 'But I won't sing.'

'You're already in.'

'I know. But I'm not singing.'

'Not much point in saying you won't go in if you're already in.'

'I can't sing.'

'You telling me I inherited all the musical talent as well?'

'I'm telling you that if I have to open my mouth in order to sing in public, I'll throw up.'

Spider squeezed his arm, reassuringly. 'You watch how I do it,' he said.

The birthday girl and two of her friends stumbled up on to the little dais, and giggled their way through 'Dancing Queen'. Fat Charlie drank a gin and tonic somebody had put into his hand, and he winced at every note they missed, at every key-change that didn't happen. There was a round of applause from the rest of the birthday group.

Another of the women took the stage. It was the pixyish one who had asked Fat Charlie where they were going. The opening chords sounded to 'Stand By Me', and she began, using the phrase in its most approximate and all-encompassing way, to sing along: she missed every note, came in too soon or too late on every line, and misread most of them. Fat Charlie felt for her.

She climbed down from the stage, and came towards the bar.

Fat Charlie was going to say something sympathetic, but she was glowing with joy. 'That was *so* great,' she said. 'I mean, that was just amazing.' Fat Charlie bought her a drink, a large vodka and orange. 'That was *such* a laugh,' she told him. 'Are you going to do it? Go on. You have to do it. I bet you won't be any crapper than I was.'

Fat Charlie shrugged, in a way that, he hoped, indicated that he contained within him depths of crap as yet unplumbed.

Spider walked over to the little stage as if a spotlight was following him.

'I bet this will be good,' said the vodka and orange. 'Did someone say you were his brother?'

'No,' muttered Fat Charlie, ungraciously. 'I said that *he* was *my* brother.'

Spider began to sing. It was 'Under the Boardwalk'.

It wouldn't have happened if Fat Charlie had not liked the song so much. When Fat Charlie was thirteen he had believed that 'Under the Boardwalk' was the greatest song in the world. (By the time he was a jaded and world-weary fourteen-year-old, it had become Bob Marley's 'No Woman No Cry'.) And now Spider was singing his song, and singing it well. He sang it in tune, he sang it as if he meant it. People stopped drinking, stopped talking, and they looked at him, and they listened.

When Spider finished singing, people cheered. Had they been wearing hats, they might well have flung them into the air.

'I can see why you wouldn't want to follow that,' said the vodka and orange to Fat Charlie. 'I mean, you can't follow that, can you?'

'Well . . .' said Fat Charlie.

'I mean,' she said with a grin, 'you can see who's got all the talent in your family.' She tipped her head, as she said it, and tilted her chin. It was the chin-tilt that did it.

Fat Charlie headed toward the stage, putting one foot in front of the other in an impressive display of physical dexterity. He was sweating.

The next few minutes passed in a blur. He spoke to the DJ, chose his song from the list – 'Unforgettable' – waited for what seemed like a brief eternity, and was handed a microphone.

His mouth was dry. His heart was fluttering in his chest.

On the screen was his first word: *Unforgettable* . . .

Now, Fat Charlie could *really* sing. He had range and power and expression. When he sang his whole body became an instrument.

The music started . . .

In Fat Charlie's head, he was all ready to open his mouth, and to sing. '*Unforgettable*,' he would sing. He would sing it to his dead father and to his brother and the night, telling them all that they were things it was impossible to forget.

Only he couldn't do it. There were people looking up at him. Barely two dozen of them, in the upstairs room of a pub. Many of them were women. In front of an audience, Fat Charlie couldn't even open his mouth.

He could hear the music playing, but he just stood there. He felt very cold. His feet seemed a long way away.

He forced his mouth open.

'I think,' he said, very distinctly, into the microphone, over the music, and heard his words echoing back from every corner of the room. 'I think I'm going to be sick.'

There was no graceful exit from the stage.

After that, everything got a bit wobbly.

* * *

There are myth-places. They exist, each in their own way. Some of them are overlaid on the world; others exist beneath the world as it is, like an underpainting.

There are mountains. They are the rocky places you will reach before you come to the cliffs that border the end of the world, and there are caves in those mountains, deep caves that were inhabited long before the first men walked the earth.

They are inhabited still.

Chapter Five

In Which We Examine the Many Consequences of the Morning After

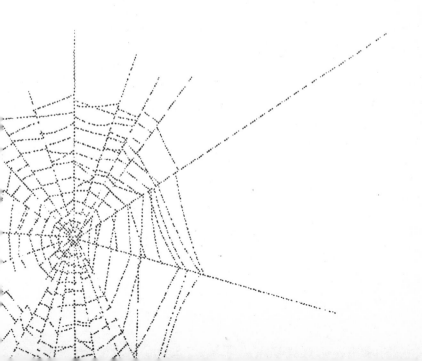

F at Charlie was thirsty.

Fat Charlie was thirsty and his head hurt.

Fat Charlie was thirsty and his head hurt and his mouth tasted evil and his eyes were too tight in his head and all his teeth twinged and his stomach burned and his back was aching in a way that started around his knees and went up to his forehead and his brains had been removed and replaced with cotton balls and needles and pins which was why it hurt to try and think, and his eyes were not just too tight in his head but they must have rolled out in the night and been reattached with roofing nails; and now he noticed that anything louder than the gentle Brownian motion of air molecules drifting softly past each other was above his pain threshold. Also, he wished he were dead.

Fat Charlie opened his eyes, which was a mistake, in that it let daylight in, which hurt. It also told him where he was (in his own bed, in his bedroom) and because he was staring at the clock on his bedside table, it told him that the time was 11.30.

That, he thought, one word at a time, was about as bad as things could get: he had the kind of hangover that an Old

Testament God might have smitten the Midianites with, and the
next time he saw Grahame Coats he would undoubtedly learn
that he had been fired.

He wondered if he could sound convincingly sick over the
phone, then realised that the challenge would be convincingly
sounding anything else.

He could not remember getting home last night.

He would phone the office, the moment he was able to
remember the telephone number. He would apologise – crippling
twenty-four-hour flu, flat on his back, nothing that could be
done . . .

'You know,' said someone in the bed next to him, 'I think
there's a bottle of water on your side. Could you pass it over
here?'

Fat Charlie wanted to explain that there was no water on his
side of the bed, and that there was, in fact, no water closer than
the bathroom sink, if he disinfected the toothbrush mug first, but
he realised he was staring at one of several bottles of water, sitting
on the bedside table. He reached his hand out, and closed fingers
that felt like they belonged to someone else around one of them,
then, with the sort of effort people usually reserve for hauling
themselves up the final few feet of a sheer rock face, he rolled
over in bed.

It was the vodka and orange.

Also, she was naked. At least, the bits of her he could see were.

She took the water, and pulled the sheet up to cover her chest.
'Ta. He said to tell you,' she said, 'when you woke, not to worry
about calling work and telling them you were ill. He said to tell
you he's already taken care of it.'

Fat Charlie's mind was not put at rest. His fears and worries
were not allayed. Then again, in the condition he was in, he only
had room in his head for a single thing to worry about at once,
and right now he was worrying about whether or not he would
make it to the bathroom in time.

'You'll need more liquids,' said the girl. 'You'll need to
replenish your electrolytes.'

Fat Charlie made it to the bathroom in time. Afterwards, seeing
he was there already, he stood under the shower until the room

stopped undulating, and then he brushed his teeth without throwing up.

When he returned to the bedroom, the vodka and orange was no longer there, which was a relief to Fat Charlie, who had started to hope that she might have been an alcohol-induced delusion, like pink elephants or the nightmarish idea that he had taken to the stage to sing on the previous evening.

He could not find his dressing gown, so he pulled on a tracksuit, in order to feel dressed enough to visit the kitchen, at the far end of the hall.

His phone chimed, and he rummaged through his jacket, which was on the floor beside the bed, until he found it, and flipped it open. He grunted into it, as anonymously as he could, just in case it was someone from the Grahame Coats Agency trying to discern his whereabouts.

'It's me,' said Spider's voice. 'Everything's OK.'

'You told them I was dead?'

'Better than that. I told them I was you.'

'But.' Fat Charlie tried to think clearly. 'But you're not me.'

'Hey. I know that. I told them I was.'

'You don't even look like me.'

'Brother of mine, you are harshing a potential mellow here. It's all taken care of. Oops. Gotta go. The big boss needs to talk to me.'

'Grahame Coats? Look, Spider—'

But Spider had put down the phone, and the screen blanked.

Fat Charlie's dressing gown came through the door. There was a girl inside it. It looked significantly better on her than it ever had on him. She was carrying a tray, on which was a water-glass with a fizzing Alka-Seltzer in it, along with something in a mug.

'Drink both of these,' she told him. 'The mug first. Just knock it back.'

'What's in the mug?'

'Egg yolk, Worcestershire sauce, Tabasco, salt, dash of vodka, things like that,' she said. 'Kill or cure. Now,' she told him, in tones that brooked no argument. 'Drink.'

Fat Charlie drank.

'Oh my God,' he said.

'Yeah,' she agreed. 'But you're still alive.'

He wasn't sure about that. He drank the Alka-Seltzer anyway. Something occurred to him.

'Um,' said Fat Charlie. 'Um. Look. Last night. Did we. Um.'

She looked blank.

'Did we what?'

'Did we. You know. *Do* it?'

'You mean you don't remember?' Her face fell. 'You said it was the best you'd ever had. That it was as if you'd never made love to a woman before. You were part god, part animal, and part unstoppable sex machine . . .'

Fat Charlie didn't know where to look. She giggled.

'I'm just winding you up,' she said. 'I'd helped your brother get you home, we cleaned you up, and, after that, you know.'

'No,' he said. 'I don't know.'

'Well,' she said, 'you were completely out cold, and it's a big bed. I'm not sure where your brother slept. He must have the constitution of an ox. He was up at the crack of dawn, all bright and smiling.'

'He went into work,' said Fat Charlie. 'He told them he was me.'

'Wouldn't they be able to tell the difference? I mean, you're not exactly twins.'

'Apparently not.' He shook his head. Then he looked at her. She stuck out a small, extremely pink tongue at him.

'What's your name?'

'You mean you've forgotten? I remember your name. You're Fat Charlie.'

'Charles,' he said. 'Just Charles is fine.'

'I'm Daisy,' she said, and stuck out her hand. 'Pleased to meet you.'

They shook hands solemnly.

'I feel a bit better,' said Fat Charlie.

'Like I said,' she said. 'Kill or cure.'

***

Spider was having a great day at the office. He almost never worked in offices. He almost never worked. Everything was new, everything was marvellous and strange, from the tiny lift that lurched him up to the fifth floor, to the warrenlike offices of the Grahame Coats Agency. He stared, fascinated, at the glass case in the lobby filled with dusty awards. He wandered through the offices, and when anyone asked him who he was, he would say 'I'm Fat Charlie Nancy', and he'd say it in his god-voice, which would make whatever he said practically true.

He found the tea-room, and made himself several cups of tea. Then he carried them back to Fat Charlie's desk, and arranged them around it in an artistic fashion. He started to play with the computer network. It asked him for a password. 'I'm Fat Charlie Nancy,' he told the computer, but there were still places it didn't want him to go, so he said, 'I'm Grahame Coats,' and it opened to him like a flower.

He looked at things on the computer until he got bored.

He dealt with the contents of Fat Charlie's in-basket. He dealt with Fat Charlie's pending basket.

It occurred to him that Fat Charlie would be waking up around now, so he called him at home, in order to reassure him; he just felt that he was making a little headway when Grahame Coats put his head round the door, ran his fingers across his stoat-like lips, and beckoned.

'Gotta go,' Spider said to his brother. 'The big boss needs to talk to me.' He put down the phone.

'Making private phone calls on company time, Nancy,' stated Grahame Coats.

'Abso-friggin'-lutely,' agreed Spider.

'And was that myself you were referring to as "the big boss"?' asked Grahame Coats. They walked to the end of the hallway, and into his office.

'You're the biggest,' said Spider. 'And the bossest.'

Grahame Coats looked puzzled; he suspected he was being made fun of, but he was not certain, and this disturbed him.

'Well, sit ye down, sit ye down,' he said.

Spider sat him down.

It was Grahame Coats's custom to keep the turnover of staff at the Grahame Coats Agency fairly constant. Some people came and went. Others came, and remained until just before their jobs would begin to carry some kind of employment protection. Fat

Charlie had been there longer than anyone: one year and eleven months. One month to go before redundancy payments or industrial tribunals could become a part of his life.

There was a speech that Grahame Coats gave, before he fired someone. He was very proud of his speech.

'Into each life,' he began, 'a little rain must fall. There's no cloud without a silver lining.'

'It's an ill wind,' offered Spider, 'that blows no one good.'

'Ah. Yes. Yes indeed. Well. As we pass through this vale of tears, we must pause to reflect that—'

'The first cut,' said Spider, 'is the deepest.'

'What? Oh.' Grahame Coats scrabbled to remember what came next. 'Happiness,' he pronounced, 'is like a butterfly.'

'Or a bluebird,' agreed Spider.

'Quite. If I may finish?'

'Of course. Be my guest,' said Spider, cheerfully.

'And the happiness of every soul at the Grahame Coats Agency is as important to me as my own.'

'I cannot tell you,' said Spider, 'how happy that makes me.'

'Yes,' said Grahame Coats.

'Well, I better get back to work,' said Spider. 'It's been a blast, though. Next time you want to share some more, just call me. You know where I am.'

'Happiness,' said Grahame Coats. His voice was taking on a faintly strangulated quality. 'And what I wonder, Nancy, Charles, is this – are you happy here? And do you not agree that you might be rather happier elsewhere?'

'That's not what I wonder,' said Spider. 'You want to know what I wonder?'

Grahame Coats said nothing. It had never gone like this before. Normally, at this point, their faces fell, and they went into shock. Sometimes they cried. Grahame Coats had never minded when they cried.

'What I wonder,' said Spider, 'is what the accounts in the Cayman Islands are for. You know, because it almost sort of looks like money that should go to our client accounts sometimes just goes into the Cayman Island accounts instead. And it seems a funny sort of way to organise the finances, for the money coming in to rest in those accounts. I've never seen anything like it before. I was hoping you could explain it to me.'

Grahame Coats had gone off-white – one of those colours that turn up in paint catalogues with names like Parchment or Magnolia. He said, 'How did you get access to those accounts?'

'Computers,' said Spider. 'Do they drive you as nuts as they drive me? What can you do?'

Grahame Coats thought for several long moments. He had always liked to imagine that his financial affairs were so deeply tangled that, even if the Fraud Squad were ever able to conclude that financial crimes had been committed, they would find it extremely difficult to explain to a jury exactly what kind of crimes they were.

'There's nothing illegal about having offshore accounts,' he said, as carelessly as possible.

'Illegal?' said Spider. 'I should hope not. I mean, if I saw anything illegal, I should have to report it to the appropriate authorities.'

Grahame Coats picked up a pen from his desk, then he put it down again. 'Ah,' he said. 'Well, delightful though it is to chat, converse, spend time and otherwise hobnob with you, Charles, I suspect that both of us have work we should be getting on with. Time and tide, after all, wait for no man. Procrastination is the thief of time.'

'Life is a rock,' suggested Spider, 'but the radio rolled me.'

'Whatever.'

* * *

Fat Charlie was starting to feel human again. He was no longer in pain; slow, intimate waves of nausea were no longer sweeping over him. While he was not yet convinced that the world was a fine and joyous place, he was no longer in the ninth circle of hangover hell, and this was a good thing.

Daisy had taken over the bathroom. He had listened to the taps running, and then to some contented splashes.

He knocked on the bathroom door.

'I'm in here,' said Daisy. 'I'm in the bath.'

'I know,' said Fat Charlie. 'I mean, I didn't know, but I thought you probably were.'

'Yes?' said Daisy.

'I just wondered,' he said, through the door. 'I wondered why you came back here. Last night.'

'Well,' she said. 'You were a bit the worse for wear. And your brother looked like he needed a hand. I'm not working this morning, so. *Voilà.*'

'*Voilà,*' said Fat Charlie. On the one hand, she felt sorry for him. And on the other, she really liked Spider. Yes. He'd only had a brother for a little over a day, and already he felt there would be no surprises left in this new family relationship. Spider was the cool one; he was the other one.

She said, 'You have a lovely voice.'

'What?'

'You were singing in the taxi, when we were going home. "Unforgettable". It was lovely.'

He had somehow put the karaoke incident out of his mind, placed it in the dark places one disposes of inconvenient things. Now it came back, and he wished it hadn't.

'You were great,' she said. 'Will you sing to me, later?'

Fat Charlie thought desperately, and then was saved from thinking desperately by the doorbell.

'Someone at the door,' he said.

He went downstairs and opened the door and things got worse. Rosie's mother gave him a look that would have curdled milk. She said nothing. She was holding a large white envelope.

'Hello,' said Fat Charlie. 'Mrs Noah. Nice to see you. Um.'

She sniffed and held the envelope in front of her. 'Oh,' she said. 'You're here. So. You going to invite me in?'

That's right, thought Fat Charlie. *Your kind always have to be invited. Just say no, and she'll have to go away.* 'Of course, Mrs Noah. Please, come in.' *So that's how vampires do it.* 'Would you like a cup of tea?'

'Don't think you can get around me like that,' she said. 'Because you can't.'

'Er. Right.'

Up the narrow stairs and into the kitchen. Rosie's mother

looked around and made a face as if to indicate that it did not meet her standards of hygiene, containing, as it did, edible foodstuffs. 'Coffee? Water?' *Don't say wax fruit.* 'Wax fruit?' *Damn.*

'I understand from Rosie that your father recently passed away,' she said.

'Yes. He did.'

'When Rosie's father passed, they did a four-page obituary in *Cooks and Cookery*. They said he was solely responsible for the arrival of Caribbean Fusion Cuisine in this country.'

'Oh,' he said.

'It's not like he left me badly off, neither. He had life insurance, and he owned a share of two successful restaurants. I'm a very well-off woman. When I die, it will all go to Rosie.'

'When we're married,' said Fat Charlie, 'I'll be looking after her. Don't you worry.'

'I'm not saying you're only after Rosie for my money,' said Rosie's mother, in a tone of voice that made it clear that that was exactly what she did believe.

Fat Charlie's headache started coming back. 'Mrs Noah, is there anything I can help you with?'

'I've been talking to Rosie, and we've decided that I should start helping with your wedding plans,' she said, primly. 'I need a list of your relations and friends. The ones you were hoping to invite. Names, addresses, e-mail and phone numbers. I've made a form for you to fill out. I thought I'd save on postage and drop it off myself, since I was going to be passing by Maxwell Gardens anyway. I was not expecting to find you home.' She handed him the large white envelope. 'There will be a total of ninety people at the wedding. You will be permitted a total of eight family members and six personal friends. The personal friends, and four family members will comprise Table H. The rest of your group will be at Table C. Your father would have been seated with us at the head table, but seeing that he has passed over, we have allocated his seat to Rosie's Aunt Winifred. Have you decided on your best man, yet?'

Fat Charlie shook his head.

'Well, when you do, make certain he knows that there won't be any crude stuff in his speech. I don't want to hear nothing from your best man I wouldn't hear in a church. You understand me?'

Fat Charlie wondered what Rosie's mother would usually hear in a church. Probably just cries of 'Back! Foul beast of Hell!' followed by gasps of 'Is it alive?' and a nervous enquiry as to whether anybody had remembered to bring the stakes and hammers.

'I think,' said Fat Charlie, 'I have more than eight relations. I mean, there are cousins, and great-aunts and things.'

'What you obviously fail to grasp,' said Rosie's mother, 'is that weddings cost money. I've allocated £175 a person to tables A to D – Table A is the head table – which takes care of Rosie's closest relations and my women's club, and £125 to tables E to G, which are, you know, more distant acquaintances, the children and so on and so forth.'

'You said my friends would be at Table H,' said Fat Charlie.

'That's the next tier down. They won't be getting the avocado shrimp starters or the sherry trifle.'

'When Rosie and I talked about it last, we thought we'd be going for a sort of a general West Indian theme to the food.'

Rosie's mother sniffed. 'She sometimes doesn't know her own mind, that girl. But she and I are now in full agreement.'

'Look,' said Fat Charlie, 'I think maybe I ought to talk to Rosie about all this, and get back to you.'

'Just fill out the forms,' said Rosie's mother. Then she said, suspiciously, 'Why aren't you at work?'

'I'm. Um. I'm not in. That is to say, I'm off this morning. Not going in today. I'm. Not.'

'I hope you told Rosie that. She was planning to see you for lunch, she told me. That was why she could not have lunch with me.'

Fat Charlie took this information in. 'Right,' he said. 'Well, thanks for popping over, Mrs Noah. I'll talk to Rosie, and—'

Daisy came into the kitchen. She wore a towel wrapped around her head, and Fat Charlie's dressing gown, which clung to her damp body. She said 'There's orange juice, isn't there? I know I saw some, when I was poking around before. How's your head?

Any better?' She opened the fridge door, and poured herself a tall glass of orange juice.

Rosie's mother cleared her throat. It did not sound like a throat being cleared. It sounded like pebbles rattling down a beach.

'Hullo,' said Daisy. 'I'm Daisy.'

The temperature in the kitchen began to drop. 'Indeed?' said Rosie's mother. Icicles hung from the final D.

'I wonder what they would have called oranges,' said Fat Charlie into the silence, 'if they weren't orange. I mean, if they were some previously unknown blue fruit, would they have been called *blues*? Would we be drinking blue juice?'

'What?' asked Rosie's mother.

'Bless. You should hear the things that come out of your mouth,' said Daisy, cheerfully. 'Right. I'm going to see if I can find my clothes. Lovely meeting you.'

She went out. Fat Charlie did not resume breathing.

'Who,' said Rosie's mother, perfectly calmly. 'Was. That.'

'My sis-cousin. My cousin,' said Fat Charlie. 'I just think of her as my sister. We were very close, growing up. She just decided to crash here last night. She's a bit of a wild child. Well. Yes. You'll see her at the wedding.'

'I'll put her down for Table H,' said Rosie's mother. 'She'll be more comfortable there.' She said it in the same way most people would say things like, 'Do you wish to die quickly, or shall I let Mongo have his fun first?'

'Right,' said Fat Charlie. 'Well,' he said. 'Lovely to see you. Well,' he said, 'you must have lots of things to be getting on with. And,' he said, 'I need to be getting to work.'

'I thought you had the day off.'

'Morning. I've got the morning off. And it's nearly over. And I should be getting off to work now so goodbye.'

She clutched her handbag to her, and she stood up. Fat Charlie followed her out into the hall.

'Lovely seeing you,' he said.

She blinked, as a nictitating python might blink before striking. 'Goodbye, Daisy,' she called. 'I'll see you at the wedding.'

Daisy, now wearing panties and a bra, and in the process of

pulling on a T-shirt, leaned out into the hall. 'Take care,' she said, and went back into Fat Charlie's bedroom.

Rosie's mother said nothing else as Fat Charlie led her down the stairs. He opened the door for her, and as she went past him, he saw on her face something terrible, something that made his stomach knot more than it was knotting already: the thing that Rosie's mother was doing with her mouth. It was pulled up at the corners in a ghastly rictus. Like a skull with lips, Rosie's mother was smiling.

He closed the door behind her and he stood and shivered in the downstairs hall. Then, like a man going to the electric chair, he went back up the hall steps.

'Who was that?' asked Daisy, who was now almost dressed.

'My fiancée's mother.'

'She's a real bundle of joy, isn't she?' She was dressed in the same clothes she had worn the previous night.

'You going to work like that?'

'Oh. Bless. No, I'll go home and change. This isn't how I look at work, anyway. Can you ring a taxi?'

'Where are you headed?'

'Hendon.'

He called a local taxi service. Then he sat on the floor in the hallway and contemplated various future scenarios, all of them uncontemplatable.

Someone was standing next to him. 'I've got some B vitamins in my bag,' she said. 'Or you could try sucking on a spoonful of honey. It's never done anything for me, but my flatmate swears by it for hangovers.'

'It's not that,' said Fat Charlie. 'I told her you were my cousin. So she wouldn't think you were my, that we, you know, a strange girl in the apartment, all that.'

'Cousin, is it? Well, not to worry. She'll probably forget all about me, and if she doesn't, tell her I left the country mysteriously. You'll never see me again.'

'Really? Promise?'

'You don't have to sound so pleased about it.'

A car horn sounded in the street outside. 'That'll be my taxi. Stand up and say goodbye.'

He stood up.

'Not to worry,' she said. She hugged him.

'I think my life is over,' he said.

'No. It's not.'

'I'm doomed.'

'Thanks,' she said. She leaned up, and she kissed him on the lips, longer and harder than could possibly fit within the bounds of recent introduction. Then she smiled, and walked jauntily down the stairs and let herself out.

'This,' said Fat Charlie out loud, when the door closed, 'probably isn't really happening.'

He could still taste her on his lips, all orange-juice and raspberries. That was a kiss. That was a serious kiss. There was an oomf behind that kiss that he had never in his whole life had before, not even from—

'Rosie,' he said.

He flipped open his phone, and speed-dialled her.

'This is Rosie's phone,' said Rosie's voice. 'I'm busy or I've lost the phone again. And you're in voicemail. Try me at home or leave me a message.'

Fat Charlie closed the phone. Then he put on his coat over his tracksuit and, wincing just a little at the terrible unblinking daylight, he went out into the street.

* * *

Rosie Noah was worried, which in itself worried her. It was, as so many things in Rosie's world were, whether she would admit it to herself or not, Rosie's mother's fault.

Rosie had become quite used to a world in which her mother hated the idea of her marrying Fat Charlie Nancy. She took her mother's opposition to the marriage as a sign from the heavens that she was probably doing something right, even when she was not entirely sure in her own mind that this was actually the case.

And she loved him, of course. He was solid, reassuring, sane . . .

Her mother's about-turn on the matter of Fat Charlie had Rosie worried, and her mother's sudden enthusiasm for wedding organisation troubled her deeply.

She had phoned Fat Charlie the previous night to discuss the matter, but he was not answering his phones. Rosie thought perhaps he had had an early night.

It was why she was giving up her lunch time to talk to him.

The Grahame Coats Agency occupied the top floor of a grey Victorian building in the Aldwych, and was at the top of five flights of stairs. There was a lift, though, which had been installed a hundred years before by theatrical agent Rupert 'Binky' Butterworth. It was an extremely small, slow, juddery lift, whose design and function peculiarities only became comprehensible when you discovered that Binky Butterworth had possessed the size, shape and ability to squeeze into small spaces of a portly young hippopotamus, and had designed the lift to fit, at a squeeze, Binky Butterworth and one other, much slimmer, person – a chorus girl, for example, or a chorus boy, Binky was not picky. All it took to make Binky happy was someone seeking theatrical representation squeezed into the lift with him, and a very slow and juddery journey up all six storeys to the top. It was often the case that by the time he reached the top floor, Binky would be so overcome by the pressures of the journey that he would need to go and have a little lie-down, leaving the chorus girl or chorus boy to cool his or her heels in the waiting room, concerned that the red-faced panting and uncontrolled gasping for breath that Binky had been suffering from as they reached the final floors meant that he had been having some kind of early Edwardian embolism.

People would go into the lift with Binky Butterworth once, but after that they used the stairs.

Grahame Coats, who had purchased the remains of the Butterworth Agency from Binky's granddaughter more than twenty years before, maintained the lift was part of history.

Rosie slammed the inner accordion door, closed the outer door, and went into reception, where she told the receptionist she wanted to see Charles Nancy. She sat down, beneath the photographs of Grahame Coats with people he had represented: she recognised Morris Livingstone, the comedian; some once-famous boy bands; and a clutch of sports stars who had, in their later years, become 'personalities' – the kind who got as much fun out of life as they could until a new liver became available.

A man came into reception. He did not look much like Fat Charlie. He was darker, and he was smiling as if he were amused by everything – deeply, dangerously amused.

'I'm Fat Charlie Nancy,' said the man.

Rosie walked over to Fat Charlie and gave him a peck on the cheek. He said, 'Do I know you?' which was an odd thing to say, and then he said, 'Of course I do. You're Rosie. And you get more beautiful every day,' and he kissed her in return, touching his lips to hers. Their lips only brushed, but Rosie's heart began to beat like Binky Butterworth's after a particularly juddery lift-journey pressed up against a chorine.

'Lunch,' squeaked Rosie. 'Passing. Thought maybe we could. Talk.'

'Yeah,' said the man who Rosie now thought of as Fat Charlie. 'Lunch.'

He put a comfortable arm around Rosie. 'Anywhere you want to go for lunch?'

'Oh,' she said. 'Just. Wherever you want.' It was the way he smelled, she thought. Why had she never before noticed how much she liked the way he smelled?

'We'll find somewhere,' he said. 'Shall we take the stairs?'

'If it's all the same to you,' she said, 'I think I'd rather take the lift.'

She banged home the accordion door, and they rode down to street level slowly and shakily, pressed up against each other.

Rosie couldn't remember the last time she had been so happy.

When they got out on to the street Rosie's phone beeped to let her know she had missed a call. She ignored it.

They went into the first restaurant they came to. Until the previous month it had been a high-tech sushi restaurant, with a conveyor belt that ran around the room carrying small raw-fishy nibbles priced according to plate colour. The Japanese restaurant had gone out of business, and had been instantly replaced, in the way of London restaurants, by a Hungarian restaurant, which had kept the conveyor belt as a high-tech addition to the world of Hungarian cuisine, which meant that rapidly cooling bowls of goulash, paprika dumplings, and pots of sour cream made their way in stately fashion around the room.

Rosie didn't think it was going to catch on.

'Where were you last night?' she asked.

'I went out,' he said. 'With my brother.'

'You're an only child,' she said.

'I'm not. It turns out I'm half of a matched set.'

'Really? Is this more of your dad's legacy?'

'Honey,' said the man she thought of as Fat Charlie, 'you don't know the half of it.'

'Well,' she said. 'I hope he'll be coming to the wedding.'

'I don't believe he would miss it for the world.' He closed his hand around hers, and she nearly dropped her goulash spoon. 'What are you doing for the rest of the afternoon?'

'Not much. Things are practically dead back at the office right now. Couple of fund-raising phone calls to make, but they can wait. Is there. Um. Were you. Um. Why?'

'It's such a beautiful day. Do you want to go for a walk?'

'That,' said Rosie, 'would be quite lovely.'

They wandered down to the Embankment, and began to walk along the northern back of the Thames, a slow, hand-in-hand amble, talking about nothing much in particular.

'What about *your* work?' asked Rosie, when they stopped to buy an ice cream.

'Oh,' he said. 'They won't mind. They probably won't even notice that I'm not there.'

* * *

Fat Charlie ran up the stairs to the Grahame Coats Agency. He always took the stairs. It was healthier, for a start, and it meant he would never again have to worry about finding himself wedged into the lift with someone else, too close to pretend they weren't there.

He walked into reception, panting slightly. 'Has Rosie been in, Annie?'

'Did you lose her?' said the receptionist.

He walked back to his office. His desk was peculiarly tidy. The clutter of undealt-with correspondence was gone. There was a yellow Post-it note on his computer screen, with 'See me. GC' on it.

He knocked on Grahame Coats's office door. This time a voice said 'Yes?'

'It's me,' he said.

'Yes,' said Grahame Coats. 'Come ye in, Master Nancy. Pull up a pew. I've been giving our conversation of this morning a great deal of thought. And it seems to me that I have misjudged you. You have been working here, for, how long . . . ?'

'Nearly two years.'

'You have been working long and hard. And now your father's sad passing . . .'

'I didn't really know him.'

'Ah. Brave soul, Nancy. Given that it is currently the fallow season, how would you react to an offer of a couple of weeks off? With, I hardly need to add, full pay?'

'Full pay?' said Fat Charlie.

'Full pay, but, yes, I see your point. Spending money. I'm sure you could do with a little spending money, couldn't you?'

Fat Charlie tried to work out what universe he was in. 'Am I being fired?'

Grahame Coats laughed then, like a weasel with a sharp bone stuck in its throat. 'Absatively not. Quite the reverse. In fact I believe,' he said, 'that we now understand each other perfectly. Your job is safe and sound. Safe as houses. As long as you remain the model of circumspection and discretion you have been so far.'

'How safe are houses?' asked Fat Charlie.

'Extremely safe.'

'It's just that I read somewhere that most accidents occur in the home.'

'Then,' said Grahame Coats, 'I think it vitally important that you are encouraged to return to your own house with all celerity.' He handed Fat Charlie a piece of rectangular paper. 'Here,' he said. 'A small thank you for two years of devoted service to the Grahame Coats Agency.' Then, because it was what he always said when he gave people money, 'Don't spend it all at once.'

Fat Charlie looked at the piece of paper. It was a cheque. 'Two thousand pounds. Gosh. I mean, I won't.'

Grahame Coats smiled at Fat Charlie. If there was triumph in that smile, Fat Charlie was too puzzled, too shaken, too bemused, to see it.

'Go well,' said Grahame Coats.

Fat Charlie went back to his office.

Grahame Coats leaned around the door, casually, like a mongoose leaning idly against a snake-den. 'An idle question. If, while you are off enjoying yourself and relaxing – a course of action I cannot press upon you strongly enough – if, during this time, I should need to access your files, could you let me know your password?'

'I think your password should get you anywhere in the system,' said Fat Charlie.

'Without doubt it will,' agreed Grahame Coats, blithely. 'But just in case. You know computers, after all.'

'It's Mermaid,' said Fat Charlie. 'M-E-R-M-A-I-D.'

'Excellent,' said Grahame Coats. 'Excellent.' He didn't rub his hands together, but he might as well have done.

Fat Charlie walked down the stairs with a cheque for two thousand pounds in his pocket, wondering how he could have so misjudged Grahame Coats for the last two years.

He walked round the corner to his bank, and deposited the cheque into his account.

Then he walked down to the Embankment, to breathe, and to think.

He was two thousand pounds richer. His headache of this morning had completely gone. He was feeling solid and prosperous. He wondered if he could talk Rosie into coming on a short holiday with him. It was short notice, but still . . .

And then he saw Spider and Rosie, walking hand in hand, on the other side of the road. Rosie was finishing an ice cream. Then she stopped, and dropped the remainder of the ice cream into a bin, and pulled Spider towards her and, with an ice-creamy mouth, began to kiss him with enthusiasm and gusto.

Fat Charlie could feel his headache coming back. He felt paralysed.

He watched them kissing. He was of the opinion that sooner or later they would have to come up for air, but they didn't, so he walked in the other direction, feeling miserable, until he reached the tube.

And he went home.

By the time he got home, Fat Charlie felt pretty wretched, so he got on to a bed that still smelled faintly of Daisy, and he closed his eyes.

Time passed, and now Fat Charlie was walking along a sandy beach with his father. They were barefoot. He was a kid again, and his father was ageless.

So, his father was saying, *how are you and Spider getting on?*

This is a dream, pointed out Fat Charlie, *and I don't want to talk about it.*

You boys, said his father, shaking his head. *Listen. I'm going to tell you something important.*

What?

But his father did not answer. Something on the edge of the waves had caught his eye, and he reached down and picked it up. Five pointed legs flexed languidly.

Starfish, said his father, musing. *When you cut one in half, they just grow into two new starfish.*

I thought you said you were going to tell me something important.

His father clutched his chest, and he collapsed on to the sand, and stopped moving. Worms came out of the sand and devoured him in moments, leaving nothing but bones.

Dad?

Fat Charlie woke up in his bedroom, his cheeks wet with tears. Then he stopped crying. He had nothing to be upset about. His father had not died; it had simply been a bad dream.

He decided that he would invite Rosie over tomorrow night. They would have steak. He would cook. All would be well.

He got up and got dressed.

He was in the kitchen, twenty minutes later, spooning down a Pot Noodle, when it occurred to him that, although what had happened on the beach had been a dream, his father was still dead.

***

Rosie stopped in at her mother's flat in Wimpole Street, late that afternoon.

'I saw your boyfriend today,' said Mrs Noah. Her given name had been Eutheria, but in the last three decades nobody had used it to her face but her late husband, and following his death it had atrophied, and was unlikely to be used again in her lifetime.

'So did I,' said Rosie. 'My God I love that man.'

'Well, of course. You're marrying him, aren't you?'

'Well, yes. I mean, I always knew I loved him, but today I really saw how much I loved him. Everything about him.'

'Did you find out where he was last night?'

'Yes. He explained it all. He was out with his brother.'

'I didn't know he had a brother.'

'He hadn't mentioned him before. They aren't very close.'

Rosie's mother clicked her tongue. 'Must be quite a family reunion going on. Did he mention his cousin, too?'

'Cousin?'

'Or maybe his sister. He didn't seem entirely sure. Pretty thing, in a trashy sort of way. Looked a bit Chinese. No better than she should be, if you ask me. But that's that whole family for you.'

'Mum. You haven't met his family.'

'I met her. She was in his kitchen this morning, walking about that place damn near naked. Shameless. *If* she was his cousin.'

'Fat Charlie wouldn't lie.'

'He's a man, isn't he?'

'*Mum!*'

'And why wasn't he at work today, anyway?'

'He was. He was at work today. We had lunch together.'

Rosie's mother examined her lipstick in a pocket mirror, then, with her forefinger, rubbed the scarlet smudges off her teeth.

'What else did you say to him?' asked Rosie.

'We just talked about the wedding, how I didn't want his best man making one of them near-the-knuckle speeches. He looked to me like he'd been drinking. You know how I warned you about marrying a drinking man.'

'Well, he looked perfectly fine when I saw him,' said Rosie, primly. Then, 'Oh, Mum, I had the most wonderful day. We walked and we talked and – oh, have I told you how wonderful he *smells*? And he has the softest hands.'

'You ask me,' said her mother, 'he smells fishy. Tell you what, next time you see him, you ask him about this cousin of his. I'm not saying she is his cousin, and I'm not saying she's not. I'm just saying that if she is, then he has hookers and strippers and good-time girls in his family, and is not the kind of person you should be seeing romantically.'

Rosie felt more comfortable, now her mother was once more coming down against Fat Charlie. 'Mum. I won't hear another word.'

'All right. I'll hold my tongue. It's not me that's marrying him, after all. Not me that's throwing my life away. Not me that'll be weeping into my pillow while he's out all night drinking with his fancy women. It's not me that'll be waiting, day after day, night after empty night, for him to get out of prison.'

'Mum!' Rosie tried to be indignant, but the thought of Fat Charlie in prison was too funny, too silly, and she found herself stifling a giggle.

Rosie's phone trilled. She answered it, and said, 'Yes,' and, 'I'd love to. That would be wonderful.' She put her phone away.

'That was him,' she said to her mother. 'I'm going over there tomorrow night. He's cooking for me. How sweet is that?' And then she said, 'Prison indeed.'

'I'm a mother,' said her mother, in her foodless flat where the dust did not dare to settle, 'and I know what I know.'

* * *

Grahame Coats sat in his office, while the day faded into dusk, staring at a computer screen. He brought up document after document, spreadsheet after spreadsheet. Some of them he changed. Most of them he deleted.

He was meant to be travelling to Birmingham that evening, where a former footballer, a client of his, was to open a nightclub. Instead he called and apologised: some things were unavoidable.

Soon the light outside the window was gone entirely. Grahame Coats sat in the cold glow of the computer screen, and he changed, and he overwrote, and he deleted.

* * *

Here's another story they tell about Anansi.

Once, long long ago, Anansi's wife planted a field of peas. They were the finest, the fattest, the greenest peas you ever did see. It would have made your mouth water just to look at them.

From the moment Anansi saw the pea field, he wanted them. And he didn't just want some of them, for Anansi was a man of enormous appetites. He did not want to share them. He wanted them all.

So Anansi lay down on his bed and he sighed, long and loud, and his wife and his sons all came a-running. 'I'm a-dying,' said Anansi, in this little weeny-weedy-weaky voice, 'and my life is all over and done.'

At this his wife and his sons began to cry hot tears.

In his weensy-weak voice, Anansi says, 'On my deathbed, you have to promise me two things.'

'Anything, anything,' says his wife and his sons.

'First, you got to promise me you will bury me down under the big breadfruit tree.'

'The big breadfruit tree down by the pea patch, you mean?' asks his wife.

'Of course that's the one I mean,' says Anansi. Then, in his weensy-weak voice, he says, 'And you got to promise something else. Promise me that, as a memorial to me, you going to make a little fire at the foot of my grave. And, to show you ain't forgotten me, you going to keep the little fire burning, and not ever let it go out.'

'We will! We will!' said Anansi's wife and children, wailing and sobbing.

'And on that fire, as mark of your respect and your love, I want to see a lickle pot, filled with salt water, to remind you all of the hot salt tears you shed over me as I lay dying.'

'We shall! We shall!' they wept, and Anansi, he closed his eyes, and he breathed no more.

Well, they carried Anansi down to the big breadfruit tree that grew beside the pea patch, and they buried him six feet down, and at the foot of the grave they built a little fire, and they put a pot beside it, filled with salt water.

Anansi, he waits down there all the day but when night falls he climbs out of the grave, and he goes into the pea patch, where he picks him the fattest, sweetest, ripest peas. He gathers them up and he boils them up in his pot, and he stuffs himself with them till his tummy swells and tightens like a drum.

Then, before dawn, he goes back under the ground, and he goes back to sleep. He sleeps as his wife and his sons find the peas gone, he sleeps through them seeing the pot empty of water and refilling it, he sleeps through their sorrow.

Each night Anansi comes out of his grave, dancing and delighting at the cleverness of him, and each night he fills the pot with peas, and he fills his tummy with peas, and he eats until he cannot eat another thing.

Days go by, and Anansi's family gets thinner and thinner, for nothing ever ripens that isn't picked in the night by Anansi, and they got nothing to eat.

Anansi's wife, she looks down at the empty plates, and she says to her sons, 'What would your father do?'

Her sons, they think and they think, and they remember every tale that Anansi ever told them. Then they go down to the tar-pits, and they buy them sixpennyworth of tar, enough to fill four big buckets, and they take that tar back to the pea patch. And down in the middle of the pea patch, they make them a man out of tar: tar face, tar eyes, tar arms, tar fingers, and tar chest. It was a fine man, as black and as proud as Anansi himself.

That night, old Anansi, fat as he has ever been in his whole life, he scuttles up out of the ground, and, plump and happy, stomach swollen like a drum, he strolls over to the pea patch.

'Who you?' he says to the tar man.

The tar man, he don't say one word.

'This is my place,' said Anansi to the tar man. 'It's my pea patch. You better get going, if you know what's good for you.'

The tar man, he don't say one word, he don't move a muscle.

'I'm the strongest, mightiest, most powerful fellow there is or was or ever will be,' says Anansi to the tar man. 'I'm fiercer than Lion, faster than Cheetah, stronger than Elephant, more terrible than Tiger.' He swelled up with pride at his power and strength and fierceness, and he forgot he was just a little spider. 'Tremble,' says Anansi. 'Tremble and run.'

The tar man, he didn't tremble and he didn't run. Tell the truth, he just stood there.

So Anansi hits him.

Anansi's fist, it sticks solid.

'Let go of my hand,' he tells the tar man. 'Let go my hand, or I'm going to hit you in the face.'

The tar man, he says not a word, and he doesn't move the tiniest muscle, and Anansi hits him, bash, right in the face.

'OK,' says Anansi, 'a joke's a joke. You can keep hold of my hands if you like, but I got four more hands, and two good legs, and you can't hold them all, so you let me go and I'll take it easy on you.'

The tar man, he doesn't let go of Anansi's hands, and he doesn't say a word, so Anansi hits him with all his hands and then kicks him with his feet, one after another.

'Right,' says Anansi. 'You let me go, or I *bite* you.' The tar fills his mouth, and covers his nose and his face.

So that's how they find Anansi, the next morning, when his wife and his sons come down to the pea patch, by the old breadfruit tree: all stuck to the tar man, and dead as history.

They weren't surprised to see him like that.

Those days, you used to find Anansi like that all the time.

Chapter Six

In Which Fat Charlie
Fails to Get Home,
Even by Taxi

D aisy woke up to the alarm. She stretched in her bed like a kitten. She could hear the shower, which meant that her flatmate was already up. She put on a pink fuzzy dressing gown and went into the hall.

'You want porridge?' she called through the bathroom door.

'Not much. If you're making it, I'll eat it.'

'You certainly know how to make a girl feel wanted,' said Daisy, and she went into the kitchenette and put the porridge on to cook.

She went back into her bedroom, pulled on her work clothes, then looked at herself in the mirror. She made a face. She put her hair up into a tight bun at the back.

Her flatmate, Carol, a thin-faced white woman from Preston, stuck her head around the bedroom door. She was towelling her hair vigorously. 'Bathroom's all yours. What's the word on the porridge?'

'Probably needs a stir.'

'So where were you the other night anyway? You said you were going off to Sybilla's birthday drinks, and I know you never came back.'

'None of your beeswax, innit.' Daisy went into the kitchen and stirred the porridge. She added a pinch of salt and stirred it some more. She glopped the porridge into bowls and placed them on the counter.

'Carol? Porridge is getting cold.'

Carol came in, sat down, stared at the porridge. She was only half-dressed. ''S not a proper breakfast, is it? You ask me, a proper breakfast is fried eggs, sausages, black pudden and grilled tomatoes.'

'You cook it,' said Daisy, 'I'll eat it.'

Carol sprinkled a dessertspoonful of sugar on her porridge. She looked at it. Then she sprinkled another one on. 'No, you bloody won't. You say that you will. But you'll start rabbiting on about cholesterol or what fried food is doing to your kidneys.' She tasted the porridge as if it might bite her back. Daisy passed her a cup of tea. 'You and your kidneys. Actually, that might be nice for a change. You ever eaten kidneys, Daisy?'

'Once,' said Daisy. 'If you ask me, you can get the same effect by grilling half a pound of liver, then weeing all over it.'

Carol sniffed. 'That wasn't called for,' she said.

'Eat your porridge.'

They finished their porridge, and their tea. They put the bowls in the dishwasher, and, because it was not yet full, did not turn it on. Then they drove in to work. Carol, who was now in uniform, did the driving.

Daisy went up to her desk, in a room filled with empty desks.

The phone rang as she sat down. 'Daisy? You're late.'

She looked at her watch. 'No,' she said. 'I'm not, sir. Now is there anything else I can do for you this morning?'

'Too right. You can call a man named Coats. He's a friend of the chief super. Fellow Crystal Palace supporter. He's already texted me about it twice this morning. Who taught the chief super to text, that's what I want to know?'

Daisy took down the details, and called the number. She put on her most businesslike and efficient tone of voice, and said, 'Detective Constable Day. How can I help you?'

'Ah,' said a man's voice. 'Well, as I was telling the chief superintendent last night, a lovely man, old friend. Good man. He suggested I talk to someone in your office. I wish to report. Well, I'm not actually certain that a crime has been committed. Probably a perfectly sensible explanation. There have been certain irregularities, and, well, to be perfectly frank with you, I've given my book-keeper a couple of weeks' leave, while I try to come to grips with the possibility that he may have been involved in certain, mm, financial irregularities.'

'Suppose we get the details,' said Daisy. 'What's your full name, sir? And the book-keeper's name?'

'My name is Grahame Coats,' said the man on the other end of the telephone. 'Of the Grahame Coats Agency. My book-keeper is a man named Nancy. Charles Nancy.'

She wrote both names down. They did not ring any bells.

* * *

Fat Charlie had planned to have an argument with Spider as soon as Spider came home. He had rehearsed the argument in his head, over and over, and had won it, both fairly and decisively, every time.

Spider had not, however, come home last night, and Fat Charlie had eventually fallen asleep in front of the television, half watching a raucous game show for horny insomniacs, which seemed to be called *Show Us Your Bum!*

He woke up on the sofa, when Spider pulled open the curtains. 'Beautiful day,' said Spider.

'You!' said Fat Charlie. 'You were kissing Rosie. Don't try to deny it.'

'I had to,' said Spider.

'What do you mean, you had to? You didn't have to.'

'She thought I was you.'

'Well, you knew you weren't me. You shouldn't have kissed her.'

'But if I had refused to kiss her, she would have thought it was you not kissing her.'

'But it wasn't me.'

'She didn't know that. I was just trying to be helpful.'

'Being helpful,' said Fat Charlie, from the sofa, 'is something you do that, generally speaking, involves *not* kissing my fiancée. You could have said you had a toothache.'

'That,' said Spider, virtuously, 'would have been lying.'

'But you were lying already! You were pretending to be me!'

'Well, it would have been compounding the lie, anyway,' explained Spider. 'Something I only did because you were in no shape to go to work. No,' he said, 'I couldn't have lied further. I would have felt dreadful.'

'Well, I *did* feel dreadful. I had to watch you kissing her.'

'Ah,' said Spider. 'But she *thought* she was kissing *you*.'

'Don't keep saying that!'

'You should feel flattered,' Spider said. 'Do you want lunch?'

'Of course I don't want lunch. What time is it?'

'Lunch time,' said Spider. 'And you're late for work again. It's a good thing I didn't cover for you again, if this is all the thanks I get.'

''S OK,' said Fat Charlie. 'I've been given two weeks off. And a bonus.'

Spider raised an eyebrow.

'Look,' said Fat Charlie, feeling like it was time to move to the second round of the argument, 'it's not like I'm trying to get rid of you or anything, but I was wondering when you were thinking of leaving.'

Spider said, 'Well, when I came here, I'd only planned to visit for a day. Maybe two days. Long enough to meet my little brother and then I'd be on my way. I'm a busy man.'

'So you're leaving today.'

'That *was* my plan,' said Spider. 'But then I met you. I cannot believe that we have let almost an entire lifetime go by without each other's company, my brother.'

'I can.'

'The ties of blood,' said Spider, 'are stronger than water.'

'Water's not strong,' objected Fat Charlie.

'Stronger than vodka, then. Or volcanoes. Or, or ammonia. Look, my point is that meeting you – well, it's a privilege. We've never been part of each other's lives, but that was yesterday. Let's start a new tomorrow, today. We'll put yesterday behind us and forge new bonds – the bonds of brotherhood.'

'You're totally after Rosie,' said Fat Charlie.

'Totally,' agreed Spider. 'What do you plan to do about it?'

'Do about it? Well, she's *my* fiancée.'

'Not to worry. She thinks I'm you.'

'Will you stop saying that . . . ?'

Spider spread his hands, in a saintly gesture, then ruined the effect by licking his lips.

'So,' said Fat Charlie, 'what are you planning to do next? Marry her, pretending to be me?'

'Marry?' Spider paused and thought for a moment. 'What. A horrible. Idea.'

'Well, I was quite looking forward to it, actually.'

'Spider does not marry. I'm not the marrying kind.'

'So my Rosie's not good enough for you, is that what you're saying?'

Spider did not answer. He walked out of the room.

Fat Charlie felt like he'd scored, somehow, in the argument. He got up from the sofa, picked up the empty foil cartons that had, the previous evening, held a chicken chow mein and crispy pork balls, and he dropped them into the bin. He went into his bedroom, where he took off the clothes he had slept in in order to put on clean clothes, discovered that, due to not doing the laundry, he had no clean clothes, so brushed yesterday's clothes down vigorously – dislodging several stray strands of chow mein – and put them back on.

He went into the kitchen.

Spider was sitting at the kitchen table, enjoying a steak large enough for two people.

'Where did you get that from?' said Fat Charlie, although he was certain that he already knew.

'I asked you if you wanted lunch,' said Spider, mildly.

'Where did you get the steak?'

'It was in the fridge.'

'That,' declaimed Fat Charlie, wagging his finger like a prosecuting attorney going in for the kill, '*that* was the steak I bought for dinner tonight. For dinner tonight for me and Rosie. The dinner I was going to be cooking for her! And you're just sitting there like a, a person eating a steak, and, and eating it, and—'

'It's not a problem,' said Spider.

'What do you mean, not a problem?'

'Well,' said Spider, 'I called Rosie this morning already, and I'm taking her out to dinner tonight. So you wouldn't have needed the steak anyway.'

Fat Charlie opened his mouth. He closed it again. 'I want you out,' he said.

'It's a good thing for man's desire to out-strip his something or other – grasp or reach or something – or what else is Heaven for?' said Spider, cheerfully, between mouthfuls of Fat Charlie's steak.

'What the hell does that mean?'

'It means I'm not going anywhere. I like it here. ' He hacked off another lump of steak, shovelled it down.

'Out,' said Fat Charlie, and then the hall telephone rang. Fat Charlie sighed, walked into the hall and answered it. '*What?*'

'Ah. Charles. Good to hear your voice. I know you're currently enjoying your well-earned, but do you think it might be within the bounds of possibility for you to swing by for, oh, half an hour or so, tomorrow morning? Say, around ten-ish?'

'Yeah. Course,' said Fat Charlie. 'Not a problem.'

'Delighted to hear it. I'll need your signature on some papers. Well, until then.'

'Who was that?' asked Spider. He had cleaned his plate, and was blotting his mouth with a paper towel.

'Grahame Coats. He wants me to pop in tomorrow.'

Spider said, 'He's a bastard.'

'So? You're a bastard.'

'Different kind of bastard. He's not good news. You should find another job.'

'I love my job!' Fat Charlie meant it when he said it. He had managed entirely to forget how much he disliked his job, and the Grahame Coats Agency, and the ghastly, lurking-behind-every-door presence of Grahame Coats.

Spider stood up. 'Nice piece of steak,' he said. 'I've set my stuff up in your spare room.'

'You've what?'

Fat Charlie hurried down to the end of the hall, where there was a room that technically qualified his residence as a two-bedroom flat. The room contained several boxes of books, a box containing an elderly Scalextric set, a tin box filled with Hot Wheels cars (most of them missing tyres), and various other battered remnants of Fat Charlie's childhood. It might have been a good-sized bedroom for a normal-sized garden gnome or an undersized dwarf, but for anyone else it was a closet with a window.

Or rather, it used to be, but it wasn't. Not any more.

Fat Charlie pulled the door open and stood in the hallway, blinking.

There was a room, yes; that much was still true, but it was an enormous room. A magnificent room. There were windows at the far end, huge picture windows, looking out over what appeared to be a waterfall. Beyond the waterfall, the tropical sun was low on the horizon, and it burnished everything in its golden light. There was a fireplace large enough to roast a pair of oxen, upon which three burning logs crackled and spat. There was a hammock in one corner, along with a perfectly white sofa and a four-poster bed. Near the fireplace was something that Fat Charlie, who had only ever seen them in magazines, suspected was probably some kind of Jacuzzi. There was a zebra-skin rug, and a bear-pelt hanging on one wall, and there was the kind of advanced audio equipment that mostly consists of a black piece of polished plastic that you wave at. On one wall hung a flat television screen that was the width of the room that should have been there. And there was more . . .

'What have you done?' asked Fat Charlie. He did not go in.

'Well,' said Spider from behind him, 'seeing as I'm going to be here for a few days, I thought I'd bring my stuff over.'

'Bring your stuff? "Bringing your stuff" is a couple of carrier bags filled with laundry, some PlayStation games and a spider plant. This is . . . *this* is . . .' He was out of words.

Spider patted Fat Charlie's shoulder as he pushed past. 'If you need me,' he said to his brother, 'I'll be in my room.' And he shut the door behind him.

Fat Charlie shook the doorknob. The door was now locked.

He went into the TV room, got the phone from the hall, and dialled Mrs Higgler's number.

'Who the hell is this at this time of the morning?' she said.

'It's me. Fat Charlie. I'm sorry.'

'Well? What you callin' about?'

'Well, I was calling to ask your advice. You see, my brother came out here.'

'Your brother.'

'Spider. You told me about him. You said to ask a spider if I wanted to see him, and I did and he's here.'

'Well,' she said, noncommittally, 'that's good.'

'It's not.'

'Why not? He's family, isn't he?'

'Look, I can't go into it now. I just want him to go away.'

'Have you tried asking him nicely?'

'We just got through with all that. He says he isn't going. He's set up something that looks like the pleasure dome of Kublai Khan in my boxroom, and I mean, round here you need the council's permission just to put in double glazing. He's got some kind of waterfall in there. Not in there, it's on the other side of the window. And he's after my fiancée.'

'How do you know?'

'He said so.'

Mrs Higgler said, 'I'm not at my best before I have my coffee.'

'I just need to know how to make him go away.'

'I don't know,' said Mrs Higgler. 'I will talk to Mrs Dunwiddy about it.' She hung up.

Fat Charlie went back down to the end of the corridor, and knocked on the door.

'What is it now?'

'I want to talk.'

The door clicked and swung open. Fat Charlie went inside. Spider was reclining, naked, in the hot tub. He was drinking something more or less the colour of electricity from a long, frosted glass. The huge picture windows were now wide open, and the roar of the waterfall contrasted with the low, liquid jazz that emanated from hidden speakers somewhere in the room.

'Look,' said Fat Charlie, 'you have to understand, this is my house.'

Spider blinked. *'This?'* he asked. *'This* is your house?'

'Well, not exactly. But the principle's the same. I mean, we're in my spare room, and you're a guest. Um.'

Spider sipped his drink, and luxuriated deeper in the hot water. 'They say,' he said, 'that house guests are like fish. They both stink after three days.'

'Good point,' said Fat Charlie.

'But it's hard,' said Spider. 'Hard when you've gone a lifetime not seeing your brother. Hard when he didn't even know you existed. Harder still when you finally see him and learn that, as far as he's concerned, you're no better than a dead fish.'

'But,' said Fat Charlie.

Spider stretched in the tub. 'I'll tell you what,' he said. 'I can't stay here for ever. Chill. I'll be gone before you know it. And, for my part, I will never think of you as a dead fish. And I appreciate that we're both under a lot of stress. So let's say no more about it. Why don't you go and get yourself some lunch – leave your front-door key behind – and then go and see a movie?'

Fat Charlie put on his jacket and went outside. He put his door-key down beside the sink. The fresh air was wonderful, although the day was grey and the sky was spitting drizzle. He bought a newspaper to read. He stopped at the chippie and bought a large bag of chips and a battered saveloy for his lunch. The drizzle stopped, so he sat on a bench in a churchyard, and read his newspaper and ate his saveloy and chips.

He very much wanted to see a film.

He wandered into the Odeon, bought a ticket for the first thing showing. It was an action adventure, and it was already on when he went inside. Things blew up. It was great.

Halfway through the film it occurred to Fat Charlie that there was something that he was not remembering. It was in his head somewhere, like an itch an inch behind his eyes, and it kept distracting him.

The film ended.

Fat Charlie realised that, although he had enjoyed it, he had not actually managed to keep much of the film he had just seen in his head. So he bought a large bag of popcorn and sat through it again. It was even better the second time.

And the third.

After that, he thought that perhaps he ought to think about getting home, but there was a late-night double feature of *Eraserhead* and *True Stories*, and he had never actually seen either film, so he watched them both, although he was, by now, really quite hungry, which meant that by the end he was unsure of what *Eraserhead* had actually been about, or what the lady was doing in the radiator and he wondered if they'd let him stay and watch it again, but they explained, very patiently, over and over, that they were going to close for the night, and enquired as to whether he didn't have a home to go to, and wasn't it time for him to be in bed?

And of course, he did, and it was, although the fact of it had slipped his mind for a while. So he walked back to Maxwell Gardens, and was slightly surprised to see that the light was on in his bedroom.

The curtains were drawn as he reached the house. Still, there were silhouettes on the window, moving about. He thought he recognised both of the silhouettes.

They came together; they blended into one shadow.

Fat Charlie uttered one deep and terrible howl.

***

In Mrs Dunwiddy's house there were many plastic animals. The dust moved slowly through the air in that place, as if it were better used to the sunbeams of a more leisurely age, and could not be bothered with all this fast modern light. There was a transparent plastic cover on the sofa, and chairs that crackled when you sat down on them.

In Mrs Dunwiddy's house there was pine-scented hard toilet paper. Mrs Dunwiddy believed in economy, and pine-scented hard toilet paper was at the bottom of her economy drive. You could still get hard toilet paper, if you looked long enough and were prepared to pay more for it.

Mrs Dunwiddy's house smelled of violet-water. It was an old house. People forget that the first children born to settlers in Florida were already old men and women when the dour Puritans landed at Plymouth Rock. The house didn't go that far back; it had

been built in the 1920s, during a Florida land development
scheme, to be the show house, to represent the hypothetical
houses that all the other buyers would find themselves eventually
unable to build on the plots of gatory swamp they were being
sold. Mrs Dunwiddy's house had survived hurricanes without
losing a roof-tile.

When the doorbell rang, Mrs Dunwiddy was stuffing a small
turkey. She tutted, and washed her hands, then walked down the
corridor to her front door, peering out at the world through her
thick, thick glasses, her left hand trailing on the wallpaper.

She opened the door a crack and peered out.

'Louella? It's me.' It was Callyanne Higgler.

'Come in.' Mrs Higgler followed Mrs Dunwiddy back to the
kitchen. Mrs Dunwiddy ran her hands under the tap, then
recommenced taking handfuls of soggy corn-bread stuffing and
pushing them deep into the turkey.

'You expectin' company?'

Mrs Dunwiddy, made a noncommittal noise. 'It always a good
idea to be prepared,' she said. 'Now, suppose you tell me what's
going on?'

'Nancy's boy. Fat Charlie.'

'What about him?'

'Well, I tell him about his brother, when he out here last week.'

Mrs Dunwiddy pulled her hand out of the turkey. 'That's not
the end of the world,' she said.

'I tell him how he can contact his brother.'

'Ahh,' said Mrs Dunwiddy. She could disapprove with just that
one syllable. 'And?'

'He's turned up in Hingland. Boy's at his wits' end.'

Mrs Dunwiddy took a large handful of wet cornbread and
rammed it into the turkey with a force that would have made the
turkey's eyes water, if it still had any. 'Can't get him to go away?'

'Nope.'

Sharp eyes peered through thick lenses. Then Mrs Dunwiddy
said, 'I done it once. Can't do it again. Not that way.'

'I know. But we got to do something.'

Mrs Dunwiddy sighed. 'It's true what they say. Live long
enough, you see all your birds come home to roost.'

'Isn't there another way?'

Mrs Dunwiddy finished stuffing the turkey. She picked up a skewer, pinned the flap of skin closed. Then she covered the bird with silver foil.

'I reckon,' she said, 'I put it on to cook late tomorrow morning. It be done in the afternoon, then I put it back into a hot oven early evening, to get it all ready for dinner.'

'Who you got comin' to dinner?' asked Mrs Higgler.

'You,' said Mrs Dunwiddy, 'Zorah Bustamonte, Bella Noles. And Fat Charlie Nancy. By the time that boy gets here, he have a real appetite.'

Mrs Higgler said, 'He's coming here?'

'Aren't you listening, girl?' said Mrs Dunwiddy. Only Mrs Dunwiddy could have called Mrs Higgler 'girl' without sounding foolish. 'Now, help me get this turkey into the fridge.'

***

It would be fair to say that Rosie had, that evening, just had the most wonderful night of her life: magical, perfect, utterly fine. She could not have stopped smiling, not even if she had wanted to. The food had been fabulous and, once they had eaten, Fat Charlie had taken her dancing. It was a proper dance hall, with a small orchestra, and people in pastel clothes who glided across the floor. She felt as if they had travelled in time together and were visiting a gentler age. Rosie had enjoyed dancing lessons from the age of five, but had no one to dance with.

'I didn't know you could dance,' she told him.

'There are so many things about me you do not know,' he said.

And that made her happy. Soon enough, she and this man would be married. There were things about him she did not know? Excellent. She would have a lifetime in which to find them out. All sorts of things.

She noticed the way other women, and other men, looked at Fat Charlie as she walked beside him, and she was happy she was the woman on his arm.

They walked through Leicester Square, and Rosie could see the stars shining up above them, the starlight somehow crisply twinkling, despite the glare of the streetlights.

For a brief moment, she found herself wondering why it had never been like this with Fat Charlie before. Sometimes, somewhere deep inside herself, Rosie had suspected that perhaps she had only kept going out with Fat Charlie because her mother disliked him so much; that she had only said 'yes' when he had asked her to marry him because her mother would have wanted her to say 'no' . . .

Fat Charlie had taken her out to the West End, once. They'd gone to the theatre. It was a birthday surprise for her, but there had been a mix-up on the tickets, which, it turned out, had actually been issued for the day before; the management were both understanding and extremely helpful, and they had managed to find Fat Charlie a seat behind a pillar in the stalls, while Rosie took a seat in the upper circle behind a violently giggly hen party from Norwich. It had not been a success, not as these things were counted.

This evening, though, this evening had been magic. Rosie had not had many perfect moments in her life, but whatever the total was, it had just gone up by one.

She loved how she felt, when she was with him.

And once the dancing was done, after they had stumbled out into the night, giddy on movement and champagne, then Fat Charlie – and, she thought, why did she think of him as Fat Charlie anyway? for he wasn't the least bit fat – put his arm around her and said, 'Now, you're coming back to my place,' in a voice so deep and real it made her abdomen vibrate; and she said nothing about working the next day, nothing about there'd be time enough for that kind of thing when they were married, nothing at all, in fact, while all the time she thought about how much she didn't want the evening to end, and how very very much she wished, no, she *needed*, to kiss this man on the lips, and to hold him.

And then, remembering she had to say something, she said 'Yes'.

In the cab back to his flat, her hands held his, and she leaned against him and stared at him as the light from passing cars and streetlamps illuminated his face.

'You have a pierced ear,' she said. 'Why didn't I ever notice before that you have a pierced ear?'

'Hey,' he said with a smile, his voice a deep bass thrum, 'how do you think it makes me feel, when you've never even noticed something like that, even when we've been together for, what is it now?'

'Eighteen months,' said Rosie.

'For eighteen months,' said her fiancé.

She leaned against him, breathed him in. 'I love the way you smell,' she told him. 'Are you wearing some kind of cologne?'

'That's just me,' he told her.

'Well, you should bottle it.'

She paid the taxi, while he opened the front door. They went up the stairs together. When they got to the top of the stairs, he seemed to be heading along the corridor, towards the spare room at the back.

'You know,' she said, 'the bedroom's here, silly. Where are you going?'

'Nowhere. I knew that,' he said. They went into Fat Charlie's bedroom. She closed the curtains. Then she just looked at him, and was happy.

'Well,' she said, after a while, 'aren't you going to try to kiss me?'

'I guess I am,' he said, and he did. Time melted and stretched and curved. She might have kissed him for a moment, or for an hour, or for a lifetime. And then—

'What was that?'

He said, 'I didn't hear anything.'

'It sounded like someone in pain.'

'Cats fighting, maybe?'

'It sounded like a person.'

'Could have been an urban fox. They can sound a lot like people.'

She stood there with her head tipped to one side, listening intently. 'It's stopped now,' she said. 'Hmm. You want to know the strangest thing?'

'Uh-huh,' he said, his lips now nuzzling her neck. 'Sure, tell me the strangest thing. But I've made it go away now. It won't bother you again.'

'The strangest thing,' said Rosie, 'is that it sounded like you.'

* * *

Fat Charlie walked the streets, trying to clear his head. The obvious course of action was to bang on his own front door until Spider came down and let him in, then to give Spider and Rosie a piece of his mind. That was obvious. Perfectly, utterly obvious.

He just needed to go back to his flat and explain the whole thing to Rosie, and shame Spider into leaving him alone. That was all he had to do. How hard could that be?

Harder than it ought to be, that was for certain. He was not quite sure why he had walked away from his flat. He was even less certain how to find his way back. Streets he knew, or thought he knew, seemed to have reconfigured themselves. He found himself walking down dead ends, exploring endless cul-de-sacs, stumbling through the tangle of late-night London residential streets.

Sometimes, he saw the main road. There were traffic lights on it, and the lights of fast-food places. He knew that once he got on to the main road he would be able to find his way back to his house, but whenever he walked to the main road he would wind up somewhere else.

Fat Charlie's feet were starting to hurt. His stomach rumbled, violently. He was angry, and as he walked he became angrier and angrier.

The anger cleared his head. The cobwebs surrounding his thoughts began to evaporate; the web of streets he was walking began to simplify. He turned a corner and found himself on the main road, next to the all-night New Jersey Fried Chicken outlet. He ordered a family pack of chicken, and sat and finished it off without any help from anyone else in his family. When that was done he stood on the pavement until the friendly orange light of a FOR HIRE sign, attached to a large black cab, came into view, and he hailed the cab. It pulled up next to him, and the window rolled down.

'Where to?'

'Maxwell Gardens,' said Fat Charlie.

'You taking the mickey or something?' asked the cab driver. 'That's just round the corner.'

'Will you take me there? I'll give you an extra fiver. Honest.'

The cabbie breathed in loudly through his clenched teeth: it was the noise a car mechanic makes before asking you whether you're particularly attached to that engine for sentimental reasons.

'It's your funeral,' said the cabbie. 'Hop in.'

Fat Charlie hopped. The cabbie pulled out, waited for the lights to change, went around the corner.

'Where did you say you wanted to go?' asked the cabbie.

'Maxwell Gardens,' said Fat Charlie. 'Number thirty-four. It's just past the off-licence.'

He was wearing yesterday's clothes, and he wished he wasn't. His mother had always told him to wear clean underwear, in case he was hit by a car, and to brush his teeth, in case they needed to identify him by his dental records.

'I know where it is,' said the cabbie. 'It's just before you get to Park Crescent.'

'That's right,' said Fat Charlie. He was falling asleep in the back seat.

'I must have taken a wrong turning,' said the cabbie. He sounded irritated. 'I'll turn off the meter, all right? Call it a fiver.'

'Sure,' said Fat Charlie, and he snuggled down on the back seat of the taxi, and he slept. The taxi drove on through the night, trying to get just round the corner.

***

Detective Constable Day, currently on a twelve-month secondment to the Fraud Squad, arrived at the offices of the Grahame Coats Agency at 9.30 a.m. Grahame Coats was waiting for her in reception, and he walked her back into his office.

'Would you care for a coffee, tea?'

'No, thank you. I'm fine.' She pulled out a notebook, and sat looking at him expectantly.

'Now, I cannot stress enough that discretion must needs be the essence of your investigations. The Grahame Coats Agency has a reputation for probity and fair dealing. At the Grahame Coats Agency, a client's money is a sacrosanct trust. I must tell you, that when I first began to entertain suspicions about Charles Nancy, I dismissed them as unworthy of a decent man and a hard worker. Had you asked me a week ago what I thought about Charles Nancy, I would have told you that he was the very salt of the earth.'

'I'm sure you would. So when did you become aware that money might have been diverted from clients' accounts?'

'Well, I'm still not certain. I hesitate to cast aspersions. Or first stones, for that matter. Judge not, lest ye be judged.'

On television, thought Daisy, they say 'just give me the facts'. She wished she could say it, but she didn't.

She did not like this man.

'I've printed out all the anomalous transactions here,' he said. 'As you'll see, they were all made from Nancy's computer. I must again stress that discretion is of the essence here: clients of the Grahame Coats Agency include a number of prominent public figures, and, as I said to your superior, I would count it as a personal favour if this matter could be dealt with as quietly as possible. Discretion must be your watchword. If, perchance, we can persuade our Master Nancy simply to return his ill-gotten gains, I would be perfectly satisfied to let the matter rest there. I have no desire to prosecute.'

'I can do my best, but at the end of the day, we gather information and turn it over to the Crown Prosecution Service.' She wondered how much pull he really had with the chief super. 'So what attracted your suspicions?'

'Ah, yes. Frankly and in all honesty, it was certain peculiarities of behaviour. The dog that failed to bark in the night time. The depth the parsley had sunk into the butter. We detectives find significance in the smallest things, do we not, Detective Day?'

'Er. Detective Constable Day, really. So, if you can give me the print-outs,' she said, 'along with any other documentation, bank records all that. We may actually need to pick up his computer, to look at the hard disk.'

'Absatively,' he said. His desk phone rang, and – 'If you'll excuse me?' – he answered it. 'He is? Good Lord. Well, tell him to just wait for me in reception. I'll come out and see him in a moment.'

He put down the phone. 'That,' he said to Daisy, 'is what I believe you would call, in police circles, a right turn-up for the books.'

She raised an eyebrow.

'That is the aforementioned Charles Nancy himself, here to see me. Shall we show him in? If you need to, you may use my offices as an interview room. I'm sure I even have a tape recorder you might borrow.'

Daisy said, 'That won't be necessary. And the first thing I'll need to do is go through all the paperwork.'

'Righto,' he said. 'Silly of me. Um, would you . . . would you like to look at him?'

'I don't see that that would accomplish anything,' said Daisy.

'Oh, I wouldn't tell him you were investigating him,' Grahame Coats assured her. 'Otherwise he'd be off to the Costa Del Crime before we could say "prima-facie evidence". Frankly, I like to think of myself as being extremely sympathetic to the problems of contemporary policing.'

Daisy caught herself thinking that anyone who would steal money from this man could not be all bad, which was, she knew, no way for a police officer to think.

'I'll lead you out,' he said to her.

In the waiting room a man was sitting. He looked as if he had slept in his clothes. He was unshaven, and he looked a little confused. Grahame Coats nudged Daisy, and inclined his head towards the man. Aloud, he said, 'Charles, Good Lord, man, look at the state of you. You look terrible.'

Fat Charlie looked at him blearily. 'Didn't get home last night,' he said. 'Bit of a mix-up with the taxi.'

'Charles,' said Grahame Coats, 'this is Detective Constable Day, of the Metropolitan Police. She is just here on routine business.'

Fat Charlie realised there was someone else there. He focused, saw the sensible clothes that might as well have been a uniform. Then he saw the face. 'Er,' he said.

'Morning,' said Daisy. That was what she said with her mouth. Inside her head she was going *ohbollocks ohbollocks ohbollocks*, over and over.

'Nice to meet you,' said Fat Charlie. Puzzled, he did something he had never done before: he imagined a plain-clothes police

officer with no clothes on, and found his imagination was
providing him with a fairly accurate representation of the young
lady beside whom he had woken up in bed, the morning after his
father's wake. The sensible clothes made her look slightly older,
more severe, and much scarier, but it was her all right.

Like all sentient beings, Fat Charlie had a weirdness quotient.
For some days the needle had been over in the red, occasionally
banging jerkily against the pin. Now the meter broke. From this
moment on, he suspected, nothing would surprise him. He could
no longer be outweirded. He was done.

He was wrong, of course.

Fat Charlie watched Daisy leave, and he followed Grahame
Coats back into his office.

Grahame Coats closed the door firmly. Then he perched his
bottom against his desk, and smiled like a weasel who has just
realised that he's been accidentally locked into the henhouse for
the night.

'Let us be blunt,' he said. 'Cards on the table. No beating about
the bush. Let us,' he elaborated, 'let us call a spade a spade.'

'All right,' said Fat Charlie, 'let's. You said you had something
for me to sign?'

'No longer an operative statement. Dismiss it from your mind.
No, let us now discuss something you pointed out to me several
days ago. You alerted me to certain unorthodox transactions
occurring here.'

'I did?'

'Two, as they say, Charles, two can play at that game. Naturally,
my first impulse was to investigate. Thus the visit this morning
from Detective Constable Day. And what I found will, I suspect,
not come as a shock to you.'

'It won't?'

'No indeed. There are, as you pointed out, definite indicators of
financial irregularities, Charles. But alas, there is only one place
to which the fickle finger of suspicion unerringly points.'

'There is?'

'There is.'

Fat Charlie felt completely at sea. 'Where?'

Grahame Coats attempted to look concerned, or at least, to look as if he were trying to look concerned, managing an expression which, in babies, always indicates that they are in need of a good burping. 'You, Charles. The police suspect you.'

'Yes,' said Fat Charlie. 'Of course they do. It's been that sort of a day.'

And he went home.

* * *

Spider opened the front door. It had started raining, and Fat Charlie stood there looking rumpled and wet.

'So,' said Fat Charlie. 'I'm allowed home now, am I?'

'I wouldn't do anything to stop you,' said Spider. 'It's your home, after all. Where were you all night?'

'You know perfectly well where I was. I was failing to come home. I don't know what kind of magic 'fluence you were using on me.'

'It wasn't magic,' said Spider, offended. 'It was a miracle.'

Fat Charlie pushed past him and stomped up the stairs. He walked into the bathroom, put in the plug and turned on the taps. He leaned out into the hall. 'I don't care what it's called. You're doing it in my house, and you stopped me coming home last night.'

He took off the day-before-yesterday's clothes. Then he put his head back around the door. 'And the police are investigating me at work. Did you tell Grahame Coats that there were financial irregularities going on?'

'Of course I did,' said Spider.

'Hah! Well, he only suspects me, that's what.'

'Oh, I don't think he does,' said Spider.

'Shows all you know,' said Fat Charlie. 'I talked to him. The police are involved. And then there's Rosie. And you and I are going to have a very long conversation about Rosie, when I get out of the bath. But first of all, I'm going to get into the bath. I spent yesterday night wandering around. I got the only sleep of the night in the back seat of a taxi. By the time I woke up it was five in the morning and my taxi driver was turning into Travis Bickle. He was conducting a monologue. I told him he might as well give up looking for Maxwell Gardens, and that it obviously wasn't a

Maxwell Gardens kind of night, and eventually he agreed so we went and had breakfast in one of those places taxi drivers have breakfast. Eggs and beans and sausages and toast, and tea you could stand a spoon up in. When he told the other taxi drivers he'd been driving all around last night looking for Maxwell Gardens, well, I thought blood was going to be spilled. It wasn't. But it looked a pretty close thing for a minute there.'

Fat Charlie stopped to take a breath. Spider looked guilty.

'*After*,' said Fat Charlie. '*After* my bath.' He shut the bathroom door.

He climbed into the bath.

He made a whimpering noise.

He climbed out of the bath.

He turned off the taps.

He wrapped a towel around his midriff and opened the bathroom door. 'No hot water,' he said, much, much too calmly. 'Do you have any idea why we have no hot water?'

Spider was still standing in the hallway. He hadn't moved. 'My hot tub,' he said. 'Sorry.'

Fat Charlie said, 'Well, at least Rosie doesn't. I mean, she wouldn't have—' And then he caught the expression on Spider's face.

Fat Charlie said, 'I want you out of here. Out of my life. Out of Rosie's life. Gone.'

'I like it here,' said Spider.

'You're ruining my bloody life.'

'Tough.' Spider walked down the hallway and opened the door to Fat Charlie's spare room. Golden tropical sunlight flooded the hallway momentarily, then the door was closed.

Fat Charlie washed his hair in cold water. He brushed his teeth. He rummaged through his laundry hamper until he found a pair of jeans and a T-shirt that were, by virtue of being at the bottom, practically clean once more. He put them on, along with a purple sweater with a teddy bear on it his mother had once given him that he had never worn but had never got around to giving away.

He went down to the end of the corridor.

The *boom-chagga-boom* of a bass and drums penetrated the door.

Fat Charlie rattled the doorhandle. It didn't budge. 'If you don't open this door,' he said, 'I'm going to break it down.'

The door opened, without warning, and Fat Charlie lurched inward, into the empty boxroom at the end of the hall. The view through the window was the back of the house behind, what little you could see of it through the rain that was now lashing the windowpane.

Still, from somewhere only a wall's thinness away, a stereo was playing too loudly: everything in the boxroom vibrated to a distant *boom-chagga-boom*.

'Right,' said Fat Charlie conversationally. 'You realise, of course, that this means war?' It was the traditional war-cry of the rabbit when pushed too far. There are places in which people believe that Anansi was a trickster rabbit. They are wrong, of course; he was a spider. You might think the two creatures would be easy to keep separate, but they still get confused more often than you would expect.

Fat Charlie went into his bedroom. He retrieved his passport from the drawer by his bed. He found his wallet where he had left it, in the bathroom.

He walked down to the main road, in the rain, and hailed a taxi.

'Where to?'

'Heathrow,' said Fat Charlie.

'Right you are,' said the cabbie. 'Which terminal?'

'No idea,' said Fat Charlie, who knew that, really, he ought to know. It had only been a few days, after all. 'Where do they leave for Florida?'

* * *

Grahame Coats had begun planning his exit from the Grahame Coats Agency back when John Major was Prime Minister. Nothing good lasts for ever, after all. Sooner or later, as Grahame Coats himself would have delighted in assuring you, even if your goose habitually lays golden eggs, it will still be cooked. While his planning had been good – one never knew when one might need to leave at a moment's notice – and he was not unaware that events were massing, like grey clouds on the horizon, he wished to put off the moment of leaving until it could be delayed no longer.

What was important, he had long ago decided, was not leaving, but vanishing, evaporating, disappearing without trace.

In the concealed safe in his office – a walk-in room he was extremely proud of – on a shelf he had put up himself, and had recently needed to put up again when it fell down, was a leather vanity case, containing two passports, one in the name of Basil Finnegan, the other in the name of Roger Bronstein. Each of the men had been born about fifty years ago, just as Grahame Coats had, but had died in their first year of life. Both of the passport photographs in the passports were of Grahame Coats. The case also contained two wallets, each with its own set of credit cards and photographic identification in the name of one of the names of the passport holders. Each name was a signatory to the funnel accounts in the Caymans, which themselves funnelled to other accounts in the British Virgin Islands, Switzerland and Liechtenstein.

Grahame Coats had been planning to leave for good on his fiftieth birthday, a little more than a year from now, and he was brooding on the matter of Fat Charlie.

He did not actually expect Fat Charlie to be arrested or imprisoned, although he would not have greatly objected to either scenario, had it occurred. He wanted him scared, discredited, and gone.

Grahame Coats truly enjoyed milking the clients of the Grahame Coats Agency, and he was good at it. He had been pleasantly surprised to discover that, as long as he picked his clientele with care, the celebrities and performers he represented had very little sense of money, and were relieved to find someone who would represent them and manage their financial affairs and make sure that they didn't have to worry. And if sometimes statements or cheques were late in coming, or if they weren't always what the clients were expecting, or if there were unidentified direct debits from client accounts, well, Grahame Coats had a high staff turnover, particularly in the book-keeping department, and there was nothing that couldn't easily be blamed on the incompetence of a previous employee, or, rarely, made right with a case of champagne and a large and apologetic cheque.

It wasn't that people liked Grahame Coats, or that they trusted him. Even the people he represented thought he was a weasel. But they believed that he was *their* weasel, and in that they were wrong.

Grahame Coats was his own weasel.

The telephone on his desk rang and he picked it up. 'Yes?'

'Mr Coats? It's Maeve Livingstone on the phone. I know you said to put her through to Fat Charlie, but he's off this week, and I wasn't sure what to say. Shall I tell her you're out?'

Grahame Coats pondered. Before a sudden heart attack had carried him off, Morris Livingstone, once the best-loved short Yorkshire comedian in the country, had been the star of such television series as *Short Back and Sides* and his own Saturday night variety-game show, *Morris Livingstone, I Presume*. He had even had a top-ten single back in the eighties, with the novelty song, 'It's Nice Out (But Put It Away)'. Amiable, easy-going, he had not only left all his financial affairs in the control of the Grahame Coats Agency, but he had also appointed, at Grahame Coats's suggestion, Grahame Coats himself as trustee of his estate.

It would have been criminal not to give in to a temptation like that.

And then there was Maeve Livingstone. It would be fair to say that Maeve Livingstone had, without knowing it, featured for many years in starring and co-starring roles in a number of Grahame Coats's most treasured and private fantasies.

Grahame Coats said, 'Please. Put her through,' and then, solicitously, 'Maeve, how lovely to hear from you. How are you?'

'I'm not sure,' she said.

Maeve Livingstone had been a dancer when she met Morris, and had always towered over the little man. They had adored each other.

'Well, why don't you tell me about it?'

'I spoke to Charles a couple of days ago. I was wondering. Well, the bank manager was wondering. The money from Morris's estate. We were told we would be seeing something by now.'

'Maeve,' said Grahame Coats, in what he thought of as his dark velvet voice, the one he believed that women responded to, 'the problem is not that the money is not there – it's merely a matter of liquidity. As I've told you, Morris made a number of unwise investments towards the end of his life, and although, following my advice, he made some sound ones as well, we do need to allow the good ones to mature: we cannot pull out now without losing almost everything. But worry ye not, worry ye not. Anything for a good client. I shall write you a cheque from my own bank account in order to keep you solvent and comfortable. How much does the bank manager require?'

'He says that he's going to have to start bouncing cheques,' she said. 'And the BBC tell me that they've been sending money from the DVD releases of the old shows. *That's* not invested, is it?'

'That's what the BBC said? Actually, *we've* been chasing *them* for money. But I wouldn't want to put all the blame on BBC Worldwide. Our book-keeper's pregnant, and things have been all at sixes and sevens. And Charles Nancy, who you spoke to, has been rather distraught – his father died, and he has been out of the country a great deal—'

'Last time we spoke,' she pointed out, 'you were putting in a new computer system.'

'Indeed we were, and please, do not get me started on the subject of book-keeping programs. What is it they say – to err is human, but to really, er, mess things up, you need a computer. Something like that. I shall investigate this forcefully, by hand if necessary, the old-fashioned way, and your moneys shall be wending their way to you. It's what Morris would have wanted.'

'My bank manager says I need ten thousand pounds in right now, just to stop them bouncing cheques.'

'Ten thousand pounds shall be yours. I am writing a cheque for you even as we speak.' He drew a circle on his note-pad, with a line going off the top of it. It looked a bit like an apple.

'I'm very grateful,' said Maeve, and Grahame Coats preened. 'I hope I'm not becoming a bother.'

'You are never a bother,' said Grahame Coats. 'No sort of bother at all.'

He put down the phone. The funny thing, Grahame Coats

always thought, was that Morris's comedic persona had always been that of a hard-headed Yorkshireman, proud of knowing the location of every penny.

It had been a fine game, thought Grahame Coats, and he added two eyes to the apple, and a couple of ears. It now looked, he decided, more or less like a cat. Soon enough it would be time to exchange a life of milking hard-to-please celebrities for a life of sunshine, swimming pools, fine meals, good wines and, if possible, enormous quantities of oral sex. The best things in life, Grahame Coats was convinced, could all be bought and paid for.

He drew a mouth on the cat, and filled it with sharp teeth, so it looked a little like a mountain lion, and as he drew he began to sing, in a reedy tenor voice,

> *'When I were a young man my father would say*
> *It's lovely outside, you should go out to play,*
> *But now that I'm older, the ladies all say,*
> *It's nice out, but put it away . . .'*

Morris Livingstone had bought and paid for Grahame Coats's penthouse flat on the Copacabana, and for the installation of the swimming pool on the island of Saint Andrews, and you must not imagine that Grahame Coats was not grateful.

> *'It's nice out, but put it awaaaay.'*

***

Spider felt odd.

There was something going on: a strange feeling, spreading like a mist through his life, and it was ruining his day. He could not identify it, and he did not like it.

And if there was one thing that he was definitely *not* feeling, it was guilty. It simply wasn't the kind of thing he ever felt. He felt excellent. Spider felt cool. He did not feel guilty. He would not have felt guilty if he was caught red-handed holding up a bank.

And yet there was, all about him, a faint miasma of discomfort.

Until now Spider had believed that gods were different: they had no consciences, nor did they need them. A god's relationship to the world, even a world in which he was walking, was about as emotionally connected as that of a computer gamer playing with knowledge of the overall shape of the game, and armed with a complete set of cheat codes.

Spider kept himself amused. That was what he did. That was the important bit. He would not have recognised guilt if he had an illustrated guide to it, with all the component parts clearly labelled. It was not that he was feckless – more that he had simply not been around the day they handed out feck. But something had changed – inside him or outside, he was not sure – and it bothered him. He poured himself another drink. He waved a hand and made the music louder. He changed it from Miles Davis to James Brown. It still didn't help.

He lay on the hammock, in the tropical sunshine, listening to the music, basking in how extremely cool it was to be him . . . and for the first time even that, somehow, wasn't enough.

He climbed out of the hammock and wandered over to the door. 'Fat Charlie?'

There was no answer. The flat felt empty. Outside the windows of the flat there was a grey day, and rain. Spider liked the rain. It seemed appropriate.

Shrill and sweet, the telephone rang. Spider picked it up.

Rosie said, 'Is that you?'

'Hullo, Rosie.'

'Last night,' she said. Then she didn't say anything. Then she said, 'Was it as wonderful for you as it was for me?'

'I don't know,' said Spider. 'It was pretty wonderful for me. So, I mean, that's probably a yes.'

'Mmm,' she said.

They didn't say anything.

'Charlie?' said Rosie.

'Uh-huh?'

'I even like not saying anything, just knowing you're on the other end of the phone.'

'Me too,' said Spider.

They enjoyed the sensation of not saying anything for a while longer, savouring it, making it last.

'Do you want to come over to my place tonight?' asked Rosie. 'My flatmates are in the Cairngorms.'

'That,' said Spider, 'may be a candidate for the most beautiful phrase in the English language. *My flatmates are in the Cairngorms*. Perfect poetry.'

She giggled. 'Twit. Um. Bring your toothbrush . . . ?'

'Oh. *Oh*. OK.'

And after several minutes of 'you put down the phone', and 'no *you* put down the phone' that would have done credit to a pair of hormonally intoxicated fifteen-year-olds, the phone was eventually put down.

Spider smiled like a saint. The world, given that it had Rosie in it, was the best world that any world could possibly be. The fog had lifted, the world had ungloomed.

It did not even occur to Spider to wonder where Fat Charlie had gone. Why should he care about such trivia? Rosie's flatmates were in the Cairngorms, and tonight? Why, tonight he would be bringing his toothbrush.

***

Fat Charlie's body was on a plane to Florida; it was crushed in a seat in the middle of a row of five people, and it was fast asleep. This was a good thing: the rear toilets had malfunctioned as soon as the plane was in the air, and although the cabin attendants had hung 'out of order' signs on the doors, this did nothing to alleviate the smell which spread slowly across the back of the plane like a low-level chemical fug. There were babies crying, and adults grumbling and children whining. One faction of the passengers, en route to Walt Disney World, who felt that their holidays began the moment they got on the plane, had got settled into their seats then began a sing-song. They sang 'Bibbidi-Bobbidi-Boo' and 'The Wonderful Thing about Tiggers', and 'Under the Sea' and 'Heigh-Ho, Heigh-Ho, It's Off to Work We Go', and even, under the impression that it was a Disney song as well, 'We're Off to See the Wizard'.

Once the plane was in the air it was discovered that, due to a catering confusion, no coach class lunch meals had been put on board. Instead, only breakfasts had been packed, which meant there would be individual packs of cereal and a banana for all passengers, which they would have to eat with plastic knives and forks, because there were, unfortunately, no spoons, which may have been a good thing, because pretty soon there wasn't any milk for the cereal either.

It was a hell-flight, and Fat Charlie was sleeping through it.

In Fat Charlie's dream he was in a huge hall, and he was wearing a morning suit. Next to him was Rosie, wearing a white wedding dress, and on the other side of her on the dais was Rosie's mother, who was, a little jarringly, also wearing a wedding dress, although this one was covered with dust and with cobwebs. Far away, at the horizon, which was the distant edge of the hall, there were people firing guns and waving white flags.

It's just the people at Table H, said Rosie's mother. Don't pay them no attention.

Fat Charlie turned to Rosie. She smiled at him with her soft sweet smile, then she licked her lips.

Cake, said Rosie, in his dream.

This was the signal for an orchestra to begin to play. It was a New Orleans jazz band, playing a funeral march.

The people at Table B, who were not people but cartoon mice and rats and barnyard animals, human-size, and celebrating – began to sing songs from Disney cartoons. Fat Charlie knew that they wanted him to join in with them. Even asleep he could feel himself panicking at the simple idea of having to sing in public, his limbs becoming numb, his lips prickling.

I can't sing with you, he told them, desperate for an excuse. I have to cut this cake.

At this, the hall fell into silence. And in the silence, a chef entered, wheeling a little trolley with something on it. The chef wore Grahame Coats's face, and on the trolley was an extravagant white wedding cake: an ornate, many-tiered confection. A tiny bride and tiny groom perched precariously on the topmost tier of the cake, like two people trying to keep their balance on top of a sugar-frosted Chrysler Building.

The chef's assistant was a police officer. She was holding a pair of handcuffs. The chef wheeled the cake up on to the dais.

Now, *said Rosie to Fat Charlie, in his dream. Cut the cake.*

Rosie's mother reached under the table, and produced a long wooden-handled knife – almost a machete – with a rusty blade. She passed it to Rosie, who reached for Fat Charlie's right hand and placed it over her own, and, together, they pressed the rusty knife into the thick white icing on the topmost tier of the cake, pushed it in between the groom and the bride. The cake resisted the blade at first, and Fat Charlie pressed harder, putting all his weight on the knife. He felt the cake beginning to give. He pushed harder.

The blade sliced through the topmost tier of the wedding cake. It slipped and sliced down the cake, through every layer and tier, and as it did so, the cake opened . . .

In his dream, Fat Charlie supposed that the cake was filled with black beads, with beads of black glass or of polished jet, and then, as they tumbled out of the cake, he realised that the beads had legs, each bead had eight clever legs, and they came out of the inside of the cake like a black wave. The spiders surged forward and covered the white tablecloth; they covered Rosie's mother and Rosie herself, turning their white dresses black as ebony; then, as if controlled by some vast and malignant intelligence, they flowed, in their hundreds, towards Fat Charlie. He turned to run, but his legs were trapped in some kind of rubbery tanglefoot, and he tumbled to the floor.

Now they were upon him, their tiny legs crawling over his bare skin, and he tried to get up but he was drowning in spiders.

Fat Charlie wanted to scream, but his mouth was filled with spiders. They covered his eyes, and his world went dark . . .

Fat Charlie opened his eyes and saw nothing but blackness, and he screamed and he screamed and he screamed. Then he realised the lights were off, and the window-shades were drawn, because people were watching the film.

It was already a flight from hell. Fat Charlie had just made it a little worse for everyone else.

He stood up, and tried to get out to the aisle, tripping over people as he went past, then, when he was almost at the gangway, straightening up and banging the overhead locker with his forehead, which knocked open the locker door and tumbled someone's hand-luggage down on to his head.

People nearby, the ones who were watching, laughed. It was an elegant piece of slapstick, and it cheered them all up no end.

Chapter Seven

In Which Fat Charlie Goes a Long Way

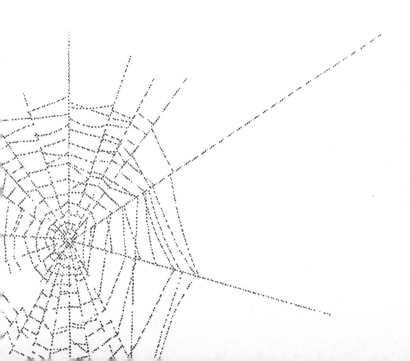

The immigration officer squinted at Fat Charlie's American passport as if she were disappointed he was not a foreign national of the kind she could simply stop coming into the country, then, with a sigh, she waved him through.

He wondered what he was going to do once he got through Customs. Rent a car, he supposed. And eat.

He got off the tram and walked through the security barrier, out into the wide shopping concourse of Orlando airport, and was nowhere nearly as surprised as he should have been to see Mrs Higgler standing there, scanning the faces of the arrivals, her enormous mug of coffee clutched in her hand. They saw each other at more or less the same moment, and she headed towards him.

'You hungry?' she asked him.

He nodded.

'Well,' she said, 'I hope you like turkey.'

* * *

Fat Charlie wondered if Mrs Higgler's maroon station wagon was the same car he remembered her driving when he was a boy. He suspected that it was. It must have been new once, that stood to reason. Everything was new once, after all. The seats were cracked and flaking leather, the dashboard was a dusty wooden veneer.

A brown-paper shopping bag sat between them, on the seat.

There was no cup-holder in Mrs Higgler's ancient car, and she clamped the jumbo mug of coffee between her thighs as she drove. The car appeared to pre-date air conditioning, and she drove with the windows down. Fat Charlie did not mind. After the damp chill of England, the Florida heat was welcome. Mrs Higgler headed south, towards the toll-road. She talked as she drove: she talked about the last hurricane, and about how she took her nephew Benjamin to Sea World and to Walt Disney World and how none of the tourist resorts were what they once were, about building codes, the price of gas, exactly what she had said to the doctor who had suggested a hip replacement, why tourists kept feeding 'gators, and why newcomers built houses on the beaches and were always surprised when the beach or the house went away or the 'gators ate their dogs. Fat Charlie let it all wash over him. It was just talk.

Mrs Higgler slowed down and took the ticket that would take her down the toll road. She stopped talking. She seemed to be thinking.

'So,' she said. 'You met your brother.'

'You know,' said Fat Charlie, 'you could have warned me.'

'I did warn you that he is a god.'

'You didn't mention that he was a complete and utter pain in the arse, though.'

Mrs Higgler sniffed. She took a swig of coffee from her mug.

'Is there anywhere we can stop and get a bite to eat?' asked Fat Charlie. 'They only had cereal and bananas on the plane. No spoons. And they ran out of milk before they got to my row. They said they were sorry and gave us all food vouchers to make up for it.'

Mrs Higgler shook her head.

'I could have used my voucher to get a hamburger in the airport.'

'I tell you already,' said Mrs Higgler. 'Louella Dunwiddy been cooking you a turkey. How do you think she feels if we get there and you fill up already at McDonald's and you ain't got no appetite. Eh?'

'But I'm *star*ving. And it's over two hours away.'

'Not,' she said firmly, 'the way I drive.'

And with that she put her foot down. Every now and then, as the maroon station wagon shuddered down the freeway, Fat Charlie would close his eyes tightly, while at the same time pushing his own left foot down on an imaginary brake pedal. It was exhausting work.

In significantly less than two hours they reached the tollway exit, and got on to a local highway. They drove towards the city. They drove past the Barnes and Noble and the Office Depot. They went past the seven-figure houses with security gates. They went down the older residential streets, which Fat Charlie remembered as being much better cared for when he was a boy. They went past the West Indian takeaway, and the restaurant with the Jamaican flag in the windows, with handwritten signs pushing the oxtail and rice specials and the homemade ginger beer and the curry chicken.

Fat Charlie's mouth watered; his stomach made a noise.

A lurch and a bounce. Now the houses were older, and this time everything was familiar.

The pink plastic flamingos were still striking attitudes in Mrs Dunwiddy's front yard, although the sun had faded them almost white over the years. There was a mirrored gazing ball as well, and when Fat Charlie spotted it he was, only for a moment, as scared as he had ever been of anything.

'How bad is it, with Spider?' asked Mrs Higgler, as they walked up to Mrs Dunwiddy's front door.

'Put it this way,' said Fat Charlie. 'I think he's sleeping with my fiancée. Which is rather more than I ever did.'

'Ah,' said Mrs Higgler. 'Tch.' And she rang the doorbell.

***

It was sort of like *Macbeth*, thought Fat Charlie, an hour later; in fact, if the witches in Macbeth had been four little old ladies, and if instead of stirring cauldrons and intoning dread incantations they had just welcomed Macbeth in and fed him turkey, and rice and peas spread out on white china plates on a red-and-white-patterned plastic tablecloth, not to mention sweet potato pudding and spicy cabbage, and encouraged him to take second helpings, and thirds, and then, when Macbeth had declaimed that nay, he was stuffed nigh unto bursting and on his oath could truly eat no more, the witches had pressed upon him their own special island rice pudding and a large slice of Mrs Bustamonte's famous pineapple upside-down cake, it would have been exactly like *Macbeth*.

'So,' said Mrs Dunwiddy, scratching a crumb of pineapple upside-down cake from the corner of her mouth, 'I understand your brother come to see you.'

'Yes. I talked to a spider. I suppose it was my own fault. I never expected anything to happen.'

A chorus of *tuts* and *tsks* and *tchs* ran around the table as Mrs Higgler and Mrs Dunwiddy and Mrs Bustamonte and Miss Noles clicked their tongues and shook their heads. 'He always used to say you were the stupid one,' said Miss Noles. 'Your father, that is. I never believed him.'

'Well, how was I to know?' Fat Charlie protested. 'It's not as if my parents ever said to me, "By the way son, you have a brother you don't know about. Invite him into your life and he'll have you investigated by the police, he'll sleep with your fiancée, he'll not just move into your home but bring an entire extra house into your spare room. And he'll brainwash you and make you go to films and spend all night trying to get home and—"' He stopped. It was the way they were looking at him.

A sigh went around the table. It went from Mrs Higgler to Miss Noles to Mrs Bustamonte to Mrs Dunwiddy. It was extremely unsettling and quite spooky, but Mrs Bustamonte belched and ruined the effect.

'So what do you want?' asked Mrs Dunwiddy. 'Say what you want.'

Fat Charlie thought about what he wanted, in Mrs Dunwiddy's little dining room. Outside, the daylight was fading into a gentle twilight.

'He's made my life a misery,' said Fat Charlie. 'I want you to make him go away. Just go away. Can you do that?'

The three younger women said nothing. They simply looked at Mrs Dunwiddy.

'We can't actually make him go away,' said Mrs Dunwiddy. 'We already . . .' and she stopped herself, and said, 'Well, we done all we can about that, you see.'

It is to Fat Charlie's credit that he did not, as, deep down he might have wished to, burst into tears, or wail, or collapse in on himself like a problematic soufflé. He simply nodded. 'Well, then,' he said. 'Sorry to have bothered you all. Thank you for the dinner.'

'We can't make him go away,' said Mrs Dunwiddy, her old brown eyes almost black behind her pebble-thick spectacles. 'But we can send you to somebody who can.'

* * *

It was early evening in Florida, which meant that in London it was the dead of night. In Rosie's big bed, where Fat Charlie had never been, Spider shivered.

Rosie pressed close to him, skin to skin. 'Charles,' she said, 'are you all right?' She could feel the goose pimples bumping the skin of his arms.

'I'm fine,' said Spider. 'Sudden creepy feeling.'

'Somebody walking over your grave,' said Rosie.

He pulled her close then, and he kissed her.

And Daisy was sitting in the small common room of the house in Hendon, wearing a bright green nightdress and fluffy, vivid pink carpet slippers. She was sitting in front of a computer screen, shaking her head and clicking the mouse.

'You going to be much longer?' asked Carol. 'You know, there's a whole computer unit that's meant to be doing that. Not you.'

Daisy made a noise. It was not a yes-noise and it was not a no-noise. It was an I-know-somebody-just-said-something-to-me-and-if-I-make-a-noise-maybe-they'll-go-away sort of noise.

Carol had heard that noise before.

'Oy,' she said. 'Big bum. Are you going to be much longer? I want to do my blog.'

Daisy processed the words. Two of them sank in. 'Are you saying I've got a big bum?'

'No,' said Carol. 'I'm saying that it's getting late, and I want to do me blog. I'm going to have him shagging a supermodel in the loo of an unidentified London nightspot.'

Daisy sighed. 'All right,' she said. 'It's just fishy, that's all.'

'What's fishy?'

'Embezzlement. I think. Right, I've logged out. It's all yours. You know you can get into trouble for impersonating a member of the royal family.'

'Bog off.'

Carol blogged as a member of the British royal family, young, male and out of control. There had been arguments in the press about whether or not she was the real thing, many of them pointing to things that she wrote that could only have been known to an actual member of the British royal family, or to someone who read the glossy gossip magazines.

Daisy got up from the computer, still pondering the financial affairs of the Grahame Coats Agency.

While fast asleep in his bedroom, in a large but certainly not ostentatious house in Purley, Grahame Coats slept. If there was any justice in the world, he would have moaned and sweated in his sleep, tortured by nightmares, the furies of his conscience lashing him with scorpions. Thus it pains me to admit that Grahame Coats slept like a well-fed milk-scented baby, and he dreamed of nothing at all.

Somewhere in Grahame Coats's house, a grandfather clock chimed politely, twelve times. In London, it was midnight. In Florida it was seven in the evening.

Either way, it was the witching hour.

* * *

Mrs Dunwiddy removed the plasticated red-and-white-check tablecloth, and put it away.

She said, 'Who's got the black candles?'

Miss Noles said, 'I got the candles.' She had a shopping bag at her feet, and she rummaged about in it, producing four candles.

They were mostly black. One of them was tall and undecorated. The other three were in the shape of a cartoon black-and-yellow penguin, with the wick coming out of his head. 'It was all they got,' she said apologetically. 'And I had to go to three stores until I found anything.'

Mrs Dunwiddy said nothing, but she shook her head. She arranged the four candles at the four ends of the table, taking the single non-penguin at the head of the table, where she sat. Each of the candles sat on a plastic picnic plate. Mrs Dunwiddy took a large box of kosher salt, and she opened the spout and poured salt crystals on the table, in a pile. Then she glared at the salt, and pushed at it with a withered forefinger, prodding it into heaps and whorls.

Miss Noles came back from the kitchen with a large glass bowl, which she placed at the centre of the table. She unscrewed the top from a bottle of sherry, and poured a generous helping of sherry into the bowl.

'Now,' said Mrs Dunwiddy, 'the devil-grass, the St John the Conqueror root, and the love-lies-bleeding.'

Mrs Bustamonte rummaged in her shopping bag and took out a small glass jar. 'It's mixed herbs,' she explained. 'I thought it would be all right.'

'Mixed herbs!' said Mrs Dunwiddy. 'Mixed herbs!'

'Will that be a problem?' said Mrs Bustamonte. 'It's what I always use when the recipe says basil this or oregano that. I can't be doin' with it. You ask me, it's all mixed herbs.'

Mrs Dunwiddy sighed. 'Pour it in,' she said.

Half a bottle of mixed herbs was poured into the sherry. The dried leaves floated on the top of the liquid.

'Now,' said Mrs Dunwiddy, 'the four earths. I hope,' she said, choosing her words with care, 'that no one here going to tell me that they could not get the four earths, and now we have to make do with a pebble, a dead jellyfish, a refrigerator magnet and a bar of soap.'

'I got the earths,' said Mrs Higgler. She produced the brown paper bag, and pulled from it four zip-lock bags each containing what looked like sand, or dried clay, each of a different colour. She emptied each bag at one of the four corners of the table.

'Glad somebody is payin' attention,' said Mrs Dunwiddy.

Miss Noles lit the candles, pointing out as she did so how easily the penguins lit, and how cute and funny they were.

Mrs Bustamonte poured out a glass of leftover sherry for each of the four women.

'Don't I get a glass?' asked Fat Charlie, but he didn't really want one. He didn't like sherry.

'No,' said Mrs Dunwiddy, firmly, 'you don't. You'll need your wits about you.' She reached into her purse and took out a small golden-coloured pill-case.

Mrs Higgler turned off the lights.

The five of them sat around the table in the candlelight.

'Now what?' asked Fat Charlie. 'Shall we all join hands and contact the living?'

'We do not,' whispered Mrs Dunwiddy. 'And I do not want to hear another word out of you.'

'Sorry,' said Fat Charlie, then wished he hadn't said it.

'Listen,' said Mrs Dunwiddy. 'You will go where they may help you. Even so, give away nothing you own, and make no promises. You understand? If you have to give somebody something, then make sure you get something of equal value in return. Yes?'

Fat Charlie nearly said 'yes', but he caught himself in time and simply nodded.

'It is good.' And with that, Mrs Dunwiddy began to hum tunelessly, in her old old voice, which quavered and faltered.

Miss Noles also began to hum, rather more melodically. Her voice was higher, and stronger.

Mrs Bustamonte did not hum. She hissed instead, an intermittent, snake-like hissing, which seemed to find the rhythm of the humming and weave through it and beneath it.

Mrs Higgler started up, and she did not hum and she did not hiss. She buzzed, like a fly against a window, making a vibrating noise with her tongue and her teeth as odd and as unlikely as if she had a handful of angry bees in her mouth, buzzing against her teeth, trying to get out.

Fat Charlie wondered if he should join in, but he had no idea what sort of thing he ought to do if he did, so he concentrated on sitting there and trying not to be weirded out by all the noises.

Mrs Higgler threw a pinch of red earth into the bowl of sherry and mixed herbs. Mrs Bustamonte threw in a pinch of the yellow earth. Miss Noles threw in the brown earth, while Mrs Dunwiddy leaned over, painstakingly slowly, and dropped in a lump of black mud.

Mrs Dunwiddy took a sip of her sherry. Then, with arthritic fingers fumbling and pushing, she took something from the pill-case, and she dropped it into the candle flame. For a moment the room smelled of lemons, and then it simply smelled as if something was burning.

Miss Noles began to drum on the tabletop. She did not stop humming. The candle flames flickered, dancing huge shadows across the walls. Mrs Higgler began to tap on the tabletop as well, her fingers knocking out a different beat to Miss Noles, faster, more percussive, the two drum-beats twining to form a new rhythm.

In Fat Charlie's mind all the sounds began to blend into one strange sound: the humming and the hissing and the buzzing and the drums. He was starting to feel light-headed. Everything was funny. Everything was unlikely. In the noises of the women he could hear the sound of wildlife in the forest, hear the crackling of enormous fires. His fingers felt stretched and rubbery, his feet were an immensely long way away.

It seemed then that he was somewhere above them, somewhere above everything, and that beneath him there were five people around a table. Then one of the women at the table gestured and dropped something into the bowl in the middle of the table, and it flared up so brightly that Fat Charlie was momentarily blinded. He shut his eyes, which, he found, did no good at all. Even with his eyes closed, everything was much too bright for comfort.

He rubbed his eyes against the daylight. He looked around.

A sheer rock face skyscrapered up behind him, the side of a mountain. Ahead of him was a sheer drop: cliffs, going down. He walked to the cliff-edge and, warily, looked over. He saw some white things, and he thought they were sheep until he realised that they were clouds; large white fluffy clouds, a very long way below him. And then, beneath the clouds, there was nothing: he could see the blue sky, and it seemed that if he kept looking he could see the blackness of space, and beyond that nothing but the chill twinkling of stars.

He took a step back from the cliff-edge.

Then he turned and walked back towards the mountains, which rose up and up, so high that he could not see the tops of them, so high that he found himself convinced that they were falling on him, that they would tumble down and bury him for ever. He forced himself to look down again, to keep his eyes on the ground, and in so doing, he noticed holes in the rock face, near ground level, which looked like entrances to natural caves.

The place between the mountainside and the cliffs, on which he was standing, was, he guessed, less than quarter of a mile wide: a boulder-strewn sandy path dotted with patches of greenery and with, here and there, a dusty brown tree. The path seemed to follow the mountainside until it faded into a distant haze.

Someone is watching me, thought Fat Charlie. 'Hello?' he called, lifting his head back. 'Hello, is anybody there?'

The man who stepped out of the nearest cave mouth was much darker of skin than Fat Charlie, darker even than Spider, but his long hair was a tawny yellow and it framed his face like a mane. He wore a ragged yellow lion-skin around his waist, with a lion's tail hanging down from it behind, and the tail swished a fly from his shoulders.

The man blinked his golden eyes.

'Who are you?' he rumbled. 'And on whose authority do you walk in this place?'

'I'm Fat Charlie Nancy,' said Fat Charlie. 'Anansi the Spider was my father.'

The massive head nodded. 'And why do you come here, Compé Anansi's child?'

They were alone on the rocks, as far as Fat Charlie knew, yet it felt as if there were many people listening, many voices saying nothing, many ears twitching. Fat Charlie spoke loudly, so that anyone listening could hear. 'My brother. He is ruining my life. I don't have the power to make him leave.'

'So you seek our help?' asked the lion.

'Yes.'

'And this brother. He is, like you, of Anansi's blood?'

'He's not like me at all,' said Fat Charlie. 'He's one of you people.'

A fluid golden movement; the man-lion bounded down lightly, lazily, from the cave mouth, over the grey rocks, covering fifty yards in moments. Now he stood beside Fat Charlie. His tail swished impatiently.

His arms folded, he looked down at Fat Charlie and said, 'Why do you not deal with this matter yourself?'

Fat Charlie's mouth had dried. His throat felt extremely dusty. The creature facing him, taller than any man, did not smell like a man. The tips of his canine teeth rested on his lower lips.

'Can't,' squeaked Fat Charlie.

From the mouth of the next cave along, an immense man leaned out. His skin was a brownish grey, and he had rumpled, wrinkled skin, and round round legs. 'If you and your brother quarrel,' he said, 'then you must ask your father to judge between you. Submit to the will of the head of the family. That is the law.' He threw his head back, and made a noise then, in the back of his nose and in his throat, a powerful trumpeting noise, and Fat Charlie knew he was looking at Elephant.

Fat Charlie swallowed. 'My father is dead,' he said, and now his voice was clear again, cleaner and louder than he expected. It echoed from the cliff-wall, bounced back at him from a hundred cave mouths, a hundred jutting outcrops of rock. Dead *dead* dead *dead* dead, said the echo. 'That's why I came here.'

Lion said, 'I have no love for Anansi the Spider. Once, long ago, he tied me to a log, and had a donkey drag me through the dust, to the seat of Mawu who made all things.' He growled at the memory, and Fat Charlie wanted to be somewhere else.

'Walk on,' said Lion. 'There may be someone here who will help you, but it is not I.'

Elephant said, 'Nor I. Your father tricked me and ate my belly fat. He told me he was making me some shoes to wear, and he cooked me, and he laughed as he filled his stomach. I do not forget.'

Fat Charlie walked on.

In the next cave mouth along stood a man wearing a natty green suit and a sharp hat with a snake-skin band around it. He wore snake-skin boots and a snake-skin belt. He hissed as Fat Charlie came past. 'Walk on, Anansi's boy,' Snake said, his voice a dry rattle. 'Your whole damn family nothing but trouble. I ain't gettin' mixed up in your messes.'

The woman in the next cave mouth was very beautiful, and her eyes were black oil-drops, and her whiskers were snowy-white against her skin. She had two rows of breasts down her chest.

'I knew your father,' she said. 'Long time back. Hoo-ee.' She shook her head, in memory, and Fat Charlie felt like he had just read a private letter. She blew Fat Charlie a kiss, but shook her head when he made to approach closer.

He walked on. A dead tree stuck up from the ground before him like an assemblage of old grey bones. The shadows were getting longer now, as the sun was slowly descending in the endless sky, past where the cliffs cragged down into the end of the world; the eye of the sun was a monstrous golden-orange ball, and all the little white clouds beneath it were burnished with gold and with purple.

The Assyrian came down like a wolf on the fold, thought Fat Charlie, the line of the poem surfacing from some long-forgotten English lesson. *And his cohorts were gleaming in purple and gold*. He tried to remember what a cohort was, and failed. Probably, he decided, it was some kind of chariot.

Something moved, close to his elbow, and he realised that what he had thought was a brown rock, beneath the dead tree, was a man, sandy-coloured, his back spotted like a leopard's. His hair was very long and very black, and when he smiled his teeth were a big cat's teeth. He only smiled briefly, and it was a smile without warmth or humour or friendship in it. He said, 'I am Tiger. Your father, he injured me in a hundred ways and he insulted me in a thousand ways. Tiger does not forget.'

'I'm sorry,' said Fat Charlie.

'I'll walk along with you,' said Tiger. 'For a short while. You say that Anansi is dead?'

'Yes.'

'Well. Well, well. He played me for a fool so many times. Once, everything was mine – the stories, the stars, everything. He stole it all away from me. Maybe now he is dead people will stop telling those damn stories of his. Laughing at me.'

'I'm sure they will,' said Fat Charlie. 'I've never laughed at you.'

Eyes the colour of polished emeralds flashed in the man's face. 'Blood is blood,' was all he said. 'Anansi's bloodline is Anansi.'

'I am not my father,' said Fat Charlie.

Tiger bared his teeth. They were very sharp. 'You don't go around making people laugh at things,' explained Tiger. 'It's a big, serious world out there; nothing to laugh about. Not ever. You must teach the children to fear, teach them to tremble. Teach them to be cruel. Teach them to be the danger in the dark. Hide in the shadows, then pounce or spring or leap or drop, and always kill. You know what the true meaning of life is?'

'Um,' said Fat Charlie. 'Is it love one another?'

'The meaning of life is the hot blood of your prey on your tongue, the meat that rends beneath your teeth, the corpse of your enemy left in the sun for the carrion-eaters to finish. That is what life is. I am Tiger, and I am stronger than Anansi ever was, bigger, more dangerous, more powerful, crueller, wiser . . .'

Fat Charlie did not want to be in that place, talking to Tiger. It was not that Tiger was mad; it was that he was so earnest in his convictions, and that all his convictions were uniformly unpleasant. Also, he reminded Fat Charlie of someone, and while he could not have told you who, he knew it was someone he disliked. 'Will you help me get rid of my brother?'

Tiger coughed, as if he had a feather, or perhaps a whole blackbird, stuck in his throat.

'Would you like me to get you some water?' asked Fat Charlie.

Tiger eyed Fat Charlie with suspicion. 'Last time Anansi offered me water, I wound up trying to eat the moon out of a pond, and I drowned.'

'I was just trying to help.'

'That was what *he* said.' Tiger leaned in to Fat Charlie, stared him in the eye. Close-up, he did not look even faintly human – his nose was too flat, his eyes were positioned differently, and he smelled like a cage at the zoo. His voice was a rumbling growl.

'This is how you help me, Anansi's child. You and all your blood. You keep well away from me. Understand? If you want to keep the meat on those bones.' He licked his lips then, with a tongue the red of fresh-killed flesh, and longer than any human tongue had ever been.

Fat Charlie backed away, certain that if he turned, if he ran, he would feel Tiger's teeth in his neck. There was nothing remotely human about the creature now: it was the size of a real tiger. It was every big cat that had turned man-eater, every tiger that had broken a human's neck like a house-cat dispatching a mouse. So he stared at Tiger as he edged backwards, and soon enough the creature padded back to its dead tree, and stretched out on the rocks, and vanished into the patchy shadows, only the impatient swish of its tail betraying its position.

'Don't you worry yourself about him,' said a woman, from a cave mouth. 'Come here.'

Fat Charlie could not decide if she was attractive or monstrously ugly. He walked towards her.

'He come on all high-and-so-mighty, but he's a-scairt of his own shadow. And he's scairter of your daddy's shadow. He got no strength in his jaws.'

There was something doglike about her face. No, not doglike . . .

'Now, me,' she continued, as he reached her, 'me, I crush the bone. That's where the good stuff is hid. That's where the sweetest meats are hid, and nobody knows it but me.'

'I'm looking for someone to help me to get rid of my brother.'

The woman threw back her head and laughed, a wild bray of a laugh, loud, long and insane, and Fat Charlie knew her then.

'You won't find anyone here to help you,' she said. 'They all suffered, when they went up against your father. Tiger hates you and your kind more than anyone has ever hated anything, but even he won't do anything while your father's out there in the world. Listen: walk this path. You ask me, and I got a stone of prophecy behind my eye, you won't find nobody to help you till you find an empty cave. Go in. Talk to whoever you find there. Understand me?'

'I think I do.'

She laughed. It was not a good laugh. 'You want to stop with me for a while first? I'm an education. You know what they say – nothing leaner, meaner, or obscener than Hyena.'

Fat Charlie shook his head, and kept walking, past the caves that line the rocky walls at the end of the world. As he passed the darkness of each cave, he would glance inside. There were people of all shapes and all sizes, tiny people and tall people, men and women. And as he passed, and as they moved in and out of the shadows, he would see flanks or scales, horns or claws.

Sometimes he scared them as he passed, and they would retreat into the back of the cave. Others would come forward, stare aggressively or curiously.

Something tumbled through the air from the rocks above a cave mouth, and landed beside Fat Charlie. 'Hello,' it said breathlessly.

'Hello,' said Fat Charlie.

The new one was excitable and hairy. Its arms and legs seemed all *wrong*. Fat Charlie tried to place it. The other animal-people were animals, yes, and people too, and there was nothing strange or contradictory about this – the animalness and the humanness combined like the stripes on a zebra to make something *other*. This one, however, seemed both human and almost-human, and the oddness of it made Fat Charlie's teeth hurt. Then he got it.

'Monkey,' he said. 'You're Monkey.'

'Got a peach?' said Monkey. 'Got a mango? Got a fig?'

''Fraid not,' said Fat Charlie.

'Give me something to eat,' said Monkey. 'I'll be your friend.'

Mrs Dunwiddy had warned him about this. *Give nothing away*, he thought. *Make no promises.*

'I'm not giving you anything, I'm afraid.'

'Who are you?' asked Monkey. 'What are you? You seem like half a thing. Are you from here or from there?'

'Anansi was my father,' said Fat Charlie. 'I'm looking for someone to help me deal with my brother, to make him go away.'

'Might get Anansi mad,' said Monkey. 'Very bad idea that. Get Anansi mad, you never in any more stories.'

'Anansi's dead,' said Fat Charlie.

'Dead there,' said Monkey. 'Maybe. But dead here? That's another stump of grubs entirely.'

'You mean, he could be here?' Fat Charlie looked up at the mountainside more warily: the idea that he might, in one of the cave mouths, find his father creaking back and forwards in a rocking chair, fedora hat pushed back on his head, sipping from a can of brown ale and stifling a yawn with his lemon-yellow gloves, was troubling indeed.

'Who? What?'

'Do you think he's here?'

'Who?'

'My father.'

'Your father?'

'Anansi.'

Monkey leaped to the top of a rock in terror, then he pressed himself against the rock, his gaze flicking from side to side, as if keeping an eye out for sudden tornadoes. 'Anansi? He's here?'

'I was asking you that,' said Fat Charlie.

Monkey swung suddenly, so he was hanging upside down from his feet, his upside-down face staring straight into Fat Charlie's. 'I go back to the world sometimes,' he said. 'They say, Monkey, wise Monkey, come, come. Come eat the peaches we have for you. And the nuts. And the grubs. And the figs.'

'Is my father here?' asked Fat Charlie, patiently.

'He doesn't have a cave,' said Monkey. 'I would know if he had a cave. I think. Maybe he had a cave and I forgot. If you gave me a peach, I would remember better.'

'I don't have anything on me,' said Fat Charlie.

'No peaches?'

'Nothing, I'm afraid.'

Monkey swung himself up to the top of his rock and he was gone.

Fat Charlie continued along the rocky path. The sun had sunk until it was level with the path, and it burned a deep orange. It shone its old light straight into the caves, and showed each cave to be inhabited. That must be Rhinoceros, grey of skin, staring out short-sightedly; there, the colour of a rotten log in shallow water, was Crocodile, his eyes as black as glass.

There was a rattle behind him, of stone scuttering against

stone, and Fat Charlie turned with a jerk. Monkey stared up at him, his knuckles brushing the path.

'I really haven't got any fruit,' said Fat Charlie. 'Or I'd give you some.'

Monkey said, 'Felt sorry for you. Maybe you should go home. This is a bad bad bad bad *bad* idea. Yes?'

'No,' said Fat Charlie.

'Ah,' said Monkey. 'Right. Right right right right *right*.' He stopped moving, then a sudden burst of loping speed, and he bounded past Fat Charlie, and stopped in front of a cave some little distance away.

'Not to go in there,' he called. 'Bad place.' He pointed to the cave opening.

'Why not?' asked Fat Charlie. 'Who's in there?'

'Nobody's in there,' said Monkey, triumphantly. 'So it's not the one you want, is it?'

'Yes,' said Fat Charlie. 'It is.'

Monkey chittered and bounced, but Fat Charlie walked past him, and clambered up the rocks until he reached the mouth of the empty cave, as the crimson sun fell below the cliffs at the end of the world.

Walking the path along the edge of the mountains at the beginning of the world (it's only the mountains at the end of the world if you're coming from the other direction) reality seemed strange and strained. These mountains and their caves are made from the stuff of the oldest stories (this was long before human-people, of course; whatever made you imagine that people were the first things to tell stories?) and stepping off the path, into the cave, Fat Charlie felt as if he were walking into someone else's reality entirely. The cave was deep; its floor was splashed white with bird-droppings. There were feathers on the cave floor too, and, here and there, like a desiccated and abandoned feather duster, was the corpse of a bird, flattened and dried.

At the back of the cave, nothing but darkness.

Fat Charlie called, 'Hello?' and the echo of his voice came back to him from the interior of the cave. *Hello hello hello hello.* He kept walking. Now the darkness in the cave seemed almost palpable, as if something thin and dark had been laid over his eyes. He walked slowly, a step at a time, his arms outstretched.

Something moved.

'Hello?'

His eyes were learning to use what little light there was, and he could make something out. *It's nothing. Rags and feathers, that's all.* Another step, and the wind stirred the feathers and flapped the rags on the floor of the cave.

Something fluttered about him, fluttered *through* him, beating the air with the clatter of a pigeon's wings.

Swirling. Dust stung his eyes and his face, and he blinked in the cold wind, and took a step back as it rose up before him, a storm of dust and rags and feathers. Then the wind was gone, and where the feathers had been blowing was a human figure, which reached out a hand and beckoned to Fat Charlie.

He would have stepped back, but it reached out and took him by the sleeve. Its touch was light and dry, and it pulled him towards it . . .

He took one step forward into the cave –

– and was standing in the open air, on a treeless, copper-coloured plain, beneath a sky the colour of sour milk.

Different creatures have different eyes. Human eyes (unlike, say, a cat's eyes, or an octopus's) are only made to see one version of reality at a time. Fat Charlie saw one thing with his eyes, and he saw something else with his mind, and in the gulf between the two things, madness waited. He could feel a wild panic welling up inside him, and he took a deep breath and held it in while his heart thudded against his ribcage. He forced himself to believe his eyes, not his mind.

So while he knew that he was seeing a bird, mad-eyed, ragged-feathered, bigger than any eagle, taller than an ostrich, its beak the cruel tearing weapon of a raptor, its feathers the colour of slate overlaid with an oilslick sheen, making a dark rainbow of purples and greens, he really only knew that for an instant, somewhere in the very back of his mind. What he saw with his eyes was a woman with raven-black hair, standing where the idea of a bird had been. She was neither young nor old, and she stared at him with a face that might have been carved from obsidian in ancient times, when the world was young.

She watched him, and she did not move. Clouds roiled across the sour-milk sky.

'I'm Charlie,' said Fat Charlie. 'Charlie Nancy. Some people, well, most people, call me Fat Charlie. You can too. If you like.'

No response.

'Anansi was my father.'

Still nothing. Not a quiver; not a breath.

'I want you to help me make my brother go away.'

She tilted her head at this. Enough to show that she was listening, enough to show that she was alive.

'I can't do it on my own. He's got magic powers and stuff. I spoke to a spider, and the next thing you know, my brother turns up. Now I can't make him go away.'

Her voice, when she spoke, was as rough and as deep as a crow's. 'What do you wish me to do about it?'

'Help me?' he suggested.

She appeared to be thinking.

Later, Fat Charlie tried, and failed, to remember what she had been wearing. Sometimes he thought it must have been a cloak of feathers; at other times he believed it must have been rags of some kind, or perhaps a tattered raincoat, of the kind she wore when he saw her in Piccadilly, later, when it had all started to go bad. She was not naked, though: of that he was nearly certain. He would have remembered if she had been naked, wouldn't he?

'Help you,' she echoed.

'Help me get rid of him.'

She nodded. 'You wish me to help you get rid of Anansi's bloodline.'

'I just want him to go away and leave me alone. I don't want you to hurt him or anything.'

'Then promise me Anansi's bloodline for my own.'

Fat Charlie stood on the vast coppery plain, which was somehow, he knew, inside the cave in the mountains at the end of the world, and was, in its turn, in some sense, inside Mrs Dunwiddy's violet-scented front room, and he tried to make sense of what she was asking for.

'I can't give things away. And I can't make promises.'

'You want him to go,' she said. 'Say it. My time is precious.' She folded her arms, stared at him with mad eyes. 'I am not scared of Anansi.'

He remembered Mrs Dunwiddy's voice. 'Um,' said Fat Charlie. 'I mustn't make promises. And I have to ask for something of equal value. I mean, it has to be a trade.'

The Bird Woman looked displeased, but she nodded. 'Then I shall give you something of equal value in trade. I give my word.' She put her hand over his hand, as if she was giving him something, then squeezed his hand closed. 'Now say it.'

'I give you Anansi's bloodline,' Fat Charlie said.

'It is good,' said a voice, and at that she went, quite literally, to pieces.

Where a woman had been standing, there was now a flock of birds, which were flying, as if startled by a gunshot, all in different directions. Now the sky filled with birds, more birds than Fat Charlie had ever imagined, brown birds and black, wheeling and crossing and flowing like a cloud of black smoke vaster than the mind could hold, like a cloud of midges as big as the world.

'You'll make him go away, now?' called Fat Charlie, shouting the words into the darkening milky sky. The birds slipped and slid in the air. Each moved only a fraction, and they kept flying, but suddenly Fat Charlie was staring up at a face in the sky, a face made of swirling birds. It was very big.

It said his name in the screams and caws and calls of a thousand, thousand, thousand birds, and lips the size of tower blocks formed the words in the sky.

Then the face dissolved into madness and chaos as the birds that made it flew down from that pale sky, flew straight towards him. He covered his face with his hands, trying to protect himself.

The pain in his cheek was harsh and sudden. For an instant he believed that one of the birds must have gashed him, torn at his cheek with its beak or talons. Then he saw where he was.

'Don't hit me again!' he said. 'It's all right. You don't have to hit me!'

On the table, the penguins were guttering low; their heads and shoulders were gone, and now the flames were burning in the shapeless black and yellow blobs that had once been their bellies, their feet in frozen pools of blackish candlewax. There were three old women staring at him.

Miss Noles threw the contents of a glass of water into his face. 'You didn't have to do that either,' he said. 'I'm here, aren't I?'

Mrs Dunwiddy came into the room. She was holding a small brown glass bottle triumphantly. 'Smelling salts,' she announced. 'I know I got some somewhere. I buy these in, oh, 'sixty-seven, 'sixty-eight. I don't know if they still any good.' She peered at Fat Charlie, then scowled. 'He wake up. Who did wake him up?'

'He wasn't breathing,' said Mrs Bustamonte. 'So I give him a slap.'

'And I pour water on him,' said Miss Noles, 'which help bring him around the rest of the way.'

'I don't need smelling salts,' said Fat Charlie. 'I'm already wet and in pain.' But, with elderly hands, Mrs Dunwiddy had removed the cap from the bottle, and she was pushing it under his nose. He breathed in as he moved back, and inhaled a wave of ammonia. His eyes watered, and he felt as if he had been punched in the nose. Water dripped down his face.

'There,' said Mrs Dunwiddy. 'Feeling better now?'

'What time is it?' asked Fat Charlie.

'It's almost five in the morning,' said Mrs Higgler. She took a swig of coffee from her gigantic mug. 'We all worried about you. You better tell us what happened.'

Fat Charlie tried to remember. It was not that it had evaporated, as dreams do, more as if the experience of the last few hours had happened to somebody else, someone who was not him, and he had to contact that person by some hitherto unpractised form of telepathy. It was all a jumble in his mind, the technicolor Ozness of the other place dissolving back into the sepia tones of reality. 'There were caves. I asked for help. There were lots of animals there. Animals who were people. None of them wanted to help. They were all scared of my daddy. Then one of them said she would help me.'

'She?' said Mrs Bustamonte.

'Some of them were men, and some of them were women,' said Fat Charlie. 'This one was a woman.'

'Do you know what she was? Crocodile? Hyena? Mouse?'

He shrugged. 'I might have remembered before people started hitting me and pouring water on me. And putting things in my nose. It drives stuff out of your head.'

Mrs Dunwiddy said, 'Do you remember what I tell you? Not giving anything away? Only trade?'

'Yes,' he said, vaguely proud of himself. 'Yes. There was a monkey who wanted me to give him things, and I said no. Look, I think I need a drink.'

Mrs Bustamonte took a glass of something from the table. 'We thought maybe you need a drink. So we put the sherry through the strainer. There may be a few mixed herbs in there, but nothin' big.'

His hands were fists in his lap. He opened his right hand to take the glass from the old woman. Then he stopped, and he stared.

'What?' asked Mrs Dunwiddy. 'What is it?'

In the palm of his hand, black and crushed out of shape, and wet with sweat, Fat Charlie was holding a feather. He remembered, then. He remembered all of it.

'It was the Bird Woman,' he said.

* * *

Grey dawn was breaking as Fat Charlie climbed into the passenger seat of Mrs Higgler's station wagon.

'You sleepy?' she asked him.

'Not really. I just feel weird.'

'Where do you want me to take you? My place? Your dad's house? A motel?'

'I don't know.'

She put the car into gear and lurched out into the road.

'Where are we going?'

She did not answer. She slurped some coffee from her megamug. Then she said. 'Maybe what we do tonight is for the best and maybe it ain't. Sometimes family things, they best left for families to fix. You and your brother. You're too similar. I guess that is why you fight.'

'I take it this is some obscure West Indian usage of the word "similar" which means "nothing at all alike"?'

'Don't you start going all British on me. I know what I'm sayin'. You and him, you both cut from the same cloth. I remember your father sayin' to me, Callyanne, my boys, they stupider than— You know, it don't matter what he actually said, but the point is, he said it about both of you.' A thought struck her. 'Hey. When you go to the place where the old gods are, you see your father in that place?'

'I don't think so. I'd remember.'

She nodded, and said nothing, as she drove.

She parked the car, and they got out.

It was chilly in the Florida dawn. The Garden of Rest looked like something from a movie: there was a low ground mist which threw everything into soft focus. Mrs Higgler opened the small gate, and they walked through the cemetery.

Where there had been only fresh earth filling his father's grave, now there was turf, and at the head of the grave was a metal plaque with a metal vase built into it, and in the vase a single yellow silk rose.

'Lord have mercy on the sinner in this grave,' said Mrs Higgler, with feeling. 'Amen, amen, amen.'

They had an audience: the two red-headed cranes, which Fat Charlie had observed on his previous visit, strutted towards them, heads bobbing, like two aristocratic prison visitors.

'Shoo!' said Mrs Higgler. The birds started at her, incuriously, and did not leave.

One of them ducked its head down into the grass, came up again with a lizard struggling in its beak. A gulp and a shake, and the lizard was a bulge in the bird's neck.

The dawn chorus was beginning: grackles and orioles and mockingbirds were singing in the day in the wilderness beyond the Garden of Rest. 'It'll be good to be home again,' said Fat Charlie. 'With any luck she'll have made him leave by the time I get there. Then everything will be all right. I can sort everything out with Rosie.' A mood of gentle optimism welled up within him. It was going to be a good day.

***

In the old stories, Anansi lives just like you do or I do, in his house. He is greedy, of course, and lustful, and tricky, and full of lies. And he is good-hearted, and lucky, and sometimes even honest. Sometimes he is good, sometimes he is bad. He is never evil. Mostly, you are on Anansi's side. This is because Anansi owns all the stories. Mawu gave him the stories, back in the dawn days, took them from Tiger and gave them to Anansi, and he spins the web of them so beautifully.

In the stories, Anansi is a spider, but he is also a man. It is not hard to keep two things in your head at the same time. Even a child could do it.

Anansi's stories are told by grandmothers and by aunts in the West Coast of Africa and across the Caribbean, and all over the world. The stories have made it into books for children: big old smiling Anansi playing his merry tricks upon the world. Trouble is, grandmothers and aunts and writers of books for children tend to leave things out. There are stories that aren't appropriate for little children any more.

This is a story you won't find in the nursery tales. I call it,

ANANSI AND BIRD

Anansi did not like Bird, because when Bird was hungry she ate many things, and one of the things that Bird ate was spiders, and Bird, she was always hungry.

They used to be friends, but they were friends no longer.

One day Anansi was walking, and he saw a hole in the ground, and that gave him an idea. He puts wood in the bottom of the hole, and he makes a fire, and he puts a cookpot in the hole and drops in roots and herbs. Then he starts running around the pot, running and dancing and calling and shouting, going, I feel good. I feel *soooo* good. Oh boy, all my aches and pains be gone and I never felt so good in my whole damn life!

Bird hears the commotion. Bird flies down from the skies to see what all the fuss is about. She goes, What you singing about? Why you carrying on like a madman, Anansi?

Anansi sings, I had a pain in my neck, but now it's gone. I had a pain in my belly, but not any longer. I had creaks in my joints, but now I'm supple as a young palm tree, I'm smooth as Snake the morning after he sheds his skin. I'm powerful happy, and now I shall be perfect, for I know the secret, and nobody else does.

What secret? asks Bird.

My secret, says Anansi. Everyone's going to give me their favourite things, their most precious things, just to learn my secret. *Whoo! Whee!* I do feel good!

Bird hops a little closer, and she puts her head on one side. Then she asks, Can I learn your secret?

Anansi looks at Bird with suspicion on his face, and he moves to stand in front of the pot in the hole, bubbling away.

I don't think so, Anansi says. May not be enough to go around. Don't bother yourself about it.

Bird says, Now, Anansi, I know we haven't always been friends. But I'll tell you what. You share your secret with me, and I promise you no bird will never eat no spider ever again. We'll be friends until the end of time.

Anansi scratches his chin, and he shakes his head. It's a mighty big secret, he says, making people young and spry and lusty and free from all pain.

Bird, she preens. Bird, she says, Oh, Anansi, I'm sure you know that I have always found you a particularly handsome figure of a man. Why don't we lie by the side of the road for a little while, and I'm sure I can make you forget all your reservations about telling me your secret.

So they lie by the side of the road, and they get to canoodling and laughing and getting all silly, and once Anansi has had what he wants Bird says, Now, Anansi, what about your secret?

Anansi says, Well, I wasn't going to tell anyone. But I'll tell you. It's a herbal bath, in this hole in the ground. Watch, I'll drop in these leaves, and these roots. Now, anyone who goes into the bath they going to live for ever, feeling no pain. I had the bath, and now I'm frisky as a young goat. But I don't think I should let anyone else use the bath.

Bird, she looks down at the bubbling water, and quick as anything she slips down into the pot.

It's awful hot, Anansi, she says.

It's got to be hot for the herbs to do their good things, says

Anansi. Then he takes the lid of the pot and he covers the pot with it. It's a heavy lid, and Anansi, he puts a rock on top of it, to weigh it down more.

Bam! Bem! Bom! comes the knocking from inside the cookpot.

If I let you out now, calls Anansi, all the good work of the bubbling bath will be undone. You just relax in there and feel yourself getting healthier.

But maybe Bird did not hear him, or believe him, because the knocking and the pushing kept on coming from inside the pot, for a while longer. And then it stopped.

That evening Anansi and his family had the most delicious Bird soup, with boiled Bird. They did not go hungry again for many days.

Since that time, birds eat spiders every chance they get, and spiders and birds aren't never going to be friends.

There's another version of the story where they talk Anansi into the cookpot too. The stories are all Anansi's, but he doesn't always come out ahead.

Chapter Eight

In Which a Pot of Coffee Comes in Particularly Useful

If anything was making Spider go away, Spider didn't know about it. On the contrary, Spider was having an excellent time being Fat Charlie. He was having such a good time being Fat Charlie he began to wonder why he hadn't been Fat Charlie before. It was more fun than a barrelful of monkeys.*

The bit of being Fat Charlie that Spider liked best was Rosie.

Until now Spider had regarded women as more or less interchangeable. You didn't give them a real name, or an address that would work for longer than a week, of course, or anything more than a disposable mobile number. Women were fun, and decorative, and terrific accessories, but there would always be more of them; like bowls of goulash coming along a conveyor belt, when you were done with one, you simply picked up the next, and spooned in your sour cream.

*Several years earlier Spider had actually been tremendously disappointed by a barrelful of monkeys. It had done nothing he had considered particularly entertaining, apart from emit interesting noises, and eventually, once the noises had stopped and the monkeys were no longer doing anything at all – except possibly on an organic level – had needed to be disposed of in the dead of night.

But Rosie . . .

Rosie was different.

He couldn't have told you how she was different. He had tried, and failed. Partly it was how he felt when he was with her: as if, seeing himself in her eyes, he became a wholly better person. That was part of it.

Spider liked knowing that Rosie knew where to find him. It made him feel comfortable. He delighted in the pillowy curves of her, the way she meant nothing but good to the world, the way she smiled. There was really nothing at all wrong with Rosie, apart from having to spend time away from her, and of course, he was beginning to discover, the little matter of Rosie's mother. On this particular evening, while Fat Charlie was in an airport, four thousand miles away, in the process of being bumped up to first class, Spider was in Rosie's mother's flat in Wimpole Street, and he was learning about her the hard way.

Spider was used to being able to push reality around a little, just a little but that was always enough. You just had to show reality who was boss, that was all. Having said that, he had never met anyone who inhabited her own reality quite so firmly as Rosie's mother.

'Who's this?' she asked, suspiciously, as they walked in.

'I'm Fat Charlie Nancy,' said Spider.

'Why is he saying that?' asked Rosie's mother. 'Who is he?'

'I'm Fat Charlie Nancy, your future son-in-law, and you really like me,' said Spider, with utter conviction.

Rosie's mother swayed and blinked and stared at him. 'You may be Fat Charlie,' she said, uncertainly, 'but I don't like you.'

'Well,' said Spider, 'you should. I am remarkably likeable. Few people have ever been as likeable as I am. There is, frankly, no end to my likeability. People gather together in public assemblies to discuss how much they like me. I have several awards, and a medal from a small country in South America which pays tribute both to how much I am liked and my general all-round wonderfulness. I don't have it on me, of course. I keep my medals in my sock drawer.'

Rosie's mother sniffed. She did not know what was going on, but whatever it was, she did not like it. Until now, she felt that she had got the measure of Fat Charlie. She might, she admitted to herself, have mishandled things a little in the beginning: it was quite possible that Rosie would not have attached herself to Fat Charlie with such enthusiasm if, following the first meeting of her mother and Fat Charlie, her mother had not expressed her opinion quite so vociferously. He was a loser, Rosie's mother had said, for she could smell fear like a shark scenting blood across the bay. But she had failed to persuade Rosie to dump him, and now her main strategy involved assuming control of the wedding plans, making Fat Charlie as miserable as possible, and contemplating the national divorce statistics with a certain grim satisfaction.

Something different was now happening, and she did not like it. Fat Charlie was no longer a large vulnerable person. This new, sharp creature confused her.

Spider, for his part, was having to work.

Most people do not notice other people. Rosie's mother did. She noticed everything. Now, she sipped her hot water from a bone china cup. She knew that she had just lost a skirmish, even if she could not have told you how, or what the battle was about. So she moved her next assault to higher ground.

'Charles, dear,' she said, 'tell me about your cousin Daisy. I worry that your family is under-represented. Would you like her to be given a larger role in the wedding party?'

'Who?'

'Daisy,' said Rosie's mother, sweetly. 'The young lady I met at your house the other morning, wandering around in her scanties. If she *was* your cousin, of course.'

'Mother! If Charlie says she was his cousin . . .'

'Let him talk for himself, Rosie,' said her mother, and she took another sip of hot water.

'Right,' said Spider. 'Daisy,' said Spider.

He cast his mind back to the night of wine, women and song: he had brought the prettiest and funniest of the women back to the flat with them, after telling her that it was her idea, and then had needed her help in getting the semi-conscious bulk of Fat Charlie up the stairs. Having already enjoyed the attentions of several of the other women during the course of the evening, he had brought the little funny one back with him rather as one might set aside an after-dinner mint, but he had found, on getting home and putting a cleaned-up Fat Charlie to bed, that he was no longer hungry. That one.

'Sweet little cousin Daisy,' he continued, without a pause. 'I am certain that she would love to be involved in the wedding, should she be in the country. Alas, she's a courier. Always travelling. One day she's here, the next, she's dropping off a confidential document in Murmansk.'

'You don't have her address? Or her phone number?'

'We can look for her together, you and I,' agreed Spider. 'Zooming around the world. She comes, she goes.'

'Then,' said Rosie's mother, much as Alexander the Great might have ordered the sacking and pillaging of a little Persian village, 'the next time she is in the country, you must invite her over. I thought she was such a pretty little thing, and I am sure that Rosie would just love to meet her.'

'Yes,' said Spider. 'I must. I really must.'

***

Each person who ever was or is or will be has a song. It isn't a song that anybody else wrote. It has its own melody, it has its own words. Very few people get to sing their own song. Most of us fear that we cannot do it justice with our voices, or that our words are too foolish or too honest, or too odd. So people live their songs instead.

Take Daisy, for example. Her song, which had been somewhere in the back of her head for most of her life, had a reassuring marching sort of beat, and words that were about protecting the weak, and it had a chorus that began 'Evildoers beware!' and was thus much too silly ever to be sung out loud. She would hum it to herself sometimes, though, in the shower, during the soapy bits.

And that is, more or less, everything you need to know about Daisy. The rest is details.

Daisy's father was born in Hong Kong. Her mother came from Ethiopia, of a family of wealthy carpet exporters: they owned a

house in Addis Ababa, and another house and lands outside
Nazret. Daisy's parents met at Cambridge – he was studying
computing before that was something that was seen as being a
sensible career path, and she was devouring molecular chemistry
and international law. They were two young people who were
equally studious, naturally shy, and generally ill-at-ease. They
were both homesick, but for very different things; however, they
both played chess, and they met on a Wednesday afternoon, at the
chess club. They were, as novices, encouraged to play together,
and during their first game Daisy's mother beat Daisy's father
with ease.

Daisy's father was nettled by this, enough that he shyly asked
for a rematch on the following Wednesday, and on every
successive Wednesday after that (excluding vacations and public
holidays) for the next two years.

Their social interaction increased as their social skills and her
spoken English improved. Together, they held hands as part of a
human chain and protested the arrival of large trucks loaded with
missiles. Together, although as part of a much larger party, they
travelled to Barcelona in order to protest the unstoppable flood of
international capitalism, and to register stern protests at
corporate hegemonies. This was also the time they got to
experience officially squirted tear gas, and Mr Day's wrist was
sprained as he was being pushed out of the way by the Spanish
police.

And then, one Wednesday, at the beginning of their third year
at Cambridge, Daisy's father beat Daisy's mother at chess. He was
made so happy by this, so elated and triumphant that, buoyed
and emboldened by his conquest, he proposed marriage; and
Daisy's mother, who had been, deep down, afraid that as soon as
he won a game he would lose interest in her, said yes, of course.

They stayed in England, and remained in academia, and they
had one daughter, whom they called Daisy because at the time
they owned (and, to Daisy's later amusement, actually rode) a
tandem – a bicycle built for two. They moved from university to
university across Britain: he taught computer sciences while his
wife wrote books that nobody wanted to read about international
corporate hegemonies, and books that they did want to read

about chess, its strategies and its history, and thus in a good year she would make more money than he did, which was never very much. Their involvement in politics waned as they grew older, and as they approached middle age they had become a happy couple with no interests beyond each other, chess, Daisy, and the reconstruction and debugging of forgotten operating systems.

Neither of them understood Daisy, not even a little.

They blamed themselves for not having nipped her fascination with the police force in the bud when it first began to manifest, more or less at the same time that she began talking. Daisy would point out police cars in the same excited way that other little girls might point out ponies. Her seventh birthday party was held in fancy dress, to allow her to wear her junior policewoman's costume, and there are still photographs in a box in her parents' attic of her face suffused with a seven-year-old's perfect joy at the sight of her birthday cake – seven candles ringing a flashing blue light.

Daisy was a diligent, cheerful, intelligent teenager, who made both her parents happy when she went to the University of London to study law and computing. Her father had dreams of her becoming a lecturer in law; her mother nurtured dreams of her daughter taking silk, perhaps even becoming a judge and then using the law to crush corporate hegemonies whenever they appeared. And then Daisy went and ruined everything by taking the entry exams and joining the police force. The police welcomed her with open arms: on the one hand there were directives on the need to improve the diversity of the force, while on the other computer crime and computer-related fraud was on the increase. They needed Daisy. Frankly, they needed a whole string of Daisies.

At this point, four years on, it would be fair to say that a career in the police force had failed to live up to Daisy's expectations. It was not, as her parents had warned her repeatedly, that the police force was an institutionally racist and sexist monolith that would crush her individuality into something soul-destroying and uniform, that would make her as much a part of the canteen culture as instant coffee. No, the frustrating part of it was getting other coppers to understand that she was a copper too. She had come to the conclusion that, for most coppers, police work was something you did to protect Middle England from scary people of the wrong social background, who were probably out to steal their mobile phones. From where Daisy stood it was about something else. Daisy knew that a kid in his den in Germany could send out a virus that would shut down a hospital, cause more damage than a bomb. Daisy was of the opinion that the real bad guys these days understood FTP sites and high-level encryption and disposable pre-paid mobile phones. She was not sure that the good guys did.

She took a sip of coffee from a plastic cup, and made a face; while she had been scanning through screen after screen, her coffee had gone cold.

She had gone through all the information that Grahame Coats had given her. There was certainly a prima-facie case for thinking that something was wrong – if nothing else there was a cheque for two thousand pounds that Charles Nancy had apparently written to himself, the previous week.

Except. Except something did not feel right.

She walked down the corridor, knocked on the super-intendent's door.

'Come!'

Camberwell had smoked a pipe at his desk for thirty years, until the building had instituted a no-smoking policy. Now he made do with a lump of Plasticine, which he balled and squashed and kneaded and prodded. As a man with a pipe in his mouth, he had been placid, good-natured and, as far as those beneath him were concerned, the salt of the earth. As a man with a lump of Plasticine in his hand, he was uniformly irritable and short-tempered. On a good day he made it as far as tetchy.

'Yes?'

'The Grahame Coats Agency case.'

'Mm?'

'I'm not sure about it.'

'Not sure about it? What on earth is there not to be sure about?'

'Well, I think maybe I should take myself off the case.'

He did not look impressed. He stared at her. Down on the desk, unwatched, his fingers were kneading the blue Plasticine into the shape of a meerschaum. 'Because?'

'I've met the suspect socially.'

'And? You've been on holiday with him? You're godmother to his kids? What?'

'No. I met him once. I stayed overnight at his house.'

'So are you saying you and he did the nasty?' A deep sigh, in which world-weariness, irritation and a craving for half an ounce of Condor ready-rubbed mingled in equal parts.

'No, sir. Nothing like that. I just slept there.'

'And that's your total involvement with him?'

'Yes, sir.'

He crushed the Plasticine pipe back into a shapeless blob. 'You realise you're wasting my time?'

'Yes, sir. Sorry, sir.'

'Do whatever you have to do. Don't bother me.'

* * *

Maeve Livingstone rode the lift up to the fifth floor alone, the slow jerky journey giving her plenty of time to rehearse in her head what she would say to Grahame Coats when she got there.

She was carrying a slim brown briefcase, which had belonged to Morris: a peculiarly masculine object. She wore a white blouse, and a blue denim skirt, and over it, a grey coat. She had very long legs and extremely pale skin, and hair which remained, with only minimal chemical assistance, quite as blonde as it had been when Morris Livingstone had married her, twenty years earlier.

Maeve had loved Morris very much. When he died, she did not delete him from her mobile phone, not even after she had cancelled his service and returned his phone. Her nephew had taken the photo of Morris that was on her phone, and she did not want to lose that. She wished she could phone Morris now, ask his advice.

She had told the speakerphone who she was, to be buzzed in downstairs, and when she walked into reception Grahame Coats was already waiting for her.

'How de do, how de do, good lady?' he said.

'We need to talk privately, Grahame,' said Maeve. 'Now.'

Grahame Coats smirked; oddly enough, many of his favourite fantasies began with Maeve saying something fairly similar, before she went on to utter such statements as, 'I need you, Grahame, right now', and, 'Oh, Grahame, I've been such a bad bad bad bad girl who needs to be taught some discipline', and, on rare occasions, 'Grahame, you are too much for one woman, so let me introduce you to my identical naked twin sister, Maeve II.'

They went into his office.

Maeve, slightly disappointingly as far as Grahame Coats was concerned, said nothing about needing it right here, right now. She did not take off her coat. Instead she opened her briefcase and took out a sheaf of papers, which she placed upon the desk.

'Grahame, at my bank manager's suggestion, I had your figures and statements for the last decade independently audited. From back when Morris was still alive. You can look at them if you like. The numbers don't work. None of them. I thought I'd talk to you about it before I called in the police. In Morris's memory, I felt I owed you that.'

'You do indeed,' agreed Grahame Coats, smooth as a snake in a butter churn. 'Indeed you do.'

'Well?' Maeve Livingstone raised one perfect eyebrow. Her expression was not reassuring. Grahame Coats liked her better in his imagination.

'I'm afraid we've had a rogue employee at the Grahame Coats Agency for quite a while, Maeve. I actually called in the police myself, last week, when I realised that something was amiss. The long arm of the law is already investigating. Due to the illustrious nature of several of the clients of the Grahame Coats agency – yourself among them – the police are keeping this as quiet as possible, and who can blame them?' She did not seem as mollified as he had hoped. He tried another tack. 'They have high hopes of recovering much, if not all of the money.'

Maeve nodded. Grahame Coats relaxed, but only a little.

'Can I ask which employee?'

'Charles Nancy. I have to say I trusted him implicitly. It came as quite a shock.'

'Oh. He's sweet.'

'Appearances,' pointed out Grahame Coats, 'can be deceptive.'

She smiled then, and a very sweet smile it was. 'It won't wash, Grahame. This has been going on for yonks. Since long before Charles Nancy started here. Probably since before my time. Morris absolutely trusted you, and you stole from him. And now you're trying to tell me that you're hoping to frame one of your employees – or blame one of your confederates – well, it won't wash.'

'No,' said Grahame Coats, contritely. 'Sorry.'

She picked up the sheaf of papers. 'Out of interest,' she said, 'how much do you think you got from Morris and me over the years? I make it about three million quid.'

'Ah.' He was not smiling at all, now. It was certainly more than that, but still. 'That sounds about right.'

They looked at each other, and Grahame Coats calculated, furiously. He needed to buy time. That was what he needed. 'What if,' he said, 'what if I were to repay it, in full, in cash, now. With interest. Let's say, fifty per cent of the amount in question.'

'You're offering me four and a half million pounds? In cash?'

Grahame Coats smiled at her, in exactly the same way that striking cobras tend not to. 'Absatively. If you go to the police, then I will deny everything, and hire excellent lawyers. In a worst-case scenario, after an extremely lengthy trial, during which I shall be forced to blacken Morris's good name in every way I possibly can, I will be sentenced at most to ten to twelve years in prison. I might actually serve five years, with good behaviour – and I should be a model prisoner. Given the general overcrowding of the prison services, I'd serve most of my sentence in an open prison, or even on day release. I don't see this as being too problematic. On the flipside, I can guarantee that, if you go to the police, you will never get a penny of Morris's money. The alternative is to keep your mouth shut, get all the money you need, and more, while I buy myself a little time to . . . to do the decent thing. If you see what I mean.'

Maeve thought about it. 'I *would* like to see you rot in prison,' she said. And then she sighed, and nodded. 'All right,' she said. 'I take the money. I never have to see or deal with you again. All future royalty cheques come directly to me.'

'Absatively. The safe is over here,' he told her.

There was a bookcase on the far wall, on which were uniform leatherbound editions of Dickens, Thackeray, Trollope and Austen, all unread. He fumbled with a book, and the bookcase slipped to one side, revealing a door behind it, painted to match the wall.

Maeve wondered if it would have a combination, but no, there was just a small keyhole, which Grahame Coats unlocked with a large brass key. The door swung open.

He reached in and turned on the light. It was a narrow room, lined with rather amateurishly fixed shelves. At the far end was a small, fireproof filing cabinet.

'You can take it in cash, or in jewellery, or in a combination of the two,' he said, bluntly. 'I'd advise the latter. Lots of nice antique gold back there. Very portable.'

He unlocked several strongboxes, and displayed the contents. Rings and chains and lockets glittered and gleamed and shone.

Maeve's mouth opened. 'Take a look,' he told her, and she squeezed past him. It was a treasure cave.

She pulled out a golden locket on a chain, held it up, stared at it in wonder. 'This is gorgeous,' she said. 'It must be worth—' and she broke off. In the polished gold of the locket she saw something moving behind her, and she turned, which meant that the hammer did not hit her squarely on the back of the head, as Grahame Coats had intended, but instead glanced off the side of her cheek.

'You little shit!' she said, and she kicked him. Maeve had good legs and a powerful kick, but she and her attacker were at close quarters.

Maeve's foot connected with his shin, and she reached for the hammer he was holding. Grahame Coats smashed out with it; this time it connected, and Maeve stumbled to one side. Her eyes seemed to unfocus. He hit her again, squarely on the top of the head, and again, and again, and she went down.

Grahame Coats wished that he had a gun. A nice, sensible handgun. With a silencer, like in the films. Honestly, if it had ever occurred to him that he would need to kill someone in his office he would have been much better prepared for it. He might even

have laid in a supply of poison. That would have been wise. No
need for any of this nonsense.

There was blood and blonde hair adhering to the end of the
hammer. He put it down with distaste, and, stepping around the
woman on the floor, he grabbed the safe-deposit boxes containing
the jewellery. He tipped them out on to his desk, and returned
them to the safe, where he removed an attaché case, containing
bundles of hundred-dollar bills and of five-hundred euro notes,
and a small black velvet bag half full of unset diamonds. He
removed some files from the filing cabinet. And, last but, as he
would have pointed out, by no means least, he took out from the
secret room a small leather vanity case, containing two wallets
and two passports.

Then he pushed the heavy door closed, and locked it, and
swung the bookcase back into position.

He stood there, panting somewhat, and caught his breath.

All in all, he decided, he was rather proud of himself. Good job,
Grahame. Good man. Good show. He had improvised with the
materials at hand, and come out ahead: bluffed and been bold
and creative – ready, as the poet said, to risk it all on a turn of
pitch and toss. He had risked, and he had won. He was the
pitcher. He was the tosser. One day, on his tropical paradise, he
would write his memoirs, and people would learn how he had
bested a dangerous woman. Although, he thought, it might be
better if she had actually been holding a gun.

Probably, he realised, on reflection, she *had* pulled a gun on
him. He was fairly sure he had seen her reach for it. He had been
extremely fortunate that the hammer had been there, that he had
a toolkit in the room for moments of necessary DIY, or he would
not have been able to act in self-defence with it so swiftly or so
effectively.

Only now did it occur to him to lock the main door to his office.

There was, he noticed, blood on his shirt and on his hand, and
on the sole of one shoe. He took off his shirt, and wiped down his
shoe with it. Then he dropped the shirt into the bin beneath his
desk. He surprised himself by putting his hand to his mouth and
licking the gobbet of blood off it, like a cat, with his red tongue.

And then he yawned. He took Maeve's papers from the desk,

ran them through the shredder. She had a second set of documents in her briefcase, and he shredded them as well. He reshredded the shreddings.

He had a closet in the corner of his office, with a suit hanging in it, and spare shirts, socks, underpants and so on. You never knew when you would need to head to a first night from the office, after all. Be prepared.

He dressed, with care.

There was a small suitcase with wheels in it in the closet too, of the kind that is meant to be placed in overhead lockers, and he put things into it, moving them around to make room.

He called reception. 'Annie,' he said. 'Would you pop out and get me a sandwich? Not from Prêt, no. I thought the new place in Brewer Street? I'm just wrapping up with Mrs Livingstone. I may actually wind up taking her out for a spot of real lunch, but best to be prepared.'

He spent several minutes on the computer, running the kind of disk-cleaning program that takes your data, over-writes it with random ones and zeroes, then grinds it up extremely small before finally depositing it at the bottom of the Thames wearing concrete overshoes. Then he walked down the hall, pulling his wheeled suitcase behind him.

He put his head around one office door. 'Popping out for a bit,' he said. 'I'll be back in about three, if anyone asks.'

Annie was gone from reception, which, he thought, was a good thing. People would assume that Maeve Livingstone had already left the agency, just as they would expect Grahame Coats to return at any time. By the time they started looking for him, he would be a long way away.

He descended in the lift. This was all happening early, he thought. He would not turn fifty for more than a year. But the exit mechanisms were already in place. He needed simply to think of it as a golden handshake, or perhaps a golden parachute.

And then, pulling the wheelie suitcase behind him, he walked out of the front door into the sunny Aldwych morning, and out of the Grahame Coats Agency for ever.

* * *

Spider had slept peacefully in his own enormous bed, in his place
in Fat Charlie's spare room. He had begun to wonder, in a vague
sort of way, whether Fat Charlie had gone for good, and had
resolved to investigate the matter the next time that he could in
any way be bothered to do so, unless something more interesting
distracted him or he forgot.

He had slept late, and was now on his way to meet Rosie for
lunch. He would pick her up at her flat, and they would go
somewhere good. It was a beautiful day in early autumn, and
Spider's happiness was infectious. This was because Spider was,
give or take a little, a god. When you're a god, your emotions are
contagious – other people can catch them. When people stood
near Spider on a day that he was this happy, their worlds would
seem a little brighter. If he hummed a song, other people around
him would start humming, in key, like something from a musical.
Of course, if he yawned, a hundred people nearby would yawn,
and when he was miserable it spread like a damp river-mist,
making the world even gloomier for everyone caught up in it. It
wasn't anything he did; it was something that he *was*.

Right now, the only thing casting a damper on his happiness
was that he had resolved to tell Rosie the truth.

Spider was not terribly good at telling the truth. He regarded
truth as fundamentally malleable, more or less a matter of
opinion, and Spider was able to muster some pretty impressive
opinions when he had to.

Being an imposter was not the problem. He liked being an
imposter. He was good at it. It fitted in with his plans, which were
fairly simple and could until now have been summarised more or
less as: a) go somewhere, b) enjoy yourself and c) leave before you
get bored. And it was now, he knew deep down, definitely time to
leave. The world was his lobster, his bib was round his neck, and
he had a pot of melted butter and an array of grotesque but
effective lobster-eating implements and devices at the ready.

Only . . .

Only he didn't want to go.

He was having second thoughts about all this, something
Spider found fairly disconcerting. Normally he didn't even have
first thoughts about things. Life without thinking had been

perfectly pleasant – instinct, impulse and an obscene amount of luck had served him quite well up to now. But even miracles can only take you so far. Spider walked down the street, and people smiled at him.

He had agreed with Rosie that he would meet her at her flat, so he was pleasantly surprised to see her standing at the end of the road, waiting for him. He felt a pang of something that was still not entirely guilt, and waved.

'Rosie? Hey!'

She came towards him, along the pavement, and he began to grin. They would sort things out. Everything would work out for the best. Everything would be fine. 'You look like a million dollars,' he told her. 'Maybe two million. What are you hungry for?'

Rosie smiled, and shrugged.

They were passing a Greek restaurant. 'Is Greek OK?' She nodded. They walked down some steps, and went inside. It was dark, and empty, having only just opened, and the proprietor pointed them towards a nook, or possibly a cranny, towards the rear.

They sat opposite each other, at a table just big enough for two. Spider said, 'There's something that I wanted to talk to you about.' She said nothing. 'It's not bad,' he went on. 'Well, it's not good. But. Well. It's something you ought to know.'

The proprietor asked them if they were ready to order anything. 'Coffee,' said Spider, and Rosie nodded her agreement. 'Two coffees,' said Spider. 'And if you can give us, um, five minutes? I need a little privacy here.'

The proprietor withdrew.

Rosie looked at Spider enquiringly.

He took a deep breath. 'Right. OK. Let me just say this, because it isn't easy and I don't know that I can . . . right. OK. Look, I'm not Fat Charlie. I know you think I am, but I'm not. I'm his brother, Spider. You think I'm him because we sort of look alike.'

She did not say anything.

'Well, I don't really look like him. But. Y'know, none of this really comes easy to me. Uh. I can't stop thinking about you. So I mean, I know you're engaged to my brother, but I'm sort of asking if you, well, if you'd think about maybe dumping him and possibly going out with me.'

A pot of coffee arrived, on a small silver tray, with two cups.

'Greek coffee,' said the proprietor, who had brought it.

'Yes. Thanks. I *did* ask for a couple of minutes . . .'

'Is very hot,' said the proprietor. 'Very hot coffee. Strong. Greek. Not Turkish.'

'That's great. Listen, if you don't mind – five minutes. Please?'

The proprietor shrugged and walked away.

'You probably hate me,' said Spider. 'If I was you I'd probably hate me too. But I mean this. More than I've ever meant anything in my life.' She was just looking at him, without expression, and he said, 'Please. Just say something. Anything.'

Her lips moved, as if she were trying to find the right words to say.

Spider waited.

Her mouth opened.

His first thought was that she was eating something, because the thing he saw between her teeth was brown, and was certainly not a tongue. Then it moved its head and its eyes, little black-bead eyes, stared at him. Rosie opened her mouth impossibly wide and the birds came out.

Spider said, 'Rosie?' and then the air was filled with beaks and feathers and claws. One after the other, birds poured out from her throat, each accompanied by a tiny coughing-choking noise, in a stream directed at him.

He threw up an arm to protect his eyes, and something hurt his wrist. He flailed out, and something flew at his face, heading for his eyes. He jerked his head backwards, and the beak punctured his cheek.

A moment of nightmare clarity: there was still a woman sitting opposite him. What he could no longer understand was how he could ever have mistaken her for Rosie. She was older than Rosie for a start, her blue-black hair streaked here and there with silver. Her skin was not the warm brown of Rosie's skin but black as flint. She was wearing a ragged ochre raincoat. And she grinned and opened her mouth wide once more, and now inside her mouth he could see the cruel beaks and crazy eyes of seagulls . . .

Spider did not stop to think. He acted. He grabbed the handle of the coffee-pot, swept it up in one hand, while with the other he pulled off the lid; then he jerked the pot towards the woman in the seat opposite him. The contents of the pot, scalding hot black coffee, went all over her.

She hissed in pain.

Birds crashed and flapped through the air of the cellar restaurant, but now there was nobody sitting opposite him, and the birds flew without direction, flapping into walls wildly.

The proprietor said, 'Sir? Are you hurt? I am sorry. They must have come in from the street.'

'I'm fine,' said Spider.

'Your face is bleeding,' said the man. He handed Spider a napkin, and Spider pressed it against his cheek. The cut stung.

Spider offered to help the man get the birds out. He opened the door to the street, but now the place was as empty of birds as it had been before his arrival.

Spider pulled out a five-pound note. 'Here,' he said. 'For the coffee. I've got to go.'

The proprietor nodded, gratefully. 'Keep the napkin.'

Spider stopped and thought. 'When I came in,' he asked, 'was there a woman with me?'

The proprietor looked puzzled – possibly even scared, Spider could not be sure. 'I do not remember,' he said, as if dazed. 'If you had been alone, I would not have seated you back there. But I do not know.'

Spider went back out into the street. The day was still bright, but the sunlight no longer seemed reassuring. He looked around. He saw a pigeon, shuffling and pecking at an abandoned ice-cream cone; a sparrow on a windowledge; and high above, a flash of white in the sunlight, its wings extended, a seagull circled.

Chapter Nine

In Which Fat Charlie Answers the Door and Spider Encounters Flamingos

Fat Charlie's luck was changing. He could feel it. The plane on which he was returning home had been oversold, and he had found himself bumped up to first class. The meal was excellent. Halfway across the Atlantic, a flight attendant came over to inform him that he had won a complimentary box of chocolates, and presented it to him. He put it in his overhead locker, and ordered a Drambuie on ice.

He would get home. He would sort everything out with Grahame Coats – after all, if there was one thing that Fat Charlie was certain of, it was the honesty of his own accounting. He would make everything good with Rosie. Everything was going to be just great.

He wondered if Spider would already be gone when he got home, or whether he would get the satisfaction of throwing him out. He hoped it would be the latter. Fat Charlie wanted to see his brother apologise, possibly even grovel. He started to imagine the things that he was going to say.

'Get out!' said Fat Charlie, 'And take your sunshine, your Jacuzzi and your bedroom with you!'

'Sorry?' said the flight attendant.

'Talking,' said Fat Charlie. 'To myself. Just um.'

But even the embarrassment he felt at this wasn't really that bad. He didn't even hope the plane would crash and end his mortification. Life was definitely looking up.

He opened the little kit of useful amenities he had been given, and put on his eye-shade, and pushed his seat back as far as it would go, which was most of the way. He thought about Rosie, although the Rosie in his mind kept shifting, morphing into someone smaller, who wasn't really wearing much of anything. Fat Charlie guiltily imagined her dressed, and was mortified when he realised that she seemed to be wearing a police uniform. He felt terrible about this, he told himself, but it didn't seem to make much of an impression. He ought to feel ashamed of himself. He ought to . . .

Fat Charlie shifted in his seat, and emitted one, small, satisfied snore.

He was still in an excellent mood when he landed at Heathrow. He took the Heathrow Express into Paddington, and was pleased to note that in his brief absence from England the sun had decided to come out. *Every little thing*, he told himself, *is going to be all right*.

The only odd note, which added a flavour of wrongness to the morning, occurred halfway through the train journey. He was staring out of the window, wishing he had bought a newspaper at Heathrow. The train was passing an expanse of green – a school playing field, perhaps – when the sky seemed, momentarily, to darken, and, with a hiss of brakes, the train stopped at a signal.

That did not disturb Fat Charlie. It was England in the autumn: the sun was, by definition, something that only happened when it wasn't cloudy or raining. But there was a figure standing on the edge of the green, by a stand of trees.

At first glance, he thought it was a scarecrow.

That was foolish. It could not have been a scarecrow. Scarecrows are found in fields, not on football pitches. Scarecrows certainly aren't left on the edge of the woodland. Anyway, if it was a scarecrow it was doing a very poor job.

There were crows everywhere, after all, big black ones.

And then it moved.

It was too far away to be anything more than a shape, a slight figure in a tattered brown raincoat. Still, Fat Charlie knew it. He knew that if he had been close enough, he would have seen a face chipped from obsidian, and raven-black hair, and eyes that held madness.

Then the train jerked, and began to move, and in moments the woman in the brown raincoat was out of sight.

Fat Charlie felt uncomfortable. He had practically convinced himself by now that what had happened, what he *thought* had happened, in Mrs Dunwiddy's front room, had been some form of hallucination, a high-octane dream, true on some level but not a real thing. Not something that had happened; rather, it was symbolic of a greater truth. He could not have gone to a real place, nor struck a real bargain, could he?

It was only a metaphor, after all.

He did not ask himself why he was now so certain that everything would soon begin to improve. There was reality, and there was *reality*, and some things were more real than others.

Faster and faster, the train rattled him further into London.

***

Spider was almost home from the Greek restaurant, napkin pushed against his cheek, when someone touched him on the shoulder.

'Charles?' said Rosie.

Spider jumped, or at least, he jerked and made a startled noise.

'Charles? Are you all right? What happened to your cheek?'

He stared at her. 'Are you you?' he asked.

'What?'

'Are you Rosie?'

'What kind of a question is that? Of course I'm Rosie. What did you do to your cheek?'

He pressed the napkin against his cheek. 'I cut it,' he said.

'Let me see.' She took his hand away from his cheek. The centre of the white napkin was stained crimson, as if he had bled into it, but his cheek was whole and untouched. 'There's nothing there.'

'Oh.'

'Charles? Are you all right?'

'Yes,' he said. 'I am. Unless I'm not. I think we should go back to my place. I think I'll be safer there.'

'We were going to have lunch,' said Rosie, in the tone of voice of one who worries that she'll only understand what's actually going on when a TV presenter leaps out and reveals the hidden cameras.

'Yes,' said Spider. 'I know. I think someone just tried to kill me, though. And she pretended she was you.'

'Nobody's trying to kill you,' said Rosie, failing to sound like she wasn't humouring him.

'Even if nobody's trying to kill me, can we skip lunch and go back to my place? I've got food there.'

'Of course.'

Rosie followed him down the road, wondering when Fat Charlie had lost all that weight. He looked good, she thought. He looked really good. They walked into Maxwell Gardens, in silence.

He said, 'Look at that.'

'What?'

He showed her. The fresh bloodstain had vanished from the napkin. It was now perfectly white.

'Is it a magic trick?'

'If it is, I didn't do it,' he said. 'For once.' He dropped the napkin into a bin. As he did so, a taxi pulled up in front of Fat Charlie's house, and Fat Charlie got out, rumpled and blinking and carrying a white plastic bag.

Rosie looked at Fat Charlie. She looked at Spider. She looked back at Fat Charlie, who had opened the bag and pulled out an enormous box of chocolates.

'They're for you,' he said.

Rosie took the chocolates and said, 'Thank you.' There were two men and they looked and sounded completely different, and she still could not work out which one of them was her fiancé. 'I'm going mad, aren't I?' she said, her voice taut. It was easier, now she knew what was wrong.

The thinner of the two Fat Charlies, the one with the earring, put his hand on her shoulder. 'You need to go home,' he said. 'Then you need a nap. When you wake up, you'll have forgotten all about this.'

Well, she thought, *that makes life easier. It's better with a plan.* She walked back to her flat with a spring in her step, carrying her box of chocolates.

'What did you do?' asked Fat Charlie. 'She just seemed to turn off.'

Spider shrugged. 'I didn't want to upset her,' he said.

'Why didn't you tell her the truth?'

'It didn't seem appropriate.'

'Like you'd know what was appropriate?'

Spider touched the front door and it opened.

'I have keys, you know,' said Fat Charlie. 'It's *my* front door.'

They walked into the hallway, walked up the stairs.

'Where have you been?' asked Spider.

'Nowhere. Out,' said Fat Charlie, as if he were a teenager.

'I was attacked by birds in the restaurant this morning. Do you know anything about that? You do, don't you?'

'Not really. Maybe. It's just time for you to leave, that's all.'

'Don't start anything,' said Spider.

'Me? *Me* start anything? I think I've been a model of restraint. You came into my life. You got my boss upset, and got the police on to me. You, you've been kissing my girlfriend. You screwed up my life.'

'Hey,' said Spider. 'You ask me, you've done a great job of screwing up your life on your own.'

Fat Charlie clenched his fist, swung back, and hit Spider in the jaw, like they do on the movies. Spider staggered back, more surprised than hurt. He put his hand to his lip, then looked down at the blood on his hand. 'You hit me,' he said.

'I can do it again,' said Fat Charlie, who wasn't sure that he could. His hand hurt.

Spider said, 'Yeah?' and launched himself at Fat Charlie, pummelling him with his fists, and Fat Charlie went over, his arm around Spider's waist, pulling Spider down with him.

They rolled up and down the hallway floor, hitting and flailing at each other. Fat Charlie half expected Spider to launch some kind of magical counterattack or to be supernaturally strong, but the two of them seemed fairly evenly matched. Both of them fought unscientifically, like boys – like brothers – and as they fought, Fat Charlie thought he remembered doing this once before, a long, long time ago. Spider was smarter and faster, but if Fat Charlie could just get on top of him, and get Spider's hands out of the way . . .

Fat Charlie grabbed for Spider's right hand, twisted it behind Spider's back, then sat on his brother's chest, putting all his weight on him.

'Give in?' he asked.

'No.' Spider wriggled and twisted, but Fat Charlie was solidly in position, sitting on Spider's chest.

'I want you to promise,' said Fat Charlie, 'to get out of my life, and to leave me and Rosie alone for ever.'

At this, Spider bucked, angrily, and Fat Charlie was dislodged. He landed, sprawled, on the kitchen floor. 'Look,' said Spider. 'I *told* you.'

There was a banging on the door downstairs, an imperious knocking of the kind that indicated someone needed to come in rather urgently. Fat Charlie glared at Spider, and Spider scowled at Fat Charlie, and slowly they got to their feet.

'Shall I answer it?' said Spider.

'No,' said Fat Charlie. 'It's *my* bloody house. And *I'm* going to bloody answer my *own* front door, thank you very much.'

'Whatever.'

Fat Charlie edged towards the stairs. Then he turned round. 'Once I've dealt with this,' he said, 'I'm dealing with you. Pack your stuff. You are on your way out.' He walked downstairs, tucking himself in, brushing the dust off, and generally trying to make it look as if he hadn't been brawling on the floor.

He opened the door. There were two large uniformed policemen, and one, smaller rather more exotic policewoman in extremely plain clothes.

'Charles Nancy?' said Daisy. She looked at him as if he was a stranger, her eyes expressionless.

'Glumph,' said Fat Charlie.

'Mr Nancy,' she said, 'you are under arrest. You have the right—'

Fat Charlie turned back to the interior of the house. 'Bastard!' he shouted up the stairs. 'Bastard bastard bastarding bastardy *bastard*!'

Daisy tapped him on the arm. 'Do you want to come quietly?' she asked, quietly. 'Only if you don't, we can subdue you first. I wouldn't recommend it, though. They're very enthusiastic subduers.'

'I'll come quietly,' said Fat Charlie.

'That's good,' said Daisy. She walked Fat Charlie outside and locked him into the back of a black police van.

The police searched the flat. The rooms were empty of life. At the end of the hall was a little spare bedroom, containing several boxes of books and toy cars. They poked around in there, but they didn't find anything interesting.

***

Spider lay on the couch in his bedroom, and sulked. He had gone to his room when Fat Charlie went off to answer the door. He needed to be on his own. He didn't do confrontations terribly well. When it got to that point was normally when he went away, and right now Spider knew it was time to go, but he still didn't want to leave.

He wasn't sure that sending Rosie home was the right thing to have done.

What he wanted to do – and Spider was driven entirely by *wants*, never by *oughts* or *shoulds* – was to tell Rosie that he wanted her – *he*, Spider. That he wasn't Fat Charlie. That he was something quite different. And that, in itself, wasn't the problem. He could simply have said to her, with enough conviction, 'I'm actually Spider, Fat Charlie's brother, and you're completely OK with this. It doesn't bother you,' and the universe would have pushed Rosie just a little, and she would have accepted it, just as she'd gone home earlier. She'd be fine with it. She would not have minded it, not at all.

Except, he knew, somewhere deep inside, she would.

Human beings do not like being pushed about by gods. They may seem to, on the surface, but somewhere on the inside, underneath it all, they sense it and they resent it. They know. Spider could tell her to be happy about the situation, and she would be happy, but it would be as real as painting a smile on her face – a smile that she would truly believe, in every way that mattered, was her own. In the short term (and until now Spider had only ever thought in the short term) none of this would be important, but in the long term it could only lead to problems. He didn't want some kind of seething, furious creature, someone who, though she hated him way down deep, was perfectly placid and doll-like and normal on the surface. He wanted Rosie.

And that wouldn't be Rosie, would it?

Spider stared out of the window, at the glorious waterfall and the tropical sky beyond it, and Spider began to wonder when Fat Charlie would come knocking on his door. Something had happened this morning in the restaurant, and he was certain that his brother knew more about it than he was saying.

After a while, he got bored with waiting, and wandered back into Fat Charlie's flat. There was nobody there. The place was a mess – it looked like it had been turned upside down by trained professionals. Spider decided that, in all probability, Fat Charlie had messed the place up himself, to indicate how upset he was that Spider had beaten him in their fight.

He looked out of the window. There was a police car parked outside, beside a black police van. As he watched, they drove away.

He made himself some toast, and he buttered it and ate it. Then he walked through the flat, carefully ensuring that all the curtains were closed.

The doorbell rang. Spider closed the last of the curtains, then he walked downstairs.

He opened the door and Rosie looked at him. She still seemed a little dazed. He looked at her. 'Well? Aren't you going to invite me in?'

'Of course. Come in.'

She walked up the stairs. 'What happened here? It looks like an earthquake hit.'

'Yeah?'

'Why are you just sitting in the dark?' She went to open the curtains.

'Don't do that! Just keep them closed.'

'What are you scared of?' asked Rosie.

Spider looked out of the window. 'Birds,' he said, eventually.

'But birds are our friends,' said Rosie, as if addressing a small child.

'Birds,' Spider said, 'are the last of the dinosaurs. Tiny velociraptors with wings. Devouring defenseless wiggly things and, and nuts, and fish, and, and other birds. They get the early worms. And have you ever watched a chicken eat? They may look innocent, but birds are, well, they're vicious.'

'There was a thing on the news the other day,' said Rosie, 'about a bird who saved a man's life.'

'That doesn't change the fact that—'

'It was a raven, or a crow. One of those big black ones. The man was lying on the lawn in his home in California, reading a magazine, and he hears this cawing and cawing, and it's a raven, trying to attract his attention. So he gets up and goes over to the tree it's perched on, and down beneath it is a mountain lion, that had been getting all ready to pounce on him. So he went inside. If that raven hadn't warned him, he would have been lion-food.'

'I don't think that's usual raven behaviour,' said Spider. 'But whether one raven once saved someone's life or not, it doesn't change anything. Birds are still out to get me.'

'Right,' said Rosie, trying to sound as if she wasn't humouring him. 'Birds are out to get you.'

'Yes.'

'And this is because . . . ?'

'Um.'

'There must be a reason. You can't tell me the great plurality of birds has just decided to treat you as an enormous early worm for no particular reason.'

He said, 'I don't think you'd believe me,' and he meant it.

'Charlie. You've always been really honest. I mean, I've trusted you. If you tell me something, I'll do my best to believe it. I'll try *really* hard. I love you and I believe in you. So why don't you let me find out if I believe you or not?'

Spider thought about this. Then he reached out for her hand, and he squeezed it.

'I think I ought to show you something,' he said.

He led her to the end of the corridor. They stopped outside the door to Fat Charlie's spare room. 'There's something in here,' he said. 'I think it'll explain it a bit better than I can.'

'You're a superhero,' she said, 'and this is where you keep the batpoles?'

'No.'

'Is it something kinky? You like to dress up in a twinset and pearls and call yourself Dora?'

'No.'

'It's not . . . a model trainset, is it?'

Spider pushed open the door to Fat Charlie's spare room, and at the same time he opened the door to his bedroom. The picture windows at the end of the room showed a waterfall, which crashed down into a jungle pool far below. The sky through the windows was bluer than sapphires.

Rosie made a small noise.

She turned round, walked back down the hall, into the kitchen, and looked out of the window at the grey London sky, doughy and unwelcoming. She came back. 'I don't understand,' she said. 'Charlie? What's happening?'

'I'm not Charlie,' said Spider. 'Look at me. *Really* look at me. I don't even look like him.'

She made no pretence of humouring him any longer. Her eyes were wide and scared.

'I'm his brother,' said Spider. 'I've screwed everything up. Everything. And I think probably the best thing I can do is just get out of all your lives and go away.'

'So where's Fat – where's Charlie?'

'I don't know. We were having a fight. He went off to answer the door, and I went off to my room, and he didn't come back.'

'He didn't come back? And you didn't even *try* to find out what had happened to him?'

'Er. He might have been taken away by the police,' said Spider. 'It's just an idea. I have no proof or anything.'

'What's your name?' she demanded.

'Spider.'

Rosie repeated it. 'Spider.' Outside the window, above the spray of the waterfall, she could see a flock of flamingos in the air, the sunlight blurring their wings in pink and white. They were stately and uncountable, and it was one of the most beautiful things Rosie had ever seen. She looked back at Spider, and looking at him, she could not understand how she had ever believed that this man was Fat Charlie. Where Fat Charlie was easygoing, open and uncomfortable, this man was like a steel rod bent back and ready to snap. 'You really aren't him, are you?'

'I told you I wasn't.'

'So. So who did I. Who have I. Who was it – who did I sleep with?'

'That would be me,' said Spider.

'I thought so,' said Rosie. She slapped him, as hard as she could, across his face. He could feel his lip start bleeding once more.

'I guess I deserved that,' he said.

'Of course you deserved it.' She paused. Then she said, 'Did Fat Charlie know about this? About you? That you were going out with me?'

'Well, yes. But he—'

'You are both sick,' she said. 'Sick, sick evil men. I hope you rot in Hell.'

She took one last puzzled glance around the enormous bedroom, and then out of the bedroom window at the jungle trees and the huge waterfall and the flock of flamingos, and walked away down the hall.

Spider sat down on the floor, with a thin trickle of blood coming from his lower lip, feeling stupid. He heard the front door slam. He walked over to the hot tub, and dipped the end of a fluffy towel into the hot water. Then he wrung it out and put it on his mouth. 'I don't need any of this,' said Spider. He said it aloud; it's easier to lie to yourself when you say things out loud. 'I didn't need any of you people a week ago and I don't need you now. I don't care. I'm done.'

The flamingos hit the window-glass like feathery, pink cannonballs, and the glass shattered, fragments of window flying across the room, scattering themselves and embedding themselves in the walls, the floor, the bed. The air was filled with plummeting pale-pink bodies, a confusion of huge pink wings and curved black beaks. The roar of a waterfall exploded into the room.

Spider pushed back against the wall. There were flamingos between him and the door, hundreds of them: five-foot-tall birds, all legs and neck. He got to his feet, and took several steps through a minefield of angry pink birds, each of them glowering at him through mad pink eyes. From a distance, they might have been beautiful. One of them snapped at Spider's hand. It didn't break the skin, but it hurt.

Spider's bedroom was a large room, but it was rapidly filling with crash-landing flamingos. And there was a dark cloud in the blue sky above the waterfall, that appeared to be another flock on its way.

They were pecking at him, and clawing at him, and buffeting him with their wings, and he knew that that was not actually the problem. The problem would be being suffocated under a fluffy pink blanket of feathers, with birds attached. It would be an astonishingly undignified way to go, crushed by birds, and not even particularly intelligent birds.

Think, he told himself. *They're flamingos. Bird-brains. You're Spider.*

So? he thought back at himself, irritated. *Tell me something I don't know.*

The flamingos on the ground were mobbing him. The ones in the air were diving towards him. He pulled his jacket over his head, and then the airborne flamingos began hitting him. It was like having someone firing chickens at you. He staggered and went down. *Well, trick them, stupid.*

Spider pushed himself to his feet, and waded through the sea of wings and beaks, until he reached the window, now an open jaw of jagged glass.

'Stupid birds,' he said, cheerfully. He pulled himself up on to the windowledge.

Flamingos are not famed for their cutting intelligence, nor for their problem-solving abilities: confronted with a twist of wire, and a bottle with something edible in it, a crow might try to make a tool out of the wire in order to get at the contents of the bottle. A flamingo, on the other hand, would try and eat the wire, if it looked like a shrimp, or possibly even if it didn't, just in case it was a new kind of shrimp. So if there was something slightly *smoky* and insubstantial about the man who stood on the windowledge insulting them, the flamingos failed to perceive it. They glared at him with the crazed pink eyes of killer rabbits, and they rushed towards him.

The man dived from the window, down into the spray of the waterfall, and a thousand flamingos launched themselves into the air after him, many of them, given the run-up a flamingo needs to get properly airborne, tumbling like stones.

Soon the bedroom contained only injured or dead flamingos: the ones who had broken the windows, the ones who had crashed into the walls, the ones who had been crushed beneath other flamingos. Those of the birds who were still alive watched the bedroom door open, apparently by itself, and close again, but, being flamingos, they thought very little of it.

Spider stood in the corridor of Fat Charlie's flat and tried to catch his breath. He concentrated on letting the bedroom stop existing, which was something that he hated to do, mostly because he was incredibly proud of his sound system, and also because it was where he kept his stuff.

You can always get more stuff, though.

If you're Spider, all you really have to do is ask.

* * *

Rosie's mother was not a woman given to gloating loudly, so when Rosie broke down in tears on the Chippendale sofa her mother refrained from whooping, from singing or from doing a small victory dance and then shimmying around the room. A careful observer, however, might have noticed a glint of triumph in her eyes.

She gave Rosie a large glass of vitaminised water with an ice-cube in it, and listened to her daughter's tearful litany of heartbreak and deception. By the end of it, the glint of triumph had been replaced with a look of confusion, and her head was starting to spin.

'So Fat Charlie wasn't really Fat Charlie?' said Rosie's mother.

'No. Well, yes. Fat Charlie *is* Fat Charlie, but for the last week I've been seeing his brother.'

'They are twins?'

'No. I don't even think they look alike. I don't know. I'm so confused.'

'So which one of them did you break up with?'

Rosie blew her nose. 'I broke up with Spider. That's Fat Charlie's brother.'

'But you weren't engaged to him.'

'No, but I thought I was. I thought he was Fat Charlie.'

'So you broke up with Fat Charlie as well?'

'Sort of. I just haven't told him yet.'

'Did he, did he know about this, this brother thing? Was it some kind of evil kinky conspiracy they did to my poor girl?'

'I don't think so. But it doesn't matter. I can't marry him.'

'No,' agreed her mother. 'You certainly cannot. Not one bit.' Inside, in her head, she did a victory jig, and set off a large but tasteful celebratory display of fireworks. 'We can find you a good boy. Don't you worry. That Fat Charlie. He was always up to no good. I knew it the first moment I saw him. He ate my wax fruit. I knew he was trouble. Where is he now?'

'I'm not sure. Spider said he might have been taken away by the police,' said Rosie.

'*Hah!*' said her mother, who increased the fireworks in her head to New Year's Eve at Disneyland proportions, and mentally sacrificed a dozen flawless black bulls for good measure. Aloud, all she said was, 'Probably in prison, if you ask me. Best place for him. I always said that was where that young man would end up.'

Rosie began to cry, if anything even harder than before. She pulled out another wodge of paper tissues and blew her nose with an extreme honk. She swallowed bravely. Then she cried some more. Her mother patted the back of Rosie's hand as reassuringly as she knew how. 'Of course you can't marry him,' she said. 'You can't marry a convict. But if he's in prison you can easily break off the engagement.' A spectre of a smile haunted the corners of her lips as she said, 'I could call on him for you. Or go there on a visitors' day and tell him he's a lousy crook and you never want to see him again. We could get a restraining order, as well,' she added helpfully.

'Th-that's not why I can't marry Fat Charlie,' said Rosie.

'No?' asked her mother, raising one perfectly pencilled eyebrow.

'No,' said Rosie. 'I can't marry Fat Charlie because I'm not in love with him.'

'Of course you aren't. I always knew that. It was a girlish infatuation, but now you see the true—'

'I'm in love,' continued Rosie, as if her mother had not spoken, 'with Spider. His brother.' The expression that made its way across her mother's face then was a cloud of wasps arriving at a picnic. 'It's OK,' said Rosie. 'I'm not going to marry him, either. I've told him I never want to see him again.'

Rosie's mother pursed her lips. 'Well,' she said, 'I can't pretend I understand any of this, but I can't say it's bad news either.' The gears in her head shifted and the cogs interlocked in new and interesting ways: ratchets ratcheted and springs resprung. 'You know,' she said, 'what would be the best thing for you right now? Have you thought about taking a little holiday? I'm happy to pay for it, all the money I'm saving on the wedding after all . . .'

That may have been the wrong thing to say. Rosie began to sob into her tissues once again. Her mother went on, 'Anyway, it would be my treat. I know you've got holiday time you haven't used at work. And you said things were quiet right now. At a time like this, a girl needs to get away from everything and simply relax.'

Rosie wondered whether she'd misjudged her mother all these years. She sniffed and swallowed and said, 'That would be nice.'

'Then it's settled,' said her mother. 'I shall come with you, to take care of my baby.' In her head, underneath the grand finale of the fireworks display, she added, *And to make sure that my baby only meets the right sort of man.*

'Where are we going?' asked Rosie.

'We're going to go,' said her mother, 'on a cruise.'

＊

Fat Charlie was not handcuffed. That was good. Everything else
was bad, but at least he wasn't in handcuffs. Life had become a
confused blur, filled with too-sharp details: the duty sergeant
scratching his nose and signing him in – 'Cell six is free' – through
a green door and then the smell of the cells, a low-level stench
he had never before encountered but which was immediately
and horribly familiar, a pervasive fug of yesterday's vomit and
disinfectant and smoke and stale blankets and unflushed toilets
and despair. It was the smell of things at the bottom, and that was
where Fat Charlie seemed to have ended up.

'When you need to flush the lavvy,' said the policeman
accompanying him down the corridor, 'you press the button in
your cell. One of us'll be by, sooner or later, to pull the chain for
you. Stops you trying to flush away the evidence.'

'Evidence of what?'

'Leave it out, sunshine.'

Fat Charlie sighed. He'd been flushing away his own bodily
waste products since he'd been old enough to take a certain pride
in the activity, and the loss of that, more than the loss of his
liberty, told him that everything had changed.

'It's your first time,' said the policeman.

'Sorry.'

'Drugs?' said the policeman.

'No, thank you,' said Fat Charlie.

'Is that what you're in for?'

'I don't know what I'm in for,' said Fat Charlie. 'I'm innocent.'

'White-collar crime, eh?' said the policeman, and he shook his
head. 'I'll tell you something the blue-collar boys know without
being told. The easier you make it on us, the easier we make it on
you. You white-collar people. Always standing up for your rights.
You just make it harder on yourselves.'

He opened the door to cell six. 'Home, sweet home,' he said.

The cell-stench was worse inside the room, which had been
painted in the kind of speckled paint that resists graffiti, and
which contained only a shelf-like bed, low to the ground, and a
lidless toilet in the corner.

Fat Charlie put the blanket he'd been issued down on the bed.

'Right,' said the policeman. 'Well. Make yourself at home. And if you get bored, please don't block the toilet with your blanket.'

'Why would I do that?'

'I often wonder that myself,' said the policeman. 'Why indeed? Perhaps it breaks the monotony. I shouldn't know. Being a law-abiding sort with a police pension waiting for me, I've never actually had to spend much time in the cells.'

'You know, I didn't do it,' said Fat Charlie. 'Whatever it was.'

'That's good,' said the policeman.

'Excuse me,' said Fat Charlie. 'Do I get anything to read?'

'Does this look like a lending library to you?'

'No.'

'When I was a young copper, bloke asked me for a book, I went and found him the book I'd been reading. J. T. Edson, it was, or maybe Louis L'Amour. He only went and blocked up his toilet with it, didn't he? Won't catch me doing that again in a hurry.'

Then he went out, and locked the door, with Fat Charlie on the inside and himself on the outside.

***

The oddest thing, thought Grahame Coats, who was not given to self-inspection, was how normal, and chipper, and generally good he felt.

The captain told them to fasten their safety belts, and mentioned that they would be landing soon on Saint Andrews. Saint Andrews was a small Caribbean island which, on declaring independence in 1962, had elected to demonstrate its freedom from colonial rule in a number of ways, including the creation of its own judiciary and a singular lack of extradition treaties with the rest of the world.

The plane landed. Grahame Coats got off and walked across the sunny tarmac dragging his wheeled bag behind him. He produced the appropriate passport – Basil Finnegan's – and had it stamped, collected the rest of his luggage from the carousel, and walked out through an unattended customs hall, into the tiny airport and from there into the glorious sunshine. He wore a T-shirt and shorts and sandals and looked like a British Holidaymaker Abroad.

His groundskeeper was waiting for him outside the airport, and Grahame Coats sat himself in the back of the black Mercedes and said, 'Home, please.' On the road out of Williamstown, the road to his clifftop estate, he stared out at the island with a satisfied and proprietorial smile on his face.

It occurred to him that before he left England he had left a woman for dead. He wondered if she was still alive; he rather doubted it. It did not bother him to have killed. It felt instead, immensely satisfying, like something he had needed to do to feel complete. He wondered if he would ever get to do it again.

He wondered if it would be soon.

Chapter Ten

In Which Fat Charlie Sees the World, and Maeve Livingstone Is Dissatisfied

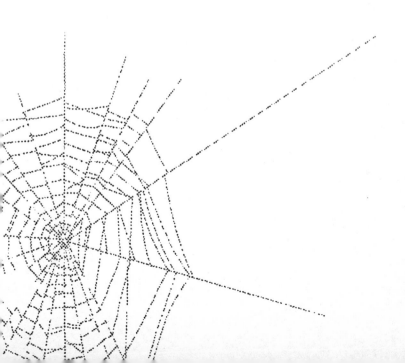

Fat Charlie sat on the blanket on the metal bed and waited for something to happen, but it didn't. What felt like several months passed, extremely slowly. He tried to go to sleep but he couldn't remember how.

He banged on the door.

Someone shouted 'Shut up!' but he couldn't tell whether it was an officer or a fellow inmate.

He walked around the cell for what, at a conservative estimate, he felt must have been two or three years. Then he sat down and let eternity wash over him. Daylight was visible through the thick glass block at the top of the wall that did duty as a window, by all appearances the same daylight that had been visible when the door was locked behind him that morning.

Fat Charlie tried to remember what people did in prison to pass the time, but all he could come up with was keeping secret diaries and hiding things in their bottoms. He had nothing to write on, and felt that a definite measure of how well one was getting on in life was not having to hide things in one's bottom.

Nothing happened. Nothing continued to happen. More

Nothing. The Return of Nothing. Son of Nothing. Nothing Rides Again. Nothing and Abbott and Costello meet the Wolfman . . .

When the door was unlocked, Fat Charlie nearly cheered.

'Right. Exercise yard. You can have a cigarette if you need one.'

'I don't smoke.'

'Filthy habit anyway.'

The exercise yard was an open space in the middle of the police station, surrounded by walls on all sides and topped by wire mesh, which Fat Charlie walked around while deciding that, if there was one thing he didn't like being in, it was police custody. Fat Charlie had had no real liking for the police, but, until now, he had still managed to cling to a fundamental trust in the natural order of things, a conviction that there was some kind of power – a Victorian might have thought of it as Providence – that ensured that the guilty would be punished, while the innocent would be set free. This faith had collapsed in the face of recent events, and had been replaced by the suspicion that he would spend the rest of his life pleading his innocence to a variety of implacable judges and tormenters, many of whom would look like Daisy, and that he would in all probability wake up in cell six the following morning to find that he had been transformed into an enormous cockroach. He had definitely been transported to the kind of maleficent universe that transformed people into cockroaches . . .

Something dropped out of the sky above him, on to the wire mesh. Fat Charlie looked up. A blackbird stared down at him, with lofty disinterest. There was more fluttering, and the blackbird was joined by several sparrows, and by something that Fat Charlie thought was probably a thrush.

They stared at him, he stared back at them.

More birds came.

It would have been hard for Fat Charlie to say exactly when the accumulation of birds on the wire mesh moved from interesting to terrifying. It was somewhere in the first hundred or so, anyway. And it was in the way they didn't coo, or caw, or trill, or sing. They simply landed on the wire and they watched him.

'Go away,' said Fat Charlie.

As one bird, they didn't. Instead, they spoke. They said his name.

Fat Charlie went over to the door in the corner. He banged on it. He said, 'Excuse me,' a few times, and then he started shouting 'Help!'

A clunk. The door was opened, and a heavy-lidded member of Her Majesty's constabulary said, 'This had better be good.'

Fat Charlie pointed upwards. He didn't say anything. He didn't need to. The constabular mouth dropped open peculiarly wide, and it hung there slackly. Fat Charlie's mother would have told the man to shut his mouth or something would fly into it.

The mesh sagged under the weight of thousands of birds. Tiny avian eyes stared down, unblinkingly.

'Christ on a bike,' said the policeman, and he ushered Fat Charlie back into the cell-block without saying another word.

* * *

Maeve Livingstone was in pain. She was sprawled on the floor. She woke, and her hair and face were wet and warm, and then she slept, and when next she woke her hair and face were sticky and cold. She dreamed and woke and dreamed again, woke enough to be conscious of the hurt at the back of her head, and then, because it was easier to sleep, and because when she slept it did not hurt, she allowed sleep to embrace her like a comfortable blanket.

In her dreams she was walking through a television studio, looking for Morris. Occasionally she would catch glimpses of him on the monitors. He always looked concerned. She tried to find her way out, but all ways led her back to the studio floor.

I'm so cold, she thought, and knew that she was awake once more. The pain, though, had subsided. All things considered, thought Maeve, she felt pretty good.

There was something she was upset about, but she was not entirely sure what it was. Perhaps it had been another part of her dream.

It was dark, wherever she was. It seemed to be some kind of broom closet, and she put out her arms to avoid bumping into anything in the darkness. She took a few nervous steps with her arms outstretched and her eyes closed, then she opened her eyes. Now she was in a room she knew. It was an office.

Grahame Coats's office.

She remembered then. The just-awake grogginess was still there – she wasn't yet thinking clearly, knew she wouldn't be properly all there until she had had her morning cup of coffee – but still, it came to her: Grahame Coats's perfidiousness, his treachery, his criminality, his . . .

. . . *why*, she thought, *he assaulted me. He hit me.* And then she thought, *The police. I should call the police.*

She reached down for the phone on the table and picked it up, or tried to, but the phone seemed very heavy, or slippery, or both, and she was unable to grasp it properly. It felt wrong for her fingers.

I must be weaker than I thought, Maeve decided. *I had better ask them to send a doctor as well.*

In the pocket of her jacket was a small silver phone which played 'Greensleeves' when it rang. She was relieved to find the phone still there, and that she had no problems at all in holding it. She dialled the emergency services. As she waited for someone to answer she wondered why they still called it 'dialling' when there weren't dials on telephones, not since she was much younger, and then after the phones with dials came the Trimphones with buttons on them and a particularly annoying ring. She had, as a teenager, had a boyfriend who could and continually did imitate the *breep* of a Trimphone, an ability that was, Maeve decided, looking back, his only real achievement. She wondered what had happened to him. She wondered how a man who could imitate a Trimphone coped in a world in which telephones could and did sound like *anything* . . .

'We apologise for the delay in placing your call,' said a mechanical voice. 'Please hold the line.'

Meave felt oddly calm, as if nothing bad could ever happen to her again.

A man's voice came on the line. 'Hello?' it said. It sounded extremely efficient.

'I need the police,' said Maeve.

'You do not need the police,' said the voice. 'All crimes will be dealt with by the appropriate and inevitable authorities.'

'You know,' said Maeve, 'I think I may have dialled the wrong number.'

'Likewise,' said the voice, 'all numbers are, ultimately, correct. They are simply numbers, and cannot thus be right or wrong.'

'That's all very well for you to say,' said Maeve. 'But I *do* need to speak to the police. I may also need an ambulance. And I have obviously called a wrong number.' She ended the call. Perhaps, she thought, 999 didn't work from a mobile. She pulled up her onscreen address book and called her sister's number. The phone rang once, and a now-familiar voice said, 'Let me clarify: I am not saying that you dialled a wrong number on purpose. What I trust that I am saying, is that all numbers are by their nature correct. Well, except for *pi*, of course. I can't be doing with *pi*. Gives me a headache just thinking about it, going on and on and on and on and on . . .'

Maeve pressed the red button and ended the call. She dialled her bank manager.

The voice that answered said, 'But here am I, wittering on about the correctness of numbers, and you're undoubtedly thinking that there's a time and a place for everything . . .'

Click. Called her best friend.

'. . . and right now what we should be discussing is your ultimate disposition. I'm afraid traffic is extremely heavy this afternoon, so if you wouldn't mind waiting where you are for a little while, you will be collected . . .' It was a reassuring voice, the voice of a radio vicar in the process of telling you his thought for the day.

If Maeve had not felt so placid, she would have panicked then. Instead, she pondered. Seeing that her phone had been – what would they call it, *hacked*? – then she would simply have to go down to the street and find a police officer and make a formal complaint. Nothing happened when Maeve pressed the button for the lift, so she walked down the stairs, thinking that there was probably never a police officer about when you wanted one anyway, they were always zooming about in those cars, the ones that went *neenorneenor*. The police, Maeve thought, should be strolling around in pairs telling people the time, or waiting at the bottom of drainpipes as burglars with bags of swag over their shoulder make their descent . . .

At the very bottom of the stairs, in the hallway, were two police officers, a man and a woman. They were out of uniform, but they were police all right. There was no mistaking them. The man was stout and red-faced, the woman was small and dark, and might, in other circumstances, have been extremely pretty. 'We know she came this far,' the woman was saying. 'The receptionist remembered her coming in, just before lunchtime. When she got back from lunch, they'd both gone.'

'You think they ran off together?' asked the stout man.

'Um, excuse me,' said Maeve Livingstone, politely.

'It's possible. There's got to be some kind of simple explanation. The disappearance of Grahame Coats. The disappearance of Maeve Livingstone. At least we've got Nancy in custody.'

'We certainly did *not* run off together,' said Maeve, but they ignored her.

The two police officers got into the lift and slammed the doors behind them. Maeve watched them judder up and away, towards the top floor.

She was still holding her mobile phone. It vibrated in her hand now, and then began to play 'Greensleeves'. She glanced down at it. Morris's photograph filled the screen. Nervously, she answered the phone. 'Yes?'

''Ullo, love. How's tricks?'

She said, 'Fine, thank you.' Then she said, 'Morris?' And then, 'No, it's not fine. It's all awful, actually.'

'Aye,' said Morris. 'I thought it might be. Still, nothing that can be done about that now. Time to move on.'

'Morris? *Where* are you calling from?'

'It's a bit complicated,' he said. 'I mean, I'm not actually on the phone. Just really wanted to help you along.'

'Grahame Coats,' she said. 'He was a crook.'

'Yes, love,' said Morris. 'But it's time to let all that go. Put it behind you.'

'He hit me on the back of the head,' she told him. 'And he's been stealing our money.'

'It's only material things, love,' said Morris, reassuringly. 'Now you're beyond the vale . . .'

'Morris,' said Maeve. 'That pestilent little worm attempted to murder your wife. I *do* think you should try to show a little more concern.'

'Don't be like that, love. I'm just trying to explain . . .'

'I have to tell you, Morris, that if you're going to take that kind of attitude, I'll simply deal with this myself. I'm certainly not going to forget about it. It's all right for you, you're dead. You don't have to worry about these things.'

'You're dead too, love.'

'That is *quite* beside the point,' she said. Then, 'I'm what?' And then, before he could say anything, Maeve said, 'Morris, I said that he *attempted* to murder me. Not that he succeeded.'

'Erm,' the late Morris Livingstone sounded lost for words. 'Maeve. Love. I know this may come as a bit of a shock to you, but the truth of the matter is that—'

The telephone made a 'plibble' noise, and the image of an empty battery appeared on the screen.

'I'm afraid I didn't get that, Morris,' she told him. 'I think the telephone battery is going.'

'You don't have a phone battery,' he told her. 'You don't have a phone. All is illusion. I keep trying to tell you, you've now transcended the vale of oojamaflip, and now you're becoming, oh heck, it's like worms and butterflies, love. You know.'

'Caterpillars,' said Maeve. 'I think you mean caterpillars and butterflies.'

'Er, that sounds right,' said Morris's voice, over the telephone. 'Caterpillars. That was what I meant. So what do worms turn into, then?'

'They don't turn into anything, Morris,' said Maeve, a little testily. 'They're just worms.' The silver phone emitted a small noise, like an electronic burp, showed the picture of an empty battery again, and turned itself off.

Maeve closed it and put it back into her pocket. She walked over to the nearest wall and, experimentally, pushed a finger against it. The wall felt clammy and gelatinous to the touch. She exerted a little more pressure, and her whole hand went into it. Then it went through it.

'Oh dear,' she said, and felt herself, not for the first time in her existence, wishing that she had listened to Morris, who after all, she admitted to herself, by now probably knew rather more about being dead than she did. *Ah well*, she thought. Being dead was probably just like everything else in life: you pick some of it up as you go along, and you just make up the rest.

She walked out the front door, and found herself coming through the wall at the back of the hall, into the building. She tried again, with the same result. Then she walked into the travel agency that occupied the bottom floor of the building, and tried pushing through the wall on the west of the building.

She went through it, and came out in the front hall again, entering from the east. It was like being in a TV set and trying to walk off the screen. Topographically speaking, the office building seemed to have become her universe.

She went back upstairs to see what the detectives were doing. They were staring at the desk, at the debris that Grahame Coats had left when he was packing.

'You know,' said Maeve helpfully, 'I'm in a room behind the bookcase. I'm in there.'

They ignored her.

The woman crouched down and rummaged in the bin. 'Bingo,' she said, and pulled out a man's white shirt, spattered with dried blood. She placed it into a plastic bag. The stout man pulled out his mobile phone.

'I want Forensic down here,' he said.

*　*　*

Fat Charlie now found himself viewing his cell as a refuge rather than as a prison. Cells were deep inside the building, for a start, far from the haunts of even the most adventurous birds. And his brother was nowhere to be seen. He no longer minded that nothing ever happened in cell six. Nothing was infinitely preferable to most of the somethings he found himself coming up with. Even a world populated exclusively with castles and cockroaches and people named K was preferable to a world filled with malignant birds that whispered his name in chorus.

The door opened.

'Don't you knock?' asked Fat Charlie.

'No,' said the policeman. 'We don't, actually. Your solicitor's finally here.'

'Mr Merryman?' said Fat Charlie, and then he stopped. Leonard Merryman was a rotund gentleman with small gold spectacles, and the man behind the cop most definitely wasn't.

'Everything's fine,' said the man who wasn't his solicitor. 'You can leave us here.'

'Buzz when you're done,' said the policeman, and he closed the door.

Spider took Fat Charlie by the hand. He said, 'I'm busting you out of here.'

'But I don't want to be busted out of here. I didn't *do* anything.'

'Good reason for getting out.'

'But if I leave then I *will* have done something. I'll be an escaped prisoner.'

'You're not a prisoner,' said Spider, cheerfully. 'You've not been charged with anything yet. You're just helping them with their inquiries. Look, are you hungry?'

'A bit.'

'What do you want? Tea? Coffee? Hot chocolate?'

Hot chocolate sounded extremely good to Fat Charlie. 'I'd love a hot chocolate,' he said.

'Right,' said Spider. He grabbed Fat Charlie's hand, and said, 'Close your eyes.'

'Why?'

'It makes it easier.'

Fat Charlie closed his eyes, although he was not certain what it would make easier. The world stretched and squeezed and Fat Charlie was certain that he was going to be sick. Then the inside of his mind settled down and he felt a warm breeze touch his face.

He opened his eyes.

They were in the open air, in a large market square, somewhere that looked extremely un-English.

'Where is this?'

'I think it's called Skopsie. Town in Italy or somewhere. I started coming here years ago. They do amazing hot chocolate here. Best I've ever had.'

They sat down at a small wooden table. It was painted fire-engine red. A waiter approached and said something to them in a language that didn't sound like Italian to Fat Charlie. Spider said, '*Dos Chocolatos*, dude,' and the man nodded and went away.

'Right,' said Fat Charlie. 'You've got me into even deeper trouble. Now they'll probably have to do a manhunt or something. It'll be in the papers.'

'What are they going to do?' asked Spider, with a smile. 'Send you to gaol?'

'Oh please.'

The hot chocolate arrived, and the waiter poured it into small cups. It was roughly the same temperature as molten lava, was halfway between a chocolate soup and a chocolate custard, and it smelled astonishingly good.

Spider said, 'Look, we've made rather a mess of this whole family reunion business, haven't we?'

'*We*'ve made rather a mess of it?' Fat Charlie managed outrage extremely well. '*I* wasn't the one who stole my fiancée. *I* wasn't the one who got me sacked from work. *I* wasn't the one who got me arrested—'

'No,' said Spider. 'But you were the one who brought the birds into it, weren't you?'

Fat Charlie took a very small initial sip of his hot chocolate. 'Ow. I think I've just burned my mouth.' He looked at his brother and saw his own expression staring back at him: worried, tired, frightened. 'Yes, I was the one who brought the birds into it. So what do we do now?'

Spider said, 'They do a really nice sort of noodly-stew thing here, by the way.'

'Are you sure we're in Italy?'

'Not really.'

'Can I ask you a question?'

Spider nodded.

Fat Charlie tried to think of the best way to put it. 'The bird thing. Where they all turn up and pretend they've escaped from an Alfred Hitchcock film. Do you think it's something that only happens in England?'

'Why?'

'Because I think those pigeons have noticed us.' He pointed to the far end of the square.

The pigeons were not doing the things that pigeons usually do. They were not pecking at sandwich crusts or bobbing along with their heads down hunting for tourist-dropped food. They were standing quite still, and they were staring. A clatter of wings and they were joined by another hundred birds, most of them landing on the statue of a fat man wearing an enormous hat that dominated the centre of the square. Fat Charlie looked at the pigeons, and the pigeons looked back at him. 'So what's the worst that could happen?' he asked Spider, in an undertone. 'They crap all over us?'

'I don't know. But I expect they can do worse than that. Finish your hot chocolate.'

'But it's *hot.*'

'And we'll need a couple of bottles of water, won't we? *Garçon?*'

A low susurrus of wings; the clack of more arriving birds; and beneath it all, low, burbling secretive coos.

The waiter brought them bottles of water. Spider, who was, Fat Charlie observed, now wearing his black and red leather jacket once more, put them into his pockets.

'They're only pigeons,' said Fat Charlie, but even as he said it, he knew the words were inadequate. They were not just pigeons. They were an army. The statue of the fat man had almost vanished from view beneath the grey and purple feathers.

'I think I preferred birds before they thought about ganging up on us.'

Spider said, 'And they're everywhere.' Then he grabbed Fat Charlie's hand. 'Close your eyes.'

The birds rose as one bird, then. Fat Charlie closed his eyes.

The pigeons came down like the wolf on the fold . . .

There was silence, and distance, and Fat Charlie thought, *I'm in an oven.* He opened his eyes and realised that it was true: an oven with red dunes that receded into the distance until they faded into a sky the colour of mother-of-pearl.

'Desert,' said Spider. 'Seemed like a good idea. Bird-free zone. Somewhere to finish a conversation. Here.' He handed Fat Charlie a bottle of water.

'Thanks.'

'So. Would you like to tell me where the birds come from?'

Fat Charlie said, 'There's this place. I went there. There were lots of animal-people there. They, um. They all knew Dad. One of them was a woman, a sort of bird woman.'

Spider looked at him. ' "There's this place"? That's not exactly very helpful.'

'There's a mountainside with caves in it. And then there are these cliffs, and they go down into nothing. It's like the end of the world.'

'It's the beginning of the world,' corrected Spider. 'I've heard of the caves. A girl I knew once told me all about them. Never been there, though. So you met the Bird Woman, and . . . ?'

'She offered to make you go away. And, um. Well, I took her up on it.'

'That,' said Spider, with a movie-star smile, 'was really stupid.'

'I didn't tell her to *hurt* you.'

'What did you think she was going to do to get rid of me? Write me a stiff letter?'

'I don't know. I didn't think. I was upset.'

'Great. Well, if she has her way, you'll be upset and I'll be dead. You could have simply asked me to leave, you know.'

'I did!'

'Er. What did I say?'

'That you liked it in my house and you weren't going anywhere.'

Spider drank some of the water. 'So what *exactly* did you say to her?'

Fat Charlie tried to remember. Now he thought about it, it seemed an odd sort of thing to say. 'Just that I was going to give her Anansi's bloodline,' he said, reluctantly.

'You what?'

'It was what she asked me to say.'

Spider looked incredulous. 'But that's not just me. That's both of us.'

Fat Charlie's mouth was suddenly very dry. He hoped it was the desert air, and sipped his bottled water.

'Hang on. Why the desert?' asked Fat Charlie.

'No birds. Remember?'

'So what are those?' He pointed. At first they looked tiny, and then you realised that they were simply very high: they were circling, and wobbling on the wing.

'Vultures,' said Spider. 'They don't attack living things.'

'Right. And pigeons are scared of people,' said Fat Charlie. The dots in the sky circled lower, and the birds appeared to grow as they descended.

Spider said, 'Point taken.' Then, 'Shit.'

They weren't alone. Someone was watching them on a distant dune. A casual observer might have mistaken the figure for a scarecrow.

Fat Charlie shouted, 'Go away!' His voice was swallowed by the sand. 'I take it all back. We don't have a deal! Leave us alone!'

A flutter of overcoat on the hot wind, and the dune was now deserted.

Fat Charlie said, 'She went away. Who would have thought it was going to be that simple?'

Spider touched his shoulder, and pointed. Now the woman in the brown overcoat was standing on the nearest ridge of sand, so close that Fat Charlie could see the glassy blacks of her eyes.

The vultures were raggedy black shadows, and then they landed: their naked mauve necks and scalps – featherless because that's so much easier when you're putting your head into rotting carcasses – extended as they stared short-sightedly at the brothers, as if wondering whether to wait until the two men died or if they should do something to hurry the process along.

Spider said, 'What else was there in the deal?'

'Um?'

'Was there anything else? Did she give you something to seal the bargain? Sometimes things like this involve a trade.'

The vultures were edging forward, a step at a time, closing their ranks, tightening the circle. There were more black slashes in the sky, growing and wobbling towards them. Spider's hand closed around Fat Charlie's hand.

'Close your eyes.'

The cold hit Fat Charlie like a punch to the gut. He took a deep breath and felt like someone had iced his lungs. He coughed and coughed, while the wind howled like a great beast.

He opened his eyes. 'Can I ask where we are this time?'

'Antarctica,' said Spider. He zipped up the front of his leather jacket, and did not seem to mind the cold. 'It's a bit chilly, I'm afraid.'

'Don't you have any middle gears? Straight from desert to ice field.'

'No birds here,' said Spider.

'Wouldn't it be easier just to go and sit inside a building that's nice and bird free? We could have lunch.'

Spider said, 'Right. Now you're complaining, just because it's a little bit nippy.'

'It's *not* a little bit nippy. It's fifty below. And anyway, *look.*'

Fat Charlie pointed at the sky. A pale squiggle, like a miniature letter m chalked on to the sky, hung unmoving in the cold air. 'Albatross,' he said.

'Frigate,' said Spider.

'Pardon?'

'It's not an albatross. It's a frigate. He probably hasn't even noticed us.'

'Possibly not,' admitted Fat Charlie. 'But *they* have.'

Spider turned, and said something else that sounded a lot like 'frigate'. There may not have been a million penguins waddling and slipping and bellysliding towards the brothers, but it certainly looked that way. As a general rule, the only things properly terrified by the approach of penguins tend to be smallish fish, but when the numbers get large enough . . .

Fat Charlie reached out without being told, and he held Spider's hand. He closed his eyes.

When he opened them, he was somewhere warmer, although opening his eyes made no difference to what he saw. Everything was the colour of night. 'Have I gone blind?'

'We're in a disused coal mine,' said Spider. 'I saw a photo of this place in a magazine a few years back. Unless there are flocks of sightless finches who have evolved to take advantage of the darkness and eat coal-chips, we're probably fine.'

'That's a joke isn't it? About the sightless finches?'

'More or less.'

Fat Charlie sighed, and the sigh echoed through the underground cavern. 'You know,' he said, 'if you'd just gone away, if you'd left my house when I asked you to, we'd not be in this mess.'

'That isn't very helpful.'

'It wasn't meant to be. God knows how I'm going to explain all this to Rosie.'

Spider cleared his throat. 'I don't think you'll have to worry about that.'

'Because . . . ?'

'She's broken up with us.'

There was a long silence. Then Fat Charlie said, 'Of course she has.'

'I made a kind of a sort of a mess of that part of things.' Spider sounded uncomfortable.

'But what if I explain it to her? I mean, if I tell her that I wasn't you, that you were pretending to be me—'

'I already did. That was when she decided she didn't want to see either of us ever again.'

'Me as well?'

''Fraid so.'

'Look,' said Spider's voice in the darkness. 'I really never meant to make . . . Well, when I came to see you, all I wanted to do was say hello. Not to. Um. I've pretty much completely cocked this all up, haven't I?'

'Are you trying to say sorry?'

Silence. Then, 'I guess. Maybe.'

More silence. Fat Charlie's said, 'Well, then I'm really sorry I called the Bird Woman to get rid of you.' Not seeing Spider while they were talking made it easier, somehow.

'Yeah. Thanks. I just wish I knew how to get rid of her.'

'*A feather!*' said Fat Charlie.

'No, you've lost me.'

'You asked if she gave me anything to seal the deal. She did. She gave me a feather.'

'Where is it?'

Fat Charlie tried to remember. 'I'm not sure. I had it when I woke up in Mrs Dunwiddy's front room. I didn't have it when I got on the plane. I suppose that Mrs Dunwiddy must still have it.'

The silence that met this was long and dark and unbroken. Fat Charlie began to worry that Spider had gone away, that he had been left abandoned in the darkness under the world. Eventually, he said 'Are you still there?'

'Still here.'

'That's a relief. If you abandoned me down here I don't know how I'd get out.'

'Don't tempt me.'

More silence.

Fat Charlie said, 'What country are we in?'

'Poland, I think. Like I said, I saw a picture of it. Only they had the lights on in the photo.'

'You need to see photos of places to go to them?'

'I need to know where they are.'

It was astounding, thought Fat Charlie, how truly quiet it was in the mine. The place had its own special silence. He started to wonder about silences. Was the silence of the grave different in kind to the silence of, say, outer space?

Spider said, 'I remember Mrs Dunwiddy. She smells of violets.' People have said, 'All hope has fled. We're going to die,' with more enthusiasm.

'That's her,' said Fat Charlie. 'Small, old as the hills. Thick glasses. I suppose we'll just have to go and get the feather from her. Then we'll give it back to the Bird Woman. She'll call off this nightmare.' Fat Charlie finished the last of the bottled water, carried here from the little square somewhere that wasn't Italy. He screwed the top back on to the bottle, and put the empty bottle down into the darkness, wondering if it was littering if no one was ever going to see it. 'So let's hold hands and go and see Mrs Dunwiddy.'

Spider made a noise. The noise was not cocky. It was unsettled and unsure. In the darkness Fat Charlie imagined Spider deflating, like a bullfrog or a week-old balloon. Fat Charlie had wanted to see Spider taken down a peg; he had not wanted to hear him make a noise like a terrified six-year-old. 'Hang on. You're scared of Mrs Dunwiddy?'

'I . . . I can't go near her.'

'Well, if it's any consolation I was scared of her too when I was a kid, and then I met her again at the funeral and she wasn't that bad. Not really. She's just an old lady.' In his mind she lit the black candles once more, and sprinkled the herbs into the bowl. 'Maybe a bit spooky. But you'll be OK when you see her.'

'She made me go away,' said Spider. 'I didn't want to go. But I broke this ball in her garden. Big glass thing, like a giant Christmas tree ornament.'

'I did that too. She was pissed.'

'I know.' The voice from the dark was small and worried and confused. 'It was the same time. That was when it all started.'

'Well. Look. It's not the end of the world. You take me to Florida, I can go and get the feather back from Mrs Dunwiddy. I'm not scared. You can stay away.'

'I can't do that. I can't go to where she is.'

'So, what are you trying to say? She's taken out some kind of magical restraining order?'

'More or less. Yes.' Then Spider said, 'I miss Rosie. I'm sorry about. You know.'

Fat Charlie thought about Rosie. He found it peculiarly hard to remember her face. He thought about not having Rosie's mother as his mother-in-law; about the two silhouettes on the curtains in his bedroom window. He said, 'Don't feel bad about it. Well, you can feel bad about it if you want, because you behaved like a complete bastard. But maybe it was all for the best.' There was a twinge in the general region of Fat Charlie's heart, but he knew that he was speaking the truth. It's easier to say true things in the dark.

Spider said, 'You know what doesn't make sense here?'

'Everything?'

'No. Only one thing. I don't understand why the Bird Woman got involved. It doesn't make sense.'

'Dad pissed her off—'

'Dad pissed *everybody* off. She's wrong, though. And if she wanted to kill us, why doesn't she just try to do it?'

'I gave her our bloodline.'

'So you said. No, something else is going on, and I don't get it.' Silence. Then Spider said, 'Hold my hand.'

'Do I need to close my eyes?'

'May as well.'

'Where are we going? The moon?'

'I'm going to take you somewhere safe,' said Spider.

'Oh good,' said Fat Charlie. 'I like safe. Where?'

But then, without even opening his eyes, Fat Charlie knew. The smell was a dead giveaway: unwashed bodies and unflushed toilets, disinfectant, old blankets and apathy.

'I bet I would have been just as safe in a luxury hotel room,' he said aloud, but there was nobody there to hear him. He sat down on the shelf-like bed of cell six, and wrapped the thin blanket around his shoulders. He might have been there for ever.

Half an hour later, someone came and led him to the inter-rogation room.

* * *

'Hello,' said Daisy, with a smile. 'Would you like a cup of tea?'

'You might as well not bother,' said Fat Charlie. 'I've seen the telly. I know how it goes. This is that whole good-cop bad-cop thing, isn't it? You'll give me a cup of tea and some Jaffa cakes, then some big hard-bitten bastard with a hair-trigger temper comes in and shouts at me and pours the tea away and starts eating my Jaffa cakes and then you stop him from physically attacking me, and make him give me my tea and Jaffa cakes back, and in my gratitude I tell you everything you want to know.'

'We could skip all that,' said Daisy, 'and you could just tell us what we want to know. Anyway, we don't have any Jaffa cakes.'

'I told you everything I know,' said Fat Charlie. 'Everything. Grahame Coats gave me a cheque for two grand and told me to take two weeks off. He said he was pleased I'd brought some irregularities to his attention. Then he asked for my password and waved me goodbye. End of story.'

'And you still say you don't know anything about the disappearance of Maeve Livingstone?'

'I don't think I ever actually met her properly. Maybe once when she came through the office. We talked on the phone a few times. She'd want to talk to Grahame Coats. I'd have to tell her the cheque was in the post.'

'Was it?'

'I don't know. I thought it was. Look, you can't believe I had anything to do with her disappearance.'

'No,' she said, cheerfully. 'I don't.'

'Because I honestly don't know what could have – you what?'

'I don't think you had anything to do with Maeve Livingstone's disappearance. I also don't believe that you had anything to do with the financial irregularities being perpetrated at the Grahame Coats Agency, although someone seems to have worked very hard to make it look like you did. But it's pretty obvious that the weird accounting practices and the steady syphoning off of money predates your arrival. You've only been there two years.'

'About that,' said Fat Charlie. He realised that his jaw was open. He closed it.

Daisy said, 'Look, I know that cops in books and movies are mostly idiots, especially if it's the kind of book with a crime-fighting pensioner or a hard-arsed private eye in it. And I'm really sorry that we don't have any Jaffa cakes. But we're not all completely stupid.'

'I didn't say you were,' said Fat Charlie.

'No,' she said. 'But you were thinking it. You're free to go. With an apology if you'd like one.'

'Where did she, um, disappear?' asked Fat Charlie.

'Mrs Livingstone? Well, the last time anyone saw her, she was accompanying Grahame Coats into his office.'

'Ah.'

'I meant it about the cup of tea. Would you like one?'

'Yes. Very much. Um. I suppose your people already checked out the secret room in his office. The one behind the bookcase?'

It is to Daisy's credit that all she said, perfectly calmly, was, 'I don't believe they did.'

'I don't think we were supposed to know about it,' said Fat Charlie, 'but I went in once, and the bookshelf was pushed back, and he was inside. I went away again,' he added. 'I wasn't spying on him or anything.'

Daisy said, 'We can pick up some Jaffa cakes on the way.'

* * *

Fat Charlie wasn't certain that he liked freedom. There was too much open air involved.

'Are you OK?' asked Daisy.

'I'm fine.'

'You seem a bit twitchy.'

'I suppose I am. You'll think this is silly, but I'm a bit. Well, I have a thing about birds.'

'What, a phobia?'

'Sort of.'

'Well, that's the common term for an irrational fear of birds.'

'What do they call a rational fear of birds, then?' He nibbled the Jaffa cake.

There was silence. Daisy said, 'Well, anyway, there aren't any birds in this car.'

She parked the car on the double yellow lines outside the Grahame Coats Agency offices and they went inside together.

* * *

Rosie lay in the sun by the pool on the aft deck of a Korean cruise ship* with a magazine over her head and her mother beside her, trying to remember why she had ever thought a holiday with her mother would be a good idea.

There were no English newspapers on the cruise ship, and Rosie did not miss them. She missed everything else, though. In her mind the cruise was a form of floating purgatory, made bearable only by the islands they visited every day or so. The

---

*The ship had been the *Sunny Archipelago* until an attack of gastric flu had made international news. A cheap attempt to rebrand it without changing the ship's initials done by the chairman of the board, who did not speak English as well as he believed he did, had left the cruise ship rejoicing in the name of the *Squeak Attack*.

other passengers would go ashore and shop, or parasail, or go for rum-sodden trips on floating pirate ships. Rosie, on the other hand, would walk, and talk to people.

She would see people in pain, see people who looked hungry or miserable, and she wanted to help. Everything seemed very fixable to Rosie. It just needed someone to fix it.

* * *

Maeve Livingstone had expected death to be a number of things, but *irritating* had never been one of them. Still, she was irritated. She was tired of being walked through, tired of being ignored and, most of all, tired of not being able to leave the offices in the Aldwych.

'I mean, if I *have* to haunt anywhere,' she said to the receptionist, 'why can't I haunt Somerset House, over the road? Lovely buildings, excellent view over the Thames, several architecturally impressive features. Some very nice little restaurants as well. Even if you don't need to eat any longer, it'd be good for people-watching.'

Annie the receptionist, whose job since the vanishment of Grahame Coats had been to answer the phone in a bored voice and say, 'I'm afraid I don't know' to pretty much any question she was asked, and who, when she was not performing this function, would phone her friends and discuss the mystery in hushed but excitable tones, did not reply to this, as she had not replied to anything Maeve had said to her.

The monotony was broken by the arrival of Fat Charlie Nancy accompanied by the female police officer.

Maeve had always rather liked Fat Charlie, even when his function had been to assure her that a cheque would soon be in the mail, but now she saw things she had never seen before: there were shadows that fluttered about him, always keeping their distance: bad things coming. He looked like a man on the run from something, and it worried her.

She followed them into Grahame Coats's office, and was delighted to see Fat Charlie head straight over to the bookshelf at the back of the room.

'So where's the secret panel?' asked Daisy.

'It's not a panel. It was a door. Behind the bookshelf over here. I don't know. Maybe there's a secret catch or something.'

Daisy looked at the bookshelf. 'Did Grahame Coats ever write an autobiography?' she asked Fat Charlie.

'Not that I've ever heard about.'

She pushed on the leatherbound copy of *My Life by Grahame Coats*. It clicked, and the bookshelf swung away from the wall, revealing a locked door behind it.

'We'll need a locksmith,' she said. 'And I don't really think we need you here any longer, Mr Nancy.'

'Right,' said Fat Charlie. 'Well,' he said, 'it's been, um. Interesting.'

And then he said, 'I don't suppose you'd like. To get some food. With me. One day?'

'Dim sum,' she said. 'Sunday lunchtime. We'll go Dutch. You'll need to be there when they open the doors at eleven-thirty, or we'll have to queue for ages.' She scribbled down the address of a restaurant, and handed it to Fat Charlie. 'Watch out for birds on the way home,' she said.

'I will,' he said. 'See you Sunday.'

***

The locksmith unfolded a black cloth wallet, and took out several slim pieces of metal.

'Honestly,' he said, 'you'd think they'd learn. It's not like good locks are expensive. I mean, you look at that door, lovely piece of work. Solid that is. Take you half a day to get through it with a blow torch. And then they let the whole thing down with a lock that a five-year-old could open with a spoon-handle . . . There we go . . . Easy as falling off the wagon.'

He pulled on the door. The door opened and they saw the thing on the floor.

'Well, for goodness' sake,' said Maeve Livingstone. 'That's not *me*.' She thought she'd have more affection for her body, but she didn't; it reminded her of a dead animal at the side of the road.

Soon enough the room was filled with people. Maeve, who had

never had much patience for detective dramas, was quickly bored, only taking an interest in what was happening when she felt herself being pulled, unarguably, downstairs and out the front door, as the human remains were taken away in a discreet blue plastic bag.

'This is more like it,' said Maeve Livingstone.

She was out.

At least she was out of the office in the Aldwych.

Obviously, she knew, there were rules. There had to be rules. It's just that she wasn't very sure what they were.

She found herself wishing she'd been more religious in life, but she'd never been able to manage it: as a small girl, she had been unable to envision a God who disliked anyone enough to sentence them to an eternity of torture in Hell, mostly for not believing in Him properly, and as she grew up her childhood doubts had solidified into a rocky certainty that Life, from birth to grave, was all there was and that everything else was imaginary. It had been a good belief, and it had allowed her to cope, but now it was being severely tested.

Honestly, she wasn't sure that even a life spent attending the right sort of church would have prepared her for this. Maeve was rapidly coming to the conclusion that in a well-organised world, Death should be like the kind of all-expenses-included luxury vacation where they give you a folder at the start filled with tickets, discount vouchers, schedules, and several phone numbers to ring if you get into trouble.

She didn't walk. She didn't fly. She moved like the wind, like a cold autumn wind that made people shiver as she passed, that stirred the fallen leaves on the pavements.

She went where she always went first, when she came to London, to Selfridges, the department store in Oxford Street. Maeve had worked in the cosmetic department of Selfridges when she was much younger, between dancing jobs, and she had always made a point of going back whenever she could, and buying expensive make-up, just as she had promised herself she would in the old days.

She haunted the make-up department until she was bored, then took a look around home furnishings. She wasn't ever going to get another dining-room table, but really, there wasn't any harm in looking . . .

Then she drifted through the Selfridges home entertainment department, surrounded by television screens of all sizes. Some of the screens were showing the news. The volume was off on each set, but the picture that filled each screen was Grahame Coats. The dislike rose burning hot within her, like molten lava. The picture changed and now she was looking at herself – a clip of her at Morris's side. She recognised it as the 'Give me a fiver and I'll snog you rotten' sketch from *Morris Livingstone, I Presume*.

She wished she could figure out a way to recharge her phone. Even if the only person she could find was the irritating voice that had sounded like a vicar, she thought, she would even have spoken to him. But mostly she just wanted to talk to Morris. He'd know what to do. This time, she thought, she'd let him talk. This time, she'd listen.

'Maeve?'

Morris's face was looking out at her from a hundred television screens. She thought for a heartbeat that she was imagining it, then that it was part of the news, but he looked at her with concern, and said her name again, and she knew it was him.

'Morris . . . ?'

He smiled his famous smile, and every face on every screen focused on her. 'Hullo, love. I was wondering what was taking you so long. Well, it's time for you to come on over.'

'Over?'

'To the other side. Move beyond the vale. Or possibly the veil. Anyway, that.' And he held out a hundred hands from a hundred screens.

She knew that all she needed to do was reach out and take his hand. She surprised herself by saying, 'No, Morris. I don't think so.'

A hundred identical faces looked perplexed. 'Maeve, love. You need to put the flesh behind you.'

'Well, obviously, dear. And I will. I promise I will. As soon as I'm ready.'

'Maeve, you're dead. How much more ready can you be?'

She sighed. 'I've still got a few things to sort out at this end.'

'For instance?'

Maeve pulled herself up to her full height. 'Well,' she said. 'I was planning on finding that Grahame Coats creature and then doing . . . well, whatever it is that ghosts do. I could haunt him or something.'

Morris sounded slightly incredulous. 'You want to haunt Grahame Coats? Whatever for?'

'Because,' she said, 'I'm not done here.' She set her mouth into a line and raised her chin.

Morris Livingstone looked at her from a hundred television screens at the same time, and he shook his head, in a mixture of admiration and exasperation. He had married her because she was her own woman, and had loved her for that reason, but he wished he could, just for once, persuade her of something. Instead, he said, 'Well, I'm not going anywhere, pet. Let us know when you're ready.'

And then he began to fade.

'Morris. Do you have any idea how I go about finding him?' she asked. But the image of her husband had vanished completely, and now the televisions were showing the weather.

* * *

Fat Charlie met Daisy for Sunday dim sum, in a dimly lit restaurant in London's tiny Chinatown.

'You look nice,' he said.

'Thank you,' she said. 'I feel miserable. I've been taken off the Grahame Coats case. It's now a full-scale murder investigation. I reckon I was probably lucky to have been with it as long as I was.'

'Well,' he said brightly, 'if you hadn't been part of it you would never have had the fun of arresting me.'

'There is that.' She had the grace to look slightly rueful.

'Are there any leads?'

'Even if there were,' she said, 'I couldn't possibly tell you about them.' A small cart was trundled over to their table, and Daisy selected several dishes from it. 'There's a theory that he threw himself off the side of a Channel Ferry. That was the last purchase on one of his credit cards – a day-ticket to Dieppe.'

'Do you think that's likely?'

She picked a dumpling up from her plate with her chopsticks, popped it into her mouth.

'No,' she said. 'My guess is that he's gone somewhere with no extradition treaty. Probably Brazil. Killing Maeve Livingstone might have been a spur-of-the-moment thing, but everything else was so meticulous. He had a system in place. Money went into client accounts. Grahame took his fifteen per cent off the top and standing orders ensured that a whole lot more came off the bottom. Lot of foreign cheques never even made it into the client accounts in the first place. What's remarkable is how long he had kept it up.'

Fat Charlie chewed a rice ball with somethng sweet inside it. He said, 'I think you know where he is.'

Daisy stopped chewing her dumpling.

'It was something about the way you said he'd gone to Brazil. Like you know he wasn't there.'

'That would be police business,' she said. 'And I'm afraid I cannot possibly comment. How's your brother?'

'I don't know. I think he's gone. His room wasn't there when I got home.'

'His room?'

'His stuff. He'd taken his stuff. And no sign of him since.' Fat Charlie sipped his jasmine tea. 'I hope he's all right.'

'You think he wouldn't be?'

'Well, he's got the same phobia that I have.'

'The birds thing. Right.' Daisy nodded sympathetically. 'And how's the fiancée, and the future mother-in-law?'

'Um. I don't think either description is, um, currently operative.'

'Ah.'

'They've gone away.'

'Was this because of the arrest?'

'Not as far as I know.'

She looked across at him like a sympathetic pixie. 'I'm sorry.'

'Well,' he said. 'Right now I don't have a job, I don't have a love life, and – thanks mostly to your efforts – the neighbours are now all convinced I'm a yardie hit man. Some of them have started crossing the road to avoid me. On the other hand, my newsagent wants me to make sure the bloke who knocked up his daughter is taught a lesson.'

'What did you tell him?'

'The truth. I don't think he believed me, though. He gave me a free bag of cheese and onion crisps and a pack of Polo mints, and told me there would be more where that came from once I'd done the job.'

'It'll blow over.'

Fat Charlie sighed. 'It's mortifying.'

'Still,' she said. 'It's not as if it's the end of the world.'

They split the bill, and the waiter gave them two fortune cookies with their change.

'What does yours say?' asked Fat Charlie.

' "Persistence will pay off",' she read. 'What about yours?'

'It's the same as yours,' he said. 'Good old persistence.' He crumpled up the fortune into a pea-size ball, and dropped it into his pocket. He walked her down to Leicester Square tube station.

'Looks like it's your lucky day,' said Daisy.

'How do you mean?'

'No birds around,' she said.

As she said it, Fat Charlie realised it was true. There were no pigeons, no starlings. Not even any sparrows.

'But there are *always* birds in Leicester Square.'

'Not today,' she said. 'Maybe they're busy.'

They stopped at the tube, and for one foolish moment Fat Charlie thought that she was going to kiss him goodbye. She didn't. She just smiled and said, 'Bless', and he half-waved at her, an uncertain hand-movement that might have been a wave and could as easily have been an involuntary gesture, and then she was down the stairs and out of sight.

Fat Charlie walked back across Leicester Square, heading for Piccadilly Circus.

He pulled out the fortune cookie slip from his pocket and uncrumpled it. 'Meet you by Eros,' it said, and next to that was a hasty little drawing of something that looked like large asterisk, and might, conceivably, have been a spider.

He scanned the skies and the buildings as he walked, but there

were no birds, and that was strange because there were always
birds in London. There were always birds everywhere.

Spider was sitting beneath the statue, reading the *News of the
World*. He looked up as Fat Charlie approached.

'It's not actually Eros, you know,' said Fat Charlie. 'It's the
statue of Christian Charity.'

'So why is it naked and holding a bow and arrow? That doesn't
seem a particularly charitable or Christian thing to do.'

'I'm just telling you what I read,' said Fat Charlie. 'Where have
you been? I was worried about you.'

'I'm all right. I've just been avoiding birds, trying to get my head
around all this.'

'You've noticed there aren't any birds around today?' said Fat
Charlie.

'I've noticed. I don't really know what to make of it. But I've
been thinking. And you know,' said Spider, 'there's something
wrong with this whole thing.'

'Everything, for a start,' said Fat Charlie.

'No. I mean there's something wrong with the Bird Woman
trying to hurt us.'

'Yup. It's wrong. It's a very, very bad thing to do. Do you want
to tell her, or shall I?'

'Not wrong like that. Wrong like – well, think about it. I mean,
despite the Hitchcock film, birds aren't the best thing to hurt
someone with. They may be death-on-wings for insects but they
really aren't very good at attacking people. Millions of years of
learning that, on the whole, people will probably eat you first.
Their first instinct is to leave us alone.'

'Not all of them,' said Fat Charlie. 'Not vultures. Or ravens. But
they only turn up on the battlefield, when the fighting's done.
Waiting for you to die.'

'What?'

'I said, except for vultures and ravens. I didn't mean
anything . . .'

'No.' Spider concentrated. 'No, it's gone. You made me think of
something, and I almost had it. Look, have you got hold of Mrs
Dunwiddy yet?'

'I phoned Mrs Higgler, but there isn't any answer.'

'Well, go and talk to them.'

'It's all very well for you to say that, but I'm skint. Broke. Cleaned out. I can't keep flying back and forwards across the Atlantic. I don't even have a job any longer. I'm—'

Spider reached into his black and scarlet jacket and pulled out a wallet. He took out a sheaf of notes in an assortment of currencies, pushed them into Fat Charlie's hand. 'Here. This should be enough to get you there and back. Just get the feather.'

Fat Charlie said, 'Listen. Has it occurred to you that maybe Dad isn't dead after all?'

'What?'

'Well, I was thinking. Maybe all this was one of his jokes. It feels like the kind of thing he'd do, doesn't it?'

Spider said, 'I don't know. Could be.'

Fat Charlie said, 'I'm sure it is. That's the first thing I'm going to do. I'm going to head down to his grave and—'

But he said nothing else, because that was when the birds came. They were city birds: sparrows and starlings, pigeons and crows, thousands upon thousands of them, and they wove and wound as they flew like a tapestry, forming a wall of birds coming towards Fat Charlie and Spider down Regent Street. A feathered phalanx huge as the side of a skyscraper, perfectly flat, perfectly impossible, all of it in motion weaving and fluttering and swooping; Fat Charlie saw it, but it would not fit inside his mind, slipping and twisting and thinning the whole time inside his head. He looked up at it and tried to make sense of what he was seeing.

Spider jerked at Fat Charlie's elbow. He shouted, 'Run!'

Fat Charlie turned to run. Spider was methodically folding his newspaper, putting it down on the bin.

'You run too!'

'It doesn't want *you*. Not yet,' said Spider, and he grinned. It was a grin that had, in its time, persuaded more people than you can imagine to do things they did not want to do; and Fat Charlie really wanted to run. 'Get the feather. Get Dad too, if you think he's still around. Just *go*.'

Fat Charlie went.

The wall of birds swirled and transformed, became a

whirlwind of birds, heading for the statue of Eros and the man beneath it. Fat Charlie ran into a doorway and watched as the base of the dark tornado slammed into Spider. Fat Charlie imagined he could hear his brother screaming over the deafening whirr of wings. Maybe he could.

And then the birds dispersed and the street was empty. The wind teased a handful of feathers along the grey pavement.

Fat Charlie stood there and felt sick. If any of the passers-by had noticed what had happened, they had not reacted. Somehow, he was certain that no one had seen it but him.

There was a woman standing beneath the statue, near where his brother had been. Her ragged brown coat flapped in the wind. Fat Charlie walked back to her. 'Look,' he said, 'when I said to make him go away, I meant just to get him out of my life. Not do whatever it is you've done to him.'

She looked into his face and said nothing. There is a madness in the eyes of some birds of prey, a ferocity that can be perfectly intimidating. Fat Charlie tried not to be intimidated by it. 'I made a mistake,' he said. 'I'm willing to pay for it. Take me instead. Bring him back.'

She continued to stare. Then she said, 'Do not doubt your turn shall come, Compé Anansi's child. In time.'

'Why do you want him?'

'I don't want him,' she told him. 'Why would I want him? I had an obligation to another. Now I shall deliver him, and then my obligation shall be done.'

The newspaper fluttered, and Fat Charlie was alone.

Chapter Eleven

In Which Rosie Learns to Say No to Strangers and Fat Charlie Acquires a Lime

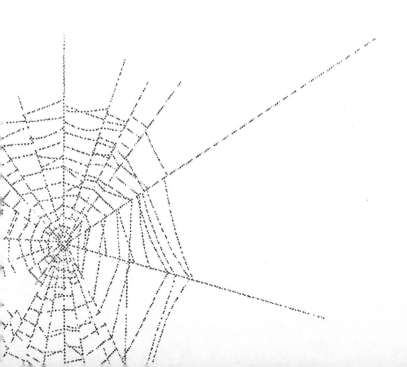

Fat Charlie looked down at his father's grave. 'Are you in there?' he said aloud. 'If you are, come out. I need to talk to you.'

He walked over to the floral grave marker and looked down. He was not certain what he was expecting – a hand to push up through the soil, perhaps, punching up and grabbing his leg – but nothing of the kind seemed to be about to happen.

He had been so certain.

Fat Charlie walked back through the Garden of Rest feeling stupid, like a game show contestant who had just made the mistake of betting his million dollars on the Mississippi being a longer river than the Amazon. He should have known. His father was as dead as roadkill, and he had wasted Spider's money on a wild-goose chase. By the windmills of Babyland he sat down and wept, and the mouldering toys seemed even sadder and lonelier than he remembered.

She was waiting for him in the parking lot, leaning against her car, smoking a cigarette. She looked uncomfortable.

'Hello, Mrs Bustamonte,' said Fat Charlie.

She took one final drag on the cigarette, then dropped it to the asphalt, and ground it out beneath the sole of her flat shoe. She was wearing black. She looked tired. 'Hello, Charles.'

'I think if I'd expected to see anyone here, it would be Mrs Higgler. Or Mrs Dunwiddy.'

'Callyanne's gone away. Mrs Dunwiddy sent me. She wants to see you.'

It's like the mafia, thought Fat Charlie. *A post-menopausal mafia*. 'She's going to make me an offer I can't refuse?'

'I doubt it. She is not very well.'

'Oh.'

He climbed into his rental, followed Mrs Bustamonte's Camry along the Florida streets. He had been so certain about his father. Certain he'd find him alive. Sure that he'd help . . .

They parked outside Mrs Dunwiddy's house. Fat Charlie looked at the front yard, at the faded plastic flamingos and the gnomes and the red mirrored gazing ball, like the one he had broken when he was a boy, sitting on a small concrete plinth like an enormous Christmas tree ornament. He walked over to the ball and saw himself, distorted, staring back from it.

'What's it for?' he said.

'It's not for anything. She liked it.'

Inside the house the smell of violets hung thick and cloying. Fat Charlie's Great Aunt Alanna had kept a tube of parma violet candies in her handbag, and, even as a chunky kid with a sweet tooth, Fat Charlie would eat them only if there wasn't anything else. This house smelled like those sweets had tasted. Fat Charlie hadn't thought of parma violets in twenty years. He wondered if they still made them. He wondered why anyone had ever made them in the first place . . .

'She's at the end of the hall,' said Mrs Bustamonte, and she stopped, and she pointed. Fat Charlie went into Mrs Dunwiddy's bedroom.

It was not a big bed, but Mrs Dunwiddy lay in it like an oversized doll. She wore her glasses, and above them something that Fat Charlie realised was the first nightcap he had ever seen, a yellowing tea-cosy-like affair, trimmed in lace. She was propped up on a mountain of pillows, her mouth open, and she was snoring gently as he walked in.

He coughed.

Mrs Dunwiddy jerked her head up, opened her eyes and stared at him. She pointed her finger to the nightstand beside the bed, and Fat Charlie picked up the glass of water sitting there and passed it to her. She took it with both hands, like a squirrel holding a nut, and she took a long sip before handing it back to him.

'My mouth get all dry,' she said. 'You know how old I am?'

'Um.' There was, he decided, no right answer. 'No.'

'Hunnert and four.'

'That's amazing. You're in such good shape. I mean, that's quite marvellous—'

'Shut up, Fat Charlie.'

'Sorry.'

'Don't say sorry like that neither, like a dog that get tell off for messin' on the kitchen floor. Hold your head up. Look the world in the eye. You hear me?'

'Yes. Sorry. I mean, just yes.'

She sighed. 'They want to take me to the hospital. I tell them, when you get to be hunnert and four, you earn the right to die in your own bed. I make babies in this bed long time back, and I birth babies in this bed, and damned if I going to die anywhere else. And another thing . . .' She stopped talking, closed her eyes and took a slow, deep breath. Just as Fat Charlie was convinced she had fallen asleep, her eyes opened and she said, 'Fat Charlie, if someone ever ask if you want to live to be hunnert and four, say no. Everything hurt. Everything. I hurt in places nobody ain't discover yet.'

'I'll bear that in mind.'

'None of your back talk.'

Fat Charlie looked at the little woman in her white wooden bed. 'Shall I say sorry?' he asked.

Mrs Dunwiddy looked away, guiltily. 'I do you wrong,' she said. 'Long time ago, I do you wrong.'

'I know,' said Fat Charlie.

Mrs Dunwiddy might have been dying, but she still shot Fat

Charlie the kind of look that would have sent children under the age of five screaming for their mothers. 'What you mean, you know?'

Fat Charlie said, 'I figured it out. Probably not all of it, but some of it. I'm not stupid.'

She examined him coldly through the thick glass of her spectacles, then she said, 'No. You not. True thing, that.'

She held out a gnarled hand. 'Give me the water back. That's better.' She sipped her water, dabbing at it with a small, purple tongue. 'Is a good thing you're here today. Tomorrow the whole house be fill with grievin' grandchildren and great-grandchildren, all of them tryin' to make me to die in the hospital, makin' up to me so I give them things. They don't know me. I outlive all my own children. Every one of them.'

Fat Charlie said, 'Are you going to talk about the bad turn you did to me?'

'You should never have break my garden mirror ball.'

'I'm sure I shouldn't.'

He remembered it, in the way you remember things from childhood, part memory, part memory of the memory: following the tennis ball into Mrs Dunwiddy's yard, and once he was there, experimentally picking up her mirrored ball to see his face in it, distorted and huge, feeling it tumble to the stone path, watching it smash into a thousand tiny shards of glass. He remembered the strong old fingers that grabbed him by the ear and dragged him out of her yard and into her house . . .

'You sent Spider away,' he said. 'Didn't you?'

Her jaw was set like a mechanical bulldog's. She nodded. 'I did a banishment,' she said. 'Didn't mean for it to go so. Everybody know a little magic back in those days. We didn't have all them kinda DVDs and cell phones and microwaves, but still, we know a lot regardless. I only wanted to teach you a lesson. You were so full of yourself, all mischief and back talk and vinegar. So I pull Spider out of you, to teach you a lesson.'

Fat Charlie heard the words, but they made no sense. 'You pulled him out?'

'I break him off from you. All the tricksiness. All the wickedness. All the devilry. All that.' She sighed. 'My mistake.

Nobody tell me that if you do magic around a, around people like your daddy's bloodline, it magnify everything. Everything get bigger.' Another sip of the water. 'Your mother never believe it. Not really. But that Spider, he worse than you. Your father never say nothing about it until I make Spider go away. Even then, all he tell me is if you can't fix it you not no son of his.'

He wanted to argue with her, to tell her how this was nonsense, that Spider was not a part of him, no more than he, Fat Charlie, was part of the sea or of the darkness. Instead, he said, 'Where's the feather?'

'What feather you talking about?'

'When I came back from that place. The place with the cliffs and the caves. I was holding a feather. What did you do with it?'

'I don't remember,' she said. 'I'm an old woman. I'm a hunnert and four.'

Fat Charlie said, 'Where is it?'

'I forget.'

'Please tell me.'

'I ain't got it.'

'Who does?'

'Callyanne.'

'Mrs Higgler?'

She leaned in, confidentially. 'The other two, they're just girls. They're flighty.'

'I called Mrs Higgler before I came out. I stopped at her house before I went to the cemetery. Mrs Bustamonte says she's gone away.'

Mrs Dunwiddy swayed gently from side to side in the bed, as if she were rocking herself to sleep. She said, 'I not going to be here for much longer. I stop eating solid food after you leave the last time. I done. Only water. Some women say they love your father, but I know him long long before them. Back when I had my looks, he would take me dancing. He come pick me up and whirl me around. He was an old man even then, but he always make a girl feel special. You don't feel . . .' She stopped, took another sip of water. Her hands were shaking. Fat Charlie took the empty glass from her. 'Hunnert and four,' she said. 'And never in my bed in the daytime except for confinements. And now I finish.'

'I'm sure you'll reach a hundred and five,' said Fat Charlie, uneasily.

'Don't you say that!' she said. She looked alarmed. *'Don't!* Your family do enough trouble already. Don't you go making things happen.'

'I'm not like my dad,' said Fat Charlie. 'I'm not magic. Spider got all that side of the family, remember?'

She did not appear to be listening. She said, 'When we would go dancing, way before the Second World War, your daddy would talk to the bandleader, and plenty times they call him up to sing with them. All the people laugh and cheer. Is so he make things happen. Singing.'

'Where is Mrs Higgler?'

'Gone home.'

'Her house is empty. Her car isn't there.'

'Gone home.'

'Er . . . you mean she's dead?'

The old woman on the white sheets wheezed and gasped for breath. She seemed unable to speak any longer. She motioned to him.

Fat Charlie said, 'Shall I get help?'

She nodded, and continued to gasp and choke and wheeze as he went out to find Mrs Bustamonte. She was sitting in the kitchen, watching Oprah on a very small countertop television. 'She wants you,' he said.

Mrs Bustamonte went out. She came back holding the empty water jug. 'What do you say to set her off like that?'

'Was she having an attack or something?'

Mrs Bustamonte gave him a look. 'No, Charles. She was laughing at you. She say you make her feel good.'

'Oh. She said Mrs Higgler had gone home. I asked if she meant she was dead.'

Mrs Bustamonte smiled, then. 'Saint Andrews,' she said. 'Callyanne's gone to Saint Andrews.' She refilled the jug in the sink.

Fat Charlie said, 'When all this started I thought that it was me against Spider, and you four were on my side. And now Spider's been taken, and it's me against the four of you.'

She turned off the water, and gazed at him sullenly.

'I don't believe anyone any more,' said Fat Charlie. 'Mrs Dunwiddy's probably faking being ill. Probably as soon as I leave here she'll be out of bed and doing the charleston around her bedroom.'

'She not eating. She say it makes her feel bad inside. Won't take a thing to fill her belly. Just water.'

'Where in Saint Andrews is she?' asked Fat Charlie.

'Just go,' said Mrs Bustamonte. 'Your family, you done enough harm here.'

Fat Charlie looked as if he was about to say something, and then he didn't, and he left without another word.

Mrs Bustamonte took the jug of water in to Mrs Dunwiddy, who lay quiet in the bed.

'Nancy's son hates us,' said Mrs Bustamonte. 'What you tell him anyhow?'

Mrs Dunwiddy said nothing. Mrs Bustamonte listened, and when she was sure that the older woman was still breathing, she took off Mrs Dunwiddy's thick spectacles, and put them down by the bed, then pulled up the sheet to cover Mrs Dunwiddy's shoulders.

After that, she simply waited for the end.

* * *

Fat Charlie drove off, not entirely certain where he was going. He had crossed the Atlantic for the third time in two weeks, and the money that Spider had given him was almost tapped out. He was alone in the car, and being alone, he hummed.

He passed a clutch of Jamaican restaurants when he noticed a sign in a storefront window: 'CUT PRICE TO THE ISLANDS'. He pulled up and went inside.

'We at A-One travel are here to serve all your travel needs,' said the travel agent, in the hushed and apologetic tone of voice doctors normally reserve for telling people that the limb in question is going to have to come off.

'Er. Yeah. Thanks. Er. What's the cheapest way to get out to Saint Andrews?'

'Will you be going on vacation?'

'Not really. I just want to go out for a day. Maybe two days.'

'Leaving when?'

'This afternoon.'

'You are, I take it, joshing with me.'

'Not at all.'

A computer screen was gazed at, lugubriously. A keyboard was tapped. 'It doesn't look like there's anything out there for less than 1200 dollars.'

'Oh.' Fat Charlie slumped.

More keyboard clicking. The man sniffed. 'That can't be right.' Then he said, 'Hold on.' A phone call, 'Is this rate still valid?' He jotted down some figures on a scratch pad. He looked up at Fat Charlie. 'If you could go out for a week, and stay at the Dolphin Hotel, I could get you a week's vacation for five hundred dollars, with your meals at the hotel thrown in. The flight will only cost you airport tax.'

Fat Charlie blinked. 'Is there a catch?'

'It's an island tourism promotion. Something to do with the music festival. I didn't think it was still going on. But then, you know what they say. You get what you pay for. And if you want to eat anywhere else it will cost you.'

Fat Charlie gave the man five crumpled hundred-dollar bills.

* * *

Daisy was starting to feel like the kind of cop you only ever see in movies: tough, hard-bitten, and perfectly ready to buck the system; the kind of cop who wants to know whether or not you feel lucky, or if you're interested in making his day, and particularly the kind of cop who says, 'I'm getting too old for this shit'. She was twenty-six years old, and she wanted to tell people she was too old for this shit. She was quite aware of how ridiculous this was, thank you very much.

At this moment, she was standing in Camberwell's office and saying, 'Yes, sir. Saint Andrew's.'

'Went there on my holidays some years back, with the former Mrs Camberwell. Very pleasant place. Rum cake.'

'That sounds like the place, sir. The closed-circuit footage from Gatwick is definitely him. Travelling under the name of Bronstein. Roger Bronstein flies to Miami, changes planes, and takes a connection to Saint Andrews.'

'You're sure it's him?'

'Sure.'

'Well,' said Camberwell. 'That buggers us good and proper, doesn't it? No extradition treaty.'

'There must be *something* we can do.'

'Mm. We can freeze his remaining accounts and grab his assets, and we will, and that'll be as much use to us as a water-soluble umbrella, because he'll have lots of cash sitting in places we can't find it or touch it.'

Daisy said, 'But that's *cheating*.'

He looked up at her as if he wasn't certain exactly what he was looking at. 'It's not a playground game of tag. If they kept the rules, they'd be on our side. If he comes back, then we arrest him.' He squashed a little Plasticine man into a Plasticine ball and began to mash it out into a flat sheet, pinching it between finger and thumb. 'In the old days,' he said, 'they could claim sanctuary in a church. If you stayed in the church the law couldn't touch you. Even if you killed a man. Of course, it limited your social life. Right.'

He looked at her as if he expected her to leave now. She said, 'He killed Maeve Livingstone. He's been cheating his clients blind for years.'

'And?'

'We should be bringing him to justice.'

'Don't let it get to you,' he said.

Daisy thought, *I'm getting too old for this shit*. She kept her mouth shut, and the words simply went round and round inside her head.

'Don't let it get to you,' he repeated. He folded the Plasticine sheet into a rough cube, then squeezed it viciously between finger and thumb. 'I don't let any of it get to me. Think of it as if you were a traffic warden. Grahame Coats is just a car that parked on the double yellow lines, but drove off before you were able to give him a ticket. Yes?'

'Sure,' said Daisy. 'Of course. Sorry.'

'Right,' he said.

She went back to her desk, went to the police internal website and examined her options for several hours. Finally, she went home. Carol was sitting in front of *Coronation Street*, eating a microwavable chicken korma.

'I'm taking a break,' said Daisy. 'I'm going on holiday.'

'You don't have any holiday time left,' pointed out Carol, reasonably.

'Too bad,' said Daisy. 'I'm too old for this shit.'

'Oh. Where are you going?'

'I'm going to catch a crook,' said Daisy.

* * *

Fat Charlie liked Caribbeair. They might have been an international airline, but they felt like a local bus company. The flight attendant called him 'darlin'' and told him jus' to sit anywhere that struck his fancy.

He stretched out across three seats, and went to sleep. In Fat Charlie's dream he was walking beneath copper skies and the world was silent and still. He was walking towards a bird vaster than cities, its eyes aflame, its beak agape, and Fat Charlie walked into the beak and down the creature's throat.

Then, in the way of dreams, he was in a room, its walls covered with soft feathers and with eyes, round like the eyes of owls, which did not blink.

Spider was in the centre of the room, his legs and arms extended. He was held up by chains made of bone, like the bones of a chicken's neck, and they ran from each corner of the room, and held him tightly, like a fly in a web.

Oh, said Spider. *It's you*.

Yes, said Fat Charlie in his dream.

The bone-chains pulled and tugged at Spider's flesh, and Fat Charlie could see the pain in his face.

Well, said Fat Charlie. *I suppose it could be worse*.

I don't think this is it, said his brother. *I think she has plans for me. Plans for us. I just don't know what they are*.

They're only birds, said Fat Charlie. *How bad could it be?*

Ever heard of Prometheus?

Er . . .

Gave fire to man. Was punished by the gods by being chained to a rock. Every day an eagle would come down and tear out his liver.

Didn't he ever run out of liver?

He grew a new one every day. It's a god thing.

There was a pause. The two brothers stared at each other.

I'll sort it out, said Fat Charlie. *I'll fix it.*

Just like you fixed the rest of your life, I suppose? Spider grinned, without mirth.

I'm sorry.

No. I'm sorry. Spider sighed. *So look, have you got a plan?*

A plan?

I'll take that as a no. Just do whatever you have to do. Get me out of here.

Are you in Hell?

I don't know where I am. If it's anywhere, this is the Hell of Birds. You have to get me out.

How?

You're Dad's son, aren't you? You're my brother. Come up with something. Just get me out of here.

Fat Charlie woke, shivering. The flight attendant brought him coffee, and he drank it gratefully. He was awake, now, and he had no desire to go back to sleep, so he read the Caribbeair magazine and learned many useful things about Saint Andrews.

He learned that Saint Andrews is not the smallest of the Caribbean Islands, but it tends to be one of the ones that people forget about, when they make lists. It was discovered by the Spanish around 1500, an uninhabited volcanic hill teeming with animal-life, not to mention a multiplicity of plants. It was said that anything that you planted on Saint Andrews would grow.

It belonged to the Spanish, and then to British, then to the Dutch, then to the British again, and then, for a short while after it was made independent in 1962, it belonged to Major F. E. Garrett, who took over the government, broke off diplomatic relations with all other countries except Albania and the Congo, and ruled the country with a rod of iron until his unfortunate

death from falling out of bed several years later. He fell out of bed
hard enough to break a number of bones, despite the presence in
his bedroom of an entire squad of soldiers, who testified that they
had all tried, but failed, to break Major Garrett's fall; and despite
their best efforts he was dead by the time that he arrived in the
island's sole hospital. Since then, Saint Andrews had been ruled
by a beneficent and elected local government, and was
everybody's friend.

It had miles of sandy beaches and an extremely small rainforest
in the centre of the island; it had bananas and sugar cane, a
banking system that encouraged foreign investment and off-shore
corporate banking, and no extradition treaties with anybody at
all, except possibly the Congo and Albania.

If Saint Andrews was known for anything, it was for its cuisine:
the inhabitants claimed to have been jerking chickens before the
Jamaicans, currying goats before the Trinidadians, frying flying
fish before the Bajans.

There were two towns on Saint Andrews – Williamstown, on
the southeast side of the island, and Newcastle, on the north.
There were street markets in which anything that grew on the
island could be bought, and several supermarkets, in which the
same foodstuffs could be bought for twice the price. One day
Saint Andrews would get a real international airport.

It was a matter of opinion whether the deep harbour of
Williamstown was a good thing or not. It was indisputable that
the deep harbour brought the cruise ships, though, floating
islands filled with people, who were changing the economy and
nature of Saint Andrews as they were changing the economy of
many Caribbean islands. At high season there would be up to half
a dozen cruise ships in Williamstown Bay, and thousands of
people waiting to disembark, to stretch their legs, to buy things.
And the people of Saint Andrews grumbled, but they welcomed
the visitors ashore, they sold them things, they fed them until
they could eat no more and then they sent them back to their
ships . . .

The Caribbeair plane landed with a bump that made Fat Charlie
drop his magazine. He put it back into the seat pocket in front of
him, walked down the steps and across the tarmac.

It was late afternoon.

Fat Charlie took a taxi from the airport to his hotel. During the taxi ride, he learned a number of things that had not been mentioned in the Caribbeair magazine.

For example, he learned that music, real music, proper music, was country-and-western music. On Saint Andrews, even the rastas knew it. Johnny Cash? He was a god. Willie Nelson? A demi-god.

He learned that there was no reason ever to leave Saint Andrews. The taxi driver himself had seen no reason ever to leave Saint Andrews, and he had given it much thought. The island had a cave, and a mountain, and a rainforest. Hotels? It had twenty. Restaurants? Several dozen. It contained a city, three towns and a scattering of villages. Food? Everything grew here. Oranges. Bananas. Nutmegs. It even, the taxi driver said, had limes.

Fat Charlie said 'No!' at this, mostly in order to feel like he was taking part in the conversation, but the driver appeared to take it as a challenge to his honesty. He slammed on the taxi's brakes, sending the car slewing over to the side of the road, got out of the car, reached over a fence, pulled something from a tree and walked back to the car.

'Look at this!' he said. 'Nobody ever tell you that I is a liar. What it is?'

'A lime?' said Fat Charlie.

'Exactly.'

The taxi driver lurched the car back into the road. He told Fat Charlie that the Dolphin was an excellent hotel. Did Fat Charlie have family on the island? Did he know anyone here?

'Actually,' said Fat Charlie, 'I'm here looking for someone. For a woman.'

The taxi driver thought this was a splendid idea, since Saint Andrews was a perfect place to come if you were looking for a woman. This was, he elaborated, because the women of Saint Andrews were curvier than the women of Jamaica, and less likely to give you grief and heartbreak than the Trinis. In addition, they were more beautiful than the women of Dominica, and they were better cooks than you would find anywhere on Earth.

If Fat Charlie was looking for a woman, he had come to the right place.

'It's not just any woman. It's a specific woman,' said Fat Charlie.

The taxi driver told Fat Charlie that this was his lucky day, for the taxi driver prided himself on knowing everyone on the Island. If you spend your life somewhere, he said, you can do that. He was willing to bet that Fat Charlie did not know by sight all the people in England, and Fat Charlie admitted that this was in fact the case.

'She's a friend of the family,' said Fat Charlie. 'Her name is Mrs Higgler. Callyanne Higgler. You heard of her?'

The taxi driver was quiet for a while. He seemed to be thinking. Then he said that, no, he hadn't ever heard of her. The taxi pulled up in front of the Dolphin Hotel, and Fat Charlie paid him.

Fat Charlie went inside. There was a young woman on reception. He showed her his passport, and the reservation number. He put the lime down on the reservation desk.

'Do you have any luggage?'

'No,' said Fat Charlie, apologetically.

'Nothing?'

'Nothing. Just this lime.'

He filled out several forms, and she gave him a key and directions to his room.

Fat Charlie was in the bath when a knock came on the door. He wrapped a towel around his midriff. It was the bellman. 'You left your lime in reception,' he said, and handed it to Fat Charlie.

'Thanks,' said Fat Charlie. He went back to his bath. Afterward, he went to bed, and dreamed uncomfortable dreams.

***

In his house on the clifftop, Grahame Coats was also having the strangest dreams, dark and unwelcome, if not actually unpleasant. He could not remember them properly when he woke, but he would open his eyes the next morning with a vague impression that he had spent the night stalking smaller creatures through the long grass, dispatching them with a blow of his paw, rending their bodies with his teeth.

In his dreams, his teeth were weapons of destruction.

He woke from the dreams feeling disturbed, with the day slightly charged.

And, each morning, a new day would begin and here, only a week away from his old life, Grahame Coats was already experiencing the frustration of the fugitive. He had a swimming pool, true, and cocoa trees and grapefruit and nutmeg trees; he had a full wine cellar and an empty meat cellar and a media centre. He had satellite television, a large DVD collection, not to mention art, thousands of dollars worth of art, all over the walls. He had a cook, who came in each day and cooked his meals, a housekeeper and a groundskeeper (a married couple who came in for a few hours each day). The food was excellent, the climate was, if you liked warm sunny days, perfect, and none of these things made Grahame Coats as happy as he felt was his due.

He had not shaved since leaving England, which had not yet endowed him with a beard, merely given him a thin covering of the kind of facial hair that makes men look shifty. His eyes sat in panda-dark sockets, and the bags beneath his eyes were so dark as to appear to be bruises.

He swam in the pool once each day, in the morning, but otherwise avoided the sun; he had not, he told himself, amassed an ill-gotten fortune to lose it to skin cancer. Or to anything else at all.

He thought about London too much. In London, each of his favourite restaurants had a maître d' who called him by name and ensured he left happy. In London there were people who owed him favours, and there was never any difficulty in getting first-night tickets, and for that matter in London there were theatres to have first nights in. He had always thought he would make a fine exile; he was starting to suspect that he had been wrong.

Needing someone to blame, he came to the conclusion that the entire affair was Maeve Livingstone's fault. She had led him on. She had attempted to rob him. She was a vixen, a minx, and a hussy. She had deserved everything she had coming to her. She had gotten off easily. Should he be interviewed on television, he could already hear the bruised innocence in his voice as he explained that he had been defending his property and his

honour from a dangerous madwoman. Frankly, it was some kind
of miracle that he'd made it out of that office alive . . .

And he had liked being Grahame Coats. He was now, as always
while he was on the island, Basil Finnegan, and it irked him. He
didn't feel like a Basil. His Basilhood had been hard-won – the
original Basil had died as an infant, and had a birthdate close to
Grahame's own. One copy of the birth certificate, along with a
letter from an imaginary clergyman, later, and Grahame possessed
a passport and an identity. He had kept the identity alive – Basil
had a solid credit history, Basil travelled to exotic places, Basil
had bought a luxury house on Saint Andrews without ever seeing
it. But in Grahame's mind, Basil had been working for him, and
now the servant had become the master. Basil Finnegan had eaten
him alive.

'If I stay here,' said Grahame Coats, 'I shall go mad.'

'What you say?' asked the housekeeper, duster in hand, leaning
in at the bedroom door.

'Nothing,' said Grahame Coats.

'Sound like you say if you stay in you go mad. You ought to go
for a walk. Walking good for you.'

Grahame Coats did not go for walks; he had people to do that
for him. But, he thought, perhaps Basil Finnegan went for walks.
He put on a broad-brimmed hat, and exchanged his sandals for
walking shoes. He took his mobile phone, instructed the
groundskeeper to come and get him when he called, and set out
from the house on the cliff-edge, heading towards the nearest
town.

It is a small world. You do not have to live in it particularly long
to learn that for yourself. There is a theory that, in the whole
world, there are only five hundred real people (the cast, as it
were. All the rest of the people in the world, the theory suggests,
are extras), and what is more, they all know each other. And it's
true, or true as far as it goes. In reality the world is made of
thousands upon thousands of groups of about five hundred
people, all of whom will spend their lives bumping into each
other, trying to avoid each other, and discovering each other in
the same unlikely teashop in Vancouver. There is an
unavoidability to this process. It's not even coincidence. It's just

the way the world works, with no regard for individuals or for propriety.

So it was that Grahame Coats walked into a small café on the road to Williamstown, in order to purchase a soft drink, and to have somewhere to sit while he called his gardener to tell him that he should come and pick him up.

He ordered a Fanta and sat down at a table. The place was practically empty: two women, one young, one older, sat in the far corner, drinking coffee and writing postcards.

Grahame Coats gazed out, across the road, at the beach. It was paradise, he thought. And it might behove him to get more deeply involved with local politics – perhaps as a sponsor of the arts. He had already made several substantial donations to the island's police force, and it might even become necessary to make sure that . . .

A voice from behind him, thrilled and tentative, said, 'Mr Coats?' and his heart lurched. The younger of the women sat down beside him. She had the warmest smile.

'Fancy running into you here,' she said. 'You on your holidays too?'

'Something like that.' He had no idea who this woman was.

'You remember me, don't you? Rosie Noah. I used to go out with Fat, with Charlie Nancy. Yes?'

'Hello. Rosie. Yes, of course.'

'I'm on a cruise, with my mum. She's still writing postcards home.'

Grahame Coats glanced back over his shoulder, to the back of the little café, and something resembling a South American mummy in a floral dress glared back at him.

'Honestly,' continued Rosie, 'I'm not really a cruise sort of person. Ten days of going from island to island. It's nice to see a familiar face, isn't it?'

'Absatively,' said Grahame Coats. 'Should I take it that you and our Charles are no longer, well, an item?'

'Yes,' she said. 'I suppose you should. I mean, we're not.'

Grahame Coats smiled sympathetically on the outside. He picked up his Fanta and walked, with Rosie, to the table in the corner. Rosie's mother radiated ill will just as an old iron radiator can radiate chill into a room, but Grahame Coats was perfectly charming and entirely helpful, and he agreed with her on every point. It was indeed appalling what the cruise companies thought they could get away with these days; it was disgusting how sloppy the administration of the cruise ship had been allowed to get; it was shocking how little there was to do in the islands; and it was, in every respect, outrageous what passengers were expected to put up with: ten days without a bathtub, with only the tiniest of shower facilities. Shocking.

Rosie's mother told him about the several quite impressive enmities she had managed to cultivate with certain American passengers whose main crime, as Grahame Coats understood it, was to overload their plates in the buffet line of the *Squeak Attack*, and to sunbathe in the spot by the aft deck pool that Rosie's mother had decided, on the first day out, was undisputedly hers.

Grahame Coats nodded, and made sympathetic noises as the vitriol dripped over him, *tch*ing and agreeing and clucking, until Rosie's mother was prepared to overlook her dislike both of strangers and people connected in some way to Fat Charlie, and she talked, and she talked, and she talked. Grahame Coats was barely listening. Grahame Coats pondered.

It would be unfortunate, Grahame Coats was thinking, if someone was to return to London at this precise point in time and inform the authorities that Grahame Coats had been encountered in Saint Andrews. It was inevitable that he would be noticed one day, but still, the inevitable could, perhaps, be postponed.

'Let me,' said Grahame Coats, 'suggest a solution to at least one of your problems. A little way up the road I have a holiday house. Rather a nice house, I like to think. And if there's one thing I have a surplus of, it's baths. Would you care to come back and indulge yourselves?'

'No, thanks,' said Rosie. Had she agreed, it is to be expected that her mother would have pointed out that they were due back at the Williamstown Port for pick-up later that afternoon, and would then have chided Rosie for accepting such invitations from virtual strangers. But Rosie said no.

'That is extremely kind of you,' said Rosie's mother. 'We would be delighted.'

The gardener pulled up outside soon after, in a black Mercedes, and Grahame Coats opened the back door for Rosie and her mother. He assured them he would absatively have them back in the harbour well before the last boat back to their ship.

'Where to, Mr Finnegan?' asked the gardener.

'Home,' he said.

'Mr Finnegan?' asked Rosie.

'It's an old family name,' said Grahame Coats, and he was sure it was. Somebody's family anyway. He closed the back door, and went around to the front.

* * *

Maeve Livingtone was lost. It had started out so well: she had wanted to be at home, in Pontefract, and there was a shimmer and a tremendous wind, and in one ectoplasmic gusting, she was home. She wandered around the house for one last time, then went out into the autumn day. She wanted to see her sister in Rye, and before she could think, there she was there in the garden at Rye, watching her sister walking her springer spaniel.

It had seemed so easy.

That was the point she had decided that she wanted to see Grahame Coats, and that was where it had all gone wrong. She was, momentarily, back in the office in the Aldwych, and then in an empty house in Purley, which she remembered from a small dinner party Grahame Coats had hosted a decade back, and then . . .

Then she was lost. And everywhere she tried to go only made matters worse.

She had no idea where she was now. It seemed to be some kind of garden.

A brief downpour of rain drenched the place and left her untouched. Now the ground was steaming, and she knew she wasn't in England. It was starting to get dark.

She sat down on the ground, and she started to sniffle.

Honestly, she told herself. *Maeve Livingstone. Pull yourself together.* But the sniffling just got worse.

'You want a tissue?' asked someone.

Maeve looked up. An elderly gentleman with a green hat and a pencil-thin moustache was offering her a tissue.

She nodded. Then she said, 'It's probably not any use, though. I won't be able to touch it.'

He smiled sympathetically and passed her the tissue. It didn't fall through her fingers, so she blew her nose with it, and dabbed at her eyes. 'Thank you. Sorry about that. It all got a bit much.'

'It happens,' said the man. He looked her up and down, appraisingly. 'What are you? A duppy?'

'No,' she said. 'I don't think so . . . What's a duppy?'

'A ghost,' he said. With his pencil moustache, he reminded her of Cab Calloway, perhaps, or Don Ameche, one of those stars who aged but never stopped being stars. Whoever the old man was, he was still a star.

'Oh. Right. Yes, I'm one of them. Um. You?'

'More or less,' he said. 'I'm dead, anyway.'

'Oh. Would you mind if I asked where I was?'

'We're in Florida.' he told her. 'In the buryin' ground. It's good you caught me,' he added. 'I was going for a walk. You want to come along?'

'Shouldn't you be in a grave?' she asked, hesitantly.

'I was bored,' he told her. 'I thought I could do with a walk. And maybe a spot of fishin'.'

She hesitated, then nodded. It was nice to have someone to talk to.

'You want to hear a story?' asked the old man.

'Not really,' she admitted.

He helped her to her feet, and they walked out of the Garden of Rest.

'Fair enough. Then I'll keep it short. Not go on too long. You know, I can tell one of these stories so it lasts for weeks. It's all in the details – what you put in, what you don't. I mean, you leave out the weather and what people are wearing, you can skip half the story. I once told a story—'

'Look,' she said, 'if you're going to tell a story, then just tell it to me, all right?' It was bad enough walking along the side of the road, in the gathering dusk. She reminded herself that she wasn't going to be hit by a passing car, but it did nothing to make her feel more at ease.

The old man started to talk, in a gentle sing-song. 'When I say Tiger,' he said, 'you got to understand it's not just the stripy cat, the India one. It's just what people call big cats – the pumas and the bobcats and the jaguars and all of them. You got that?'

'Certainly.'

'Good. So . . . a long time ago,' he began, 'Tiger had the stories. All the stories there ever were was Tiger stories, all the songs were Tiger songs, and I'd say that all the jokes were Tiger jokes, but there weren't no jokes told back in the Tiger days. In Tiger stories all that matters is how strong your teeth are, how you hunt and how you kill. Ain't no gentleness in Tiger stories, no tricksiness, and no peace.'

Maeve tried to imagine what kind of stories a big cat might tell. 'So they were violent?'

'Sometimes. But mostly what they was, was bad. When all the stories and the songs were Tiger's, that was a bad time for everyone. People take on the shapes of the songs and the stories that surround them, especially if they don't have their own song. And in Tiger times all the songs were dark. They began in tears, and they'd end in blood, and they were the only stories that the people of this world knew.

'Then Anansi comes along. Now, I guess you know all about Anansi—'

'I don't think so,' said Maeve.

'Well, if I started to tell you how clever and how handsome and how charming and how cunning Anansi was, I could start today and not finish until next Thursday,' began the old man.

'Then don't,' said Maeve. 'We'll take it as said. And what did this Anansi do?'

'Well, Anansi won the stories – won them? No. He *earned* them. He took them from Tiger, and made it so Tiger couldn't enter the real world no more. Not in the flesh. The stories people told became Anansi stories. This was, what, ten, fifteen thousand years back.

'Now, Anansi stories, they have wit and trickery and wisdom. So, all over the world, all of the people, they aren't just thinking of hunting and being hunted any more. Now they're starting to *think* their way out of problems – sometimes thinking their way into worse problems. They still need to keep their bellies full, but now they're trying to figure out how to do it without working – and *that's* the point where people start using their heads. Some people think the first tools were weapons, but that's all upside down. First of all, people figure out the tools. It's the crutch before the club, every time. Because now people are telling Anansi stories, and they're starting to think about how to get kissed, how to get something for nothing by being smarter or funnier. That's when they start to make the world.'

'It's just a folk story,' she said. 'People made up the stories in the first place.'

'Does that change things?' asked the old man. 'Maybe Anansi's just some guy from a story, made up back in Africa in the dawn days of the world by some boy with blackfly on his leg, pushing his crutch in the dirt, making up some goofy story about a man made of tar. Does that change anything? People respond to the stories. They tell them themselves. The stories spread, and as people tell them, the stories change the tellers. Because now the folk who never had any thought in their head but how to run from lions and keep far enough away from rivers that the crocodiles don't get an easy meal, now they're starting to dream about a whole new place to live. The world may be the same, but the wallpaper's changed. Yes? People still have the same story, the one where they get born and they do stuff and they die, but now the story means something different to what it meant before.'

'You're telling me that before the Anansi stories the world was savage and bad?'

'Yeah. Pretty much.'

She digested this. 'Well,' she said cheerily, 'it's certainly a good thing that the stories are now Anansi's.'

The old man nodded.

And then she said, 'Doesn't Tiger want them back?'

He nodded. 'He's wanted them back for ten thousand years.'

'But he won't get them, will he?'

The old man said nothing. He stared into the distance. Then he shrugged. 'Be a bad thing if he did.'

'What about Anansi?'

'Anansi's dead,' said the old man. 'And there ain't a lot a duppy can do.'

'As a duppy myself,' she said, 'I resent that.'

'Well,' said the old man, 'duppies can't touch the living. Remember?'

She pondered this a moment. 'So what can I touch?' she asked.

The look that flickered across his elderly face was both wily and wicked. 'I guess,' he said, 'you could touch me.'

'I'll have you know,' she told him, mock-offended, 'that I'm a married woman.'

His smile only grew wider. It was a sweet smile now, and a gentle one, as heartwarming as it was dangerous. 'Generally speaking, that kind of contract terminates in a *till death us do part.*'

Maeve was unimpressed.

'Thing is,' he told her, 'you're an immaterial girl. You can touch immaterial things. Like me. I mean, if you want, we could go dancing. There's a place just down the street here. Won't nobody notice a couple of duppies on their dance floor.'

Maeve thought about it. It had been a long time since she had gone dancing. 'Are you a good dancer?' she asked.

'I've never had any complaints,' said the old man.

'I want to find a man – a living man – called Grahame Coats,' she said. 'Can you help me find him?'

'I can certainly steer you in the right direction,' he said. 'So, are you dancing?'

A smile crept about the edges of her lips. 'You asking?' she said.

* * *

The chains that had kept Spider captive fell away. The pain, which had been searing and continuous, like a bad toothache that occupied his entire body, began to pass.

Spider took a step forward.

In front of him was what appeared to be a rip in the sky, and he moved towards it.

Ahead of him he could see an island. He could see a small

mountain in the centre of the island. He could see a pure blue sky, and swaying palm trees, a white gull high in the sky. But even as he saw it the world seemed to be receding. It was as if he was looking at it through the wrong end of a telescope. It shrank and slipped from him, and the more he ran towards it the further away it seemed to get.

The island was a reflection in a puddle of water, and then it was nothing at all.

He was in a cave. The edges of things were crisp – crisper and sharper than anywhere that Spider had ever been before. This was a different kind of place.

She was standing in the mouth of the cave, between him and the open air. He knew her. She had stared into his face in a Greek restaurant in South London, and birds had come from her mouth.

'You know,' said Spider, 'I have to say, you've got the strangest ideas about hospitality. You come to my world, I'd make you dinner, open a bottle of wine, put on some soft music, give you an evening you would never forget.'

Her face was impassive; carved from black rock it was. The wind tugged at the edges of her old brown coat. She spoke then, her voice high and lonely as the call of a distant gull.

'I took you,' she said. 'Now, you will call him.'

'Call him? Call who?'

'You will bleat,' she said. 'You will whimper. Your fear will excite him.'

'Spider does not bleat,' he said. He was not certain this was true.

Eyes as black and as shiny as chips of obsidian stared back into his. They were eyes like black holes, letting nothing out, not even information.

'If you kill me,' said Spider, 'my curse will be upon you.' He wondered if he actually had a curse. He probably did; and if he didn't, he was sure that he could fake it.

'It will not be I that kills you,' she said. She raised her hand, and it was not a hand but a raptor's talon. She raked her talon down his face, down his chest, her cruel claws sinking into his flesh, tearing his skin.

It did not hurt, although Spider knew that it would hurt soon enough.

Beads of blood crimsoned his chest and dripped down his face. His eyes stung. His blood touched his lips. He could taste it and smell the iron scent of it.

'Now,' she said in the cries of distant birds. 'Now your death begins.'

Spider said, 'We're both reasonable entities. Let me present you with a perhaps rather more feasible alternative scenario that might conceivably have benefits for both of us.' He said it with an easy smile. He said it convincingly.

'You talk too much,' she said, and shook her head. 'No more talking.'

Then she reached into his mouth with her sharp talons, and with one wrenching movement she tore out his tongue.

'There,' she said. And then she seemed to take pity on him, for she touched Spider's face in a way that was almost kindly, and she said, 'Sleep.'

He slept.

* * *

Rosie's mother, now bathed, reappeared refreshed, invigorated and positively glowing.

'Before I give you both a ride into Williamstown, can I give you a hasty guided tour of the house?' asked Grahame Coats.

'We do have to get back to the ship, thanks all the same,' said Rosie, who had not been able to convince herself that she wanted a bath in Grahame Coats's house.

Her mother checked her watch. 'We have ninety minutes,' she said. 'It won't take more than fifteen minutes to get back to the harbour. Don't be ungracious, Rosie. We would love to see your house.'

So Grahame Coats showed them the sitting room, the study, the library, the television room, the dining room, the kitchen and the swimming pool. He opened a door beneath the kitchen stairs that looked as if it would lead to a broom cupboard, and walked his guests down the wooden steps into the rock-walled wine cellar.

He showed them the wine, most of which had come with the house when he had bought it. He walked them to the far end of the wine cellar, to the bare room that had, back in the days before refrigeration, been a meat-storage locker. It was always chilly in the meat locker, where heavy chains came down from the ceiling, the empty hooks on the ends showing where once whole carcasses had hung long before. Grahame Coats held the heavy iron door open politely while both the women walked inside.

'You know,' he said, helpfully, 'I've just realised. The light switch is back where we came in. Hold on.' And then he slammed the door behind the women, and he rammed closed the bolts.

He picked out a dusty-looking bottle of 1995 Chablis Premier Cru from a wine rack.

He went upstairs with a swing in his step, and let his three employees know that he would be giving them the week off.

It seemed to him, as he walked up the stairs to his study, as if something were padding soundlessly behind him, but when he turned there was nothing there. Oddly, he found this comforting. He found a corkscrew, opened the bottle and poured himself a pale glass of wine. He drank it and, although he had never previously had much time for red wines, he found himself wishing that what he was drinking was richer and darker. *It should be*, he thought, *the colour of blood*.

As he finished his second glass of Chablis, he realised that he had been blaming the wrong person for his plight. Maeve Livingstone was, he saw it now, merely a dupe. No, the person to blame, obviously and undeniably, was Fat Charlie. Without his meddling, without his criminal trespass into Grahame Coats's office computer systems, Grahame Coats wouldn't be here, an exile, like a blond Napoleon on a perfect, sunny Elba. He wouldn't be in the unfortunate predicament of having two women imprisoned in his meat locker. *If Fat Charlie was here*, he thought, *I would tear out his throat with my teeth*, and the thought shocked him even as it excited him. You didn't want to screw with Grahame Coats.

Evening came, and Grahame Coats watched the *Squeak Attack* from his window as it drifted past his house on the cliff and off into the sunset. He wondered how long it would take them to notice that two passengers were missing. He even waved.

Chapter Twelve

In Which Fat Charlie Does Several Things for the First Time

The Dolphin Hotel had a concierge. He was young and bespectacled, and he was reading a paperback novel with a rose and a gun on the cover.

'I'm trying to find someone,' said Fat Charlie. 'On the island.'

'Who?'

'A lady named Callyanne Higgler. She's here from Florida. She's an old friend of my family.'

The young man closed his book thoughtfully, then he looked at Fat Charlie through narrowed eyes. When people do this in paperback books it gives an immediate impression of dangerous alertness, but in reality it just made the young man look like he was trying not to fall asleep. He said, 'Are you the man with the lime?'

'What?'

'The man with the lime?'

'Yes, I suppose I am.'

'Lemme see it, nuh?'

'My lime?'

The young man nodded, gravely.

'No, you can't. It's back in my room.'

'But you *are* the man with the lime?'

'Can you help me find Mrs Higgler? Are there any Higglers on the island? Do you have a phone book I could look at? I was hoping for a phone book in my bedroom.'

'It's a kinda common name, you know?' said the young man. 'The phone book not going to help.'

'How common could it be?'

'Well,' said the young man, 'for example, I'm Benjamin Higgler. She over there, on reception, she name Amerila Higgler.'

'Oh. Right. Lots of Higglers on the island. I see.'

'She on the island for the music festival?'

'What?'

'It going on all this week.' He handed Fat Charlie a leaflet, informing him that Willie Nelson (cancelled) would be headlining the Saint Andrews Music Festival.

'Why'd he cancel?'

'Same reason Garth Brooks cancel. Nobody tell them it was happening in the first place.'

'I don't think she's going to the music festival. I really need to track her down. She's got something I'm looking for. Look, if you were me, how would you go about looking for her?'

Benjamin Higgler reached into a desk drawer and pulled out a map of the island. 'We're here, just south of Williamstown . . .' he began, making a felt-pen mark on the paper. From there, he began marking out a plan of campaign for Fat Charlie: he divided the island into segments that could easily be covered in a day by a man on a bicycle, marked out each rum-shop and café with small crosses. He put a circle beside each tourist attraction.

Then he rented Fat Charlie a bicycle.

Fat Charlie pedalled off to the south.

There were information conduits on Saint Andrews that Fat Charlie, who, on some level believed that coconut palms and cellular telephones ought to be mutually exclusive, had not expected. It did not seem to make any difference who he talked to: old men playing draughts in the shade; women with breasts like watermelons and buttocks like armchairs and laughter like mockingbirds; a sensible young lady in the tourist office; a bearded rasta with a Jamaica-coloured knit cap and what appeared to be a woollen miniskirt: they all had the same response.

'You the one with the lime?'

'I suppose so.'

'Show us your lime.'

'It's back at the hotel. Look, I'm trying to find Callyanne Higgler. She's about sixty. American. Big mug of coffee in her hand.'

'Never heard of her.'

Bicycling around the island, Fat Charlie soon discovered, had its dangers. The chief mode of transportation on the island was the minibus: unlicensed, unsafe, always overfilled, the minibuses hurtled around the island tooting and squealing their brakes, slamming around corners on two wheels whilst relying on the weight of their passengers to ensure they never tipped over. Fat Charlie would have been killed a dozen times on his first morning out were it not for the low thud of drum and bass being played over each bus's sound system: he could feel them in the pit of his stomach even before he heard their engines, and he had plenty of time to wheel the bicycle over to the side of the road.

While none of the people he spoke to were exactly what you could call helpful, they were still all extremely friendly. Fat Charlie stopped several times on his day's expedition to the south and refilled his water bottle: he stopped at cafés and at private houses. Everyone was so pleased to see him, even if they didn't know anything about Mrs Higgler. He got back to the Dolphin Hotel in time for dinner.

On the following day he went north. On his way back to Williamstown, in the late afternoon, he stopped on a clifftop, dismounted and walked his bike down to the entry gate of a luxurious house that sat on its own, overlooking the bay. He pressed the speakerphone button, said hello, but no one replied. A large black car sat in the driveway. Fat Charlie wondered if perhaps the place was deserted, but a curtain twitched in an upper room.

He pressed the button again. 'Hullo,' he said. 'Just wanted to see if I could fill my water bottle here.'

There was no reply. Perhaps he had only imagined that there was someone at the window. He seemed extremely prone to imagining things here: he started to fancy that he was being watched, not by someone in the house, but by someone or something in the bushes that bordered the road. 'Sorry to have bothered you,' he said into the speaker, and clambered back on to his bike. It was downhill from here all the way to Williamstown. He was sure that he'd pass a café or two on the way, or another house, a friendly one.

He was on his way down the road – the cliffs had become a steepish hill down to the sea – when a black car came up behind him, and accelerated forward with a roar. Too late, Fat Charlie realised that the driver had not seen him, for there was a long scrape of car against the bike's handlebar, and Fat Charlie found himself tumbling, with the bike, down the hill. The black car drove on.

Fat Charlie picked himself up halfway down the hill. 'That could have been nasty,' he said aloud. The handlebars were twisted. He hauled his bike back up the hill and on to the road. A low bass rumble alerted him to the approach of a minibus, and he waved it down.

'Can I put my bike in the back?'

'No room,' said the driver, but he produced several bungee cords from beneath his seat, and used them to fasten the bike on to the roof of the bus. Then he grinned. 'You must be the Englishman with the lime.'

'I don't have it on me. It's back at the hotel.'

Fat Charlie squeezed on to the bus, where the booming bass resolved itself, extremely improbably, into Deep Purple's 'Smoke on the Water'. Fat Charlie squeezed in next to a large woman with a chicken on her lap. Behind them two white girls chattered about the parties they had attended the previous night and the shortcomings of the temporary boyfriends they had accumulated during their holiday.

Fat Charlie noticed the black car – a Mercedes – as it came back up the road. It had a long scratch along one side. He felt guilty, hoped his bike hadn't scraped the paintwork too badly. The windows were tinted so dark that the car might have been driving itself . . .

Then one of the white girls tapped Fat Charlie on the shoulder and asked him if he knew of any good parties on the island that night, and when he said he didn't, started telling him about one that she'd been to in a cave two nights before, where there was a swimming pool and a sound system and lights and everyfink, and so Fat Charlie completely failed to notice that the black Mercedes was now following the minibus into Williamstown, and that it only went on its way once Fat Charlie had retrieved his bike from the roof of the minibus ('next time, you should bring the lime') and carried the bike into the hotel lobby.

Only then did the car return to the house on the clifftop.

Benjamin the concierge examined the bike and told Fat Charlie not to worry, and they'd have it all fixed and good as new by tomorrow.

Fat Charlie went back to his hotel room, the colour of underwater, where his lime sat, like a small green Buddha, on the countertop.

'You're no help,' he told the lime. This was unfair. It was only a lime; there was nothing special about it at all. It was doing the best it could.

* * *

Stories are webs, interconnected, strand to strand, and you follow each story to the centre, because the centre is the end. Each person is a strand of story.

Daisy, for example.

Daisy could not have lasted as long as she had in the police force without having a sensible side to her nature, which was mostly all anybody saw. She respected laws, and she respected rules. She understood that many of these rules are perfectly arbitrary – decisions about where one could park, for example, or what hours shops were permitted to open – but that even these rules helped the big picture. They kept society safe. They kept things secure.

Her flatmate, Carol, thought she'd gone mad.

'You can't just leave and say you're going on holiday. It doesn't work like that. You're not on a TV cop show, you know. You can't just zoom all over the world to follow up a lead.'

'Well, then, in that case I'm not,' Daisy had retorted, untruthfully. 'I'm really just going on holiday.'

She said it so convincingly that the sensible cop who lived at the back of her head was shocked into silence, and then began to explain to her exactly what she was doing wrong, beginning with pointing out that she was about to go off on an entirely unauthorised leave – tantamount, muttered the sensible cop, to neglect of duty – and moving on from there.

It explained it on the way to the airport, and all across the Atlantic. It pointed out that even if she managed to avoid a permanent black mark in her personal files, let alone being thrown out of the police force altogether, even if she did find Grahame Coats, there was nothing she could do once she found him. Her Majesty's Constabulary look unkindly on kidnapping foreign criminals, let alone arresting them, and she rather doubted she would be able to persuade him to return to the UK willingly.

It was only when Daisy got off the little plane from Jamaica and tasted the air – earthy, spicy, wet, almost sweet – of Saint Andrews, that the sensible cop stopped pointing out the sheer ill-considered madness of what she was doing. That was because it was drowned out by another voice. 'Evildoers beware!' it sang. 'Beware! Take care! Evildoers everywhere!' and Daisy was marching to its beat. Grahame Coats had killed a woman in his office in the Aldwych, and he had walked out of there scot-free. He had done it practically under Daisy's nose.

She shook her head, collected her bag, brightly informed the immigration officer that she was here on her holidays, and went out to the taxi rank.

'I want a hotel that's not too expensive, but isn't icky, please,' she said to the driver.

'I got just the place for you, darlin',' he said. 'Hop in.'

***

Spider opened his eyes and discovered that he was staked out, face down. His arms were tied to a large stake, pounded into the earth in front of him. He could not move his legs, or twist his neck enough to see behind him, but he was willing to bet that they were similarly hobbled. The movement, as he tried to lift himself out of the dirt, to look behind him, caused his scratches to burn.

He opened his mouth, and dark blood drooled on to the dust, wetting it.

He heard a sound and twisted his head as much as he could. A white woman was looking down at him curiously.

'Are you all right? Silly question. Just look at the state of you. I suppose you're another duppy. Do I have that right?'

Spider thought about it. He didn't think he was a duppy. He shook his head.

'If you are, it's nothing to be ashamed of. Apparently, I'm a duppy myself. I hadn't heard the term before, but I met a delightful old gentleman on the way here who told me all about it. Let me see if I can be of any assistance.'

She crouched down next to him, reached out to help loosen his bonds.

Her hand slipped through him. He could feel her fingers, like strands of fog, brushing his skin.

'I'm afraid I don't seem able actually to touch you,' she said. 'Still, that means that you're not dead yet. So cheer up.'

Spider hoped this odd ghost-woman would go away soon. He couldn't think straight.

'Anyway, once I had everything sorted out, I resolved to remain walking the Earth until I take vengeance on my killer. I explained it to Morris – he was on a television screen in Selfridges – and he said he rather thought I was missing the entire point of having moved beyond the flesh, but I ask you, if they expect me to turn the other cheek they have several other thinks coming. Anyway, there are a number of precedents. And I'm sure I can do a Banquo-at-the-feast thing, given the opportunity. Do you talk?'

Spider shook his head, and blood dripped from his forehead into his eyes. It stung. Spider wondered how long it would take him to grow a new tongue. Prometheus had managed to grow a new liver on a daily basis, and Spider was pretty sure that a liver had to be a lot more work than a tongue. Livers did chemical reactions – bilirubin, urea, enzymes, all that. They broke down alcohol, and that had to be a lot of work on its own. All tongues did was talk. Well, that and lick, of course . . .

'I can't keep yattering on,' said the yellow-haired ghost lady. 'I've got a long way to go, I think.' She began to walk away, and she faded as she walked. Spider raised his head and watched her slip from one reality to another, like a photograph fading in the sunlight. He tried to call her back, but all the noises he could make were muffled, incoherent. Tongueless.

Somewhere in the distance, he heard the cry of a bird.

Spider tested his bonds. They held.

He found himself thinking, once again, of Rosie's story of the raven who saved the man from the mountain lion. It itched in his head, worse than the claw-tracks on his face and chest. *Concentrate.* The man lay on the ground, reading or sunbathing. The raven cawed in the tree. There was a big cat in the undergrowth . . .

And then the story reshaped itself, and he had it. Nothing had changed. It was all a matter of how you looked at the ingredients.

What if, he thought, the bird wasn't calling to warn the man that there was a big cat stalking him? What if it was calling to tell the mountain lion that there was a man on the ground – dead, or asleep or dying. That all the big cat had to do was finish the man off. And then the raven would feast on what it left . . .

Spider opened his mouth to moan, and blood ran from his mouth and puddled on the powdery clay.

Reality thinned. Time passed, in that place.

Spider, tongueless and furious, raised his head and twisted it to look at the ghost birds that flew around him, screaming.

He wondered where he was. This was not the bird-woman's copper-coloured universe, nor her cave, but neither was it the place he had previously tended to think of as the real world. It was closer to the real world, though, close enough that he could almost taste it, or would have tasted it if he could taste anything in his mouth but the iron tang of the blood, close enough that, if he were not staked out on the ground, he could have touched it.

If he had not been perfectly certain of his own sanity, certain to a degree that normally is only found in people who have concluded that they're definitely Julius Caesar and have been sent to save the world, he might have thought that he was going mad. First he saw a blonde woman who claimed to be a duppy, and now he heard voices. Well, he heard one voice anyway. Rosie's.

She was saying, 'I dunno. I thought it would be a holiday, but seeing those kids, without anything, it breaks your heart. There's so much they need.' And then, while Spider was trying to assess the significance of this, she said, 'I wonder how much longer she's going to be in the bath. Good thing you've got plenty of hot water here.'

Spider wondered if Rosie's words were meant to be important, whether they held the key to escaping from his predicament. He doubted it. Still, he listened harder, wondering whether the wind would carry any more words between the worlds. Apart from the crash of the waves on breakers behind and far below him, he heard nothing, only silence. But a specific kind of silence. There are, as Fat Charlie once suspected, many kinds of silences. Graves have their own silence, space has its silence, mountaintops have theirs. This was a hunting silence. It was a stalking silence. In this silence something moved on velvet-soft pads, with muscles like steel springs coiled beneath soft fur: something the colour of shadows in the long grass; something that would ensure that you heard nothing it did not wish you to hear. It was a silence that was moving from side to side in front of him, slowly and relentlessly, and with every arc it was getting closer.

Spider heard that in the silence, and the hairs on the back of his neck stiffened. He spat blood on to the dust by his face, and he waited.

* * *

In his house on the clifftop, Grahame Coats paced back and forth. He walked from his bedroom to the study, then down the stairs to the kitchen and back up to the library and from there back to his bedroom again. He was angry with himself: how could he have been so stupid as to assume that Rosie's visit was a coincidence?

He had realised it when the buzzer had sounded, and he had looked into the closed circuit TV screen at Fat Charlie's inane face. There was no mistaking it. *It was a conspiracy.*

He had imitated the action of a tiger, and climbed into the car, certain of an easy hit-and-run: if they found a mangled bicycle rider, people would blame it on a minibus. Unfortunately, he had not counted on Fat Charlie cycling so close to the road's drop-off: Grahame Coats had been unwilling to push his car any closer to the edge of the road, and now he was regretting it. No, Fat Charlie had sent in the women in the meat locker, they were his spies. They had infiltrated Grahame Coats's house. He was lucky that he had tumbled their scheme. He had known there was something *wrong* about them.

As he thought of the women, he realised that he had not fed them yet. He ought to give them something to eat. And a bucket. They would probably need a bucket after twenty-four hours. Nobody could say that he was an animal.

He had bought a handgun in Williamstown, the previous week. You could buy guns pretty easily on Saint Andrews, it was that sort of island. Most people didn't bother with buying guns, though, it was that sort of island too. He took the gun from his bedside drawer and went down to the kitchen. He took a plastic bucket from under the sink, tossed several tomatoes, a raw yam, a half-eaten lump of Cheddar cheese and a carton of orange juice into it. Then, pleased with himself for thinking of it, he fetched a toilet roll.

He went down to the wine cellar. There was no noise from inside the meat locker.

'I've got a gun,' he said. 'And I'm not afraid to use it. I'm going to open the door now. Please go over to the far wall, turn around and put your hands against it. I've brought food. Co-operate and you will both be released unharmed. Co-operate and nobody gets hurt. That means,' he said, delighted to find himself able to deploy an entire battalion of clichés hitherto off limits, 'no funny business.'

He turned on the lights inside the room, then pulled the bolts. The walls of the room were rock and brick. Rusting chains hung from hooks in the ceiling.

They were against the far wall. Rosie looked at the rock. Her mother stared over her shoulder at him like a trapped rat, furious and filled with hate.

Grahame Coats put down the bucket; he did not put down the gun. 'Lovely grub,' he said. 'And, better late than never, a bucket. I see you've been using the corner. There's toilet paper, too. Don't ever say I didn't do anything for you.'

'You're going to kill us,' said Rosie. 'Aren't you?'

'Don't antagonise him, you stupid girl,' spat her mother. Then, assuming a smile of sorts, she said, 'We're grateful for the food.'

'Of course I'm not going to kill you,' said Grahame Coats. It was only as he heard the words coming out of his mouth that he admitted to himself that, yes, of course he was going to have to kill them. What other option did he have? 'You didn't tell me that Fat Charlie sent you here.'

Rosie said, 'We came on a cruise ship. This evening we're meant to be in Barbados for the fish fry. Fat Charlie's in England. I don't even think he knows where we've gone. I didn't tell him.'

'It doesn't matter what you say,' said Grahame Coats. 'I've got the gun.'

He pushed the door closed and bolted it. Through the door he could hear Rosie's mother saying, 'The animal. Why didn't you ask him about the animal?'

'Because you're just imagining it, Mum. I keep telling you. There isn't an animal in here. Anyway, he's nuts. He'd probably just agree with you. He probably sees invisible tigers himself.'

Stung by this, Grahame Coats turned off their lights. He pulled out a bottle of red wine and went upstairs, slamming the cellar door behind him.

In the darkness beneath the house, Rosie broke the lump of cheese into four bits and ate one as slowly as she could.

'What did he mean about Fat Charlie?' she asked her mother, after the cheese had dissolved in her mouth.

'Your bloody Fat Charlie. I don't want to know about Fat Charlie,' said her mother. 'He's the reason that we're down here.'

'No, we're here because that Coats man is a total nutjob. A nutter with a gun. It's not Fat Charlie's fault.' She had tried not to let herself think about Fat Charlie, because thinking about Fat

Charlie meant that she inevitably found herself thinking about Spider . . .

'It's back,' said her mother. 'The animal is back. I heard it. I can smell it.'

'Yes, Mum,' said Rosie. She sat on the concrete floor of the meat cellar and thought about Spider. She missed him. When Grahame Coats saw reason and let them go, she'd try to locate Spider, she decided. Find out if there was room for a new beginning. She knew it was only a silly daydream, but it was a good dream, and it comforted her.

She wondered if Grahame Coats would kill them tomorrow.

* * *

A candle flame's thickness away, Spider was staked out for the beast.

It was late afternoon, and the sun was low behind him.

Spider was pushing at something with his nose and lips: it had been dry earth, before his spit and blood had soaked into it. Now it was a ball of mud, a rough marble of reddish clay. He had pushed it into a shape that was more or less spherical. Now he flicked at it, getting his nose underneath it and then jerking his head up. Nothing happened, as nothing had happened the previous how-many times. Twenty? A hundred? He wasn't keeping count. He simply kept on. He pushed his face further into the dirt, pushed his nose further under the ball of clay, jerked his head up and forward . . .

Nothing happened. Nothing was going to happen.

He needed another approach.

He closed his lips on the ball, closed them around it. He breathed in through his nose, as deeply as he could. Then he expelled the air through his mouth. The ball popped from his lips, with a pop like a champagne cork, and landed about eighteen inches away.

Now he twisted his right hand. It was bound at the wrist, with the rope pulling it tightly towards the stake. He pulled the hand back, bent it round. His fingers reached for the lump of bloody mud, and they fell short.

It was so near . . .

Spider took another deep breath, but choked on the dry dust, and began to cough. He tried again, twisting his head over to one side to fill his lungs. Then he rolled over and began to blow, in the direction of the ball, forcing the air from his lungs as hard as he could.

The clay ball rolled – less than an inch, but it was enough. He stretched, and now he was holding the clay in his fingers. He began to pinch the clay between finger and thumb, then turning it and doing it again. Eight times.

He repeated the process once more, this time squeezing the pinched clay a little tighter. One of the pinches fell off on to the dirt, but the others held. He had something in his hand that looked like a small ball with seven points coming out of it, like a child's model of the sun.

He looked at it with pride: given the circumstances, he felt as proud of it as anything a child has ever brought home from school.

The word, that would be the hardest part. Making a spider, or something quite like it, from blood and spit and clay, that was easy. Gods, even minor mischief gods like Spider, know how to do that. But the final part of Making was going to prove the hardest. You need a word to give something life. You need to name it.

He opened his mouth. 'Hrrurrrurrr,' he said, with his tongueless mouth.

Nothing happened.

He tried again. 'Hrrurrurr!' The clay sat, a dead lump in his hand.

His face fell back into the dirt. He was exhausted. Every movement tore the scabs on his face and chest. They oozed and burned and – worse – itched. *Think!* he told himself. There had to be a way of doing this . . . To talk without his tongue . . .

His lips still had a layer of clay on them. He sucked at them, moistening as well as he could, without a tongue.

He took a deep breath, and let it push through his lips, controlling it as best he could, saying it with such certainty that not even the universe could argue with him: he described the thing on his hand, and he said his own name, which was the best magic he knew: '*hhssspphhhrrriiivver*'.

And on his hand, where the lump of bloody mud had been, sat a fat spider, the colour of red clay, with seven spindly legs.

Help me, thought Spider. *Get help.*

The spider stared at him, its eyes gleaming in the sunlight. Then it dropped from his hand to the earth, and it proceeded to make its lopsided way into the grass, its gait wobbly and uneven.

Spider watched it until it was out of sight. Then he lowered his head into the dirt, and he closed his eyes.

The wind changed then, and he smelled the ammoniac scent of male cat on the air. It had marked its territory . . .

High in the air, Spider could hear birds caw in triumph.

* * *

Fat Charlie's stomach growled. If he had had any superfluous money he would have gone somewhere for dinner, just to get away from his hotel, but he was, as near as dammit, now quite broke, and evening meals were included in the cost of the room, so as soon as it turned seven, he went down to the restaurant.

The maitre d' had a glorious smile, and she told him that they would open the restaurant in just a few more minutes. They had to give the band time to finish setting up. Then she looked at him. Fat Charlie was beginning to know that look.

'Are you . . . ?' she began.

'Yes,' he said. 'I've even got it with me.' He took the lime out of his pocket and showed it to her.

'Very nice,' she said. 'That's definitely a lime you've got there. I was going to say, are you going to want the *à la carte* menu or would you rather do the buffet?'

'Buffet,' said Fat Charlie. The buffet was free. He stood in the hall outside the restaurant holding his lime.

'Just wait a moment,' said the maître d'.

A small woman came down the corridor from behind Fat Charlie. She smiled at the maître d' and said, 'Is the restaurant open yet? I'm completely starved.'

There was a final *thrum-thung-thdum* from the bass guitar and a *plunk* from the electric piano. The band put down their instruments and waved at the maître d'. 'It's open,' she said. 'Come in.'

The small woman stared at Fat Charlie with an expression of wary surprise. 'Hello, Fat Charlie,' she said. 'What's the lime for?'

'It's a long story.'

'Well,' said Daisy. 'We've got the whole of dinnertime ahead of us. Why don't you tell me all about it?'

* * *

Rosie wondered whether madness could be contagious. In the blind darkness beneath the house on the cliff, she had felt something brush past her. Something soft and lithe. Something huge. Something that growled, softly, as it circled them.

'Did you hear that too?' she said.

'Of course I heard it, you stupid girl,' said her mother. Then she said, 'Is there any orange juice left?'

Rosie fumbled in the darkness for the juice carton, passed it to her mother. She heard the sound of drinking, then her mother said, 'The animal will not be the one that kills us. *He* will.'

'Grahame Coats. Yes.'

'He's a bad man. There is something riding him, like a horse, but he would be a bad horse, and he is a bad man.'

Rosie reached out and held her mother's bony hand in her own. She didn't say anything. There wasn't anything much to say.

'You know,' said her mother, after a while, 'I'm very proud of you. You were a good daughter.'

'Oh,' said Rosie. The idea of not being a disappointment to her mother was a new one, and something about which she was not sure how she felt.

'Maybe you should have married Fat Charlie,' said her mother. 'Then we wouldn't be here.'

'No,' said Rosie. 'I should never have married Fat Charlie. I don't love Fat Charlie. So you weren't entirely wrong.'

They heard a door slam upstairs.

'He's gone out,' said Rosie. 'Quick. While he's out. Dig a tunnel.' First she began to giggle, and then she began to cry.

***

Fat Charlie was trying to understand what Daisy was doing on the island. Daisy was trying, equally as hard, to understand what Fat Charlie was doing on the island. Neither of them was having much success. A singer, in a long red slinky dress, who was too good for a little hotel restaurant's Friday Night Fun, was up on the little dais at the end of the room singing 'I've Got You Under My Skin'.

Daisy said, 'You're looking for the lady who lived next door when you were a little boy, because she may be able to help you find your brother.'

'I was given a feather. If she's still got it, I may be able to exchange it for my brother. It's worth a try.'

She blinked, slowly, thoughtfully, entirely unimpressed, and picked at her salad.

Fat Charlie said, 'Well, you're here because you think that Grahame Coats came here after he killed Maeve Livingstone. But you're not here as a cop. You just powered in under your own steam on the off chance that he's here. And if he is here, there's absolutely nothing you can do about it.'

Daisy licked a fleck of tomato seed from the corner of her lips, and looked uncomfortable. 'I'm not here as a police officer,' she said. 'I'm here as a tourist.'

'But you just walked off the job and came here after him. They could probably send you to prison for that, or something.'

'Then,' she said, drily, 'it's a good thing that Saint Andrews doesn't have any extradition treaties, isn't it?'

Under his breath Fat Charlie said 'Oh God.'

The reason Fat Charlie said 'Oh God' was because the singer had left the stage and was now starting to walk around the restaurant with a radio microphone. Right now, she was asking two German tourists where they were from.

'Why would he come *here*?' asked Fat Charlie.

'Confidential banking. Cheap property. No extradition treaties. Maybe he really likes citrus fruit.'

'I spent two years terrified of that man,' said Fat Charlie. 'I'm going to get some more of that fish-and-green-banana thing. You coming?'

'I'm fine,' said Daisy. 'I want to leave room for dessert.'

Fat Charlie walked over to the buffet, going the long way around to avoid catching the singer's eye. She was very beautiful, and her red sequined dress caught the light and glittered as she moved. She was better than the band. He wished she'd go back on to the little stage and keep singing her standards – he had enjoyed her 'Night and Day' and a peculiarly soulful 'Spoonful of Sugar' – and stop interacting with the diners. Or at least, stop talking to people on his side of the room.

He piled his plate high with more of the things he had liked the first time. The thing about bicycling around the island, he thought, was that it gave you an appetite.

When he returned to his table, Grahame Coats, with something vaguely beardish growing on the lower part of his face, was sitting next to Daisy, and he was grinning like a weasel on speed. 'Fat Charlie,' said Grahame Coats, and he chuckled, uncomfortably. 'It's amazing, isn't it? I come looking for you here, for a little tête-à-tête, and what do I find as a bonus? This glamourous little police officer. Please, sit down over there and try not to make a scene.'

Fat Charlie stood like a waxwork.

'Sit down,' repeated Grahame Coats. 'I have a gun pressed against Miss Day's stomach.'

Daisy looked at Fat Charlie imploringly, and she nodded. Her hands were on the tablecloth, pressed flat.

Fat Charlie sat down.

'Hands where I can see them. Spread them on the table, just like hers.'

Fat Charlie obeyed.

Grahame Coats sniffed. 'I always knew you were an undercover cop, Nancy,' he said. 'An *agent provocateur*, eh? You come into my offices, set me up, steal me blind.'

'I never—' said Fat Charlie, but he saw the look in Grahame Coats's eyes, and he shut up.

'You thought you were so clever,' said Grahame Coats. 'You all thought I'd fall for it. That was why you sent the other two in, wasn't it? The two at the house? Did you think I'd believe they were really from the cruise ship? You have to get up pretty early in the morning to put one over on me, you know. Who else have you told? Who else knows?'

Daisy said, 'I'm not entirely sure what you're talking about, Grahame.'

The singer was finishing 'Some of These Days': her voice was bluesy and rich, and it twined around them all like a velvet scarf.

> *'Some of these days*
> *You're gonna miss me, honey*
> *Some of these days*
> *You're gonna feel so lonely*
> *You'll miss my huggin'*
> *You'll miss my kissin' . . .'*

'You're going to pay the bill,' said Grahame. 'Then I'll escort you and the young lady out to the car. And we'll go back to my place, for a proper talk. Any funny business, and I shoot you both. *Capisce?*'

Fat Charlie *capisced*. He also *capisced* who had been driving the black Mercedes that afternoon, and just how close he had already come to death that day. He was beginning to *capisce* how utterly cracked Grahame Coats was and how little chance Daisy and he had of getting out of this alive.

The singer finished her song. The other people scattered around the restaurant clapped. Fat Charlie kept his hands palms down on the table. He stared past Graham Coats at the singer, and, with the eye that Grahame Coats could not see, he winked at her. She was tired of people avoiding her eyes; Fat Charlie's wink was extremely welcome.

Daisy said, 'Grahame, obviously I came here because of you, but Charlie's just—' She stopped and made the kind of expression you make when someone pushes a gun barrel deeper into your stomach.

Grahame Coats said, 'Listen to me. For the purposes of the innocent bystanders here assembled, we're all good friends. I'm going to put the gun into my pocket, but it will still be pointing at you. We're going to get up. We're going to my car. And I will—'

He stopped. A woman with a red spangly dress and a

microphone was heading for their table, with an enormous smile on her face. She was making for Fat Charlie. She said, into her microphone, 'What's your name, darlin'?' She put the microphone into Fat Charlie's face.

'Charlie Nancy,' said Fat Charlie. His voice caught and wavered.

'And where you from, Charlie?'

'England. Me and my friends. We're all from England.'

'And what do you do, Charlie?'

Everything slowed. It was like diving off a cliff into the ocean. It was the only way out. He took a deep breath and said it 'I'm between jobs,' he started. 'But I'm really a singer. I sing. Just like you.'

'Like me? What kind of things you sing?'

Fat Charlie swallowed. 'What have you got?'

She turned to the other people at Fat Charlie's table. 'Do you think we could get him to sing for us?' she asked, gesturing with her microphone.

'Er. Don't think so. No. Absatively out of the question,' said Grahame Coats. Daisy shrugged, her hands flat on the table.

The woman in the red dress turned to the rest of the room. 'What do we think?' she asked them.

There was a rustle of clapping from the diners at the other tables, and more enthusiastic applause from the serving staff. The barman called out, 'Sing us something!'

The singer leaned in to Fat Charlie, covered the mike and said, 'Better make it something the boys know.'

Fat Charlie said, 'Do they know "Under the Boardwalk"?' and she nodded, announced it, and gave him the microphone.

The band began to play. The singer led Fat Charlie up to the little stage, his heart beating wildly in his chest.

Fat Charlie began to sing, and the audience began to listen.

All he had wanted was to buy himself some time, but he felt comfortable. No one was throwing things. He seemed to have plenty of room in his head to think in. He was aware of everyone in the room: the tourists and the serving staff, and the people over at the bar. He could see everything: he could see the barman measuring out a cocktail, and the old woman in the rear of the room filling a large plastic mug with coffee. He was still terrified, still angry, but he took all the terror and the anger and he put it into the song, and let it all become a song about lazing and loving. As he sang, he thought.

What would Spider do? thought Fat Charlie. *What would my dad do?*

He sang. In his song he told them all exactly what he planned to do under the boardwalk, and it mostly involved making love.

The singer in the red dress was smiling, and snapping her fingers, and shimmying her body to the music. She leaned into the keyboard player's microphone and began to harmonise.

I'm actually singing in front of an audience, thought Fat Charlie. *Bugger me.*

He kept his eyes on Grahame Coats.

As he entered the last chorus, he began to clap his hands above his head, and soon the whole room was clapping along with him, diners and waiters and chefs, everyone except Grahame Coats, whose hands were beneath the tablecloth, and Daisy, whose hands were flat on the table. Daisy was looking at him as if he was not simply barking mad, but had picked an extremely odd moment to discover his inner Drifters.

The audience clapped, and Fat Charlie smiled and he sang, and as he sang he knew, without any shadow of a doubt, that everything was going to be all right. They were going to be just fine, him and Spider and Daisy and Rosie too, wherever she was, they'd be OK. He knew what he was going to do: it was foolish and unlikely and the act of an idiot, but it would work. And as the last notes of the song faded away, he said, 'There's a young lady at the table I was sitting at. Her name's Daisy Day. She's from England too. Daisy, can you wave at everyone?'

Daisy gave him a sick look, but she raised a hand from the table, and she waved.

'There's something I wanted to say to Daisy. She doesn't know I'm going to say this.' *If this doesn't work,* whispered a voice at the back of his head, *she's dead. You know that?* 'But let's hope she says yes. Daisy? Will you marry me?'

The room was quiet. Fat Charlie stared at Daisy, willing her to understand, to play along.

Daisy nodded.

The diners applauded. *This* was a floor show. The singer, the maître d' and several of the waitresses descended on the table, hauled Daisy to her feet and pulled her over to the middle of the floor. They pulled her over to Fat Charlie, and, as the band played 'I Just Called to Say I Love You' he put his arm around her.

'You got a ring for her?' asked the singer.

He put his hand into his pocket. 'Here,' he said to Daisy. 'This is for you.' He put his arms around her and kissed her. If anyone is going to get shot, he thought, it will be now. Then the kiss was over, and people were shaking his hand and hugging him – one man, in town, he said, for the music festival, insisted on giving Fat Charlie his card – and now Daisy was holding the lime he had given her with a very strange expression on her face; and when he looked back to the table they had been sitting at, Grahame Coats was gone.

Chapter Thirteen

Which Proves to Be Unlucky for Some

The birds were excited, now. They were cawing and crying and chattering in the treetops. *It's coming*, thought Spider, and he cursed. He was spent, and done. There was nothing left in him. Nothing but fatigue, nothing but exhaustion.

He thought about lying on the ground and being devoured. Overall, he decided, it was a lousy way to go. He wasn't even certain that he'd be able to regrow a liver, while he was pretty sure that whatever was stalking him had no plans to stop at just the liver anyway.

He began to wrench at the stake. He counted to three, and then, as best as he could and as much as he could, jerked both of his arms towards him so they'd tense the rope and pull the stake, then he counted to three and did it again.

It had about as much effect as if he was to try to pull a mountain across a road. One two three . . . *tug*. And *again*. And *again*.

He wondered if the beast would come soon.

One two three . . . *tug*. One two three . . . *tug*.

Somewhere, someone was singing, he could hear it. And the song made Spider smile. He found himself wishing that he still had a tongue: he'd stick it out at the tiger when it finally made its appearance. The thought gave him strength.

One two three . . . *tug.*

And the stake gave and shifted in his hands.

One more pull and the stake came out of the ground, slick as a sword sliding out of a stone.

He pulled the ropes towards him, and held the stake in his hands. It was about three feet long. One end had been sharpened, to go into the ground. He pushed it out of the loops of rope with numb hands. Ropes dangled uselessly from his wrists. He hefted the stake in his right hand. It would do. And he knew then that he was being watched: that it had been watching him for some time now, like a cat watching a mousehole.

It came to him in silence, or nearly, insinuating its way towards him like a shadow moving across the day. The only movement that caught the eye was its tail, which swished impatiently. Otherwise, it might have been a statue, or a mound of sand that looked, due to a trick of the light, like a monstrous beast, for its coat was a sandy colour, its unblinking eyes the green of the midwinter sea. Its face was the wide cruel face of a panther. In the islands they called any big cat Tiger, and this was every big cat there had ever been – bigger, meaner, more dangerous.

Spider's ankles were still hobbled, and he could barely walk. Pins and needles pricked his hands and his feet. He hopped from one foot to another and tried to look as if he was doing it on purpose, some kind of dance of intimidation, and not because standing hurt.

He wanted to crouch and untie his ankles, but he did not dare take his eyes off the beast.

The stake was heavy, and thick, but was too short to be a spear, too clumsy and large to be anything else. Spider held it by the narrower end, where it had been sharpened, and he looked away, out to sea, intentionally not looking at the place the animal was, relying on his peripheral vision for information.

What had she said? *You will bleat. You will whimper. Your fear will excite him.*

Spider began to whimper. Then he bleated, like an injured goat, lost and plump and alone.

A flash of sandy-coloured motion, barely enough time to register teeth and claws as they blurred towards him. Spider swung the stake like a baseball bat, as hard as he could, feeling it connect with a satisfying thunk across the beast's nose.

Tiger stopped, stared at him as if unable to believe its eyes, then made a noise in the back of its throat, a querulous growl, and it walked, stiff-legged, back in the direction it had come, toward the scrub, as if it had a prior appointment that it wished it could get out of. It glared back at Spider resentfully, over its shoulder, a beast in pain; gave him the look of an animal who would be returning.

Spider watched it go.

Then he sat down, and untangled and untied his ankles.

He walked, a little unsteadily, along the cliff-edge, following it gently downhill. Soon a stream crossed his path, running off the cliff-edge in a sparkling waterfall. Spider went down on his knees, cupped his hands together, and began to drink the cool water.

Then he began to collect rocks. Good, fist-sized rocks. He stacked them together, like snowballs.

* * *

'You've hardly eaten anything,' said Rosie.

'*You* eat. Keep your strength up,' said her mother. 'I had a little of that cheese. It was enough.'

It was cold in the meat cellar, and it was dark. Not the kind of dark your eyes get used to, either. There was no light. Rosie had walked the perimeter of the cellar, her fingers trailing against the whitewash and rock and crumbling brick, looking for something that would help, finding nothing.

'You used to eat,' said Rosie. 'Back when Dad was alive.'

'Your father,' said her mother, 'used to eat, too. And see where it got him? A heart attack, aged forty-one. What kind of world is that?'

'But he loved his food.'

'He loved everything,' said her mother bitterly. 'He loved food, he loved people, he loved his daughter. He loved cooking. He loved me. What did it get him? Just an early grave. You mustn't go loving things like that. I've told you.'

'Yes,' said Rosie. 'I suppose you have.'

She walked towards the sound of her mother's voice, hand in front of her face to stop it banging into one of the metal chains that hung in the middle of the room. She found her mother's bony shoulder, put an arm around her.

'I'm not scared,' said Rosie, in the darkness.

'You're crazy, then,' said her mother.

Rosie let go of her mother, moved back into the middle of the room. There was a sudden creaking noise. Dust and powdered plaster fell from the ceiling.

'Rosie? What are you doing?' asked Rosie's mother.

'Swinging on the chain.'

'You be careful. If that chain gives way, you'll be on the floor with a broken head before you can say Jack Robinson.' There was no answer from her daughter. Mrs Noah said, 'I told you. You're crazy.'

'No,' said Rosie. 'I'm not. I'm just not scared any more.'

Above them, in the house, the front door slammed.

'Bluebeard's home,' said Rosie's mother.

'I know. I heard,' said Rosie. 'I'm still not scared.'

***

People kept clapping Fat Charlie on the back, and buying him drinks with umbrellas in them; in addition to which, he had now collected five business cards from people in the music world, on the island for the festival.

All around the room, people were smiling at him. He had an arm round Daisy: he could feel her trembling. She put her lips to his ear. 'You're a complete loony, you know that?'

'It worked, didn't it?'

She looked at him. 'You're full of surprises.'

'Come on,' he said. 'We're not done yet.'

He made for the maître d'. 'Excuse me . . . There was a lady.

While I was singing. She came in, refilled her coffee mug from the pot back there, by the bar. Where did she go?'

The maître d' blinked and shrugged. She said, 'I don't know . . .'

'Yes, you do,' said Fat Charlie. He felt certain, and smart. Soon enough, he knew, he would feel like himself again, but he had sung a song to an audience, and he had enjoyed it. He had done it to save Daisy's life, and his own, and he had succeeded in doing both these things. 'Let's talk out there.' It was the song. While he had been singing, everything had become perfectly clear. It was still clear. He headed for the hallway, and Daisy and the maître d' followed.

'What's your name?' he asked the maître d'.

'I'm Clarissa.'

'Hello, Clarissa. What's your last name?'

Daisy said, 'Charlie, shouldn't we call the police?'

'In a minute. Clarissa what?'

'Higgler.'

'And what's your relationship to Benjamin? The concierge?'

'He's my brother.'

'And how exactly are you two related to Mrs Higgler. To Callyanne Higgler?'

'They're my neice and nephew, Fat Charlie,' said Mrs Higgler, from the doorway. 'Now, I think you better listen to your fiancée, and talk to the police. Don't you?'

* * *

Spider was sitting by the stream on the clifftop, with his back to the cliff and a heap of throwing stones in front of him, when a man came loping out of the long grass. The man was naked, save for a pelt of sandy fur around his waist, behind which a tail hung down; he wore a necklace of teeth, sharp and white and pointed; his hair was long and black. He walked casually towards Spider, as if he were merely out for an early morning constitutional, and Spider's appearance there was a pleasant surprise.

Spider picked up a rock the size of a grapefruit, hefted it in his hand.

'Heya, Anansi's child,' said the stranger. 'I was just passing, and

I noticed you, and wondered if there was anything I could do to help.' His nose looked crooked and bruised.

Spider shook his head. He missed his tongue.

'Seeing you there, I find myself thinking, poor Anansi's child, he must be so hungry.' The stranger smiled too widely. 'Here. I've got food enough to share with you.' He had a sack over his shoulder, and now he opened the sack, and reached his right hand into it, producing a freshly killed black-tailed lamb. He held it by the neck. Its head lolled. 'Your father and I ate together on many an occasion. Is there any reason that you and I cannot do likewise? You can make the fire and I will clean the lamb and make a spit to turn it. Can you not taste it already?'

Spider was so hungry he was light-headed. Had he still been in possession of his tongue, perhaps he would have said 'yes', confident of his ability to talk himself out of trouble; but he had no tongue. He picked up a second rock in his left hand.

'So let us feast and be friends; and let there be no more misunderstandings,' said the stranger.

And the vulture and the raven will clean my bones, thought Spider.

The stranger took another step toward Spider, who decided that this was his cue to throw the first rock. He had a good eye and an excellent arm, and the rock struck where he had intended it to strike, on the stranger's right arm; he dropped the lamb. The next rock hit the stranger on the side of the head – Spider had been aiming for a spot just between the too-widely set eyes, but the man had moved.

The stranger ran, then, a bounding run, with his tail straight out behind him. Sometimes he looked like a man when he ran, and sometimes he looked like a beast.

When he was gone, Spider walked to the place he had been, to retrieve the black-tailed lamb. It was moving, when he reached it, and for a heartbeat he imagined that it was still alive, but then he saw that the flesh was creeping with maggots. It stank, and the stench of the corpse helped Spider forget how hungry he was, for a little while.

He carried it at arm's length to the cliff-edge, and threw it down into the sea. Then he washed his hands in the stream.

He did not know how long he had been in this place. Time was stretched and squashed here. The sun was lowering on the horizon.

After the sun has set, and before the moon has risen, thought Spider. *That is when the beast will be back.*

***

The implacably cheerful representative of the Saint Andrews police force sat in the hotel front office with Daisy and Fat Charlie, and listened to everything each of them had to say with a placid, but unimpressed smile on his wide face. Sometimes he would reach up a finger and scratch his moustache.

They told the police officer that a fugitive from justice called Grahame Coats had come in to them while they were eating dinner, and threatened Daisy with a gun. Which, they were also forced to admit, nobody but Daisy had actually seen. Then Fat Charlie told him about the incident with the black Mercedes and the bicycle, earlier that afternoon, and no, he hadn't actually seen who was driving the car. But he knew where it came from. He told the officer about the house on the clifftop.

The man touched his pepper-and-salt moustache, thoughtfully. 'Indeed, there is a house where you describe. However, it does not belong to your man Coats. Far from it. You are describing the house of Basil Finnegan, an extremely respectable man. For many years, Mr Finnegan has had a healthy interest in law and order. He has given money to schools, but more important, he contributed a healthy sum toward the construction of the new police station.'

'He put a gun to my stomach,' said Daisy. 'He told me that unless we came with him, he'd shoot.'

'If this was Mr Finnegan, little lady,' said the police office, 'I'm sure that there is a perfectly simple explanation.' He opened his briefcase, produced a thick sheaf of papers. 'I'll tell you what. You think about the matter. Sleep on it. If, in the morning, you are convinced that it was more than high spirits, you simply have to fill in this form, and drop off all three copies at the police station. Ask for the new police station, at the back of the city square. Everyone knows where it is.'

He shook both of their hands and went on his way.

'You should have told him you were a cop too,' said Fat Charlie. 'He might have taken you more seriously.'

'I don't think it would have done any good,' she said. 'Anyone who calls you 'little lady' has already excluded you from the set of people worth listening to.'

They walked out into the hotel reception.

'Where did she go?' asked Fat Charlie.

Benjamin Higgler said, 'Aunt Callyanne? She's waiting for you in the conference room.'

* * *

'There,' said Rosie. 'I knew I could do it, if I just kept swinging.'

'He'll kill you.'

'He's going to kill us anyway.'

'It won't work.'

'Mum, have you got a better idea?'

'He'll see you.'

'Mum, will you please stop being so negative? If you've got any suggestions that would help, please say them. Otherwise just don't bother. OK?'

Silence.

Then, 'I could show him my bum.'

'What?'

'You heard me.'

'Er. Instead of?'

'In addition to.'

Silence. Then Rosie said, 'Well, it couldn't hurt.'

* * *

'Hello, Mrs Higgler,' said Fat Charlie. 'I want the feather back.'

'What make you think I got your feather?' she asked, arms folded across her vast bosom.

'Mrs Dunwiddy told me.'

Mrs Higgler seemed surprised by this, for the first time. 'Louella did tell you I got the feather?'

'She said you had the feather.'

'I keeping it safe.' Mrs Higgler gestured towards Daisy with her mug of coffee. 'You can't expect me to start talkin' in front of her. I don't know her.'

'This is Daisy. You can say anything to her you'd say to me.'

'She's your fiancée,' said Mrs Higgler. 'I heard.'

Fat Charlie could feel his cheeks starting to burn. 'She's not my— We aren't actually. I had to say something to get her away from the man with the gun. It seemed the simplest thing.'

Mrs Higgler looked at him. Behind her thick spectacles, her eyes began to twinkle. 'I know that,' she said. 'It was during your song. In front of an audience.' She shook her head, in the way that old people like to do when pondering the foolishness of the young. She opened her black purse, took out an envelope, passed it to Fat Charlie. 'I promised Louella I keep it safe.'

Fat Charlie took out the feather from the envelope, half crushed from where he had been holding it tightly the night of the séance. 'OK,' he said. 'Feather. Excellent. Now,' he said to Mrs Higgler, 'what exactly do I do with it?'

'You don't know?'

Fat Charlie's mother had told him, when he was young, to count to ten before he lost his temper. He counted, silently and unhurriedly, to ten, whereupon he lost his temper. 'Of course I don't know what to do with it, you stupid old woman! In the last two weeks I've been arrested, I've lost my fiancée and my job, I've watched my semi-imaginary brother get eaten by a wall of birds in Piccadilly Circus, I've flown back and forth across the Atlantic like some kind of lunatic transatlantic pingpong ball, and today I got up in front of an audience and I, and I *sang* because my psycho ex-boss had a gun barrel against the stomach of the girl I'm having dinner with. All I'm trying to do is sort out the mess my life has turned into since *you* suggested I might want to talk to my brother. So, no. No, I don't know what to do with this bloody feather. Burn it? Chop it up and eat it? Build a nest with it? Hold it out in front of me and jump out of the window?'

Mrs Higgins looked sullen. 'You have to ask Louella Dunwiddy.'

'I'm not sure that I can. She wasn't looking very well the last time I saw her. And we don't have much time.'

Daisy said, 'Great. You got your feather back. Now, can we please talk about Grahame Coats?'

'It's not only a feather. It's the feather I swapped for my brother.'

'So swap it back, and let's get on with things. We've got to do something.'

'It's not as simple as that,' said Fat Charlie. Then he stopped, and thought about what he had said and what she had said. He looked at Daisy admiringly. 'God, you're smart,' he said.

'I try,' she said. 'What did I say?'

They didn't have four old ladies, but they had Mrs Higgler, Benjamin, and Daisy. Dinner was almost finished, so Clarissa, the maître d', seemed perfectly happy to come and join them. They didn't have earths of four different colours, but there was white sand from the beach behind the hotel and black dirt from the flowerbed in front of it, red mud at the side of the hotel, multicoloured sand in test tubes in the gift shop. The candles they borrowed from the poolside bar were small and white, not tall and black. Mrs Higgler assured them that she could find all the herbs they actually needed on the island, but Fat Charlie had Clarissa borrow a pouch of bouquet garni from the kitchen.

'I think it's all a matter of confidence,' Fat Charlie explained. 'The most important thing isn't the details. It's the magical atmosphere.'

The magical atmosphere in this case was not enhanced by Benjamin Higgler's tendency to look around the table and burst into explosive giggles, nor by Daisy's continually pointing out that the whole procedure was extremely silly.

Mrs Higgler sprinkled the bouquet garni into a bowl of left-over white wine.

Mrs Higgler began to hum. She raised her hands in encouragement, and the others began to hum along with her, like drunken bees. Fat Charlie waited for something to happen.

Nothing did.

'Fat Charlie,' said Mrs Higgler. 'You hum too.'

Fat Charlie swallowed. There's nothing to be scared of, he told himself: he had sung in front of a roomful of people; he had proposed marriage in front of an audience to a woman he barely knew. Humming would be a doddle.

He found the note that Mrs Higgler was humming, and he let it vibrate in his throat . . .

He held his feather. He concentrated and he hummed.

Benjamin stopped giggling. His eyes widened. There was an expression of alarm on his face, and Fat Charlie was going to stop humming to find out what was troubling him, but the hum was inside him now, and the candles were flickering . . .

'Look at him!' said Benjamin. 'He's—'

– and Fat Charlie would have wondered what exactly he was, but it was too late to wonder.

Mists parted.

Fat Charlie was walking along a bridge, a long white footbridge across an expanse of grey water. A little way ahead of him, in the middle of the bridge, a man sat on a small wooden chair. The man was fishing. A green fedora hat covered his eyes. He appeared to be dozing, and he did not stir as Fat Charlie approached.

Fat Charlie recognised the man. He rested his hand on the man's shoulder.

'You know,' he said, 'I knew you were faking it. I didn't think you were really dead.'

The man in the chair did not move, but he smiled. 'Shows how much you know,' said Anansi. 'I'm dead as they come.' He stretched luxuriantly, pulled a little black cheroot from behind his ear, and lit it with a match. 'Yup. I'm dead. Figure I'll stay dead for a lickle while. If you don't die now and again, people start takin' you for granted.'

Fat Charlie said, 'But.'

Anansi touched his finger to his lips for silence. He picked up his fishing rod and began to wind the reel. He pointed to a small net. Fat Charlie picked it up, and held it out as his father lowered a silver fish, long and wriggling, into it. Anansi took the hook from the fish's mouth, then dropped the fish into a white pail. 'There,' he said. 'That's tonight's dinner taken care of.'

For the first time it registered with Fat Charlie that it had been dark night when he had sat down at the table with Daisy and the Higglers, but that while the sun was low wherever he was now, it had not set.

His father folded up the chair, and gave Fat Charlie the chair and the bucket to carry. They began to walk along the bridge. 'You know,' said Mr Nancy, 'I always thought that if you ever came to talk to me, I'd tell you all manner of things. But you seem to be doing pretty good on your own. So what brings you here?'

'I'm not sure. I was trying to find the Bird Woman. I want to give her back her feather.'

'You shouldn't have been messin' about with people like that,' said his father, blithely. 'No good ever comes from it. She's a mess of resentments, that one. But she's a coward.'

'It was Spider—' said Fat Charlie.

'Your own fault. Letting that old busybody send half of you away.'

'I was only a kid. Why didn't you *do* anything?'

Anansi pushed the hat back on his head. 'Ol' Dunwiddy couldn't do anything to you you didn't let her do,' he said. 'You're *my* son, after all.'

Fat Charlie thought about this. Then he said. 'But why didn't you *tell* me?'

'You're doing OK. You're figurin' it all out by yourself. You figured out the songs, didn't you?'

Fat Charlie felt clumsier and fatter and even more of a disappointment to his father, but he didn't simply say 'No'. Instead he said, 'What do you think?'

'I think you're gettin' there. The important thing about songs is that they're just like stories. They don't mean a damn unless there's people listenin' to them.'

They were approaching the end of the bridge. Fat Charlie knew, without being told, that this was the last chance they'd ever have to talk. There were so many things he needed to find out, so many things he wanted to know. He said, 'Dad. When I was a kid. Why did you humiliate me?'

The old man's brow creased. 'Humiliate you? I loved you.'

'You got me to go to school dressed as President Taft. You call that love?'

There was a high-pitched yelp of something that might have been laughter from the old man, then he sucked on his cheroot. The smoke drifted from his lips like a ghostly speech balloon. 'Your mother had something to say about that,' he said. Then he said, 'We don't have long, Charlie. You want to spend the time we got left fighting?'

Fat Charlie shook his head. 'Guess not.'

They had reached the end of the bridge. 'Now,' said his father. 'When you see your brother. I want you to give him something from me.'

'What?'

His father reached up a hand, pulled Fat Charlie's head down. Then he kissed him, gently, on the forehead. 'That,' he said.

Fat Charlie straightened up. His father was looking up at him with an expression that, if he had seen it on anyone else's face, he would have thought of as pride. 'Let me see the feather,' said his father.

Fat Charlie reached into his pocket. The feather was there, looking even more crumpled and dilapidated than it looked before.

His father made a *tch* noise, and held the feather up to the light. 'This is a beautiful feather,' said his father. 'You don't want it to get all manky. She won't take it back if it's messed up.' Mr Nancy ran his hand over the feather, and it was perfect. He frowned at it, 'Now, you'll just get it messed up again.' He breathed on his fingernails, polished them against his jacket. Then he seemed to have arrived at a decision. He removed his fedora, slipped the feather into the hatband. 'Here. You could do with a natty hat anyway.' He put the hat on to Fat Charlie's head. 'It suits you,' he said.

Fat Charlie sighed. 'Dad. I don't wear hats. It'll look stupid. I'll look a complete tit. Why do you always try to embarrass me?'

In the fading light, the old man looked at his son. 'You think I'd lie to you? Son, all you need to wear a hat is attitude. And you got that. You think I'd tell you you looked good if you didn't? You look real sharp. You don't believe me?'

Fat Charlie said, 'Not really.'

'Look,' said his father. He pointed over the side of the bridge. The water beneath them was still and smooth as a mirror, and the man looking up at him from the water looked real sharp in his new green hat.

Fat Charlie looked up to tell his father that maybe he had been wrong, but the old man was gone.

He stepped off the bridge into the dusk.

* * *

'Right. I want to know exactly where he is. Where did he go? What have you done to him?'

'I didn't do anything. Lord, child,' said Mrs Higgler. 'This never happened the last time.'

'It looked like he was beamed up to the mothership,' said Benjamin. 'Cool. Real-life special effects.'

'I want you to bring him back,' said Daisy, fiercely. 'I want him back *now*.'

'I don't even know where he is,' said Mrs Higgler. 'And I didn't send him there. He do that himself.'

'Anyway,' said Clarissa. 'What if he's off doing what he's doing and we make him come back? We could ruin it all.'

'Exactly,' said Benjamin. 'Like beaming the landing party back, halfway through their mission.'

Daisy thought about this, and was irritated to realise that it made sense – as much as anything made sense these days, anyway.

'If nothing else is happening,' said Clarissa, 'I ought to go back to the restaurant. Make sure everything's all right.'

Mrs Higgler sipped her coffee. 'Nothin' happenin' here,' she agreed.

Daisy slammed her hand down on the table. 'Excuse me. We've got a killer out there. And now Fat Charlie's beamed up to the mastership.'

'Mothership,' said Benjamin.

Mrs Higgler blinked. 'OK,' she said. 'We should do something. What do you suggest?'

'I don't know,' said Daisy. 'Kill time, I suppose.' She picked up the copy of the *Williamstown Courier* that Mrs Higgler had been reading, and began to flip through it.

The story about the missing tourists, the women who hadn't gone back to their cruise ship, was a column on page three. *The two at the house*, said Grahame Coats in her head. *Did you think I'd believe they were from the ship?*

At the end of the day, Daisy was a cop.

'Get me the phone,' she said.

'Who are you calling?'

'I think we'll start with the Minister of Tourism and the Chief of Police, and we'll go on from there.'

* * *

The crimson sun was shrinking on the horizon. Spider, had he not been Spider, would have despaired. On the island, in that place, there was a clean line between day and night, and Spider watched the last red crumb of sun being swallowed by the sea. He had his stones, and the two stakes.

He wished he had fire.

He wondered when the moon would be up. When the moon rose, he might have a chance.

The sun set – the final smudge of red sank into the dark sea, and it was night.

'Anansi's child,' said a voice from out of the darkness. 'Soon enough, I shall feed. You will not know I am there until you feel my breath on the back of your head. I stood above you, while you were staked out for me, and I could have crunched through your neck then and there, but I thought better of it. Killing you in your sleep would have brought me no pleasure. I want to feel you die. I want you to know why I have taken your life.'

Spider threw a rock towards where he thought the voice was coming from, and heard it crash harmlessly into the undergrowth.

'You have fingers,' said the voice, 'but I have claws sharper than knives. You have your two legs, but I have four legs that will never tire, that can run ten times as fast as you ever will and keep on running. Your teeth can eat meat, if it has been made soft and tasteless by the fire, for you have little monkey-teeth, good for chewing soft fruit and crawling bugs; but I have teeth that rend and tear the living flesh from the bones, and I can swallow it while the lifeblood still fountains into the sky.'

And then Spider made a noise. It was a noise that could be

made without a tongue, without even opening his lips. It was a *meh* noise, of amused disdain. *You may be all these things, Tiger, it seemed to say, but so what? All the stories there ever were are Anansi's. Nobody tells Tiger stories.*

There was a roar from the darkness, a roar of fury and frustration.

Spider began to hum the tune of the 'Tiger Rag'. It's an old song, good for teasing tigers with: 'Hold that tiger,' it goes. 'Where's that tiger?'

When the voice came next from the darkness, it was nearer.

'I have your woman, Anansi's child. When I am done with you, I shall tear her flesh. Her meat will taste sweeter than yours.'

Spider made the *hmph!* noise people make when they know they're being lied to.

'Her name is Rosie.'

Spider made an involuntary noise then.

In the darkness, someone laughed. 'And as for eyes,' it said, 'you have eyes that see the obvious, in broad daylight, if you are lucky, whereas my people have eyes that can see the hairs prickle on your arms as I talk to you, see the terror on your face, and see that in the night time. Fear me, Anansi's child, and if you have any final prayers to say, say them now.'

Spider had no prayers, but he had rocks, and he could throw them. Perhaps he might get lucky, and a rock might do some damage in the darkness. Spider knew that it would be a miracle if it did, but he had spent his entire life relying on miracles.

He reached for another rock.

Something brushed the back of his hand.

Hello, said the little clay spider, in his mind.

Hi, thought Spider. *Look, I'm a bit busy here, trying not to be eaten, so if you don't mind keeping out of the way for a while . . .*

But I brought them, thought the spider. *Like you asked.*

Like I asked?

You told me to go for help. I brought them back with me. They followed my webstrand. There are no spiders in this creation, so I slipped back and webbed from there to here and from here to there again. I brought the warriors. I brought the brave.

'A penny for your thoughts,' said the big cat voice in the

darkness. And then it said, with a certain refined amusement, 'What's the matter? Cat got your tongue?'

A single spider is silent. They cultivate silence. Even the ones that do make noises will normally remain as still as they can, waiting. So much of what spiders do is waiting.

The night was slowly filled with a gentle rustling.

Spider thought his gratitude and pride at the little seven-legged spider he had made from his blood and spittle and from the earth. The spider scuttled from the back of his hand up to his shoulder.

Spider could not see them, but he knew they were all there: the great spiders and the small spiders, venomous spiders and biting spiders: huge hairy spiders and elegant chitinous spiders. Their eyes took whatever light they could find, but they saw through their legs and their feet, constructing vibrations into a virtual image of the world about them.

They were an army.

Tiger spoke again from the darkness. 'When you are dead, Anansi's child – when all of your bloodline is dead – then the stories will be mine. Once again, people will tell Tiger stories. They will gather together and praise my cunning and my strength, my cruelty and my joy. Every story will be mine. Every song will be mine. The world will be as it once was again: a hard place. A dark place.'

Spider listened to the rustle of his army.

He was sitting at the cliff-edge for a reason. While it gave him nowhere to retreat to, it meant that Tiger could not charge, he could only creep.

Spider started to laugh.

'What are you laughing at, Anansi's child? Have you lost your reason?'

At that, Spider laughed longer and louder.

There was a yowl from the darkness. Tiger had met Spider's army.

Spider venom comes in many forms. It can often take a long while to discover the full effects of the bite. Naturalists have pondered this for years: there are even spiders whose bite can cause the place bitten to rot and to die, sometimes more than a year after it was bitten. As to why spiders do this, the answer is simple. It's because spiders think this is funny, and they don't want you ever to forget them.

Black widow bites on Tiger's bruised nose, tarantula bites on his ears: in moments his sensitive places burned and throbbed, swelled and itched. Tiger did not know what was happening: all he knew was the burning and the pain and the sudden fear.

Spider laughed, longer and louder, and listened to the sound of a huge animal bolting into the undergrowth, roaring in agony and in fright.

Then he sat and he waited. Tiger would be back, he had no doubt. It was not over yet.

Spider took the seven-legged spider from his shoulder, and stroked it, running his fingers back and forth across its broad back.

A little way down the hill something glowed with a cold green luminescence, and it flickered, like the lights of a tiny city, flashing on and off into the night. It was coming towards him.

The flickering resolved itself into a hundred thousand fireflies. Silhouetted and illuminated in the centre of the firefly-light was a dark figure, man-shaped. It was walking steadily up the hill.

Spider raised a rock, mentally readied his spider-troops for one more attack. And then he stopped. There was something familiar about the figure in the firefly-light; it wore a green fedora.

***

Grahame Coats was most of the way through a half-bottle of rum he had found in the kitchen. He had opened the rum because he had no desire to go down into the wine cellar, and because he imagined it would get him drunk faster than wine would. Unfortunately, it didn't. It did not seem to be doing much of anything, let alone providing the emotional off-switch he felt he needed. He walked around the house with a bottle in one hand and a half-full glass in the other, and sometimes he took a swig from one, and sometimes from the other. He caught sight of his reflection in the mirror, hangdog and sweaty. 'Cheer up,' he said aloud. 'Might never happen. Cloud silver lining. Life rain mus' fall. Too many cooks. 'S an ill wind.' The rum was pretty much gone.

He went back into the kitchen. He opened several cupboards before he noticed a bottle of sherry, towards the back. Grahame picked it up and cradled it gratefully, as if it were a very small old friend who had just returned after years at sea.

He unscrewed the top of the bottle. It was a sweet cooking sherry, but he drank it down like lemonade.

There were other things Graham Coats had noticed, while looking for alcohol in the kitchen. There were, for example, knives. Some of them were very sharp. In a drawer, there was even a small stainless-steel hacksaw. Grahame Coats approved. It would be the very simple solution to the problem in the basement.

'*Habeas corpus*,' he said. 'Or *habeas delicti*. One of those. If there is no body, then there was no crime. *Ergo. Quod erat demonstrandum.*'

He took his gun out of his jacket pocket, put it on the kitchen table. He arranged the knives around it in a pattern, like the spokes of a wheel. 'Well,' he said, in the same tones he had once used to use to persuade innocent boy bands that it was time to sign their contract with him and to say hello to fame if not actually fortune, 'no time like the present.'

He pushed three kitchen knives blade down through his belt, placed the hacksaw in his jacket pocket, and then, gun in hand, he went down the cellar stairs. He turned on the lights, blinked at the wine bottles on their side, each in their rack, each covered with a thin layer of dust, and then he was standing beside the iron meat-locker door.

'Right,' he shouted. 'You'll be pleased to hear that I'm not going to hurt you. I'll be letting you both go now. All a bit of a mistake. Still, no hard feelings. No use crying over spilt. Stand by the far wall. Assume the position. No funny stuff.'

It was, he reflected, as he pulled back the bolts, almost comforting how many clichés already exist for people holding guns. It made Grahame Coats feel like one of a brotherhood: Bogart stood beside him, and Cagney, and all the people who shout at each other on *COPS*.

He turned the light on and pulled open the door. Rosie's mother stood against the far wall, with her back to him. As he came in, she flipped up her skirt and waggled an astonishingly bony brown bottom.

His jaw dropped open. That was when Rosie slammed down a length of rusty chain on to Grahame Coat's wrist, sending the gun flying across the room.

With the enthusiasm and accuracy of a much younger woman, Rosie's mother kicked Grahame Coats in the groin, and as he clutched his crotch and doubled up, making noises pitched at a level that only dogs and bats could hear, Rosie and her mother stumbled out of the meat locker.

They pushed the door closed and Rosie pushed shut one of the bolts. They hugged.

They were still in the wine cellar when all the lights went off.

'It's just the fuses,' said Rosie, to reassure her mother. She was not certain that she believed it, but she had no other explanation.

'You should have locked both bolts,' said her mother. And then, 'Ow,' as she stubbed her toe on something, and cursed.

'On the bright side,' said Rosie, '*he* can't see in the dark either. Just hold my hand. I think the stairs are up this way.'

Grahame Coats was down on all fours on the concrete floor of the meat cellar, in the darkness when the lights went out. There was something hot dripping down his leg. He thought for one uncomfortable moment that he had wet himself, before he understood that the blade of one of the knives he had pushed into his belt had cut deeply into the top of his leg.

He stopped moving and lay on the floor. He decided that he had been very sensible to have drunk so much: it was practically an anaesthetic. He decided to go to sleep.

He was not alone in the meat locker. There was someone in there with him. Something that moved on four legs.

Somebody growled, 'Get up.'

'Can't get up. I'm hurt. Want to go to bed.'

'You're a pitiful little creature and you destroy everything you touch. Now get up.'

'Would love to,' said Grahame Coats in the reasonable tones of a drunk. 'Can't. Just going to lie on the floor for a bit. Anyway. She bolted the door. I heard her.'

He heard a scraping from the other side of the door, as if a bolt was slowly being released.

'The door is open. Now: if you stay here, you'll die.' An impatient rustling; the swish of a tail; a roar, half-muffled in the back of a throat. 'Give me your hand and your allegiance. Invite me inside you.'

'I don't underst—'

'Give me your hand, or bleed to death.'

In the black of the meat cellar, Grahame Coats put out his hand. Someone – something – took it, and held it, reassuringly. 'Now, are you willing to invite me in?'

A moment of cold sobriety touched Grahame Coats then. He had already gone too far. Nothing he did would make matters worse, after all.

'Absa*tively*,' whispered Grahame Coats, and as he said it he began to change. He could see through the darkness easy as daylight. He thought, but only for a moment, that he saw something beside him, bigger than a man, with sharp, sharp teeth. And then it was gone, and Grahame Coats felt wonderful. The blood no longer spurted from his leg.

He could see clearly in the darkness. He pulled the knives from his belt, dropped them on to the floor. He pulled off his shoes, too. There was a gun on the ground, but he left it there. Tools were for apes and crows and weaklings. He was no ape.

He was a hunter.

He pulled himself up on to his hands and his knees, and then he padded, four-footed, out into the wine-cellar.

He could see the women. They had found the steps up to the house, and they were edging up them blindly, hand in hand in the darkness.

One of them was old and stringy. The other was young and tender. The mouth salivated in something that was partly Grahame Coats.

* * *

Fat Charlie left the bridge, with his father's green fedora pushed back on his head, and he walked into the dusk. He walked up the rocky beach, slipping on the rocks, splashing into pools. Then he trod on something that moved. A stumble, and he stepped off it.

It rose into the air, and it kept rising. Whatever it was, it was enormous: he thought at first that it was the size of an elephant, but it grew bigger still.

Light, thought Fat Charlie. He sang aloud, and all the lightning bugs, the fireflies of that place, clustered around him, flickering off and on with their cold green luminescence, and in their light he could make out two eyes, bigger than dinner plates, staring down at him from a supercilious reptilian face.

He stared back. 'Evening,' he said, cheerfully.

A voice from the creature, smooth as buttered oil. 'He-llo,' it said. 'Ding-dong. You look remarkably like dinner.'

'I'm Charlie Nancy,' said Charlie Nancy. 'Who are you?'

'I am Dragon,' said the dragon. 'And I shall devour you in one slow mouthful, little man in a hat.'

Charlie blinked. *What would my father do?* he wondered. *What would Spider have done?* He had absolutely no idea. *Come on. After all, Spider's sort of a part of me. I can do whatever he can do.*

'Er. You're bored with talking to me now, and you're going to let me pass unhindered,' he told the dragon, with as much conviction as he was able to muster.

'Gosh. Good try. But I'm afraid I'm not,' said the dragon, enthusiastically. 'Actually, I'm going to eat you.'

'You aren't scared of limes, are you?' asked Charlie, before remembering that he'd given the lime to Daisy.

The creature laughed, scornfully. 'I,' it said, 'am frightened of nothing.'

'Nothing?'

'Nothing,' it said.

Charlie said, 'Are you *extremely* frightened of nothing?'

'Absolutely terrified of it,' admitted the Dragon.

'You know,' said Charlie, 'I have nothing in my pockets. Would you like to see it?'

'No,' said the Dragon, uncomfortably, 'I most definitely would not.'

There was a flapping of wings like sails, and Charlie was alone on the beach. 'That,' he said, 'was much too easy.'

He kept on walking. He made up a song for his walk. Charlie had always wanted to make up songs, but he never did, mostly because of the conviction that if he ever had written a song, someone would have asked him to sing it, and that would not have been a good thing, much as death by hanging would not be a good thing. Now, he cared less and less, and he sang his song to the fireflies, who followed him up the hillside. It was a song about meeting the Bird Woman and finding his brother. He hoped the fireflies were enjoying it: their light seemed to be pulsing and flickering in time with the tune.

The Bird Woman was waiting for him at the top of the hill.

Charlie took off his hat. He pulled the feather from the hatband.

'Here. This is yours, I believe.'

She made no move to take it.

'Our deal's over,' said Charlie. 'I brought your feather. I want my brother. You took him. I want him back. Anansi's bloodline was not mine to give.'

'And if I no longer have your brother?'

It was hard to tell, in the firefly light, but Charlie did not believe that her lips had moved. Her words surrounded him, however, in the cries of nightjars, and in the owls' shrieks and hoots.

'I want my brother back,' he told her. 'I want him whole and in one piece and uninjured. And I want him now. Or whatever went on between you and my father over the years was just the prelude. You know. The overture.'

Charlie had never threatened anyone before. He had no idea how he would carry out his threats – but he had no doubt that he would indeed carry them out.

'I had him,' she said, in the bittern's distant boom. 'But I left him, tongueless, in Tiger's world. I could not hurt your father's line. Tiger could, once he found his courage.'

A hush. The night-frogs and the night-birds were perfectly silent. She stared at him impassively, her face almost part of the shadows. Her hand went into the pocket of her coat. 'Give me the feather,' she said.

Charlie put it into her hand.

He felt lighter, then, as if she had taken more from him than just an old feather . . .

Then she placed something into his hand: something cold and damp. It felt like a lump of meat, and Charlie had to quell the urge to fling it away.

'Return it to him,' she said, in the voice of the night. 'He has no quarrel with me, now.'

'How do I get to Tiger's world.'

'How did you get here?' she asked, sounding almost amused, and the night was complete, and Charlie was alone on the hill.

He opened his hand and looked at the lump of meat that sat there, floppy and ridged. It looked like a tongue, and he knew whose tongue it had to be.

He put the fedora back on his head, and he thought, *Put my thinking cap on*, and as he thought it, it didn't seem so funny. The green fedora was not a thinking cap: but it was the kind of hat that would be worn by someone who not only thought but also came to conclusions of an important and vital kind.

He imagined the worlds as a web: it blazed in his mind, connecting him to everyone he knew. The strand that connected him to Spider was strong and bright, and it burned with a cold light, like a lightning bug or a star.

Spider had been a part of him, once. He held on to this knowledge, let the web fill his mind. And in his hand was his brother's tongue: that had been part of Spider until very recently, and it wished devoutly to be part of him again. Living things remember.

The wild light of the web burned about him. All Charlie needed to do was follow it . . .

He followed it, and the fireflies clustered around and travelled with him.

'Hey,' he said. 'It's me.'

Spider made a small, terrible noise.

In the glimmer of firefly light, Spider looked awful: he looked hunted and he looked hurt. There were scabs on his face and chest.

'I think this is probably yours,' said Charlie.

Spider took the tongue from his brother, with an exaggerated *thank you* gesture, placed it into his mouth, pushed it in and held it down. Charlie watched and waited as the tongue took root. Soon, Spider seemed satisfied – he moved his mouth experimentally, pushing the tongue to one side and then to the other, as if he were preparing to shave off a moustache, opening his mouth widely and waggling his tongue about. He closed his mouth and stood up.

Finally, in a voice that was still a little wobbly around the edges, he said, 'Nice hat.'

* * *

Rosie made it to the top of the steps first, and she pushed open the wine-cellar door. She stumbled into the house. She waited for her mother, then she slammed and bolted the cellar door behind her. The power was out up here as well, but the moon was high and nearly full, and, after the darkness, the pallid moonlight coming through the kitchen windows might as well have been floodlighting.

Boys and girls come out to play, thought Rosie. *The moon does shine as bright as day* . . .

'Phone the police,' said her mother.

'Where's the phone?'

'How the hell should I know where the phone is? He's still down there.'

'Right,' said Rosie, wondering whether she should find a phone to call the police, or just get out of the house, but before she had reached a decision, it was too late.

There was a bang so loud it hurt her ears, and the door to the cellar crashed open.

The shadow came out of the cellar.

It was real. She knew it was real. She was looking at it. But it was impossible: it was the shadow of a great cat, shaggy and huge. Strangely, though, when the moonlight touched it, the shadow seemed *darker*. Rosie could not see its eyes, but she knew it was looking at her, and that it was hungry.

It was going to kill her. This was where it would end.

Her mother said, 'It wants you, Rosie.'

'I know.'

Rosie picked up the nearest large object, a wooden block that had once held knives, and she threw it at the shadow as hard as she could, and then, without waiting to see if it made contact, she moved as fast as she could out of the kitchen, into the hallway. She knew where the front door was . . .

Something dark, something four-footed, moved faster: it bounded over her head, landed almost silently in front of her.

Rosie backed up against the wall. Her mouth was dry.

The beast was between them and the front door, and it was padding slowly back towards Rosie, as if it had all the time in the world.

Her mother ran out of the kitchen then, then ran past Rosie – tottered down the moonlit corridor towards the great shadow, her arms flailing. With her thin fists she punched the thing in the ribs. There was a pause, as if the world was holding its breath, and then it turned on her. A blur of motion and Rosie's mother was down on the ground, while the shadow shook her like a dog with a rag doll between its teeth.

The doorbell rang.

Rosie wanted to call for help, but instead she found she was screaming, loudly and insistently. Rosie, when confronted with an unexpected spider in a bathtub, was capable of screaming like a B-movie actress on her first encounter with a man in a rubber suit. Now she was in a dark house containing a shadowy tiger and a potential serial killer, and one, perhaps both, of those entities, had just attacked her mother. Her head thought of a couple of courses of action (the gun: the gun was down in the cellar. She ought to go down and get the gun. Or the door – she could try to get past her mother and the shadow and unlock the front door) but her lungs and her mouth would only scream.

Something banged at the front door. *They're trying to break in*, she thought. *They won't get through that door. It's solid.*

Her mother lay on the floor in a patch of moonlight, and the shadow crouched above her, and it threw back its head and it roared, a deep rattling roar of fear and challenge and possession.

I'm hallucinating, thought Rosie with a wild certainty. *I've been locked up in a cellar for two days and now I'm hallucinating. There is no tiger.*

By the same token, she was certain that there was no pale woman in the moonlight, even though she could see her walking down the corridor, a woman with blonde hair, and the long, long legs and narrow hips of a dancer. The woman stopped when she reached the shadow of the tiger. She said, 'Hello, Grahame.'

The shadow-beast lifted its massive head and growled.

'Don't think you can hide from me in that silly animal costume,' said the woman. She did not look pleased.

Rosie realised that she could see the window through the woman's upper body, and she backed up until she was pressing hard against the wall.

The beast growled again, this time a little more uncertainly.

The woman said, 'I don't believe in ghosts, Grahame. I spent my life, my whole life, not believing in ghosts. And then I met you. You let Morris's career run aground. You steal from us. You murder me. And finally, to add insult to injury, you force me to believe in ghosts.'

The shadowy big-cat-shape was whimpering now, and backing down the hall.

'Don't think you can avoid me like that, you useless little man. You can pretend to be a tiger all you like. You aren't a tiger. You're a rat. No, that's an insult to a noble and numerous species of rodent. You're less than a rat. You're a gerbil. You're a *stoat.*'

Rosie ran down the hall. She ran past the shadow-beast, past her fallen mother. She ran *through* the pale woman, and it felt like she was passing through fog. She reached the front door, and began feeling for the bolts.

In her head or in the world Rosie could hear an argument.

Someone was saying, *Pay no attention to her, idiot. She can't touch you. It's just a duppy. She's barely real. Get the girl! Stop the girl!*

And someone else was replying, *You certainly do have a valid point here. But I'm not convinced that you've taken all the circumstances into account, vis-à-vis, well, discretion, um, better part of valour, if you follow me . . .*

I *lead*. You *follow*.

But . . .

'What I want to know,' said the pale woman, 'is just how ghostly you currently are. I mean, I can't touch people. I can't really even touch things. I *can* touch ghosts.'

The pale woman aimed a serious kick at the beast's face. The shadow-cat hissed and took a step back, and the foot missed it by less than an inch.

The next kick connected, and the beast yowled. Another kick, hard against the place the cat's shadowy nose would be, and the beast made the noise of a cat being shampooed, a lonely wail of horror and outrage, of shame and defeat.

The corridor was filled with the sound of a dead woman laughing, a laugh of exultation and delight. 'Stoat,' said the pale woman's voice, again. 'Grahame Stoat.'

A cold wind blew through the house.

Rosie pulled the last of the bolts, and she turned the lock. The front door fell open. There were the beams of flashlights, blinding-bright. People. Cars. A woman's voice said, 'It's one of the missing tourists.' And then she said, 'My God.'

Rosie turned.

In the flashlight's beam Rosie could see her mother, crumpled on the tiled floor, and, beside her, shoeless and unconscious and unmistakably human, Grahame Coats. There was a red liquid splashed all around them, like crimson paint, and Rosie found herself, for a breath, unable to work out what it was.

A woman was talking to her. She was saying, 'You're Rosie Noah. My name's Daisy. Let's find somewhere for you to sit down. Would you like to sit down?'

Someone must have found the fuse box, for at that moment the lights went on all over the house.

A large man in a police uniform was bent over the bodies. He looked up and said, 'It is definitely Mr Finnegan. He is not breathing.'

Rosie said, 'Yes, please. I would like to sit down very much.'

* * *

Charlie sat beside Spider on the edge of the cliff, in the moonlight, his legs dangling over the side.

'You know,' he said, 'you used to be a part of me. When we were kids.'

Spider put his head on one side. 'Really?'

'I think so.'

'Well, that would explain a few things.' He held out his hand: a seven-legged clay spider sat on the back of his fingers, tasting the air. 'So what now? Are you going to take me back or something?'

Charlie's brow crinkled. 'I think you've turned out better than you would have done if you were part of me. And you've had a lot more fun.'

Spider said, 'Rosie. Tiger knows about Rosie. We have to do something.'

'Of course we do,' said Charlie. It was like book-keeping, he thought: you put entries in one column, deduct them from another, and if you've done it correctly, everything should come out right at the bottom of the page. He took his brother's hand.

They stood up, and took a step forward, off the cliff –

– and everything was bright –

A cold wind blew between the worlds.

Charlie said, 'You're not the magical bit of me, you know.'

'I'm not?' Spider took another step. Stars were falling now by the dozen, streaking their way across the dark sky. Someone, somewhere, was playing high sweet music on a flute.

Another step, and now distant sirens were blaring. 'No,' said Charlie. 'You're not. Mrs Dunwiddy thought you were, I think. She split us apart, but she never really understood what she was doing. We're more like two halves of a starfish. You grew up into a whole person. And so,' he said, realising it was true as he said it, 'did I.'

They stood on the cliff-edge in the dawn. An ambulance was on its way up the hill, lights flashing, and another, behind that. They parked by the side of the road, beside a cluster of police cars.

Daisy seemed to be telling everyone what to do.

'Not much that we can do here. Not now,' said Charlie. 'Come on.' The last of the fireflies left him, and blinked its way to sleep.

They rode the first minibus of the morning back to Williamstown.

* * *

Maeve Livingstone sat upstairs in the library of Grahame Coats's house, surrounded by Grahame Coats's art and books and DVDs, and she stared out of the window. Down below the island's emergency services were putting Rosie and her mother into one ambulance, Grahame Coats into another.

She had, she reflected, really enjoyed kicking the beast-thing that Grahame Coats had become. It was the most profoundly satisfying thing she had done since she had been killed – although if she were to be honest with herself, she would have to admit that dancing with Mr Nancy came in an extremely close second. He had been remarkably spry, and nimble on his feet.

She was tired.

'Maeve?'

'Morris?' She looked around her, but the room was empty.

'I wouldn't want to disturb you, if you were still busy, pet.'

'That's very sweet of you,' she said. 'But I think I'm done.'

The walls of the library were beginning to fade. They were losing colour and form. The world behind the walls was starting to show, and in its light she saw a small figure in a smart suit waiting for her.

Her hand crept into his. She said, 'Where are we going now, Morris?'

He told her.

'Oh. Well, that will be a pleasant change,' she said. 'I've always wanted to go there.'

And, hand in hand, they went.

Chapter Fourteen

Which Comes to
Several Conclusions

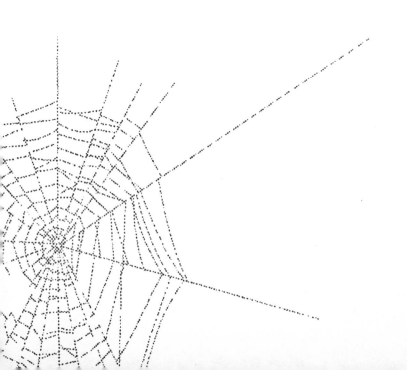

Charlie woke to a banging on a door. Disorientated, he looked around: he was in a hotel room, and various unlikely events clustered inside his head like moths around a naked bulb, and while he tried to make sense of them he let his feet get up and walk him to the hotel-room door. He blinked at the diagram on the back of the door, which told him where to go in case of fire, trying to remember the events of the previous night. Then he unlocked the door and pulled it open.

Daisy looked up at him. She said, 'Were you asleep in that hat?'

Charlie put his hand up and felt his head. There was definitely a hat on it. 'Yes,' he said. 'I think I must have been.'

'Bless,' she said. 'Well, at least you took your shoes off. You know you missed all the excitement, last night?'

'I did?'

'Brush your teeth,' she said helpfully. 'And change your shirt. Yes, you did. While you were . . .' and then she hesitated. It seemed quite improbable, on reflection, that he really had vanished in the middle of a séance. These things did not happen.

Not in the real world. 'While you weren't there. I got the police chief to go up to Grahame Coats's house. He had those tourists.'

'Tourists . . . ?'

'It was what he said at dinner, something about us sending the two people in, the two at the house. It was your fiancée and her mother. He'd locked them up in his basement.'

'Are they OK?'

'They're both in the hospital.'

'Oh.'

'Her mum's in rough shape. I think your fiancée will be OK.'

'Will you stop calling her that? She's not my fiancée. She ended the engagement.'

'Yes. But you didn't, did you?'

'She's not in love with me,' said Charlie. 'Now, I'm going to brush my teeth and change my shirt, and I need a certain amount of privacy.'

'You should shower too,' she said. 'And that hat smells like a cigar.'

'It's a family heirloom,' he told her, and he went into the bathroom and locked the door behind him.

**

The hospital was a ten-minute walk from the hotel, and Spider was sitting in the waiting room, holding a dog-eared copy of *Entertainment Weekly* magazine as if he were actually reading it.

Charlie tapped him on the shoulder, and Spider jumped. He looked up warily and then, seeing his brother, he relaxed, but not much. 'They said I had to wait out here,' Spider said. 'Because I'm not a relation or anything.'

Charlie boggled. 'Well, why didn't you just *tell* them you were a relative? Or a doctor?'

Spider looked uncomfortable. 'Well, it's easy to do that stuff if you don't *care*. If it doesn't matter if I go in or I don't, it's easy to go in. But now it matters, and I'd hate to get in the way or do something wrong, and I mean, what if I tried and they said no, and then . . . what are you grinning about?'

'Nothing really,' said Charlie. 'It just all sounds a bit familiar.

Come on. Let's go and find Rosie. You know,' he said to Daisy, as they set off down a random corridor, 'there are two ways to walk through a hospital. Either you look like you belong there – here you go, Spider. White coat on back of door, just your size. Put it on – or you should look so out of place that no one will complain that you're there. They'll just leave it for someone else to sort out.' He began to hum.

'What's that song?' asked Daisy.

'It's called "Yellow Bird",' said Spider.

Charlie pushed his hat back on his head, and they walked into Rosie's hospital room.

Rosie was sitting up in bed, reading a magazine and looking worried. When she saw the three of them come in, she looked more worried. She looked from Spider to Charlie and back again.

'You're both a long way from home,' was all she said.

'We all are,' said Charlie. 'Now, you've met Spider. This is Daisy. She's in the police.'

'I'm not sure that I am any more,' said Daisy. 'I'm probably in all kinds of hot water.'

'You're the one who was there last night? The one who got the island police to come up to the house?' Rosie stopped. She said, 'Any word on Grahame Coats?'

'He's in intensive care, just like your mum.'

'Well, if she comes to before he does,' said Rosie, 'I expect she'll kill him.' Then she said, 'They won't talk to me about my mum's condition. They just say that it's very serious, and they'll tell me as soon as there's anything to tell.' She looked at Charlie with clear eyes. 'She's not as bad as you think she is, really. Not when you get time to know her. We had a lot of time to talk, locked up in the dark. She's all right.'

She blew her nose. Then she said, 'They don't think she's going to make it. They haven't directly said that to me, but they sort of said it in a not-saying it sort of way. It's funny. I thought she'd live through anything.'

Charlie said, 'Me too. I figured even if there was a nuclear war, it would still leave radioactive cockroaches and your mum.'

Daisy stepped on his foot. She said, 'Do they know anything more about what hurt her?'

'I told them,' said Rosie. 'There was some kind of animal in the house. Maybe it was just Grahame Coats. I mean it sort of was him, but it was sort of someone else. She distracted it from me, and it went for her . . .' She had explained it all as best she could to the island police that morning. She had decided not to talk about the blonde ghost-woman. Sometimes minds snap under pressure, and she thought it best if people did not know that hers had.

Rosie broke off. She was staring at Spider as if she had only just remembered who he was. She said, 'I still hate you, you know.' Spider said nothing, but a miserable expression crept across his · face, and he no longer looked like a doctor: now he looked like a man who had borrowed a white coat from behind a door and was worried that someone would notice. A dreamlike tone came into her voice. 'Only,' she said, 'only when I was in the dark, I thought that you were helping me. That you were keeping the animal away. What happened to your face? It's all scratched.'

'It was an animal,' said Spider.

'You know,' she said, 'now I see you both at once, you don't look anything alike at all.'

'I'm the good-looking one,' said Charlie, and Daisy's foot pressed down on his toes for the second time.

'Bless,' said Daisy, quietly. And then, slightly louder, 'Charlie? There's something we need to talk about outside. Now.'

They went out into the hospital corridor, leaving Spider inside.

'What?' said Charlie.

'What what?' said Daisy.

'What have we got to talk about?'

'Nothing.'

'Then why are we out here? You heard her. She hates him. We shouldn't have left them alone together. She's probably killed him by now.

Daisy looked up at him with the kind of expression that Jesus might have given someone who had just explained that he was probably allergic to bread and fishes, so could He possibly do him a quick chicken salad: there was pity in that expression, along with almost infinite compassion.

She touched a finger to her lips and pulled him back towards the door. He looked back into the hospital room: Rosie did not appear to be killing Spider. Quite the opposite, if anything. 'Oh,' said Charlie.

They were kissing. Put like that, and you could be forgiven for presuming that this was a normal kiss, all lips and skin and possibly even a little tongue. You'd miss how he smiled, how his eyes glowed. And then, after the kiss was done, how he stood, like a man who had just discovered the art of standing and had figured out how to do it better than anyone else who would ever come along.

Charlie turned his attention back to the corridor, to find Daisy in conversation with several doctors and the police officer they had encountered the previous evening.

'Well, we always had him figured as a bad man,' the police officer was saying to Daisy. 'I mean, frankly, you only get this kind of behaviour from foreigners. The local people, they simply wouldn't do that kind of thing.'

'Obviously not,' said Daisy.

'Very. Very grateful,' said the police chief, patting her shoulder in a way that set Daisy's teeth on edge. 'This little lady saved that woman's life,' he told Charlie, giving his shoulder a patronising pat for good measure, before setting off, with the doctors, down the corridor.

'So what's happening?' asked Charlie.

'Well, Grahame Coats is dead,' she said. 'More or less. And they don't hold out any hope for Rosie's mum, either.'

'I see,' said Charlie. He thought about this. Then he finished thinking, and came to a decision. Said, 'Would you mind if I just chatted to my brother for a bit? I think he and I need to talk.'

'I'm going back to the hotel anyway. I'm going to check my e-mail. Probably going to have to say sorry on the phone a lot. Find out if I still have a career.'

'But you're a hero, aren't you?'

'I don't think that's what anyone was paying me for,' she said, a little wanly. 'Come and find me at the hotel when you're done.'

Spider and Charlie walked down the Williamstown high street in the morning sun.

'You know, that really is a good hat,' said Spider.

'You really think so?'

'Yeah. Can I try it on?'

Charlie gave Spider the green fedora. Spider put it on, looked at his reflection in a shop window. He made a face, and gave Charlie the hat back. 'Well,' he said, disappointed, 'it looks good on you, anyway.'

Charlie pushed his fedora back on to his head. Some hats can only be worn if you're willing to be jaunty, to set them at an angle and to walk beneath them with a spring in your stride, as if you're only a step away from dancing. They demand a lot of you. This hat was one of those, and Charlie was up to it. He said, 'Rosie's mum is dying.'

'Yeah.'

'I really, *really* never liked her.'

'I didn't know her as well as you did. But given time, I'm sure I would have really, really disliked her too.'

Charlie said, 'We have to try and save her life, don't we?' He said it without enthusiasm, like someone pointing out it was time to visit the dentist.

'I don't think we can do things like that.'

'Dad did something like it for Mum. He got her better, for a while.'

'But that was him. I don't know how we'd do that.'

Charlie said, 'The place at the end of the world. With the caves.'

'Beginning of the world, not the end. What about it?'

'Can we just get there? Without all that candles and herbs malarkey?'

Spider was quiet. Then he nodded, 'I think so.'

They turned together, turned in a direction that wasn't usually there, and they walked away from the Williamstown high street.

Now the sun was rising, and Charlie and Spider walked across a beach littered with skulls. They were not proper human skulls, and they covered the beach like yellow pebbles. Charlie avoided them, where he could, while Spider crunched his way through them. At the end of the beach they took a left turn that was left to absolutely everything, and the mountains at the beginning of the world towered above them and the cliffs fell away below.

Charlie remembered the last time he was here, and it seemed

like a thousand years ago. 'Where is everyone?' he said aloud, and
his voice echoed against the rocks and came back to him. He said,
loudly, 'Hello?'

And then they were there, watching him. All of them. They
seemed grander, now, less human, more animal, *wilder*. He
realised that he had seen them as people last time because he had
expected to meet people. But they were not people. Arrayed on
the rocks above them were Lion and Elephant, Crocodile and
Python, Rabbit and Scorpion, and the rest of them, hundreds of
them, and they stared at him with eyes unsmiling: animals he
recognised; animals that no one living would be able to identify.
All the animals that have ever been in stories. All the animals that
people have dreamed of, worshipped or placated.

Charlie saw all of them.

It's one thing, he thought, *singing for your life, in a room filled
with diners, on the spur-of-the-moment, with a gun barrel in the
ribs of the girl you . . .*

That you . . .

Oh.

Well, thought Charlie, *I can worry about that later.*

Right now he badly wanted either to breathe into a brown
paper bag, or to vanish.

'There must be hundreds of them,' said Spider, and there was
awe in his voice.

There was a flurry in the air, on a nearby rock, which resolved
itself into the Bird Woman. She folded her arms and stared at
them.

'Whatever it is you're going to do,' Spider said, 'you'd better do
it soon. They aren't going to wait around for ever.'

Charlie's mouth was dry. 'Right.'

Spider said, 'So. Um. What exactly do we do now?'

'We sing to them,' said Charlie, simply.

'What?'

'It's how we fix things. I figured it out. We just sing it all, you
and I.'

'I don't understand. Sing *what*?'

Charlie said, 'The *song*. You sing the song, you fix things.' Now
he sounded desperate. 'The *song*.'

Spider's eyes were like puddles, after the rain, and Charlie saw things in them he had not seen before: affection, perhaps, and confusion, and, mostly, apology. 'I don't know what you're talking about.'

Lion watched them from the side of a boulder. Monkey looked at them from the top of a tree. And Tiger . . .

Charlie saw Tiger. It was walking gingerly towards them, on four feet. Its face was swollen and bruised, but there was a glint in its eyes, and it looked as if it would be more than happy to even the score.

Charlie opened his mouth. A small croaking noise came out, as if Charlie had recently swallowed a particularly nervous frog. 'It's no use,' he whispered to Spider. 'This was a stupid idea, wasn't it?

'Yup.'

'Do you think we can just go away again?' Charlie's nervous glance swept the mountainside and the caves, took in each of the hundreds of totem creatures from before the dawn of time. There was one he had not seen the last time he had looked: a small man, with lemon-yellow gloves, and a pencil-thin moustache, and no fedora hat to cover his thinning hair.

The old man winked when he caught Charlie's gaze.

It wasn't much, but it was enough.

Charlie filled his lungs, and he began to sing. 'I am Charlie,' he sang. 'I am Anansi's son. Listen as I sing my song. Listen to my life.'

He sang them the song of a boy who was half a god, and who was broken into two by an old woman with a grudge. He sang of his father, and he sang of his mother.

He sang of names and words, of the building blocks beneath the real, the worlds that make worlds, the truths beneath the way things are; he sang of appropriate ends and just conclusions for those who would have hurt him and his.

He sang the world.

It was a good song, and it was his song. Sometimes it had words, and sometimes it didn't have any words at all.

As he sang, all the creatures listening began to clap and to stamp and to hum along; Charlie felt like he was the conduit for a great song that took in all of them. He sang of birds, of the magic of looking up and seeing them in flight, of the sheen of the sun on a wingfeather in the morning.

The totem creatures were dancing now, the dances of their kind. The Bird Woman danced the wheeling dance of birds, fanning her tailfeathers, tossing back her beak.

There was only one creature on the mountainside who did not dance.

Tiger lashed his tail. He was not clapping or singing or dancing. His face was bruised purple, and his body was covered in welts and in bite-marks. He had padded down the rocks, a step at a time, until he was close to Charlie. 'The songs aren't yours,' he growled.

Charlie looked at him, and sang about Tiger, and about Grahame Coats, and those who would prey upon the innocent. He turned: Spider was looking up at him with admiration.

Tiger roared in anger, and Charlie took the roar and wound his song around it. Then he did the roar himself, just like Tiger had done it. Well, the roar began just as Tiger's roar had, but then Charlie changed it, so it became a really goofy sort of roar, and all the creatures watching from the rocks started to laugh. They couldn't help it. Charlie did the goofy roar again. Like any impersonation, like any perfect caricature, it had the effect of making what it made fun of intrinsically ridiculous. No one would ever hear Tiger roar again without hearing Charlie's roar underneath it. 'Goofy sort of a roar,' they'd say.

Tiger turned his back on Charlie. He loped through the crowd, roaring as he ran, which only made the crowd laugh the harder; and Tiger angrily retreated back into his cave.

Spider gestured with his hands; a curt movement.

There was a rumble, and the mouth of Tiger's cave collapsed in a small rockslide. Spider looked satisfied. Charlie kept singing.

He sang the song of Rosie Noah, and the song of Rosie's mother: he sang a long life for Mrs Noah and all the happiness that she deserved.

He sang of his life, all of their lives, and in his song he saw the pattern of their lives as a web that a fly had blundered into, and with his song he wrapped the fly, made certain it would not escape, and he repaired the web with new strands.

And now the song was coming to its natural end.

Charlie realised, with no little surprise, that he enjoyed singing to other people, and he knew, at that moment, that this was what he would spend the rest of his life doing. He would sing: not big, magical songs that made worlds or recreated existence. Just small songs, that would make people happy for a breath, make them move, make them, for a little while, forget their problems. And he knew that there would always be the fear before performing, the stage-fright, that would never go away, but he also understood that it would be like jumping into a swimming pool – only uncomfortably chill for a few seconds – and then the discomfort would pass and it would be good . . .

Never *this* good. Never this good again. But good enough.

And then he was done. Charlie hung his head. The creatures on the clifftop let the last notes die away, stopped stamping, stopped clapping, stopped dancing. Charlie took off his father's green fedora and fanned his face with it.

Under his breath, Spider said, 'That was amazing.'

'You could have done it too,' said Charlie.

'I don't think so. What was happening at the end? I felt you doing *something*, but I couldn't really tell what it was.'

'I fixed things,' said Charlie. 'For us. I think. I'm not really sure . . .' And he wasn't. Now the song was over, the content of the song was unravelling like a dream in the morning.

He pointed to the cave mouth that was blocked by rocks. 'Did you do that?'

'Yeah,' said Spider. 'Seemed the least I could do. Tiger will dig his way out eventually, though. I wish I'd done something worse than just shut the door on him, to be honest.'

'Not to worry,' said Charlie. 'I did. Something much worse.'

He watched the animals disperse. His father was nowhere to be seen, which did not surprise him. 'Come on,' he said. 'We ought to be getting back.'

***

Spider went back to see Rosie at visiting time. He was carrying a large box of chocolates, the largest that the hospital gift shop sold.

'For you,' he said.

'Thanks.'

'They told me,' she said, 'that they think my mum's going to pull through. Apparently she opened her eyes and asked for porridge. The doctor said it's a miracle.'

'Yup. Your mother asking for food. Certainly sounds like a miracle to me.'

She swatted his arm with her hand, then left her hand resting on his arm.

'You know,' she said, after a while, 'you're going to think this is silly of me. But when I was in the dark, with Mum, I thought that you were helping me. I felt like you were keeping the beast at bay. That if you hadn't've done what you were doing, he would have killed us.'

'Um. I probably helped.'

'Really?'

'I don't know. I think so. I was in trouble as well, and I thought about you.'

'Were you in very big trouble?'

'Enormous. Yes.'

'Will you pour me a glass of water, please?'

He did. She said, 'Spider, what do you *do*?'

'Do?'

'For a job.'

'Whatever I feel like doing.'

'I think,' she said, 'I may stay here, for a bit. The nurses have been telling me how much they need teachers here on the island. I'd like to see that I was making a difference.'

'That might be fun.'

'And what would you do, if I did?'

'Oh. Well, if you were here, I'm sure I could find something to keep me busy.'

Their fingers twined, tight as a ship's knot.

'Do you think we can make this work?' she asked.

'I think so,' said Spider, soberly. 'And if I get bored with you, I'll just go away and do something else. So not to worry.'

'Oh,' said Rosie, 'I'm not worried.' And she wasn't. There was steel in her voice, beneath the softness. You could tell where her mother got it from.

***

Charlie found Daisy on a deck chair out on the beach. He thought she was asleep in the sun. When his shadow touched her, she said, 'Hello, Charlie.' She didn't open her eyes.

'How did you know it was me?'

'Your hat smells like a cigar. Are you going to be getting rid of it soon?'

'No,' said Charlie. 'I told you. Family heirloom. I plan to wear it till I die, then leave it to my children. So. Do you still have a job with the police force?'

'Sort of,' she said. 'My boss said that it's been decided I was suffering from nervous exhaustion brought on by overwork, and I'm on sick leave until I feel well enough to come back.'

'Ah. And when will that be?'

'Not sure,' she said. 'Can you pass the suntan oil?'

He had a box in his pocket. He took it out and put it on the arm of the deck chair. 'In a minute. Er.' He paused. 'You know,' he said, 'we've already done the big embarrassing one of these at gunpoint.' He opened the box. 'But this is for you, from me. Well, Rosie returned it to me. And we can swap it for one you like. Pick out a different one. Probably it won't even fit. But it's yours. If you want it. And um. Me.'

She reached into the box and took out the engagement ring.

'Hmph. All right,' she said. 'As long as you're not just doing it to get the lime back.'

***

Tiger prowled. His tail lashed irritably from side to side, as he paced back and forth across the mouth of his cave. His eyes burned like emerald torches in the shadows.

'Whole world and everything used to be mine,' said Tiger. 'Moon and stars and sun and stories. I owned them all.'

'I feel it incumbent on me to point out,' said a small voice from the back of the cave, 'that you said that already.'

Tiger paused in his pacing; he turned then, and insinuated himself into the back of his cave, rippling as he walked, like a fur rug over hydraulic springs. He padded back until he came to the carcass of an ox and he said, in a quiet voice, 'I *beg* your pardon.'

There was a scrabbling from inside the carcass. The tip of a nose protruded from the ribcage. 'Actually,' it said, 'I was, so to speak, agreeing with you. That was what I was doing.'

Little white hands pulled a thin strip of dried meat from between two ribs, revealing a small animal the colour of dirty snow. It might have been an albino mongoose, or perhaps some particularly shifty kind of weasel in its winter coat. It had a scavenger's eyes.

'Whole world and everything used to be mine. Moon and stars and sun and stories. I owned them all,' said Tiger. Then he said, 'Would have been mine again.'

Tiger stared down at the little beast. Then, without warning, one huge paw descended, smashing the ribcage, breaking the carcass into foul-smelling fragments, pinning the little animal to the floor; it wriggled and writhed but it could not escape.

'You are here,' said Tiger, his huge head nose to nose with the pale animal's tiny head, 'you are here under my sufferance. Do you understand that? Because the next time you say something irritating, I shall bite your head off.'

'Mmmph,' said the weaselly thing.

'You wouldn't like it if I bit off your head, would you?'

'*Nngk,*' said the smaller animal. Its eyes were a pale blue, two chips of ice, and they glinted as it twisted uncomfortably beneath the weight of the huge paw.

'So will you promise me that you will behave, and you will be quiet?' rumbled Tiger. He lifted his paw a little to allow the beast to speak.

'Indeedy,' said the small white thing, extremely politely. Then, with one stoat-like movement, it twisted and sank its sharp little teeth into Tiger's paw. Tiger bellowed in pain, whipped the paw back, sending the little animal flying through the air. It struck the rock ceiling, bounced over to a ledge and from there it darted, like a dirty white streak, to the very back of the cave, where the ceiling got low and close to the floor, and where there were many hiding places for a small animal, places a larger animal could not go.

Tiger padded as far back into the cave as it could easily walk. 'You think I can't wait?' he asked. 'You have to come out sooner or later. I'm not going anywhere.' Tiger lay down. He closed his eyes and soon began to make fairly convincing snoring noises.

After about half an hour of snoring from Tiger, the pale animal crept out from the rocks, and slipped from shadow to shadow, making for a large bone that still had plenty of good meat on it, if you didn't mind a certain rankness, and it didn't. Still, to get to the bone, it would have to pass Tiger. It lurked in the shadows, then it ventured out on little silent feet.

As it passed the sleeping Tiger, a forepaw shot out, and a claw slammed down on the creature's tail, pinning it down. Another paw held the little creature behind the neck. The great cat opened its eyes. 'Frankly,' it said, 'we appear to be stuck with each other. So all I'm asking is that you make an effort. We can both make an effort. I rather doubt that we'll ever be friends, but perhaps we could learn to tolerate each other.'

'I take your point,' said the small ferrety thing. 'Needs must, as they say, when the Devil drives.'

'That's an example of what I'm saying,' said Tiger. 'You just have to learn when to keep your mouth shut.'

'It's an ill wind,' said the little animal, 'that blows nobody any good.'

'Now you're irritating me again,' said Tiger. 'I'm trying to tell you. Don't irritate me, and I won't bite off your head.'

'You keep using the phrase "bite my head off". Now, when you say "bite my head off", I take it I can assume that this is actually some kind of metaphorical statement, implying that you'll shout at me, perhaps rather angrily?'

'Bite your head off. Then crunch it. Then chew it. Then swallow it,' said Tiger. 'Neither of us can leave until Anansi's child forgets we're here. The way that bastard seems to have arranged things, even if I kill you in the morning you'll be reincarnated back in this blasted cave by the end of the afternoon. So don't irritate me.'

'Ah well. Another day . . .' said the small white animal.

'If you say "another dollar",' said Tiger, 'I will be irritated, and there will be serious consequences. Don't. Say anything. Irritating. Do you understand?'

There was a brief silence in the cave at the end of the world. It was broken by a small, weaselly voice, saying 'Absa*tive*ly.'

It started to say, 'Oww!' but the noise was suddenly and effectively silenced.

And then there was nothing in that place but the sound of crunching.

* * *

The thing they don't tell you about coffins in the literature, because frankly it's not much of a selling point to the people who are buying them, is just how comfortable they are.

Mr Nancy was extremely satisfied with his coffin. Now that all the excitement was over, he'd gone back to his coffin, and was comfortably dozing. Every once in a while he would wake and remember where he was, then he'd roll over and go back to sleep.

The grave, as has been pointed out, is a fine place, not to mention a private one, and this is an excellent place to get a little down time. Six feet down, best kind there is. Another twenty years or so, he thought, and he would have to think about getting up.

He opened one eye when the funeral started.

He could hear them up above him: Callyanne Higgler and the Bustamonte woman and the other one, the thin one, not to mention a small horde of grandchildren, great-grandchildren and great-great-grandchildren, all of them sighing and wailing and crying their eyes out for the late Mrs Dunwiddy.

Mr Nancy thought about pushing one hand up through the turf and grabbing Callyanne Higgler's ankle. It was something he'd wanted to do ever since he saw *Carrie* at a drive-in, thirty years earlier, but now the opportunity presented itself, he found himself able to resist the temptation. Honestly, he couldn't be bothered. She'd only scream and have a heart attack and die, and then the damn Garden of Rest would get even more crowded than it already was.

Too much like hard work, anyway. There were good dreams to be dreamed, in the world beneath the soil. *Twenty years*, he thought. *Maybe twenty-five.* By that time, he might even have grandchildren. It's always interesting to see how the grandchildren turn out.

He could hear Callyanne Higgler wailing and carrying on up above him. Then she stopped her sobbing long enough to announce, 'Still. It's not as if she don't have a good life and a long one. That woman's a hundred and three years old when she passes from us.'

'Hunnert and four!' said an irritated voice from under the ground beside him.

Mr Nancy reached one insubstantial arm out and tapped the new coffin sharply on the side. 'Keep it down, there, woman,' he barked. 'Some of us is tryin' to sleep.'

* * *

Rosie had made it clear to Spider that she expected him to get a steady job, the kind that involved getting up in the morning and going somewhere.

So one morning the day before Rosie was to be discharged from the hospital, Spider got up early and went down to the town library. He logged on to the library computer, sauntered on to the internet and, very carefully, cleared out all Grahame Coats's remaining bank accounts, the ones that the police forces of several continents had so far failed to find. He arranged for the stud farm in Argentina to be sold. He bought a small, off-the-peg company, endowed it with the money, and applied for charitable status. He sent off an e-mail, in the name of Roger Bronstein, hiring a lawyer to administer the foundation's business, and suggested that the lawyer might wish to seek out Miss Rosie Noah, late of London, currently of Saint Andrews, and hire her to Do Good.

Rosie was hired. Her first task was to find office space.

Following this, Spider spent four full days walking (and, at nights, sleeping on) the beach that circled most of the island, tasting the food in each of the dining establishments he encountered along the way until he came to Dawson's Fish Shack. He tried the fried flying fish, the boiled green figs, the grilled chicken and the coconut pie, then he went back into the kitchen and found the chef, who was also the owner, and offered him money enough for partnership and cooking lessons.

Dawson's Fish Shack is now a restaurant, and Mr Dawson has retired. Sometimes Spider's out front and sometimes he's back in the kitchen: you go down there and look for him, you'll see him. The food is the best on the island. He's fatter than he used to be, though not as fat as he'll wind up if he keeps tasting everything he cooks.

Not that Rosie minds.

She does some teaching, and some helping out, and a lot of Doing Good, and if she ever misses London she never lets it show. Rosie's mother, on the other hand, misses London continually and vocally, but takes any suggestion that she might want to return there as an attempt to part her from her as-yet-unborn (and, for that matter, unconceived) grandchildren.

Nothing would give this author greater pleasure than to be able to assure you that, following her return from the valley of the shadow of death, Rosie's mother became a new person, a jolly woman with a kind word for everyone, that her new-found appetite for food was only matched by her appetite for life and all it had to offer. Alas, respect for the truth compels perfect honesty and the truth is that when she came out of hospital Rosie's mother was still herself, just as suspicious and uncharitable as ever, although significantly more frail, and now given to sleeping with the light on.

She announced that she would be selling her flat in London and would move to wherever in the world Spider and Rosie were, to be near her grandchildren; and, as time went on, she would drop pointed comments about the lack of grandchildren, the quantity and motility of Spider's spermatozoa, the frequency and positions of Spider and Rosie's sexual relations and the relative cheapness and ease of *in vitro* fertilisation, to the point where Spider seriously began to think about not going to bed with Rosie any more, just to spite Rosie's mother. He thought about this for about eleven seconds one afternoon, while Rosie's mother was handing them photocopies of an article from a magazine that she had found which suggested that Rosie should stand on her head for half an hour after sex; and he mentioned these thoughts to

Rosie that night, and she laughed, and told him that her mother wasn't allowed in their bedroom anyway, and that she wasn't going to be standing on her head after making love for anybody.

Mrs Noah has a flat in Williamstown, near Spider and Rosie's house, and twice a week one of Callyanne Higgler's many nieces looks in on her, does the vacuuming, dusts the glass fruit (the wax fruit melted in the island heat), and makes a little food and leaves it in the fridge, and sometimes Rosie's mum eats it and sometimes she doesn't.

***

Charlie's a singer these days. He's lost a lot of the softness. He's a lean man, now, with a trademark fedora hat. He has lots of different fedoras, in different colours; his favourite one is green.

Charlie has a son. His name is Marcus: he is four and a half, and possesses that deep gravity and seriousness that only small children and mountain gorillas have ever been able to master.

Nobody ever calls Charlie 'Fat Charlie' any more, and honestly, sometimes he misses it.

It was early in the morning in the summer, and it was already light. There was already noise coming from the room next door. Charlie let Daisy sleep. He climbed out of bed quietly, grabbed a T-shirt and shorts, and went through the door, to see his son naked on the floor playing with a small wooden train set. Together they pulled on their T-shirts and shorts and flip-flops, and Charlie put on a hat, and they walked down to the beach.

'Daddy?' said the boy. His jaw was set, and he seemed to be pondering something.

'Yes, Marcus?'

'Who was the shortest president?'

'You mean in height?'

'No. In, in days. Who was the shortest?'

'Harrison. He caught pneumonia during his inauguration and died. He was president for forty-something days, and he spent most of his time in office dying.'

'Oh. Well, who was the longest then?'

'Franklin Delano Roosevelt. He served three full terms. Died in office during his fourth. We'll take off our shoes here.'

They placed their shoes on a rock, carried on walking down towards the waves, their toes digging into the damp sand.

'How do you know so much about presidents?'

'Because my father thought it would do me good to find out about them, when I was a kid.'

'Oh.'

They waded out into the water, making for a boulder, one that could only be seen at low tide. After a while, Charlie picked the boy up and let him ride on his shoulders.

'Daddy?'

'Yes, Marcus.'

'P'choona says you're famous.'

'And who's Petunia?'

'At playgroup. She says her mom has all your CDs. She says she loves your singing.'

'Ah.'

'*Are* you famous?'

'Not really. A little bit.' He put Marcus down on the top of the boulder, then he clambered up it himself. 'OK. Ready to sing?'

'Yes.'

'What do you want to sing?'

'My favourite song.'

'I don't know if she'll like that one.'

'She will.' Marcus had the certainty of walls, of mountains.

'OK. One, two, three . . .'

They sang 'Yellow Bird' together, which was Marcus's favourite song that week, and then they sang 'Zombie Jamboree', which was his second favourite, and 'She'll Be Coming Round the Mountain', which was his third favourite. Marcus, whose eyes were better than Charlie's, spotted her as they were finishing 'She'll Be Coming Round the Mountain' and he began to wave.

'There she is, Daddy.'

'Are you sure?'

The morning haze blurred the sea and sky together into a pale whiteness, and Charlie squinted at the horizon. 'I don't see anything.'

'She's gone under the water. She'll be here soon.'

There was a splash, and she surfaced immediately below them; with a reach and a flip and a wiggle she was sitting on the rock beside them, her silvery tail dangling down into the Atlantic, flicking beads of water up on to her scales. She had long, orange-red hair.

They all sang together now, the man and the boy and the mermaid. They sang 'The Lady Is a Tramp' and 'Yellow Submarine' and then Marcus taught the mermaid the words to *The Flintstones* theme song.

'He reminds me of you,' she said to Charlie, 'when you were a little boy.'

'You knew me then?'

She smiled. 'You and your father used to walk down the beach, back then. Your father,' she said. 'He was quite some gentleman.' She sighed. Mermaids sigh better than anyone. Then she said, 'You should go back now. The tide's coming in.' She pushed her long hair back, and jack-knifed into the ocean. She raised her head above the waves, touched her fingertips to her lips, and blew Marcus a kiss before vanishing under the water.

Charlie put his son on to his shoulders and he waded through the sea, back to the beach, where his son slipped down from his shoulders on to the sand. He took off his old fedora hat and placed it on his son's head. It was much too big for the boy, but it still made him smile.

'Hey,' said Charlie, 'you want to see something?'

'OK. But I want breakfast. I want pancakes. No, I want oatmeal. No, I want pancakes.'

'Watch this.' Charlie began to do a sand-dance in his bare feet, soft-shoe shuffling through the sand.

'I can do that,' said Marcus.

'Really?'

'Watch me, Daddy.' He could, too.

Together the man and the boy danced their way back up the sand to the house, singing a wordless song that they made up as they went along, and which lingered in the air even after they had gone in for breakfast.

Acknowledgments

To begin with, an enormous bunch of flowers to Nalo Hopkinson, who kept a helpful eye on the Caribbean dialogue and not only told me what I needed to fix but suggested ways to fix it; and also to Lenworth Henry, who was there on the day I made it all up, and whose voice I heard in the back of my head when I was writing it (which is why I was delighted to hear that he would be narrating the audio book).

As with my last adult novel, *American Gods*, I was given two boltholes while I was writing this novel. I started writing it in Tori's spare house in Ireland, and I finished it there as well. She is a most gracious hostess and was this novel's shoe consultant. At one point in the middle, hurricanes permitting, I worked in Jonathan and Jane's spare house in Florida. It's a good thing to have friends with more houses than they have bodies, especially if they're happy to share. Most of the rest of the time I wrote in the local coffee house, and drank cup after cup of terrible tea in a rather pathetic demonstration of hope over experience.

Roger Forsdick and Graeme Baker gave up their time to answer my questions about the police, and fraud, and extradition treaties, while Roger also showed me around the cells, fed me dinner and looked over the finished manuscript. I'm very grateful.

Sharon Stiteler kept an eye on the book to make sure the birds passed muster and she answered my birding questions. Pam Noles was the first person to read any of the book, and her responses kept me going. There was a small host of other people who lent me their eyes and minds and opinions, including Olga Nunes, Colin Greenland, Giorgia Grilli, Anne Bobby, Peter Straub, John M. Ford, Anne Murphy and Paul Kinkaid, Bill Stiteler and Dan and Michael Johnson. Errors of fact or of opinion are mine, not theirs.

Thanks also go to Ellie Wylie; Thea Gilmore; The Ladies of

Lakeside; to Miss Holly Gaiman who turned up to help whenever she decided I needed a sensible daughter around; to the Petes of Hill House Publications; to Michael Morrison, Lisa Gallagher, Jack Womack and Julia Bannon; and to Dave McKean.

Jennifer Brehl, my editor at Morrow, was the person who persuaded me that the story I told her over lunch that day really would make a good novel, at a time when I really wasn't sure what the next novel was going to be, and she sat patiently when I phoned her up one night and read her the first third of the book. For these things alone she should be sainted. Jane Morpeth at Headline is the kind of editor writers hope to get if they're very good and eat all their vegetables. Merrilee Heifetz at Writers House, with the assistance of Ginger Clark, and, in the UK, Dorie Simmonds are my literary agents. I'm lucky to have them all on my side, and I know just how lucky I am.

Jon Levin keeps the world of movies running for me. My assistant Lorraine helped keep me writing and made really good cups of tea.

I don't think I could have written Fat Charlie without having had both an excellent but embarrassing father and wonderful but embarrassed children. Hurrah for families.

And a final thank you to something that didn't exist when I wrote *American Gods*: to the readers of the journal at www.neil gaiman.com, who were always there whenever I needed to know anything, and who, between them all, as far as I can tell, know everything there is to be known.

Neil Gaiman, June 2005

EXclusive Material

Contents

Author's Preface
to ANANSI BOYS Deleted Scene

Think of this as being one of those odd scenes that normally turn up as extras on DVDs – the scenes that everyone liked, but that made the film work better without them. It's one of them.

I really enjoyed writing it, and my editor at Headline, the redoubtable Jane Morpeth, was sad when I told her it was going because she liked it. And for that matter, I liked it too, only it messed up the pacing of the chapter it was in, and once I was prepared to grit my teeth and cut it, everything worked rather better.

I firmly believe that cut scenes are best left cut.

Even so, it had Spider in it, doing what Spider does best. And it had birds in. And in my head, it was the bit of the novel that was almost a Warner Brothers' cartoon.

So when Jane asked if I would be willing to let it appear – just this once – in the back of *Anansi Boys*, I found myself, slightly to my surprise, saying yes.

I've let it run into an earlier version of the scene that's still in the novel, at the end of Chapter Eleven. (This scene would have been in Chapter Eleven, split into two or three segments, and occurred between Fat Charlie arriving at the hotel and the end of the chapter.)

The Adventures of Spider
(A Deleted Scene)

S pider was imagining himself elsewhere. He was flicking, in his mind, through places he knew, or remembered, or imagined, willing himself there. Nothing happened. He remained precisely where he was, held by the chain of bones in his feathered cell.

He tried doing it the other way, thinking of a person, and trying to make himself be with them. This tended to be a fairly un-reliable method of travel for Spider at the best of times: Spider had trouble with other people. He had trouble remembering their faces, or their names, or sometimes even that they really existed at all.

He thought about Fat Charlie; he thought of old girlfriends, but they seemed peculiarly unconvincing, reconfiguring in his head into an assembly of breasts and lips and skin and smiles, and they evaporated in his mind; last of all, he thought of Rosie. He thought of her eyes, her warmth, the curve of her nostrils, the smell of her hair.

(And, on a cruise ship, dozing by the pool, Rosie shifted uncomfortably.)

Well, thought Spider, if he could not get out one way, he would get out another. There was more than one way to skin a cat, after all.*

He tried changing shape, with no result. He tried shouting. He tried shouting some more.

There was a flapping noise. Two sandhill cranes stood in front of him. They looked at him curiously.

It's not impossible to be Spider, or something like him. All you need is a complete and utter certainty that everything will work out; a cocky assurance that's just a hair's breadth away from psychosis; and the conviction that you're a monstrously clever fellow, and that the universe always looks after its own.

'You know,' said Spider to the birds, 'I don't want to cause a problem but these chains are a bit loose. One solid tug and I could fall down.'

The birds might have looked concerned. Spider couldn't be sure. It's hard to tell with birds.

'It's a shocking job,' said Spider. 'Whoever made these chains should be properly ashamed of themselves. Frankly, I could get out of them in a couple of minutes, and think of the trouble you'd all be in with herself if I simply fell out of them and wandered off. Quite appalling workmanship.'

The cranes looked at each other. One of them strutted back towards the wall. Spider watched it – a jog to the left, then it reached out its beak to the wall, and it touched a feather there, a feather paler than the others. And then it was gone.

'You know,' said Spider to the remaining crane. 'Let's just pretend I didn't say anything. I'd hate to put you all to any bother.'

A fluttering, and now the space was filled with huge crows who landed on the bone chains, then strutted about like builders examining the work of quite a different firm of builders, one that

---

* Spider had investigated this saying, and had established to his own satisfaction that while there actually were a number of ways of skinning a cat, scaring a cat out of its skin was merely a figure of speech. There are still several prematurely grey cats in the Los Angeles area who give mice an extremely wide berth, as if unsure of what they are going to turn into.

had left town with the work incomplete. They cawed and *tokked* in what Spider was certain was the corvine equivalent of, 'So what sort of cowboy put *this* together, then?'

A word from their foreman and the chains were covered in crows tapping and prodding with black beaks against the bones. A loud caw and the chains fell apart – the bones tumbled to the floor, and Spider tumbled with them. The floor was littered with twigs and tiny feathers, splashed and speckled with birdshit.

Spider got to his feet and noticed, for the first time, the geese. There were five of them, and they surrounded him, pecking at him, honking and hissing, to ensure that he stayed in the centre of them. A goose with its dander up and its neck down can cow a Doberman with a hiss, and these were the geese of nightmares.

Spider smiled at them.

Beneath the clever beaks of the crows the bone chains were expertly reassembled. The geese began to lower their necks once more, still honking and hissing, pushing Spider back to where the chains were waiting.

'Hey,' he said to the geese. 'Just give me room to breathe. I'm going back, yeah?'

He turned to the chains, he counted to three, and then he turned back and swung himself towards the wall where the sandhill crane had vanished. In the dim light he lunged for one feather paler than the others, and he hoped.

The wall became thin, almost translucent, and he pushed through it triumphantly, with angry geese pecking at his heels, and realised as he did so that he might have made a slight mistake.

Somehow, he had assumed that the cell was deep in the earth – that's where people build cells, after all. But on the whole, birds don't burrow.

The tree was enormous, higher than a giant redwood, and it was filled with a rookery of nests, including, just above him, the nest from which he had escaped. Below him, approaching with the speed of an out-of-control sports car, was the ground.

'Not a problem,' Spider told himself.

Again he tried to shift his location, with no more luck or success than before. Again he tried to change his shape – a little brown spider would simply have flown away on the air currents. Nothing happened, only the ground was rather closer.

Still, he thought, if he couldn't move and he couldn't change, the odds were that whatever kind of a place he was in, it wasn't a *real* place. It was made of mind, not world. As long as he was able to bear in mind that this was Maya, was illusion, he thought, he would be fine. He spread his arms and his legs. The cold air rushed past him.

And then he hit the ground. It's not real, he thought, as the air was knocked out of him and, for a moment, everything went dark.

***

Spider picked himself up. He hurt, all over, but nothing seemed to be broken.

He wondered if he had his own pocket universe somewhere, hung with webs and scuttling, industrious, storytelling spiders. He did not know. He was not sure where to look for it, if he did have one. His father would have known, of course . . .

The sky was the colour of beaten copper, and the earth was sandy and grey, and everything smelled of cinnamon and nutmeg. There had to be a way out. That was obvious. Ways in, ways out. He picked a direction, and did not run. Instead, he strolled, but he covered a lot of ground like that. Spider strolled like some people zoomed.

There was a large bird on a bush looking at him. The bird said, 'Spider. You know you're never going to escape from here.'

Spider said, 'I'll bet you all I own that I shall. And that you'll show me how to get away.'

Birds can't smirk, they don't have the equipment, but this one almost managed it. 'All you own?'

'Everything, if you show me the way out. So please, show me the way out of here.'

'Never,' said the bird.

'Close your eyes,' said Spider, 'and count to ten. I promise that by the time you've finished counting you'll have pointed me to the way out of here.'

The bird closed its eyes. 'One,' it said. 'Two. Three. Four.'

With one twist, Spider broke its neck, and it stopped counting. 'Still, I wouldn't want you to think me a liar,' said Spider to the bird. He plucked it, and set the feathers to one side, then he made a small fire in the earth, roasted and ate the meat, cleaned off the bones, and, last of all, he cast the bones on to the sand.

They fell higgledy-piggledy, every which way. Spider scooped them up again. 'Remember,' he said, 'you can't lie when you're dead.' This time when he cast the bones they pointed unequivocally in one direction.

'That's what I like,' said Spider. 'Someone who honours his bets.'

He put the bird's feathers on, and walked to the top of a hill. Ahead of him was a tear in the sky, a small rip in the coppery fabric of everything, and darkness spilled through it, and behind the darkness stars were twinkling. Spider no longer cared that it was uncool to run. Now he ran.

As he reached the bottom of the hill, birds descended around him.

'Stop!' they called.

He stopped. 'I'm a bird,' he told them. 'Just like you.' Even in the Bird Woman's universe, he was certain that he had enough conviction to make the things he said true for those that heard them.

'What manner of bird are you?' asked a heron, puzzled. 'An emu? An ostrich? A moa?'

'Yeah. Sure. Something like that,' said Spider. 'Hey, have any of you seen Spider anywhere? I heard that he had escaped, and I was told to guard the way out of here.'

''We're looking for him too,' said an eagle. ''Haven't seen him, though. Actually, we thought you might be him, when we saw you coming towards us.'

'No, you didn't,' said Spider. 'You thought I was just another bird.'

'Oh. Right. That was what we thought,' agreed the heron.

'So. You lot all wait here, and guard the way out,' said Spider. 'And I'll just put my head through there and make sure that he hasn't got here ahead of us.'

Spider walked forward. He walked through the rip in the sky.

Ahead of him he could see an island. He could see a small mountain in the centre of the island. He could see a pure blue sky, and swaying palm trees, a white gull high in the sky. But even as he saw it the world seemed to be receding. It was as if he was looking at it through the wrong end of a telescope. It shrank and slipped from him, and the more he ran towards it the further away it seemed to get.

The island was a reflection in a puddle of water, and then it was nothing at all.

He was in a cave. The edges of things were crisp – crisper and sharper than anywhere that Spider had ever been before. This was a different kind of place. The feathers he had worn fell to the rocky floor. He turned to the daylight.

She was standing in the mouth of the cave, between him and the open air. She had stared into his face in a Greek restaurant in South London, and birds had come from her mouth.

'You know,' said Spider, 'I was just in your world. And I have to say, you've got the strangest ideas about hospitality. You come to my world, I'd make you dinner, open a bottle of wine, put on some soft music, give you an evening you would never forget.'

Her face was impassive; carved from black rock, it was. The wind tugged at the edges of her old brown coat. She spoke then, her voice high and distant as the wrenching call of a distant gull. 'I took you,' she said. 'Now, you will call him.'

'Call him? Call who?'

'You will bleat,' she said. 'You will whimper. Your fear will excite him.'

'Spider does not bleat,' he said. He was not certain it was true.

Eyes as black and as shiny as chips of obsidian stared back into his. They were eyes like black holes, letting nothing out, not even information.

'If you kill me,' said Spider, 'my curse will be upon you.' He wondered if he actually had a curse. He probably did.

'It will not be me that kills you,' she said. She raised her hand, and it was not a hand but a raptor's talon. She raked her talon down his face, down his chest, her cruel claws sinking into his flesh, ripping his skin.

It did not hurt, although Spider knew that it would hurt soon enough.

Beads of blood crimsoned his chest and dripped down his face. His eyes stung. His blood touched his lips. He could taste it, and smell the iron scent of it.

'Now,' she said in the cries of distant birds. 'Now your death begins.'

Spider said, 'We're both reasonable entities. Let me present you with a perhaps rather more feasible alternative scenario that might conceivably have benefits for both of us.' He said it with an easy smile. He said it convincingly.

'You talk too much,' she said. Then she reached into his mouth with her sharp talons, and with one wrenching movement she tore out his tongue.

'There,' she said. And then she said, 'Sleep.'

Author's Preface
to the Notebook Extracts

I love the physical act of writing a book, of beginning writing by filling a pen, and then making marks on paper. I think that's mostly because, on paper, you have to just keep moving forward. You can't stop to polish a sentence, or revise, or fix things. And no one can send you e-mail or messages. It's just you and a notebook and a pen, and a bunch of stuff in your head.

These pages are taken from the leather-bound notebook I wrote most of *Anansi Boys* in. (I bought it in Göttingen, in Germany. I was there for a Literary Festival.) When the book was done I had forgotten what I had written on the title page. It's how the Ashanti begin their Anansi stories. 'We do not really mean, we do not really mean what we say . . .' they start. It's a fine get-out clause for an author or a storyteller.

But we do. We do.

Anansi Boys.

by

Neil Gaiman.

"we do not really mean,
we do not really mean
what we say"...
How the Ashanti
begin Ananse stories..

god is
dead.

meet the kids.

~ Anansi Boys ~

Thank
Thorne Smith.

if.

To begin a little before the beginning. I
shall write down everything I know about Anansi
Boys...

———

Mr Nancy dies at the beginning of the book.
He is singing karaoke. He has a heart attack
and carks it on a blonde ("It's how he would
have wanted to go.")

His son, Charlie, comes to the funeral, gets
there late. He talks to old lady, family
friend, learns that his dad was a god,
and that he has a brother who inherited
the side of things. He's asked how to
solve "Ask a spider," he's told.

The days pass. Charlie goes home... his
gf asks him to get a spider out of the bath.
The Brother turns up... a psychopathic but delightful
trickster - impersonates people, takes joy in
confounding Charlie's life & mucking him up.
He has to go. He won't go...

Things are getting weirder. Charlie goes back
to old ladies & implores them to help. They have
a seance, & do a spell...

Charlie's in the Dreamland. He sees the
various animals - none of them will take on
Anansi until he gets to the Bird woman's cave.
He asks her to help him get rid of
his brother - she agrees

And then it gets scary... on the run
- both of them, as she comes after Anansi's

(B) bloodline...
Boys on the run, until Charlie tells
Spider to take them back to the Florida
cemetery.
A final conflict with the boys, and
then Spider, and the spider woman...

Publisher's note: this was a blank
page in the notebook, so we have
reproduced Neil's drawing of the
seven-legged spider for visual
entertainment

It has been drawn to this
author's attention that in a book
called <u>American Gods</u> there is
also a Mr Nancy, who claims to
have two sons, and who may have
a number of the characteristics in of
the Mr Nancy in here.
The author suggests strongly that
the reader might want to ~~g~~ avoid
~~mapping~~

(or chapter Title?)
First line of the book should be
"so a man walks into a bar."
Maybe each chapter begins with a joke line...

It begins, as most things began, with a song. ~~There~~ In the beginning, after all, was the word, and it came with a tune. That was how the world was made, how the void was divided into light and darkness, how the lands and the stars and the dreams, and the little gods and the totem creatures, how all of them came into the world.

They were sung.

The great beasts were sung first, after the lands and hills and seas and oceans, and the lesser beasts. The dreamtime was sung, and the hunting grounds.

Songs ~~last~~ remain. They can turn emperors into laughing-stocks, and bring down dynasties. They can last, long after the events or the people in them are dust and dreams. That's the power of songs.

There are other things you can do with songs, apart from make worlds, ~~You can take the~~ and that was what Fat Charlie's father, ~~the reverend~~ Aloysious Nancy (deceased)

② was doing.

~~then~~ ~~&~~ He was standing on a very small stage, in the ~~front~~ upstairs room of a bar just off Highway 1, and he was belting it out, ~~such~~ a huge voice for such a ~~small~~ frail man.

The whole karaoke evening had been looking like it ~~was~~ going ~~&~~ to a utter bust before the little old man had come in. He had sent two glasses of the house champagne ~~too~~ a couple of blonde ladies, and tipped his hat to them — for he wore a hat, a white fedora, and lemon-yellow gloves — and had ~~walked~~ strolled over ~~&~~ their table awhile they sipped their drinks and giggled.

"Are you enjoyin' yourselves, ladies?" he asked.

They giggled, and told him they were having a good time, thank you. He said, just wait, to them, and flashed a grin ~~that~~ ~~barely revealed the gintest~~ wide and confident grin at them.

He walked over to the DJ, who was also the barman. "My friend," he said. "I would like to sing. What are you drinking?"

He was charm itself. He was something from long, long ago, when manners and courtly shouldness were. The barman felt relieved that he was in the bar. This was going to be a good evening.

And then the old man got up on the stage and sang, and not once but twice on the first time he raised FC's life

---

~~Fat~~ ~~handful~~ Charlie was only ever fat for a
~~couple~~ of years, from shortly before the age of nine,
when his mother decided that, if there
was one thing she was over and done
with and if he had any argument with
it he could just stick it you know where,
it was her marriage to that elderly goat
she had made the unfortunate mistake
of marrying. and she would be ~~best~~
leaving in the morning for somewhere a
long way away, and he had better not
try to follow; to the age of fourteen,
when he grew a little, and exercised
a little more. He was not fat. He
was not even chubby, merely a little
soft looking at the edges. But the name
Fat Charlie clung to him, like chewing
gum to the sole of a mishoe. He would
introduce himself as Charles, or, in
his early twenties, Chaz or, in writing,
as C. Nancy, but it was no
use: the name would creep in,
infiltrating the new part of his life like
cockroaches moving ~~into~~ behind the fridge
in a sparkling white kitchen, and

④ like it or not — and he didn't, — he would be Fat Charlie again.

It was, he knew, irrationally, because his father had ~~named him~~ given him the nickname, and when his father gave things names, they stuck. There was a dog, a prize-winning dog, who had lived on their street, when Fat Charlie was a boy. It was a boxer, long-legged and point-eared, with a face ~~that~~ looked like it had run, ~~face~~ nose-first into the wall, an ~~aristocrat~~ among ~~canines~~. It had entered dog shows. It had rosettes for Best of Breed, and Best in Class, and even one marked Best in Show. It rejoiced in the name of Campbell's Macinrory Arbuthnot the Seventh, ~~This lasted until one~~ ~~the~~ and its owners, when they were getting familiar, called it 'Tony.' This lasted until the day ~~that~~ Fat Charlie's father, sitting out on their dilapidated porch-swing, sipping his beer, noticed the dog.

"Hell of a goofy dog," he said. "Like ~~that~~ friend of Donald Duck's. Hey, Goofy."

And that had once been

best in show, suddenly shipped and
shifted. It was as if Fat Charlie
saw the dog through his father's eyes,
and darned if he wasn't a pretty
goofy dog, all things considered. almost rubbery.
It didn't take long for the name
to spread up and down their street.
Campbelli's Macinnony About that the 7th's
owners struggled with it, but it was
like they might as well 'have stood
their ground and argued with a
flood. Total strangers would pat the
once-proud Goden's head, and say
"Hello, goofy." They stopped entering the dog for shows,
took what not: they didn't have the heart.
'Goofy-looking dog" said the judge.
     Fat Charlie's father's names for things
stuck. That was how it was.
     It was why Fat Charlie he didn't think of his
father as Dad, or Papa or any
particular even as Mr Nancy, which was what
everyone else called him.
     That was far from the worst thing about
Fat Charlie's father.
     There had been a number of
candidates for the worst thing about
Fat Charlie's father - his roving eye and
equally as adventurous fingers, the little

(6) black cigarillos, which he called cheroots, which he smoked, the smell of which clung to everything he touched. His fondness for a peculiar shuffling form of tap-dancing, his total and invincible ignorance about current affairs, combined with his apparent conviction that sitcoms were half-hour long insights into the lives of and struggles of real people. These were not the worst thing about F.C.'s father (although each of them had played its part in the worst thing).

The worst thing about Fat Charlie's father was that he was embarrassing.

Of course, everybody's parents are embarrassing. It is the nature of parents to embarrass merely by existing, while it is in the nature of children to cringe with mortification should their parents so much as speak to them on the street.

Fat Charlie's father, on the other hand, had elevated this to an art form, and he rejoiced in it, just as he rejoiced in practical jokes, ranging from the simple — Fat Charlie would never

forget his first apple-pie bed — to the
unimaginable
complex...

"Like what?" asked Rosie, his fiancée, one
evening, when Fat Charlie, who normally did
not talk about his father, had started,
stumblingly, to explain why he thought
simply inviting his father to their wedding
would be a bad idea. They were in a
wine bar in South London. Fat Charlie
had long been of the opinion that three
thousand miles and the Atlantic Ocean were
both good things to have between himself
and his father.

"Well," said Fat Charlie, and he
remembered a parade of indignities, then
settled upon one of them. "Well, when I
moved from the local junior school to the
middle school, my Dad made a point of
telling me how much he had always
loved Presidents' Day when he was a boy,
because it's the law — that at school on Presidents'
Day, the kids who are dressed up as their
favourite Presidents, get a big bag of
candy."

"Oh. That's a nice law," said Rosie,
who had never been out of England, if you
didn't count a Club 18-30 Holiday

⑧ to somewhere she thought had been called
the Island — spirit and that had been on an island in,
she was fairly certain, the mediterranean.

Rosie had warm brown eyes and a good
heart, even if geography was not her
particular forte.

"No," said Fat Charlie, "it's not. He
made it up. There is no tradition of going
to school on president's Day dressed as your
favourite President. Kids dressed as presidents
do not get bags of candy by an Act of
Congress, nor was your popularity for the years
ahead decided entirely by what president
you dressed as — the average kids dressed as
the obvious presidents, the Lincolns or Washingtons,
but the ones who would become popular, they
dressed as John Quincy Adams, or Warren Gamaliel
Harding, or someone like that."

"Boys and girls?"

"Oh yes. I spent the week before presidents'
Day ~~planning the state~~ reading everything there
was to read about presidents, trying to choose
the right one."

"Didn't you think he was pulling your
leg?"

Fat Charlie shook his head. "It's not
something you think about, when you dad
starts to work you over. He's the
finest liar you'll ever meet..."

This is the story of Spider, and what happened when he was eaten by the Bird Lady and went to the Hell of Birds, and how he escaped, and what happened then.

So spider was swallowed by the wall of Birds. He felt it touch him, then he felt pain, Spider had never been to a dentist — nor had he ever needed to — but if he had he would have recognised the pain: it was a drill hitting a nerve, all over his body, and it got worse and worse until there was no respite but madness, or unconsciousness. Spider was not certain which one he chose.

When he came to, there were bones clutching his wrists, and bones about his ankles, and he was suspended in a rough X (cross?) for the corners of a room. Breathing was difficult, movement hurt.

The walls of his cell were moving gently. They were feathered.

over to other notebook. Then p 102 of other notebook, Back here.

Stories are webs, interwoven, strand to strand, and you follow each story to the centre, because the centre is the end.

~~There was a knock on the door.~~

The sun was shining on the horizon as it
sank into the sea, and Spider, had he not been
Spider, would have despaired. On the island
there was a clear line between day and night,
and once the red crumb of sun was eaten by the
sea it would all be over.

He had his stones and his sticks. He wished
he had fire; fire would help. If there was a
moon; if the moon rose soon, perhaps then
he would have a chance. *into his head.

"Anansi's boy," said a voice from the
darkness* "soon enough I shall feed on you.
You will not know that I am there until you
feel my breath on your neck. You have
fingers, but I have claws sharper than knives,
you have two legs, but I have four legs that never
tire, that run ten times as fast as yours ever
will. Your teeth can eat meat, if it has been
made soft and tasteless from heat but you have too
little monkey-teeth, good ~~for peaches and~~ soft
fruit and cracking bugs; but I have teeth that
rend and tear the living meat from the bones,
as the blood fountains up into the sky."

Spider would do brag — to talk about
his people, of their patience, their skill, their
webs, their venom. But all he said
was,

"You may have all those things, Tiger.
But all the stories there are or will

be are Anansi's. Nobody tells Tiger stories." (261)

There was a roar – of fury and of
frustration.

Spider began to sing the Tiger Rag. "Hold that
Tiger," he sang. "Where's the Tiger?"

When the voice came from the darkness, it
was nearer.

"My servant, ~~it said.~~ Has your woman,
Anansi's son. When I am done here, I
shall tear out her throat. Her meat
will be sweeter than yours / or I shall
mate with her.

"You're lying, Tiger."

"Her name... her name is Rosie."

Now Spider opened his mouth, and with a
tongueless mouth he moaned.

In ~~his~~ Spider's head, Tiger was laughing.

"And eyes," said Tiger into Spider's mind. "You
people have eyes that see the obvious, in
broad daylight. But my folk have eyes that
see the hairs prickle on your arms as I talk
to you, and see that in the darkness. Be
afraid, Anansi's boy. And if you have any
final prayers to say, say them now."
(spider on his head)

Spider had never said any prayers
and he wasn't going to start now.
But he had rocks, and even if he could
not see, he could still throw them. And
a rock might hit Tiger. Spider knew
that it could be a miracle if it did,
but he had spent his entire life relying

(262) on miracles, after all.

Something brushed his hand.

— Hello, said the yellow spider.

— Hi, said Spider. Look, I'm a bit busy here, avoiding being eaten, so if you don't mind keeping out of the way until later...

— But I brought them, said the spider. Like you asked.

— Like I asked?

— You asked for help, said the little yellow spider. I brought them.* They followed my webstrand. There are no spiders in this creation, so I slipped back, and webbed from there to here and from here to here. I brought the warriors. I brought the brave.

A single spider is silent. They cultivate silence. Even the ones that can make a noise will often remain as still as they can, waiting. So much of what spiders do is wait.

The night was slowly filling with a rustling.

When you have enough spiders in one place that you can hear them...

— Good job, said Spider to the little spider, who had clambered up from his hand to his shoulder, and from there had begun to make himself at home in Spider's ear.

* may want to do a scene of yellow spiders offering help.

There were great spiders and small spiders, venomous, spiders and bird-eating spiders; huge, hairy spiders and elegant chitinous spiders. ~~There are spiders~~ Spider venom is, too often, not like snake venom - it can take a long time (sometimes years) to discover that you've been bitten and to ~~realise~~ discover the effects of the bite. Naturalists puzzle over this - what point, they ask, can the Tasmanian [?] spider bite be, where ~~you~~ the bitee's flesh starts rotting fifteen years later. The answer is simple: they think it's funny. It's the spidery equivalent of a whoopee cushion or a rubber fried egg. Tiny eggs in clumps of eight, took whatever bright they could find.

They were an army.

"When you are dead, ~~Spider~~ Anansi child. When both of you are dead, then the stories will be mine. People will tell Tiger stories. They will gather together and praise my cunning and my bravery, my wisdom and my strength. Every story will be mine."

Spider listened to the rustle of the legs of his army, as they found their target.

If he bounds, if he runs, if he comes for me now, I am dead, thought Spider. It was why he was at the edge of the cliff - it meant there was nowhere to retreat to, but it also meant that if tiger was to come he would creep, not charge.

A yowl from the darkness made Spider smile. Tiger had met the army.

(264) Black widow bites on Tiger's left nose, innumerable bites on his ears: his sensitive places burned and throbbed, swelled and hurt... Tiger did not know what was happening: all he knew was the pain and the burning and the sudden panic.

He bolted. The sound of a huge animal lumbering through the bushes.

Spider sat on the cliff-edge and waited. Tiger would be back, he had no doubt of that.

The light was gentle and strange, and for a moment only Spider thought it was the moon. It prowled someone walking towards him.

Spider readied his troops. He hefted his rock.

The figure in the light said, "Um. Excuse me." Spider lowered the rock.

"Here," said Fat Charlie. "This is yours."

Spider reached out his hand, and took the object. It was smaller than he had thought it would be, red and cold and gloppy. He placed it in his mouth, felt it root there. It was cold and unpleasant. It did not feel like it was his. He wiggled it, salivated, was happy.

"Nice hat," he said.

"You think so?"

"Yeah. I guess. Mostly, it's how you wear it."

"Where'd you get my tongue from?"

"The Bird woman. I'll tell you later."

An Interview
with Neil Gaiman

Spiders – down the plug hole or let them be?

I am a let-them-be person, on the whole. I will move spiders that are in the wrong place because you find yourself, if you're a father, having to be the default person who moves spiders that are in the wrong place. This is one of those strange parental duties that they don't tell you about when you get married and have kids, but turns up almost immediately.

I've only failed at spider removal once, in Mexico, when a famous director knocked on the door of my hotel room and told me there was a spider 'literally as big as his hand' on his curtains, and could I remove it for him? I assumed it was just a normal-sized spider and went off to help him usher it out of his room, only to discover that this particular Mexican spider really was the size of his hand, if not larger, and that, apparently, once spiders get over a certain size, it doesn't really matter that I'm fond of the idea of spiders, this really wasn't a tumbler and a birthday card job. I walked towards it, and I froze. Eventually we wound up phoning the front desk who sent up a small man with a broom, and that was the end of that. But I am fond of spiders, even though they make me slightly uncomfortable.

Who are your top three all-time favourite gods?

I love Czernobog. I love the Slavic gods, mainly because I can't find out very much about them. I'm sure if there were lots of stories about them I'd like them less, but I made him up for

American Gods and enjoyed just improvising on the theme, so he's definitely one of my favourite gods.

From the Norse Pantheon, I'm desperately fond of Loki, even though he technically is not actually a god – he's a giant who went to live with the gods. But he used to hang around with them and get them into trouble, and I like anyone who just hangs round getting into trouble – it's enormously good fodder for a story.

And Anansi – I love Anansi. I love all trickster gods, and the delight of Anansi is he's a little trickster god. Probably the one that I like even more than him would be Coyote, who is the Native American creative trickster. He is slightly more big and powerful than Anansi. Anansi is all about the revenge of the weak. I think it's interesting that Anansi stories sometimes become Brer Rabbit stories. Rabbits and spiders are sort of small, and you can squash them – though most people don't squash rabbits and most people don't get called to take rabbits out of the bath, but I think the principle is the same.

Top three godlike geniuses?

I'm an enormous fan of Stephen Sondheim's because of what he does with words, and with music, and with words and music. So he's one of those people who make me think, 'I wish I could do that,' rather sadly.

Douglas Adams I always felt was a genius. I was lucky enough to get to work with Douglas – I did the *Hitchhiker's Guide to the Galaxy* companion, a book called *Don't Panic*, back when I was a 25-year-old journalist. I interviewed Douglas a lot and worked with him on it, and was very, very aware that he was a genius. It was a useful thing to know. He wasn't terribly happy at the time, and he didn't produce an awful lot, and he seemed to spend more time not writing than he ever did writing, which I thought was probably not a terribly good way to do it if you wanted to be a writer. But the mind on him was astonishing.

I think all geniuses – or the ones that I've run into – tend to have a faintly tenuous relationship with the real world, because so much is going on on the inside. They may be geniuses but they often need someone to walk around holding the string. They're sort of balloons, bobbing around.

I don't ever think I'm a genius. People come up and say, 'Oh, you're a genius.' No, I'm not. I'm talented, and there's a gulf between them. Like people getting to look at a hill and going, 'Oh, it's a mountain,' and the mountain's going, 'No, it's not.'

Third genius: I've just run out of geniuses. I mean, my son Mike can do things with computers that make my eyes cross, and I'm pretty sure that my friend Alan Moore is a genius, but really, it's an awful lot easier not to put people on pedestals. It's easier for everyone that way, for you and for them.

Top tips for surviving family get-togethers?

Mine was always bring a book. That was how I would survive all family get-togethers. My father would actually frisk me sometimes, though, on going in, to find and remove books, because otherwise I would just head off somewhere with my book and be dreadfully antisocial. It's still the best thing as far as I'm concerned for surviving family get-togethers.

(*Anansi Boys* actually can be used for that. If you are undergoing a family get-together simply take your copy of *Anansi Boys*, go and sit somewhere out of the way and smile at people as they come past. They will leave you alone. Or they may do. Until they come up to you and say, 'Now it's time for a nice walk,' and you have to put it away.)

Most embarrassing moment caused by a parent – possibly frisking?

The trouble with parents, and this is speaking as a parent, is that by our very nature we embarrass our children. I thought I was over it, but on this last trip to England, I found myself with my daughter Maddy – who's ten and spends much of her time being totally embarrassed by me – and with my mother – who's a wonderful lady in her seventies – in a fish and chip shop.

My mother began a conversation with the lady behind the counter which rapidly got embarrassing enough that I just fled and went to check that the car was still there. There was actually no possible way that the car could have gone anywhere, but I still decided that it was probably better that I went and checked the car than that I stood there being embarrassed.

On the other hand, my daughter didn't find her grandmother embarrassing at all; she just thinks she's hilarious.

So I think, thank heavens, that it will skip a generation and I can assume my own grandchildren will not find me anywhere near as embarrassing as my children do.

But the worst things that one looks back on are fundamentally trivial. I remember my father had a favourite pair of shoes when I was a teenager and incredibly sensitive to wearing the right kind of thing. My dad's favourite pair of shoes was European, and bright yellow, and incredibly comfortable, and looked faintly like bananas. I would try and walk far enough behind him so that no one would ever think we were together.

Which is an awful lot like my daughter being embarrassed by me driving a Mini. I have to drop my daughter off round the corner from her school so a) none of her friends can see that I'm driving a Mini, and b) none of her friends can hear what I'm playing on the car stereo, because anything I'm playing is by definition embarrassing.

And even being Neil Gaiman doesn't help with that?

No, being Neil Gaiman normally does absolutely no good at all. Every now and then it gets kids into things that they quite enjoy, but frankly all parents are embarrassing.

I'm quite sure it's the same for absolutely everybody in the whole world. You could be King, you could be President, and your own children will still say, 'Oh my God, Dad, just stop singing. We're in public. It's so embarrassing. And put that down . . .' Because that's what kids say. And they're right.

Talking of singing: top three karaoke tunes?

I actually had great fun coming up with karaoke tunes in *Anansi Boys*. While I don't think I could list a top three, I'd like to go on record grumbling about the current complexities of the copyright system, which mean that you're quoting four words of a song and you have the publishers suddenly saying, 'OK, we'd like two thousand dollars for that, please.'

And you're going, 'You must be joking,' and have to rewrite a line or two in the book instead.

Do you have any nicknames that you can't get rid of?

I never got any nicknames, and was always incredibly disappointed by this. I'd read books and everyone would have cool nicknames. Far from being unable to ever shake a nickname I never managed to acquire one.

Of course, I was always very amused watching kids that I knew through school try to shake nicknames. I had a friend who I will not name because he may one day pick up this book, whose nickname was Baggy, because of the particularly large pair of trousers that his mother sent him to school in as a small boy. And he remained Baggy, until by the time he was about seventeen he was no longer Baggy, he was now Don't Call Me Baggy, which as a nickname was even worse.

I always like the way that people mostly get rid of nicknames by going off to college or getting new jobs: just reinventing themselves completely. It was fun doing it in *Anansi Boys*, and deciding exactly at what moment in the text it would occur, and what's also nice is that no one notices while they're reading it.

What was your favourite moment of ANANSI BOYS?

As a writer your favourite moments are different to a reader's, and they're different for different reasons.

My favourite day writing was the day that I got to write Fat Charlie's hangover followed by Spider's day in the office. And I was writing it in a little coffee shop fairly near my house and I kept giggling, and they kept giving me funny looks.

My other favourite moment, oddly enough, was when Maeve Livingstone was in the lift going up to Grahame Coats's office, and I suddenly realised just what would actually happen if she got into that office, and also realised that, if I let that happen, I was going to have to completely rethink the last third of the book, because up until that point I didn't want anything quite that dark to happen to any of the characters.

And what was nice was actually letting it happen and then not writing the book for about three months while I thought about things, and researched, and then went off and wrote the last third of the book.

I had to stop at that point and figure out how a comedy worked. I knew that I wanted it to be a comic novel, and it needed to be a comedy, but also that there were places in there where I was skirting perilously close to horror.

You start realising that in horror fiction people get what they deserve, whereas in comedies people get what they need. And I felt that at the end of *Anansi Boys*, everybody got what they needed.

Reading-group
Discussion Questions

1. *Anansi Boys* combines a modern-day story with myths, legends and visions that should be unbelievable, yet Neil Gaiman creates a world in which the extraordinary becomes completely acceptable. How does he achieve this?

2. 'Comedy' is too loose a term to describe the humour in *Anansi Boys*. What are the different forms of humour in the novel, and what part do they play in the drive of the narrative? What other emotional responses are significant?

3. Fat Charlie and Spider begin as polar opposites, but during the novel Charlie incrementally, and with great subtlety, reclaims his Spider-side. Where are the turning points for Charlie's character, and when did you realise he was no longer Fat Charlie? How does Spider change?

4. What does *Anansi Boys* show about the inherent bonds between brothers, even those who believe they hate each other, and between parents and children? How is loyalty and courage rewarded, and betrayal and cowardice punished?

5. All stories are Anansi's. What is the significance of the Anansi tales that are woven into the narrative – the stories within a story? How do they link into the metaphor of the story as a web?

6. How do Fat Charlie's dreams and visions influence the story? Why are his dreams important?

7. Maeve's indignation at becoming a ghost is endearing, but her desire for vengeance is very powerful. Which other characters seek vengeance, and how does this overwhelming desire for revenge affect them?

8. What does *Anansi Boys* say about today's multicultural society? How are the characters influenced by their varied backgrounds? Do traditional attitudes conflict with or inform new ideas?